FINDING TULSA

a novel
by

Jim Provenzano

Advance Praise for *Finding Tulsa*

"*Finding Tulsa* reminds you what a good friend a novel can be. It's about friendship, about "losing men and then finding them," about brotherly love and conflict, and the possibility of resolution. It's sexy, funny, astute, panoramic—it knows about suburban Ohio basement rec rooms and glam parties in the Hollywood hills. I felt like I had met a charming guy at a cocktail party who seemed to get me, understood my past, confided his own, and then disappeared to another better party before I was ready for him to leave. And it's wrapped around a fearless, wrenching narrative about facing your childhood demons, raising the question of whether or not one of the demons might have been you. Read it twice! There's so much to savor, to argue with, reflect upon, learn from, enjoy."

— John Weir, Lambda Literary Award-winning author of
The Irreversible Decline of Eddie Socket

"Jim Provenzano must have been spying on me from my adolescence (making short films with my brother) to my adulthood (making gay movies and TV series). I identified with every twist, turn, and blow by blow of this sexy showbiz saga!"

— Sam Irvin, Director of *Dante's Cove*;
Co-Producer of *Gods And Monsters* and *The Broken Hearts Club*

"*Finding Tulsa* is sexy, romantic, witty, engaging, both cleverly current yet sweetly retrospective. It's Jim Provenzano's most complex and accomplished novel. He gets so much right and so evocatively about show business, from those school plays we all remember to Hollywood made-for-television movies, with delicious stops at boyhood Super-8 movies and out of town gay porn shoots."

— Felice Picano, author of *Justify My Sins: A Hollywood Novel in Three Acts*, and the New York Times best-seller *Like People in History*

"Jim Provenzano always keeps in mind what the original 'Tulsa' said in *Gypsy*: 'This step is good for the costume.' Provenzano never misses a step as he suavely combines aesthetics and homoerotics in a work that is throughout deeply touching."

— David Ehrenstein, author of *Open Secret: Gay Hollywood—1928-2000*

"Lights! Camera! Action! *Finding Tulsa* is a show-biz comedy told by a witty industry insider divulging how plays and movies and characters like "Tulsa" help gay boys survive adolescence, create identity, and worship beauty. What better icons could Provenzano have picked than Sondheim and *Gypsy* on which to fly his vivid characters, backstage intrigues, and dialogue sure to thrill the theater and movie queen in all of us. Writing at the top of his powers, with his striped tie and hopes high, he's got rhythm. All he needs is you to go with 'im. A splendid romp! Let him entertain you!"

— Jack Fritscher, author of *Mapplethorpe: Assault with a Deadly Camera*
and the Lammy Finalist, *Some Dance to Remember:*
A Memoir-Novel of San Francisco 1970-1982

"Everything's coming up roses in *Finding Tulsa*, Jim Provenzano's intoxicating portrait of an artist as young to middle-aged man, from a high school musical techie in torn shorts to a semi jaded independent gay filmmaker. It's a well-told yarn, full of humor and panache about a Hollywood player torn between his boyhood crush and a porn star. Spin the bottle, ride the Rolodex, and fasten your seat belt for Provenzano's sweet roller coaster ride."

— Marc Huestis, film director (*Sex Is* ...) and author of
Impresario of Castro Street: an Intimate Showbiz Memoir

"Jim Provenzano's sexy, funny and soulful new novel *Finding Tulsa* is a beautiful deep-end dive into the memory of desire, the thumping bass note that drives life and art. The novel gorgeously explores how our hearts and cocks are woven with our theatre and films as we figure out how to be the star of our own queer story."

— Tim Miller, Performer and author of *A Body in the O*

FINDING TULSA

a novel
by

Jim Provenzano

Palm Drive Publishing
Sebastopol CA

An excerpt of this work titled "The Lair of Light" was originally published in *Cast Out: Queer Lives in Theater*, Robin Bernstein, Editor, The University of Michigan Press, 2006.

Cover illustration: Getty Images
Cover design: Max Leger
Published by Palm Drive Publishing, Sebastopol CA
Email: Publisher@PalmDrivePublishing.com

Library of Congress Control Number: 2020933984
Provenzano, Jim 1961–
Finding Tulsa / Jim Provenzano

p.cm
ISBN   978-1-890834-45-6 print
         978-1-890834-46-3 ebook

1. Fiction 2. Gay Fiction 3. Literary Fiction 4. Hollywood 1990s 5. Ohio
6. Coming of Age 7. Film Directing 8. Theatre 9. Sexuality 10. Homosexuality
I. Provenzano, Jim II. Finding Tulsa.

First Printed 2020
10 9 8 7 6 5 4 3 2
Printed in the United States
Palm Drive Publishing, Sebastopol CA
www.PalmDrivePublishing.com

For

Vito Russo

ACT I

"That which we are, we are,
one equal temper of heroic hearts
made weak by time and fate."
—Alfred Lord Tennyson, *The Odyssey*

"Nobody laughs at me, because I laugh first."
—Louise, *Gypsy*

1. I trip before I board

While my next career move hinges on this meeting, I'm distracted by a looming statue about to take flight, winged at its ankles and helmet. I imagine shooting a scene here, starting with its butt. *Mercury's Rim.*

We're in the middle of The Abbey's courtyard. Barry is only halfway through his latté, but he's already waxing poetic about the screening of some friend-of-a-friend's latest epic, after which both of us had lied through our teeth: "Wonderful, excellent."

"Stan, you are a pip," Barry smirks. "With the thing about his 'use of negative space.'" Our giggles almost shatter wide-brim cups and the ears of queens nearby, who glance at us for daring to encroach on their personal audio space. We're café-ing; neutral territory.

While Barry talks about his script, I'm drawing a sketch of the statue's butt on the paper tablecloth. We try not to notice each other glance as men pass on the Robertson sidewalk. I'm comfortable under the shade of the awning, doodling nonstop, but he knows I'm paying attention. The project, the first feature film about a gay superhero, has been handed down from Singer to Barker to about six other directors. Once upon a time I was the only director he'd consider, and now I'm ready, if not a last resort choice. Actually, Hollywood's finally acknowledged gay films, even though some of us have been making them for years.

"So when's your plane tomorrow?" Barry asks.

"One' o'clock. Actually, twelve-fifty-five."

Five years ago he would have been helping me pack for this trip. Now he needs to be reminded why I'm going. "Brookside, Ohio, for a tribute to the retiring theatre director of my youth."

"Oh, god."

"Not quite. I'm the only thing close to a celebrity that came out of that town, not counting the adulterous dean. And…"

"Hmm?"

"Nothing." I almost mention Lance, but he'll be flying out later. Besides, just bringing up his name will take everything off-track for Barry.

"Do you watch the clouds or the movie?" Barry asks.

"Both. But once I watched a thunderstorm from above while listening to *Aida.*"

"Mmm," Barry hums appreciatively. He doesn't leave L.A. much, except in his Range Rover. He's an outdoor type, but hates planes. Once he fucked me on a mountaintop in the Santa Monica Mountains. I would have fallen in love with him at the time, but I had a rock poking into my back.

"Hope you don't get some bore next to you," he says. I think at one point I mentioned the idea of Barry coming with me. I was either joking at the time, or we were still sleeping together. But it's months after the broadcast, the Ace Awards, and Lance ... it's all in post-production. Everything's post—.

"Or a lousy movie," I say.

"Ugh. I hate the way they chop them up."

"Undoubtedly starring Hugh Grant."

"The English Father of the Bride."

"Who Went Up a Mountain and Came Down Busted."

Barry doesn't laugh. His jovial mood has passed. He wants to get a decision out of me before I leave. I've read it, another great one. Barry doesn't know I've already bought two copies of the graphic novel it's based on. One is for the creator to sign when we're still in our honeymoon phase, before the rabid fans trash its prospects online. The other set's already cut up and laid out on makeshift storyboards all over my house. I'm hoping my touches will more than fill up any deficiencies in the script. I will not argue it into art, like I had to last time.

"You know, Stan, you should do that cameo." Barry shifts gears to Brendan, the up and coming music video director, my former ingénue, who wants me to be in his short. I'd rather be in his shorts. We already made a movie together, so the seduction thing is backwards. Not courting, Brendan's working me for every bitmap of info he can get.

"I have an interview at the theatre with some local cub," I say, deleting Brendan as content.

"You did a lot of theatre there when you were a kid, didn't you," Barry says.

"So?"

"So, you know how to do it."

I sip my coffee. No whip plus double café poser float. Just coffee, thanks.

I consider my choices, the ones I had as a kid. Performing? Never again. I would have given my usual comfort-from-behind-the-lens spiel, but I've already been quoted on that, twice. After that, it's just dumb. "Time to put away childish things."

"Not even in a music video?" he asks.

"The last time. You want to know the last time?"

A lanky post-grunge tattoo-on-the-back-of-his-neck dude sits at a table near us. I stare. So does Barry. We smile at each other on the return glance.

"What film?" Barry asks.

We're supposed to work together again, another movie, my fourth feature, his ninth. We're fielding offers now. I love that phrase, so agricultural.

Barry writes. I point the camera, and cut, and overdub, and buy beer kegs if necessary to cram a herd of people into different rooms and beaches and sets to make them be my puppets. Barry knows I work hard. I also get pretty pent-up, and he was there for me. But after the last shoot, the TV movie about incest, we don't sleep together anymore.

"*We are Lost to Vision Altogether,*" I say, waiting for him to register recognition. It was a small, brilliant piece of film. "My last moments in front of the camera."

Barry doesn't know the title. He never knows the title, even after writing it. I don't usually like working with people who don't know the title.

"Tom Kalin," I say, naming the director. "He shot a kiss-in at Maria Maggenti's party on Tenth Street above Tompkins Square. Nineteen-eighty-something. Snowy night and the second date with the first guy I loved in New York. We're out in the hall lined up and giggling like the way Spin the Bottle should have been."

I've omitted mention of the gay porn epic I recently wrapped, which Barry refused to discuss. I'll get to that, eventually.

"Where is he?"

"Who? Tom?"

"The guy you kissed at Maria's party."

"Naples, I think. This year."

Barry lets his gaze amble. The tattooed guy catches my eye again, but then lights up a cigarette. I feel a lunge of lust for it, for him, then pity, then the thousand things that shoot through the synapses of an ex-smoker, a collective metabolic replacement for a nicotine rush, an unfilled Mad Lib.

The urge dies as I look back to Barry. His beard keeps my attention; a bit of forest in the waxed-trimmed-shaved desert we call WeHo.

Barry's beard is russet, the color of Labradors. There were times when it was gummy with smears of my spit or other liquids. Now it's clean, evenly trimmed. I resist the urge to touch him. Barry's a bit chunky, a bit too much Metrex over muscle. I miss that.

"So, are we gonna do this thing?" He taps the table.

"Huh? Oh, your script."

It's not like I'm auditioning his work. I know Barry's work like the back of his butt, which I would describe as velvet marble, one of the only non-hairy areas of his body. Barry wants to form a union, in spite of all I did to him, his last script, the one you're going to see happen, from ego wars to Lucite awards.

This time, it's different. The game isn't, *Do You Want Me?* It's, *Do You Want to Storm the Castle with Me Again?*

I smile, give him an open look. I like to stare deep into people's eyes. It makes them think I'm being truly honest. I even fool myself. "This is gonna be a lot of green screen, a lot of CGI."

"You can do that."

"It's really great and I'm like ninety-nine and nine-tenths percent sure, but I gotta go home for a while, you know, with the parent's house, and the thing at the college—"

"The retirement party for that director?"

"Yeah. Also, I gotta rip down the paneling in the basement and resurface the walls. Apparently, it's rotting like the House of Usher. Might even have to dig trenches along the outside."

"Quelle butch."

"So, lemme think about this."

Listen to me. Used to be, I'd jump at anything. Used to be I was begging Barry for a project. He carried me through post-production like no other, picking up all the slips, making it work. Had we made the shift from passion to professionalism? Would we once again share the charge of creation with the intimacy as near-partners? Would a new film with him just be one big long date?

It's late October 2000. He's already tried to recruit me to be part of his desert New Year's Eve Millennium hegira, which sounds cool; camping, food, hiking, the perfect anti-party. But under it, I'd be sharing a tent with Lance, expected to, comfortable enough to bring him, but I wonder if Barry's deciding to escape the city because he knows something we don't. We lived through the riots. We even have tapes, which we don't replay.

Even if the romance—if you can call the occasional trailer quickie or a late night on-location tumble as a romance—is over, I'll be able to work with him. I was really just playing with him, because of course I needed the gig. Despite the Ace Award, the only offers that came have been forgettable; travel documentaries, industrials, a few commercials. I'd rather hustle on Santa Monica than sign on to the torpid scripts I'd been given to read. I had to continue this 'integrity' phase. I was just gonna bust Barry's balls for not being the man I loved, when he should have been. He'll be okay. He'll wait. I've doodled so many storyboards, I take the paper table-cloth with me.

Waiting for the airport shuttle the next morning, I'm looking over the place I've called home for the last too-many years. My bags sit by the door: a small backpack (headphones and tapes in case I end up next to a yacker) and my PowerBook for onboard, along with a slightly larger bag with clothes. I don't have to check it, but I like having the freedom to move, to wander Airport World.

Brief house tour before I leave. Establish sense of place before it's abandoned.

Santa Monica bungalow, charmingly shabby, enough to deter thieves from noticing that the French doors are not wired. Pass through the garden of chaos with overgrown jade and yuccas out of a *Star Trek* set. That dusty pile of black rubber is the surf gear. The small bench and chair are the place where I used to smoke. There were jars and planters full of butts, a collection. They're gone now. I'm clean.

In the living room, there's a big-armed sofa and mismatched chairs so mushy they demand a nap. They suck you in while the CDs sing. On the walls are a few framed posters of my past films, one featuring an actor who I thought was the love of my life. On the floor is my next movie, hope-fully, now a mere pile of comic book pictures.

Near the mess, boxes have begun to grow in small stacks, since I'll soon be moving out some time after my trip back home.

The dining table next to the kitchen counter takes us into the kitchen proper, cluttered with all the gadgets capable of crushing, whirling and slicing any fruit or vegetable into a dippable pulp.

The kitchen is the cartoon art room. Walls in marker-erasable Colorforms plastic, scribble-able thought bubbles over cartoon faces, it demands jokes while you lean on the counter and watch me cook, or while I watch you cook, if you're a really nice guest. This week's best, from the dinner party last month: "I just wanna try another size, not another pierc-ing!" Northstar shouts. "Just say where," seethes Wolverine, claws aimed. Last year The Tick asked Spidey for another chance at love. I've kept that one.

I check the fridge for any perishables that may implode before my return. Not much.

On the fridge are poems, beautiful phrases put together by party guests. I have one from all my friends. It's a combination of Magnetic Poetry and another set called *X Philes*, the bootleg version, made before the guy who ripped off Fox's *X-Files* got the license to make them for Fox. It's a tough town. Only thieves get in.

Those should be put back in their little boxes, after I write them down. Anyway, that's where I got the chapter titles for this book.

The near-impenetrable front door hall is lined with bookshelves, tape shelves, but have mostly been boxed. Where the hell else could I put it? They don't do basements in L.A.

In the guest bedroom are tables and my editing console, more film canisters, videotapes, CDs and files. Atop a shelf over my desk are the awards from indie and gay film festivals, and a pair of stolen drive-in theatre speakers. Some need to be put away. I still can't decide.

Over the shelf hangs my pride and joy, a three-by-five foot poster of Hel, the gal from *Metropolis* who drove a city mad, her metallic face surrounded in lush green. It's signed by the man himself, Fritz Lang. No, I didn't pay top dollar, but it was a long time before she got into my hands.

The bathroom walls are a lovely cacophony of mixed tiles picked from leftover warehouse piles. On a plaster gargoyle-shaped sconce, the silver teardrop-shaped Cable Ace Award. Behold and wipe.

But Hel and the Ace weren't there when all this started. I'm getting ahead of myself.

If you happen to spend some extra time in my bedroom, you'll see the photo over the bed. Um, yes. That gets questions. You have to look closer to see a small framed black and white photo of a man being eaten by an alligator.

Those shoulders bared under African sun, him lying in it. A real ham, though, I mean, to stuff yourself into the guts of an alligator to have your picture taken while you're writing? Whoa. Give the man a nod.

By this time in my description of the Peter Beard photo, you may have hopefully fallen into bed with me, or something of that nature, if you are the sort of person I'd like to do that to, which is ... Well, anyway that's what this is all about, isn't it? Who do you love?

The shuttle bus is late. I pace outside and stand, breathing deep, as if smoking. Then I get the urge and decide to quell it with the better stuff.

I return to my den, open the curved plastic window of my 1965 GI Joe Apollo capsule, current resale value $460.00, and shove a silver-uniformed Joe aside to extract the plastic bag that holds a morsel of Humboldt puffy.

I return the capsule to its tabled orbit, and proceed to light, ignite, and take flight. Despite my best intentions, I'll be flying while flying.

I'm leaving home for an undecided length of time, leaving this place. No garage. The '76 Dodge Dart is in the driveway. It needs work. When Gramma died, I got it, since everyone else in the family had a car. I flew to Pittsburgh, stayed half a day, then drove back cross-country. When I opened the glove compartment somewhere in Kansas, inside was a tiny pair of her Isotoner gloves. I keep them there.

No dog, no kids, no cable, just, finally, a cell phone. What would you expect from a former underground gay film director whose main form of income has been, until recently, managing Woo Video on Pico, who's now lunching with animators about a proposed gay teen serialized action adventure series? What would you expect from a former chubby longhaired fag, now leaner and shaved, whose deepest passions are food, watching surfers come home, and capturing every bit of living and fucking and dying on tape or film?

The shuttle bus arrives to take me on a drive in which I will imagine opening credits, with music by Stone Temple Pilots, "Flies in the Vaseline," perhaps, since my story is all about being stuck in sex things and working one's way out.

This story goes back and forth, but loops around itself. My life/career/whatever, misguided as they come, is based purely on the loss and discovery of men.

The shuttle's honk makes me jump.

I fight a pang of dread, praying my home will be untouched upon my return.

That or burned to ashes.

It could happen.

2. can't have milk

I was a theatre queen before I had pubes. My teen summer tans were as pale as unwashed muslin and my skin as cool as the air-conditioned theater where I hid. In secret moments, wrapped in musty curtains or old costumes, my heart fluttered with uncontrollable surges of heat, passion, and hope.

Some may say a life in the theatre can ruin you. I say it was my salvation. In the days when walking down the street or by a playground might leave me with a bloody nose or a hurled insult that hurt even more, the theatre was my refuge, my shelter.

Although it may have given me a bit too much of a flair for the stylish and symmetrically designed, I still can't shake the flush of desire at the scent of sawdust or a freshly painted flat. I remember what those summers taught me: how to hold myself up amid despair and ridicule, how to light a room, how to see art, where to find the right clever quote, and if that failed, how to improvise.

Theater schooled me in Varsity Fagdom.

I stole a canvas once.

Welcome to Circe Airlines. Our arrival time is five hours or twenty years.

I'm typing on the plane, clacking away at my speech while the businessclone next to me pretends to sleep, his thick-fingered hand near-cradling his crotch. I look down occasionally, then out the window, regarding the rumpled blanket of earth, wishing I'd taken another glance at my city before leaving.

I turn down Frank Black on the headphones, now that the thrill of jetting over Los Angeles is over.

I'm uncomfortable in my seat, but being a visual type of person, I always want the window. Besides, plane seats are meant to annoy guys like me. I'm a bit large, not fat, but tall, what in my youth would have its own section in the Sears catalog: husky. Now I'd be a bear if I weren't naturally smooth. I wonder if I can start my own gay subcategory of chunky, smooth gays: Dolphins?

As I resume typing, the businessclone shifts his weight. Our legs graze.

I admit it. I stole a canvas, folded it away in the attic. I'd painted the last layer myself, in a light cream I'd mixed, a dual spatter of brown and beige, followed by intricate wainscoting with a wet blend wood pattern. I'd even made a small mouse hole at one corner. There was no losing that. I hated how a canvas could be lost, thrown out, how all the work disappeared and all I had were programs and memories. So, I stole it. It became my sail for the journey that never seems to end. (remember to pause dramatically here)

I'm not returning it, I'm sorry to say. I still need to hold on to a bit of my memory, to remember when I learned the secret of theatre. It wasn't in a book. It wasn't in a script or a title or a performance. It was somewhere in between that paint and those layers of signatures, glyphs of all sizes, bits of immortality and belief in a myth and a tale, enough to tell it again and again until there was no more time, when you tired of the tale and merely wanted to tell tales of the time when you were telling the tale.

Well, that's a bunch of crap.

Have to trim that last part later. The four-dollar rum and Coke is getting to me, and the businessclone is looking handsome under the plane's dim lights, having spread his legs deliberately to touch my thigh. I don't retreat.

Not here on the plane. Numbers traded like baseball cards. A meeting somewhere back home, in some field or hotel, somewhere close to home, where I can christen some haunt of my childhood's ghost with some new juice.

But of course I don't need company to do that.

This is an autobiography, the story somebody else might write about me, because after twenty years of hard work, I'm finally an overnight success.

You're saying, how old is this guy? I started doing theatre at fourteen. That's when I learned how to lie to stay alive.

Making movies is fun and don't let anyone tell you different, even me. But the worst part is dreaming movies, almost every night; brilliant Busby Berkeley nude go-go boy riot musicals; burning buildings and singing dinosaurs. These are the sad ones, doomed to an audience of one.

Take the redemption angle on last night's dream: My long-lost uncle is homeless. His teeth are rotten. Despite my efforts to dress him up and get him clean, he returns to the streets, curling himself up in a cardboard box. I woke up from that one crying, not because of my uncle's fate, but because no one would back it even if it could be a movie.

But before the industry tell-all, I've got to outline the usual bucolic revisionist memoir. Brookside, Ohio, where a boy learned the ropes. Call it Winesburg, if you like, or Ithaca. Call it anything warm and sweet and innocent where there are always thick packets of handwritten mail and store-bought pies waiting. Call it home.

3. there is luscious hidden language

When a show closed, before the last performance, everybody from the little kids like me to the older college kids signed their names on the backs of a flat. Flats were painted over and used again, so you had to label the show you were in.

Eric Shoemaker was very neat, making a small signature in paint beside each previous show he did. Mickey Steinbock used to draw cartoons, until he used a Magic Marker that bled through the other side. We had to keep putting pictures or plants in front of the stain to hide it.

Other student actors were more flamboyant, scribbling large John Hancocks or funny sayings. That kept us together more than all the latches and hinges and sandbags combined.

Whenever I was in a show as a boy, I remember pacing backstage and counting the flats with my signature. But mostly it was with my brother, our two first names stacked together above our last:

**DAN & STAN
GROZNIAK**

It was our little tribute to ourselves. I'm Stan. Stanley Valeri Grozniak, officially. Nice name for a Polish-Irish kid, huh? Those flats were littered with our names long before our first dates with girls, that activity being yet another form of acting for me.

When a flat became too laden with layers of paint, cracked, or ripped a few too many times for another patch, it was usually shoved away in a vertical file along the side of the scene shop, the giant play space of saws, hammers, drills, buckets of bolts, racks of lumber, and bins of pigment.

If we were short of wood, some techie would take out an old flat, rip off the canvas and start all over again. There was no need to rip up a well-made flat. They took too long to build.

Sometimes we scrubbed and thinned the layers of paint on a canvas so we could reuse it. Dick Thorson and I would hose the flats down, scrubbing them in the driveway of the scene shop, both of us shirtless and wet in the summer afternoons, our few hours actually spent in the sun. My chubby teenage frame was nothing compared to his burly muscles. Dick looked even better wet.

Mom always says Dick Thorson looked like a big Muppet, not a little one-hander, like Kermit or Ernie, but the big standing ones from way back. Do you remember Jim Henson's *Cinderella?* Do you remember seeing something or someone for the first time and knowing it was love without knowing the name for it? I had crushes on Muppets. Is that strange, any stranger to love a guy only six years your senior? But let's not jump to societal issues. Let's have more nostalgic backstory.

When too many layers had come and gone, Dick and I would peel the sagging canvas off the frames, prying the staples off with flathead screwdrivers to salvage the wood. Truly old canvases became floor mats for other painting projects (It was one of those, complete with foot prints, that I own). Those naked wet frames worried me. They showed what could happen if we didn't believe long enough or hard enough.

I'm thinking about this stuff as I write my speech for my homecoming. The things about me that made me an outcast are what got me this fame, this resounding revenge. Cliché, yes, but I will revel in it, soak it up like champagne at thirty thousand feet. Or I would if I weren't traveling coach and drinking a rum and Coke.

I click away at my PowerBook while the semi-cute businessclone tries his hand once more at conversation. I like seeing his uneasiness as I continue to type through our talk, the way his eyes keep darting down to the screen, as if I'm recording his blathering, as if I even know what we're chatting about. I finally notice he's leaning in closer, so I shut the damn thing and look him right in the eye, and we talk.

The movie is over. Yes, it starred Hugh Grant. While parents walk their infants up and down aisles, other folks jockey for the toilet.

He, of course, gets around to the question, which for me will open that vast cesspool of my opinions, successes, and failures, the question which will bring up the topics of homosexuality, death, AIDS, sexual frailties, poverty, and riches: "What do you do for a living?"

I tell him.

"How'd you get into that?"

I recite what I tell interviewers, when they ask, and they always do, how I got my first idea to direct films. If he'd ever had a beer and movie night in college a few years back, he might know of my *The Manipulator* trilogy, a low-budget late '80s cult classic. The rest are categorized as "gay," "experimental," or both.

I don't mind being ghettoized into the gay filmmaker category. Categories are nice. They help your audience find you. We have our own shelves. I just don't want gay people coming to my movies expecting a gay aesthetic, camp, or Bette, or poppers, or any of that, as if I'm just another Judy queen with a touching story to tell about a love affair between sero-discordant club kids in P-Town.

I'm sorry, but while this homo was being reared, so to speak, some other things took his fancy, like Aerosmith, *Battlestar Galactica,* and Aquaman.

"Puppets," I tell the businessclone.

"What?"

"How I got into directing."

"Oh."

It was on a family trip to Mexico. I was ten. In a crowded market street, I bought a set of marionettes from an old woman, her face brown and dry as terracotta. My parents had lost me in the maze of tents and shops. My mother tells me she got the inkling I would become a very efficient director when they found me haggling the old woman down to ten bucks for three puppets. "Cutting the budget even then," is her much-repeated joke.

But it wasn't about that. I only had ten dollars, and I thought those puppets were friends, that they couldn't be taken away from each other. In that dusty grotto in Nogales, a little clown with guns, a red-caped bull-fighter with tight, spangled pants, and a mustachioed cop danced under my hands. On the plane back to Ohio, I refused to check the marionettes with the luggage, insisting they each get to see the clouds.

I tell the interviewers about my movie nights, charging neighborhood kids five cents for a Halloween showing of the last reel of *Phantom of the Opera*—preadolescents couldn't take all four reels, even with our concocted rock music accompaniment—preceded by a bad horror Super8 one-reeler my brother and I made.

In our *Jekyll and Hyde,* I was transformed by downing a magic liquid of water, bicarbonate of soda, and green food dye. It foamed thanks to our crewmember, Mike Humerkauser, a chubby blond boy who would later initiate me into the joys of Kiss, Alice Cooper, and Bowie's *Diamond Dogs.* I also borrowed his fake fangs, which he let me keep when I tried to return them coated in drool.

The film also included the traditional Jekyll-goes-mad scene, in which we lit our backyard like a London park, propping up ancient black gates my dad had removed in favor of white waist-high fencing. He also played our first victim. Dressed as a bum, my Jekyll character mimed beating him with a cane.

What would a psychotherapist say to that one?

My brother lost these films in an abrupt move one cold night, as he hastily departed from Chicago to his now-wife's apartment. The landlord in Chicago did not care for non-paying tenants and did not have a polite way of expressing this dislike. Dan now lives in San Francisco with his lovely wife Gloria and their cherub, Gloria II.

Before his abrupt move and subsequent loss of our filmic property, my brother did, however, get these scenes dubbed onto video before losing them. I cursed him, spat violent threats over the phone, and swore to disown him until he made a copy for my pre-Ace Awards *Entertainment Tonight* interview.

It seemed our name just came up at a party, and some high-aired creative director met my bro, the up and coming San Francisco comic animator in town for an MTV party conference schmooze session. Before I knew it, Dan's video was on a segment of the show, and he later snagged a spot himself to promote his new video game.

On a much smaller PR scale, I'm scheduled to do an interview with my hometown newspaper before the tribute to Arthur McCabe, whom I like to call my professor. Actually, he ran the entire small but magical theatre department of Brookside College. He was also my dad's best friend. My love affair with the theatre really began there. Forget those damn puppets. None of the kids on the block liked that stuff anyway. Besides, they didn't really like me, even though I only charged them a nickel.

Brookside, Ohio, where Baptist churches emerged from the ground faster than Monolith Monsters, where Young Men's Christian Athletes could merely burp and appear in the local newspapers. Who would think that such a tiny town in Ohio could hold such treasures for an up and coming director?

Every few weeks of the summer of 1976, when my lust awoke, I passed an hour or so in the fourth floor no-action college library john, Duane Michals's first photo book in my lap or delicately placed on the toilet paper dispenser. Naked men in wings and masks and strange, timeless, mythical symbol image plays urged my boy juices up and outward. Eventually I collected enough change to photocopy the entire book and paste it together at home, then I hid it in my attic filing cabinet of eaves, between dusty pink fiberglass insulation.

Playing with the pictures of Duane Michals taught me to understand storyboarding and sidetracked me into photography for a while, but hey, learn to make a good still, then move the picture. I always wiped up the stains.

I didn't know how to move these strange non-credit, non-tuitioned skills into a career. With the exception of my wonderful years as the manager of Woo Video, I think I'm one of the least hirable people I know. While others have old lovers, I have old jobs. I quit jobs like stormy romances, lured by the security, the domesticity, bliss through repetition. Storming out in a huff always worked best. Easing off left room for reconsideration, glossed-over polite farewells, all lies.

I was forced to become a director, a maker of projects. I like to see an end, a completion to work and relationships. I'm like a lot of others who felt a great relief with the collapse of the economy, the great heavy curtain of Reagan's Oz falling in embarrassment. This unveiling gave people who always hated dumb work and dumb jobs and power structure a certain affinity. Dart in, out, take the money and go. Freelance. Free Lance.

Of course, I didn't tell the businessclone on the plane all that. I told him the Mexican puppets story. He gave me his number.

4. reincarnation proves ancient telepathic blood

Carrot top.

Through a stroke of genetics, both my brother and I inherited our father's dingy Polish gray-brown eyes and hair, and his square jaw. The cleft chin, I think, came from the Irish. It was Mother's Irish side that nestled inside, I guess.

"Never was an artist in my family before you two," Dad would say, surprised and proud of his sons' increasingly flamboyant skills. Well, maybe mine were a bit more so.

But the red hair was definitely on Mom's side.

A gang of junior high kids and I, mostly the theatre crew of Brookside, piled into Mindy Menck's mom's Cadillac to a mall movie showing of *Carrie.* I forget who hissed it first, but the moment Piper Laurie stalked up that driveway, russet red hair shining off a black cape, somebody said, "It's Mrs. Grozniak!" And it stuck.

I remember laughing too, but later, when Carrie's mom turned out to be a freak, I burned inside. Not that I was really embarrassed about my mom and her fiery red hair. People already knew we didn't go to church. She used to go door to door recruiting wives for the League of Women Voters, a several-years activity that also got her in the local yawner, *The Brookside Gazette.* She wore black and red Pendleton capes and knee-high, don't-fuck-with-me snow boots that made the plain folk in town stare. She was the pioneer of our collection of family news clippings.

I was secretly proud of my mom and her orange hair, and even more secretly thrilled by her mysterious brothers. They were from Pittsburgh, where we were all originally born. We got out before I could absorb memories. One of my mom's brothers supposedly disappeared. The other is in a grave in Piscataway, sent by one needle too many.

The most I had of them were photos in the attic, next to an eave where, possibly still hidden, is the second issue of *Playgirl,* which I'd stolen shortly after I grew pubic hair and the balls to shoplift.

Several photos of my Uncle Sean, shirtless, lay stuffed in a box in the attic of my parents' home. Him in reform school in Pittsburgh. Him at the beach. Him at a playground, holding his newborn son like a fidgeting sack of flour.

Pittsburgh is a minefield of borrowed memories. We got out of Pennsylvania before I became too big a mouth to feed. But I feel like I have roots there. I feel like going back someday. I feel like retracing things, finding things out, like why I feel like a redhead on the inside.

Sean O'Leary, the uncle, the redhead, paler freckled skin, his hair brush cut like G.I. Joe, but thin, frail and a dim brassy glow. He was my first real kiss.

Of course, at ten, a boy doesn't completely get the function of parts. I just remember one of Uncle Sean's visits with his wife, May, and their new baby, my little burble of a cousin, Mike. I was in my pajamas, sent off to bed, and the round of goodnight kisses burned in by the scrape of his cheek, by the tiny taste of spit from his lips, by the glance, the way I had to pinch my PJs on the way up the stairs to stop the mistaken feeling of having to pee.

At fourteen, what I gazed at in the attic and what I played with in the basement came together, somewhere in the middle.

Our basement tried to become a den for a while. In one back room were the washer and dryer, Dad's tool bench, and other little rooms for Christmas ornaments and spare boxes.

The front room of the basement was paneled in wood. Bookshelves lined one wall. An old sofa sat along another wall, with a few leftover end tables on either side. It was comfortable enough, but the boggy Ohio floods of the 1970s kept interrupting, and we'd have to call the Roto-Rooter guy and throw out any soggy thing left on the floor.

But at times, the space had a mystery, and when I invited friends over for sleepovers, my short-term friends and I had enough privacy to run around in our underpants, making sex jokes and peeing into the drain below the washing machine.

It became my secret space for long self-play sessions away from Dan's interruptions. I'd walk around the room, peeking through health manuals, old science journals, and *Life* magazines with nude hippies. A few times I stole a carrot from the fridge's crisper and, ever so delicately, inserted the bobbed end into my ass, trying to figure out what the big deal was about getting buttfucked.

Marty Keyhouser kept making jokes about a scene in *Deliverance*, a movie my parents wouldn't take me to see and I couldn't sneak into. I had an image of Burt Reynolds getting butt-fucked. No offense to Ned Beatty, but when I finally saw the film, I was disappointed.

When not thinking sexual thoughts about movies stars, which was most of the time, I danced off the paneled basement walls, singing George Chakiris and Richard Beymer's parts in *West Side Story*. All right, Natalie Wood's too, and Rita Moreno's, on occasion.

Dan and I often filmed our little movies in the basement, the only place where a mess was allowed to remain in progress. We'd stay up late on weekends, clicking away with an animated cartoon or Claymation four-minute masterwork while watching a late night horror movie.

Two Cleveland stations played late night horror movies, and each had hosts with their own styles. Friday nights, one of the small local stations had a strange host called The Ghoul. He wore sunglasses with one lens permanently out, a hippie Cyclops in a lab coat and a goatee.

The Ghoul helped initiate a sardonic sensibility toward our young minds. At pivotal or ridiculous scenes in *Bride of the Monster,* or possibly the best worst horror film of all time, *The Creeping Terror,* the show's studio technicians would bump in a sample of some wacky comment from The Beatles *Christmas Album*: "Look out for yourself!" "Ooooh, Get away!" or snippets of appropriate songs. When Ghidra took flight, the "Surfin' Bird" chorus blasted through the worn speaker of the black-and-white TV Dan and I had dragged down to the basement after Dad got tenure and bought a newer color set for the living room.

Once, I even dressed up an old Raggedy Andy doll to look like The Ghoul, complete with goatee, eye patch, and lab coat, and mailed it to the station as a gift. Weeks later, The Ghoul displayed it on one of his shows. "This was sent from Brookside, Ohio by Stan and Dan Groz, Groooze, Groznik!"

He messed up our name, but we screamed so loud with joy it woke our parents. Dad came downstairs just in time to watch his sons marvel as The Ghoul placed my Raggedy Ghoul on a table with his constant victim, Froggy, a plastic amphibian, atop him, and finally blow them both up with a cluster of firecrackers.

My father seemed concerned for our sanity and the content of local television, but made no protests since we usually watched it in the basement. Despite the cement floors, the carpeting was pulled up in the spring, when the drain clogged up, leaving the floor an inch high in water. But those winter nights, with the fireplace going, marshmallows roasting in our basement, we often had a few of our friends over to watch the monster movies. Sometimes I invented arguments to get Dan pissed off enough to leave me with my own friend, David Hollister or Randy Simms.

Sleepovers. I think of all the times I could have had sex.

The CBS affiliate, Channel 8, reigned on Saturdays. Big Chuck and Hoolihan showed even worse movies, and took a lot of time performing comedy sketches no better than a high school talent show. Some of the bits were so bad we couldn't even tell where the punch line was without the aid of their persistent audio laugh track.

Hoolihan was a willowy guy who later left the show and turned into a born-again Christian. I think he had a wife and kids, but that didn't bother me. What did bother me, in retrospect, were his solo comedy sketches, "Readings by Robert." They had a slightly Ernie Kovacs quality, but the bespectacled, lisping character, who read inane poems with his legs crossed, was probably one of the worst gay stereotypes of my young life. I could imitate "Robert" all too well, and often did to make Dan laugh, until I grew tired of it. I didn't realize the implications of venting my own fears of being effeminate. Things like that can fuck a kid up.

Big Chuck, on the other hand, was a large, handsome guy who looked like a retired football player. He had a strong jaw and the cleft chin of Kirk Douglas. He was often the butt of jokes, since he was Polish. That's why I loved him. The show's writers got around the possible complaints from numerous Northern Ohio Polish viewers by using the phrase, "person of a certain ethnic background." The joke could be all about bowling, white socks, flamingos on the lawn, Parma, Ohio (a center of Polish immigrants), but it was always just about "people of a certain ethnic background."

This was in the days before home VCRs, of course, so any moment had to be enjoyed right then and savored forever, since some of the show was also live. Among them was the regular reading of the letters from fans. Once the movie was over, Big Chuck and Hoolihan appeared in short nightgowns and caps to bid all viewers goodnight. Big Chuck's nightie was red, and it hung just low enough not to be indecent. A common gag among crew members, or the later replacement co-host, Little John, a cute Italian midget with a big nose, was to try to get Big Chuck's nightgown yanked up to expose him, or to get Big Chuck to fall down and expose himself.

By high school, Dan was working weekends or dating girls, so I sometimes had the run of the basement, laying on the sofa, waiting eagerly through every awful horror movie and lousy sketch for the show's closer. I'd seen brief glimpses enough times to anticipate the thrill, even though I knew Big Chuck wore undershorts. I'd already worked myself up to a hard-on just by watching the weekly joke commercial about kielbasa, the Polish sausage my mother only cooked, thankfully, on holidays.

The commercial featured a tight pan shot of Big Chuck's waist. He sported denim jeans and a holster, but instead of a gun, he had a long, pendulous link of kielbasa in it. As he walked, the thick sausage flopped against his hip. Usually I'd settle for jacking off to that image, imagining the meat to be Big Chuck's. I'd then force myself to watch the rest of the show, drowsing on the sofa huddled under a blanket, usually falling asleep for the night.

The show always ended with Big Chuck and Hoolihan standing around, sound off, while the audio guy played Peggy Lee's "Is That All There Is?" It was years before I even heard the song in its entirety, since the version they played always slowed to a halt, recorded to the sound of the turntable winding down, Peggy Lee's voice thickening to molasses. It became a theme—no exposures, no flesh flash, another dumb movie, another Saturday night with me alone in a clammy basement, perpetually waiting for a moving image of manhood.

One night, though, I felt a sense of anticipation and held off, even through the swinging sausage bit. The movie that night was *Creature from the Black Lagoon,* and I'd successfully delayed my teen orgasm through every one of the men's underwater and shirtless scenes.

I had initiated that basement so many times while watching *Wild Wild West* episodes, *Space 1999,* even an occasional *Beverly Hillbillies* scene with Jethro, I lost track of the stains, the times I knelt down and fingered my seed into evaporating patterns on the dusty cement floor. I had a private cum-shooting contest alongside the full length Mark Spitz poster with him wearing only Speedos and seven medals, hung on the wall. Twice I struck gold.

One afternoon, my brother Dan came down the stairs and caught me with a carrot.

"What are you doing?" he cried.

Well, if he didn't know, I wasn't about to explain it to him. Instead, I threw it at him. A bit of shit splatted against the paneling. He ran up the stairs, screaming. I quickly pulled my clothes on, grabbed the carrot, hid it deep in a garbage can, and raced up the stairs and out the garage door, where I continued running into the woods, a vast expanse of sub-suburban, not quite rural acreage, still undeveloped by rows of tract homes.

I didn't come home until well after nightfall. Dinner was dry but warm, a single plateful in the oven. There must have been a brief talk, "a little chat," as Mom called them, but I don't remember what was said, how she glossed over the facts until I burst out, loud enough for Dan to hear upstairs, with the fact that I was gay, and there wasn't anything they could do about it.

All I knew was I had somehow gained power over the situation by showing the enormity of my secrets. I would choose the discussion. I would direct and cut the scene as I saw fit. I think that's what gave Dan and me the biggest thrill, making things in our way, imitative of our icons and heroes, of course. But we got to make our childhoods.

That almost got ruined when Dan discovered me mid-carrot. Before that, we'd always been conspirators, collaborators. That changed when we grew apart.

Sex can do that, even when you don't have it.

Before my brother discovered my affection for produce, and before I fell in love with Dick Thorson and other college boys with tall bodies and sweet smiles, things were innocent and all crammed together with giggles and fits.

Sometimes people asked if we were non-identical twins, which is not true, though we sometimes nodded yes in response, a private joke. Between me and Dan, my mom had had a miscarriage. One of our sickest jokes was picking on the imaginary in-between brother. He was a great little buffer when we couldn't beat up on each other once we realized we only had each other.

Our first film was no masterpiece, nothing like our *Jekyll and Hyde*. The Christmas of 1974, I was twelve and Dan was thirteen-and-a-half. We got a GAF Super8 Movie Camera and a GAF Super8 Projector. They're still both up in the attic in Brookside rotting and broken, but when we got them, it was magic. We rarely fought over who shot what. Somebody had to shoot, and somebody had to be shot. We traded.

Christmas Day, we ran around the house shooting the Christmas tree, the cats, and our parents smiling, the glaring movie light attached to the tiny camera like a headlight on antlers. We kept shooting long after the film ran out, and days later, we both raced to the Giant Store photo department to get the little reel. Home again, we carefully wove it through the projector's guts as if it were precious gold thread.

We laughed at our incompetence, but inside, we both knew we'd failed. It wasn't art. We didn't even want to show it to our parents, but relented. When they mentioned showing it to some of their friends, we cringed, cashed our Christmas checks from our grandparents, and bought four more rolls of film. Then we planned.

People were boring and too hard to wrangle. We made cartoons. Using a stop motion wire, we made a clumsy cartoon with magazine cuttings flying around a series of backgrounds. In one part, I wanted to recreate the depth effect in some early Popeye cartoons. I showed Dan how to do it with a sheet of glass. I stole the idea from a chart in a special issue of *Scream Magazine* devoted to the technical details of *King Kong*. He seemed wary, but we tried it.

We created a forest of hands clipped from jewelry ads. Armless creatures with bulging eyes chased bird things with shoes for wings. The glass ended up glaring. The section with the cartoons and magazine people was funny, usually one opening its mouth to eat another. My fingers and elbows were in a few shots, but we were happy. This was magic. The audience could be summoned.

My parents used to throw parties in the '70s. Dad was a math teacher at Brookside College, and all sorts of intelligent people came to eat and drink. We sat in corners or asked precocious questions from English teachers whose breath was heavy with scotch.

Before one of these parties, I'd snuck a sip of the scotch in our dining room bar and gasped for air. I hated it and preferred sneaking my mother's sparkling cider as I stole cashews and Brazil nuts from the little nut bowls she set out on such nights.

Mom didn't drink, then. At the time, I didn't know the difference. I just knew the smoke and music would make me tired, and Dan and I would be sent off to bed, occasionally visited by bored adults who liked to peruse our room full of monster posters and books and *Star Wars* models and my growing puppet collection.

The first night we showed a film, my dad draped a white sheet over a painting, where we aimed the projector. All the adults laughed in the right places and clapped and whistled when the movie was over.

I didn't know then most other kids didn't make movies that were watched by college professors. I didn't know most other kids didn't make art, or at least didn't make a constant waterfall of it the way we did.

Forget magnetting them to the fridge. We had piles of drawings, stacks of cartoon books, clusters of clay sculptures. I want to be able to do that again, to make things without thinking once about whether anyone will like it, fund it, market it, distribute it, to just make things and do things knowing they'll make me happy, and if someone else likes it, then fine.

How nice for you. How nice for everyone.

5. lazy men want the curse

Barry prefers to say we met at a party in 1989, which is true enough, but it's not where we really connected. There were handshakes and chitchat at some semi-closeted actor's house, me worrying my palm was cold from the beer bottle I was holding. I remember some flirtatious greetings, him complimenting my past work with a funny remark. I politely waited for him to make a self-deprecating joke about his name, Barry Goldstein, before trying out a line as sacred to me as prayer for others.

We were hovering over a table laden with munchies when I said, "Have an egg roll, Mister Goldstein?"

He didn't get it until I sang the line from *Gypsy*. Then he laughed.

After hearing my last name, he asked if I was Czech. I corrected him, but that stuck. He was more interested in my grandparents than my grand projects.

"When did they leave Poland?" he asked.

"Oh, before the war."

"Which one?"

"Um, Two."

"Well, there were a lot of them, ya know."

"I guess."

"So, you're from ..." He asked, as if I still hadn't answered his question.

"My family was all born in Pittsburgh."

"Oh. And your mother?"

"Irish. Potato famine stuff."

"Right."

We connected then. I knew it. It was an oasis of reality. Out here, more people ask what you've done, not where you're from because everyone's recreated themselves. Roots are bleached. Which is why I scoff at Barry's cover-up about our next encounter. Nobody cares in L.A. The past is mist, haze. It's always where you're going, what you'll be doing, "projects."

I remember slipping away from the party, which was cast with too many industry up-and-comers eager to schmooze. I offered no ins, and therefore little fuel for gab. This was when I was really not getting any work at all, adrift without a crew.

Yet the energy of the party and the two beers filled me with that nervous antsy feeling I mistook for desire. I went to The Zone, a warehouse of a sex club, and wandered the fake sets of erotic machismo, fending off pint-size touchers and ambling after muscle boys.

And then I saw Barry. He'd taken off his party shirt or gone home to change, I don't know. Maybe he had stud gear ready in his car. He looked awkward there, out of place, his slightly burly form and hairy chest pressing out of a Brando wife-beater. A lot of guys were giving him glances. Thickness implies health, doncha know.

His beard was thinner then, but still incongruous to the nubile Marky Mark look others sported. He looked filmed, authentically preserved like a guy from a '70s porn tape I'd never gotten around to renting. I was amused at how the environment, the music and dim lighting, could change the shape of his face. In the darker light, he looked more severe, not a light-hearted Jewish stud, but a daddy.

He didn't recognize me at first, but when we nearly bumped into each other on a third pass, we both softly chuckled and stood close.

He broke to awkwardness by paraphrasing an old joke.

"Did you hear about the Polish actor? He wanted to get into movies, so he fucked the writer."

I laughed, too loud for the environs, judging by a few nearby men's glares. Barry led me to a little cubicle, but despite our erections popping out of our pants, we both felt ridiculous in the cramped booth. He didn't look like anything more than himself.

He invited me to his house. It was as if we'd saved each other from the sex club, superior for moving our first encounter to a home.

I followed in my Awful Car, a thrice-used Chrysler something, playing an old Red Hot Chili Peppers mix of slow songs. Tailing Barry's Range Rover, I smoked a cigarette with satisfaction, as if we'd already completed the act.

I remembered nights back in the '70s, when gas was cheap, driving for hours was an evening's entertainment. A few times, Dan and I played Tailgate. You arbitrarily pick a car and just follow it. We pretended we were detectives, investigating some Ed Gein-type criminal. Usually the driver pulled into a quiet driveway in a tiny town near Brookside. We'd drive on, then home.

Once, though, we followed a guy in a mint green Cadillac. Dan decided we should see his face, and we pulled up beside him and both gave him a glance. He was heavyset, poured into his seat, jowly, not at all content. He looked like the sort of man who would make a grinding cough every two minutes. We passed, then slowed and let him pass. It was a slow highway dance. We followed the Cadillac for two hours. Dan kept saying, "You wanna quit?" I'd shake my head. We made up a whole life for the guy: dead wife, weird kids, sold house, maybe a dog named Pippy. We didn't let him go until we reached the Indiana border. We'd reached a symbol of finality. Also, we were almost out of gas.

Barry's first breakfast made for me would later become a sort of symbol for apology or renewal: scrambled eggs with dill, mushrooms and a tiny bit of parmesan, plus diced potatoes not quite hash browns, just plain coffee, and fresh ground carrot juice. That got me giggling. I'd never had fresh ... ground? Squeezed seems dumb, anyway. You don't squeeze a carrot, you eviscerate it.

The juice got me to telling Barry about The Carrot Incident with my brother. After a good round of laughter at my expense, we got around to the topic of work.

"So, you did three features?" Barry was asking about *The Manipulator* trilogy.

"I wouldn't call them features, but yes, I made three movies." I didn't want to talk about them. That would get me talking about Ricky.

Barry must have sensed it, I don't know, because he just wrapped that up with, "I'll have to go out and rent them."

"Sure."

"They are on video, aren't they?"

"Yeah."

"And you know a good place to find them?"

I smiled. I was a manager at Woo Video at the time, and I liked it. I could see Barry coming into Woo Video with the regularity of any other pre- or post-sex flirting guy, and there have been a few, surprised to find me behind the counter and on the shelf, and not doing lunch at Chateau Marmont. They would keep their memberships. They would occasionally invite me over to watch their rentals. Some of them seemed to stop renting porno once they'd boinked me. That I found odd, as if, having explored their bodies, I could no longer price-code their fantasies.

"Actually, if you're in a retail mood, my movies are on sale in Walmarts."

"Whoah."

"I didn't get any of that deal, though."

"Oh."

Barry didn't think managing a video store was any sort of work for a former film director, no matter what grade. Barry asked sincerely what I wanted to do next, as in a Next that would involve returning to the hazardous environs of making films. I feigned one project or another, making the half-finished screenplays fermenting in my computer seem like more than they were. Mainly I was filling time and paying rent.

"Two free tapes a night," I said. "I'm amassing a very nice library."

"You're a film director. You shouldn't be working in a video store."

"I like it. I like my boss. Mr. Woo is very nice. We have fun. I've got benefits, dental. He let us put the Van Damme standup in a tutu for Gay Pride."

That got him. Barry laughed and understood not to harp on the caste of my employment. He did ask me if I had an agent, though, as we had round two of coffee in his yard. I threatened to sunbathe nude. He went for my shorts.

"Agents, agents." I wasn't going to dodge him that time. I knew directors had agents, but that didn't seem to fit me. I hadn't even joined the Director's Guild, since it would have cost a third of my fee from the last real film I made. I didn't want to be considered for another feature with car crashes and murders. No guns, please. Obscurity fit me.

Sometimes, at the video store, I wore my favorite T-shirt that Rick Dacker, the star of *The Manipulator* movies gave me. The T-shirt reads: "Don't You Know Who I Was?"

Barry and I finished breakfast. Despite the fact that I could have stayed since I had night shift, I made moves to leave. Being a successful producer, Barry assured me his agent would be calling. Maybe we could work on something in the future. "If you care to swim with sharks again," he said in a way that to me meant he understood why I chose to be a loser.

I didn't expect anything of it, but I was pleased Barry made the gesture. It gave me a feeling of continuance, of a future. My dreams of making a wide appeal gay film had been thus far dashed. I felt secure in the ghetto. This was pre-Ellen, pre-*Trick*, pre-*Brokeback*, before Christine Vachon and her crew even starting banging out all those fashionable queer murder flicks that annually charmed the festival circuit.

I didn't know Barry really meant it until his agent called a week later for a meeting. Sal Benedetto was nice enough, but the twenty minutes I spent watching him talk to other people on the phone didn't seem to justify the two hours driving to and from his office in Culver City.

Weeks went by. Barry would call. We'd go out, have nice sex, but make no plans to meet too soon again. I made mention of a "guy I've been seeing," a total lie, but he took it as what it was, a pushing away. I didn't want to let him think I was just fucking him as thanks for what had yet to happen, reconnecting with an actual career. I was still happy being a has-been.

"Any sexual relationship between show biz people has advantages," admonished my friend and co-worker, Jorge Oribe. Jorge ran the foreign film section at Woo Video and the Men's Erotica Section of Woo Too, in West Hollywood. Mister Woo failed to grasp the concept that merely saying Woo WeHo would give us a *Wizard of Oz* inside joke. Ya gotta get a gimmick to survive in L.A. Instant Camp, just add parking.

"Woo Two name after my son," Mister Woo stated with finality.

Jorge and I realized we needed to evolve or die.

Jorge also works on other people's films, costume assisting, mostly. For me, though, he was Costume Master. Jorge was into his leather phase then.

That bright October day in 1994, Jorge and I nibbled at the remnants of our lunch before his pre-Halloween "clean the house since neither of us have dates or the energy for a party." I'd been hinting about some sort of possibility with Barry.

Jorge stood there in a leopard-skin bikini and yellow rubber gloves. "Nude Maid. Because you're a dirty little boy." Jorge posed beside his Magic Chef in the latest money-making scheme of the day.

Jorge had a script I liked better than Barry's. It was bilingual. But try getting that financed. I told him I was moving forward on another project, but I promised to find him employment, should I have the strings to pull more than a few Mexican puppets.

"That'd be nice. Then I can afford to get a real maid." Jorge scrubbed away at the guts of his oven. He'd discovered that all that goo that spills over when you overcook gathers up in stalactite form. Jorge had recently become more aware of fire safety after his recent amour. "Ooh, honey! That fireman I dated with the big muscles and the little willy! He read my place up and down for code violations!"

Jorge collects, among many, many other flammable things, old magazines. *After Dark. Rona Barrett's Hollywood.*

We're collectible sisters.

I scraped the oven grill like a lyre. My trash shorts sported some butch grease stains. The plan was to get as grungy as possible, then crash a Halloween party and pretend we were mechanics. That was supposed to get us laid.

Watching Jorge's butt wiggle, I purred, "Che culito."

"Stuff it in, Stubbito," he hissed.

That's Jorge's private name for me. It makes reference to my, um, girth, in certain places.

"In the oven? Al Parker does Sylvia Plath!"

Jorge pulled out of the oven at that remark.

So why isn't this the story of us? There's the little matter of Jorge being so gorgeous that I'd be overshadowed. Besides, I made more friends when I went out with Jorge, especially when I clarified that we were just friends. Jorge is too popular for mating. We had sex once, and when I got all lovey-dovey, he reminded me he's a Sagittarius and then we didn't talk for a few days, until he explained that our affair was merely my rebound post-Ricky.

"This is our fifth Halloween together," he said as he plopped a sponge into the sink.

"Really?"

"Oh, you don't remember the first one, the pool party? With Ricky and ... I'm sorry."

"Why? Don't apologize."

"Okay."

Ricky had been there as well as a lot of other guys I don't see much. That year had been spent with a lot more people. I wondered about that.

Jorge is an ex-dancer who won't be coming out of retirement. "Honey, if I ever lift my legs again for *anyone*," he'd said, "it is not gonna be for a choreographer." He still moves in lots of ways: planning projects, getting people together for parties, protests, orgies.

At Woo Video, we had a secret game. Any customer who unknowingly rented one of our films got a free bag of microwave popcorn. We never sold the stuff anyway.

Unfortunately, we rarely gave it away, either.

"So, it sounds good to me," Jorge said of Barry and his project. "You're dating him. He's Mister Eggroll, and you got a brand new project to save you from the next edition of *Whatever Happened To...?*"

"Yeah, but—"

"But what?" He shifted to PeeWee Herman voice. "Everybody's got a big but."

I replaced the grills after he gave the oven's insides a final swipe with a cluster of paper towels. "The but is, I don't think I agree with his point of view on the topic."

"Daddy Knows Best?"

"Uncle."

"Mmmm. He wants to play it careful."

"Yup."

"Baby, it's a lot of money. Why don't you be careful once and see what it gets you, instead of your usual guerrilla school of directing."

I tossed a sponge at him.

He ripped off a glove, aiming for my butt. I made sure he didn't miss.

Delicately replacing the stovetop as if it were the hood of an antique car, Jorge squatted in front of the oven, replaced each of the knobs, and clicked each burner on with what seemed a sort of scientific devotion. The quartet of blue flames burped into existence.

He smiled.

"Now we cook again!"

6. true myth is real hot

A Halloween party in 1986 got me my first big break. Before *Manipulators* and some short video work, I'd gotten a reputation for my ability to convey metaphor with the arrangement of objects. The placement of roses, or just the right Hockney tells you more, gives you another clue, or reflects the scene in such a way that you cannot help but blurt an appreciative sigh. I liked doing that, even when they weren't my films.

When one director used her own house for the main setting of her film, she kept my arrangements and bought all the items I'd scrounged up. After that, a few people who weren't making films saw my work and called me to arrange their own homes. Mostly I didn't buy much, just moved things in such a way that their spaces were opened or made cozy, and their personalities blossomed. I just dug through some personal things, old mementos, photos, and the clients would return, gasping in pleasure, as if I'd unleashed their private insides and made them comfortable, souls on display.

I got an invitation to redo a friend of a friend's apartment, or two apartments. It was a scary job that helped just about finish my career as an arranger.

Bob and Bobby's apartment, or two apartments, were a pair of studios on the third and fourth floor of a small house in Malibu. Bob was a shrink. Bobby, his younger, more beautiful boyfriend, was a model of sorts. I forget. It seemed they wanted a lovely, light bedroom for Bobby above, and a dark, forbidding, murky space below for Bob. *Chaqu'un a sons gout.*

We arranged for an advance payment and supplies and colors. They left for Europe and gave me the keys. "Stay here if you like," they said, "to get a feel for the place."

I took a quivering joy in being the master of this couple's household. During the painting, they had stored all the weird stuff away, or actually never had any, which I thought creepier, so I was left to my own, to paint their new layered home in their about-to-be cliché style.

I would paint the upstairs in a soft rag roll, eggshell white against a cream, everywhere. Downstairs, like a deep netherland of Dante, was to be a burnished maroon with a fresco corrosion, faux-everything, and darker, chocolate faux-wood trim. But what sold me on the job wasn't mere wall painting, but the casual way they requested a mural. I loved the idea.

I got into the painting, completely. I was making a set where their personal life movies would be shown daily, without repeats. It exhausted me. It made me hungry.

There was a little sandwich shop down the highway where I bought lunch from a pair of swarthy Croatian brothers, and I got a sandwich every day. The sandwiches tasted better knowing their thick fingers touched them inside and out.

When I returned after my third day, one of them asked if I'd moved to the neighborhood.

"No, painting an apartment up the road."

"Ah. If ya busy, we deliver."

Either of them could have come upstairs, and I would have seduced him. I held back lustful fantasies whenever I buzzed whichever one of them in. Perhaps it was the paint fumes.

When one of the brothers brought the heavy white bag of food, I couldn't resist going for it. If he demurred or was upset, hey, it was just another memory, and although a good deal of that fluttering, that queasiness, was fear of rejection. Few were the times when I hadn't been correct in my lustful intentions.

"You like the paint job?" I asked him. His mayo and roast beef juice-smeared apron hid the pouch of his jeans. "They want it like an old Roman fresco."

"Oh, you need people then," he said.

"Yeah, I was thinking naked athletes."

"Yes, is, is nice."

"You're nice." I touched him on the arm. "You should model for me."

"Oh, I shouldn't." He half-backed away, but not too far to let me lift his apron, kneel, and unzip. The first moment I surrounded him with my mouth, his jeans fell down his hairy columns of thighs. His apron fell over my head like a tent.

Before he abruptly erupted, I aimed his cock at the mural. He obliged, and I knew the wall would be finished, his sperm splattering it. I'd swirl it in later, mixing it with the crusting, almost dry paint. I remember thinking of Mark Spitz.

I loved how he charged me for the sandwich, but refused a tip.

He never modeled for me, but I remembered enough of his body to paint him and his brother as toga-clad studs lifted from Vesuvius. The slut in me wondered if he ever told his brother, and even more, why the other brother never delivered.

The crush was when the Bob the shrink, having returned exhausted from Europe, said he was dissatisfied with the mural, that it needed to be redone. He called the toga boys "obtrusive." I refused. He paid me off, I returned the keys and other than in a few photos, I never saw my mural, or them, again.

I assume Bob had it redone, not knowing how damned authentic that Italianate effect was. Perhaps he smelled it, and it was too much for him.

I had poured my body and limbs and the fluids of that beautiful man into this wall, and that queen had decided it wasn't worthy. I think it was then I knew I would always be an independent artist, never again to let another person determine quality in my work, or what I could get out of someone else and where I would aim it.

Returning to my cramped, shared Silver Lake apartment in my mottled, coughing Honda sucked worse than before. A few grand from Bob's check in my bank account, I flew to Pittsburgh under the guise of visiting my parents, but it was really to claim my prize, Gramma's Dodge Dart, which had lain waiting in Pittsburgh at an aunt's garage almost a year after her death.

I drove through Pennsylvania to Brookside, Ohio, visited home to collect food and a few hundred in "spending money" from Dad. I also rummaged through my collection of old toys just to check that they were still waterproofed in the attic. Since I was barely housed at the time, they all had to remain vaulted with the parents.

I called Jorge from Kansas, where I discovered Gramma's gloves. He appreciated the gesture. I complained about my situation. He said he had heard about a place in Santa Monica I might like.

"Tell the landlord I'll take it."

"But you haven't even seen it."

"Do you like it?"

"Yes."

"Take it."

"But Stan—"

"I trust you, Jorge. Give him a check today. I'll pay you when I get there."

I did. Savoring the idea of driving cross-country to a new home, I took a few extra days, turned my path from a line into a squiggle. Ain't that America.

I paid two months' rent on the Santa Monica place. Jorge shouldn't have worried. I'm still there. In fact, the first thing I did before moving into the bedroom was drive to Malibu, buy a box full of those sandwiches with a mere parting smile from the Croatians, and repaint that mural from memory on a huge flat board, more out of spite than anything else.

Shortly after the unveiling of my mural on the back porch, Jorge called me with a job to decorate a Halloween party. The client, a producer whom I'll call Mr. A-List (yet another redhead) wanted his house to be transformed into something trippy, yet not grotesque or with any cobwebs. As he showed me his pristine expansive home, I knew he was using the party job as an excuse for a vague promise of actual film work, and perhaps some sexual favors.

Styrofoam graves lined the yard, each with puns on dead film stars. Lupe Garou. Hex Rarison. John Gorefield. Marlon Braindo. Maximilian Hell. Yes, totally *Simpsons* Halloween specials.

As I decorated, he finished up his orange and black cookie icing, while a few friends carved pumpkins, and the DJ collected his cross of Bauhaus, "Monster Mash," and horror film score mixes. Bathroom reading: a two-foot stack of *Scream* magazines.

But the hit was The Hallway.

Mr. A-List's house had a long hallway, too thin for hanging any real art worth standing back and enjoying. He had some tiny gelatin prints from an artist friend who'd died, but they were all images of dried branches, a sort of female Minor White collection. I took them down and put up hideous old portraits I found at a flea market.

Just before my X kicked in and his guests started arriving, a few of us played with Day-Glo paints and turned these boring rummage sale portraits into hideously painted glow-in-the-dark cartoons with extruding bones, fangs, and hollowed-out eyes. I hit the black light I'd put in the hall for the night, and we knew we'd done it.

"Just like *The Fall of the House of Usher!*" screamed one film buff queen.

"*The House of Usher*," one film historian corrected.

We couldn't keep people out of the hall.

Fortunately, one of the guests turned out to be *The House of Usher* film's production manager, one of the reigning queens with wild stories to tell about the days of Samuel Z. Arkoff, American International, B flicks, and the whole Ed Wood-ian scene. He ended up sitting in a big chair with twenty-something PAs, arty wannabes, and UCLA film students hovered around him like a Macy's Santa Claus at The Munsters.

Mr. A-List was thrilled I'd made his party practically legendary. The costume contest winners were two producer friends of his, who wore '70s suits and hair; the GuberPeters, Scariest Couple of divorced candy bars.

Before the night's end, 'Santa' tactfully asked for a ride home after some flirtatious overtures, since he was too sloshed to veer his DeSoto ten blocks downhill. On the ride to his home, before I returned to the party, Santa offered to recommend me to an old friend of his. It didn't matter who it was. It didn't matter while I was letting him blow me goodnight. I stood in his lovely home feeling like Joe Dallesandro, pants at my ankles, so benevolent was I for letting him think he still had some shred of allure. Eventually, though, it would pay off.

The next day, I returned to Mr. A-List's home to remove the props and decorations. I replaced the scary portraits with a series of small white plaster shelves. On each one I placed a vintage G.I. Joe doll. That cost him. Nearest the door to his bedroom was the red-haired number, the one who I imagined ended up nestled in some teenage boy's crotch on a few quiet 1960s afternoons. When I told Mr. A-List how the fuzzy redheaded G.I. Joe resembled him, he kissed me.

That lie may have brought us together, but I'm glad I put that Joe closest to his bedroom door. While he never got me any work after our brief tussle in bed, a certain guest of his from the previous night would prove to be my Santa Claus.

7. **what** have you did ?

As the plane descends through a cloud bank somewhere over northern Ohio, the businessclone, who's given me his card, tells me he is from Shaker Heights. He is also half-Polish, half-Greek. He says we should get together over the weekend. As I shake his strong hand, trying to ignore the people who hover nearby, grabbing bags from overhead, eavesdropping on the birth of a friendship that may go nowhere, I'm already calculating how I can maneuver myself up to visit Martin Cocotakis, consultant in Cleveland. "Not pronounced 'Cock in Tookas,'" he mutters to me suggestively.

I like a name you have to be careful with.

I'm secretly hoping my dad will be late picking me up so I can steal a smoke after five hours cramped in the plane. Then I remember I don't need it, don't even want it, and feel better.

My dad stands toward the back of the crowd, smiling. We hug hello, and he offers to take my bag. I decline. We chat, ease our way out and away. His face is splotched with age and broken blood vessels. His belly is now an overdue child. His breathing is audible. He is what I will be if I'm not careful.

Dad drives swiftly south on I-71, and I fiddle with the radio, not wanting to force anything too aggressive on him, yet not wanting to fall asleep to dentist office music. We find a balance with jazz, as always, and the conversation drifts like a sax solo. Since I can feel the fatigue of having to repeat my stories for my mother once we're home, I don't. I talk about other things: the Ace Awards, meeting famous people, investing money, cars.

I could rattle off all the famous people I've met or seen or slept with or had lunch near, but it doesn't impress him. Maybe he just can't translate it. We end up talking about the chores facing me, like tearing down the basement paneling. I ask if we'll go to the hardware store on Midland Street, but he says it's closed, and the Home Depot at the mall has a better selection anyway. With some amusement, he receives my critique of chain stores. I know he hopes I can multitask, do the hard work he no longer can.

But the gaps between the talk, the silences, for me are full of the chunks of my life I know my father will never understand: the way L.A. works, the way gay people meet and lose each other. You can try to remember the tune of a song that nearly drove you to the rocks. You can tell people over and over again that a monster appeared out of a cave and bit the heads off your crewmates, but those who didn't witness will never believe your journey.

All the while I'm anxious to be home, to see it mostly like I remembered it, but secure. I want the vault of my childhood to remain intact, accruing value.

Dad pulls up to the driveway like the thousand other times in our lives.

Home. The trees are naked and blackish; elm, oak, and that pesky acorn with all those nuts. Leaves coat the lawn in a calm blanket of oranges and reds.

"Think I oughtta rake these leaves," I say.

"Your mother has some kid to do that."

"Oh."

The house looks solid. It should be. They don't make red brick homes anymore. Sure, the garage door's been replaced, and the chimney had to be shored up, repairs I never worked on, having the excuse of adulthood to miss them. I still feel guilty for my absence.

I greet her after I drop my bags in the foyer. Mom's up from her favorite chair. The TV is on, as if she was just hanging out like normal, not fighting the impulse to call Dad's car phone, not worrying, which is her job, one she has always done well.

We hug. She smells the same, offers food, control of the TV, but, "After *NYPD*. I love that actor, what's his name, the redhead, have you ever met him?" I see his bright orange hair and can't help but compare it to hers, which came in a bottle.

I tell her even though they film that in L.A., I haven't met him.

I drag my bags up to my room, or what used to be my room. A desk is where Dan's bed was. A computer lies dormant. My mother surfs the net, chats online with women around the world.

Something's wrong.

What happened to our beds, the family heirlooms, the two twins with little wooden ships on the headboards, the beds my father and his brother slept in from the '40s through the '50s, the bed in which I learned to make love to myself in the '70s, to sail away into dreamland with my heroes in togas?

But then I remember. They just fell apart one day, as if all the years of our bouncing and fighting and playing built up until after we'd gone, and the poor old things collapsed. Maybe they died from our absence.

But weren't they almost antique? Priceless to me?

Ridiculous. They're just pieces of furniture. Pieces of boyhood. Boy wood.

I have some leftover pasta in the kitchen, not in front of the TV, where my parents both sit as if I never left, as if my coming home is no big deal. But I know it is. They're counting the hours, the days, until I say something, or he or she says something, until we share our nervousness about the upcoming election, until we've all dug up enough skeletons to get them rattling once again, and I won't be able to stand being in this home for another minute.

I finish eating and enter the living room, plop myself down and sigh.

"Isn't it nice to be home?"

"Yes," I say, with complete honesty. It is nice.

Except I just want to "arrange" everything, starting with a big garage sale. The house is filled with new knick-knacks, objects without memory for me. I resent the new furniture.

"Everyone's been asking about you," Mom says, everyone being a few of her neighbors, curious Baptists with a need for gossip on the infidel next door's activities, and our more sympathetic family friends, the tenured folk from Brookside College.

"What did you tell them?"

"Nothing that isn't in the magazines," she assures me. "I'm very proud of you and I wish you wouldn't harp on me for divulging your private life."

"Whatever." We won't go there. I switch channels. She changes the topic, eventually retires for the evening. Mom is referring to the time she dared to enter a message board on a tribute site to my 1987-1989 trilogy, *The Manipulator.* I'd seen it, but never graced them with a reply email, other than a brief thanks.

Practically the entire three scripts, with screencaps, bios of the actors and complete credits, and sound files litter the website. Mom found it by Googling her son's name. She now understands the concept of avatars, and signing one's name online as the mother of the director of a cult film— well, it just ain't kosher.

It's particularly not kosher when those rabid fans can't seem to quit speculating about the mysterious death of the trilogy's star, a death I witnessed, a death I dreaded, a death I narrowly avoided myself, and don't particularly care to chat about on a shitty little copyright-infringing website.

None of that mentioned again, Mom wisely hands me the TV remote and walks upstairs to bed.

Like every visit home since college, I stay up later than they do, surfing the channels, seeing the Ohio version of what I no longer watch in L.A., at least not in English: infomercials, mediocre mainstream films, pre-election blather. My movies have never made it to network TV. I occasionally see actors or films where I know a crew member or met one at a bagel shop.

I walk to the video shelf in the dining room. There they are, all my movies, dupes I sent, displayed proudly between Walmart copies of feature films Mom bought, along with her own copy of *Say Uncle,* right on top.

Maybe they'll want to watch it again with me. I could show them scene by scene, what I and a dozen actors and sixty crew members went through. Here's the line that almost got me fired. Here's the day I made "Mom" (Penelope) cry. The scene where the "Son" (Brendan) called me a wimp, the scene that made Barry throw things at me. Here's the day we stopped sleeping together, the shot I hemmed and hawed over for hours, making all the crew members hate me, or make me think they hated me, since I had broken down and gotten stoned before going on the set.

Whaddaya say, Mom and Pop? Want a little tour?

No way.

I sneak across the dining room, as if I'm fourteen again and a party is about to start, or has finished. I withdraw a tumbler from the little wooden cabinet of a bar, slip open the cap of a bottle of Chivas Regal, probably untouched in months. The liquor falls into the glass with a heavy glug. I sneak into the freezer, plop in a few ice cubes. They crack.

I am amazed and proud of how my mother can live in a house with alcohol and not even touch it. Me, who had to race to a Quiki Mart when I was out of cigarettes, who could last maybe a week without pot. All the shit we gave her when she slipped, Dan and I, while Dad defended her from the two little monsters she'd raised.

I pull open the side door to the porch, our lovely little screened-in verandah. I sit on the rumpled plastic outdoor furniture, sip the burn of the Chivas into my mouth, swallow, and set the glass down quietly on the deck table, afraid the tinkling ice will wake someone. But the neighborhood is silent, and cold, despite the last breath of October's Indian summer. A single car passes on a distant street. No boom boxes. No sirens. No mayhem. All psychos are comfortable in their homes.

I want to be here when I'm very, very old. I want to die here. I would like that privilege returned to me.

8. did spontaneous blue tunnel swim with butt like iron

People like to use the term "crush" for the unrequited love kids have for other kids, or adults. I think it's an appropriate term, for kids go unarmed into the battlefield of love. Of course they're going to get crushed.

Dick Thorson, however, was purely sexual—bearded, animal, sweaty, and a redhead. He wasn't a crush. He was a fantastic creature to be observed, witnessed, like a lion at the zoo. By day, I worked with him through three summers. At night, I pulled out my two-year-old March 1974 *Playgirl*, with centerfold Bill Douglas, who bore a striking resemblance to Dick Thorson.

I was a very lucky boy.

Just saying his name, of course, drew me to stutters. "Hey, Dick! Where's my hammer?" "Dick's up on the catwalk." "What color gel you want on this, Dick?" "Whaddaya want, Dick?"

I took every opportunity to shout his name across the scene shop, theater, anywhere, just to make people laugh, or make him smile, my boners nestled away in undies under shorts. The two layers were too hot for the summers, but very necessary. It also helped keep my tool belt from falling down as I strolled about the scene shop impersonating him.

Unlike other men I'd stared at who often "dressed" to one side consistently, the bulge in Dick's cut-off jeans pushed out in all directions. Sometimes it would be pressed flat over his zipper, but most times it slouched down one side or another, depending on what he was doing. I'd notice it hanging left, see him stand and move around to work, bend over, and then later see it on the other side, the hidden prize at the apex of thick furry legs that grew out of his work boots like stalks.

This is how he let me touch him.

We'd be standing together, holding up a flat, preparing to connect it to another, and need a nail. Since Dick was more than a foot taller than me, he'd hold the flat with both hands. I'd reach down into the pouch of his worn tool belt, dig out a few three-penny nails, stick a few in my mouth, and hammer a nail into the flat under his watchful gaze. Then I'd do it again, reach down, dig in, retract my sharp little prizes, put more in my mouth, every reach jostling his suede tool belt, bumping his groin, only a layer of denim and suede between us.

When I got to the bottom of the flats, he'd still be holding them together. I'd finish, kneeling below him with a nervous pause, seeing if the flat would stand on its own. His legs and his tool belt and his fiery beard and mane of hair loomed above me, saying "Good," then moving on.

The college's Spring production of *1776* was terrific, I suppose. Watching American History get up and sing didn't thrill a closeted just-pubed boy getting Cs in the subject. Since I was still in school, going through the hell of being a nobody at Brookside Middle School, I didn't participate in the show. Only summer theater for me.

I avoided the barrage of *Bicentennial Minutes* by immersing myself in stagecraft. Every morning as I walked the three blocks to the theater, I counted the hideously painted Bicentennial trolls that had once been mere fire hydrants.

Dan sometimes showed up, but he had discovered girls, while I was left to carrots and Dick. This was after The Carrot Incident. Everything from here on in is Post-Carrot.

We were making new flats. Dick handed me a scrap of paper. I couldn't read it, so I clumsily laid out the one-by-threes on the floor, careful as I cut them. I was only allowed to use the table saw with Dick hovering nearby, watching, guiding me. Dick had lost part of his "fuck finger" on the circular saw the previous year. His blood still stained the notched wood below the blade.

That night, I had taken the scrap of paper with words and signs on it and lay it on my bed, poring over it as if it was an obscure love poem. It lay next to the Bill Douglas centerfold as I worshipped in the steaming attic. Once, I even cut out a little paper tool belt from a True Value catalog for Bill/Dick to wear.

Dick was a senior at Brookside College. I was in ninth grade. I knew my body a lot better by then, and I knew Dick knew it, too. I wasn't so chubby anymore. Girls had begun flirting with me in school.

After *1776*, the summer show schedule began with *Godspell*, followed by Neil Simon's *The Star-Spangled Girl*, and, for a big finale, *Gypsy*. It was a very American summer.

I considered *Godspell* a piece of dreck, but I was charmed nevertheless. Lance Holtzer, whom I more worshipped than lusted for, played Christ. I ran a spotlight in the booth while Dick manned the light board, sifting through every cue with the expertise of a lab scientist. The previous year, another student had posted a wooden sign on the wall above the light board in Dick's honor. Below a cartoon drawing of him, it read, "The Lair of Light."

One afternoon, Dick let me help set the light cues. I stood at the board like a young *Star Trek* recruit, and he sat behind me giving cues. When I messed up, he scooted his chair in and leaned over me to pull the dimmers. I breathed in, smelling his funky warmth around me, stealing glances at the shortened middle finger missing a nail. His beard just tickled the back of my neck, and I intentionally pulled back a bit, feeling his other hand around my waist.

We stood like that for a while. I liked to think he got hard too. I don't know. He pulled back, and I was afraid to turn around, thinking maybe he was watching me, wondering.

During days in the shop, Dick would hover patiently over me, explaining the most efficient way of holding a hammer. He'd let me rest my weight on the far end of a one-by-three while he hammered away, bent over, his jeans pressing against his ass. I knew I wanted to get to that butt, although I wasn't sure what to do with it at the time.

While Dick stood high on a scaffold hanging lights that I tied to a thick scratchy rope, I felt like a young assistant to Michelangelo, hauling up buckets for his colorful ceiling endeavors. I also noticed for the first time from my lower vantage point that he didn't wear shorts beneath his cutoffs. The dull gray pouch of a jock strap hung from one leg. My mother had mutely purchased one for me when I turned thirteen the previous summer, as if I was now required to wear such a pinching elastic contraption. It lay on my bed one afternoon among a pile of new socks and white T-shirts, like White Christmas in August. Mom could be so wonderful sometimes.

Since I wasn't really a jock, it hadn't seemed a useful item until I noticed the way Dick wore his, needed it. His gonads nestled safely there.

Dad never told us about sex, except as a sort of equation whose result produced offspring. He used that term, "offspring." We read books with charts. Dan told me more variations, but every explanation left me wondering, what about guys' butts? Why do I keep thinking guys' butts add into this theorem?

It was as if they assumed we just learned these things on our own since we were so creative and mature for our ages.

Thank the gods I had access to a college library.

Even though checking the spotlight only took a minute, call for the crew was at seven, so I always showed up and signed in promptly, as if I was practicing for union work. Besides, it got me out of the house early.

But the night my parents came to see *Godspell,* they made me wait.

"I'm gonna be late!" I seethed, while Dan watched Suzanne Somers bob about on TV. Dan's darker hair and eyes, plus his slightly larger frame, gave him the upper hand in any situation, visually speaking. Our hair was at its longest in these days, me going for the Bobby Sherman look, while Dan's more closely approximated Aerosmith's guitarist, Joe Perry.

Dan was still pissed off with me for spending so much time making sets at the theater that I wouldn't work on his latest film idea. He wanted to do a *Jaws* parody, which I thought was stupid. He knew better. We could synch it to the radio novelty song, show it at a school talent show, and be the hit of the town. I told him we needed an underwater camera and sound to make it work. GAF hadn't come out with either of those yet, at least ones we could afford.

I knew his anger was something else though, a pile of somethings. Maybe he wanted to enjoy the rare privilege of being in the house alone for an evening. I knew what fun that could be. Maybe it was something else, a long-saved grudge. Maybe he would call his girlfriend over. Dan and I kept our crimes from our parents and stored them like ammo.

My mother descended the stairs, looking terrific in a paisley dress with a scarf and small gold-colored earrings. Her hair wasn't as frizzy as usual, but it was still that bright orange Dan once said "glowed in the dark." Mom didn't speak to him for days after that, just kept referring to him as "your brother," or, to my father, "your son."

Dad followed, sporting a light blue jacket, matching pants Mom must have picked out for him, and the loudest tie in his extensive collection, a red striped number with dogs on it.

"What is that?" I said, incredulous.

"It was a gift from Artie, and I'm wearing it."

"We don't even have a dog."

Mom walked through the living room, her back to Dad, giving me a glance that said, *Don't even try.*

Dad waved us all out and ceremoniously closed the door, keeping the air-conditioned comfort safely locked in. We were an odd quartet, our parents all gussied up and me and Dan in shorts and T-shirts. I didn't dress up because I was working the show, but Dan had argued that if I didn't have to dress up, neither did he. He would regret his decision later, since he didn't get to spend the performance in the overheated lighting booth, but shivering in his seat in the air-conditioned theater.

I started to cut across the lawn toward the college, but then heard my father call out, "Where are you going?"

"To the theater."

"We're driving." Mom was already being escorted into her seat. Dan was making finger drawings on the back hood.

"It's three blocks."

"Stan. Get in the car."

"But, Dad." I scowled, returned, and crossed my arms in the back.

Dan glared at me. It was bad enough they were coming to my turf. They didn't realize I never did any of these theatrical or cinematic things to please them. But that I had to be seen going with them, and in the car like we were lazy, was even more humiliating.

They were too early, and I was late. As we parked, I wanted to bolt away from them, but some invisible leash kept me close.

Other early-comers sat or stood outside, more standing about in the cool air-conditioned comfort of the theater lobby. The building was only a few years old, strangely alien with its modern angles and red brick walls. People in shorts and loud red, white, and blue shirts milled about.

At the ticket booth, my father made a silly joke about the comp tickets being worth more than the price. As a Math teacher, Dad had the sense of humor of a Math teacher.

Dan and I walked away to the little concession booth where a soda machine was always available, if not appetizing. Sometimes Dan and I would just drink the club soda, sometimes just the syrup. This time it was a real combo. He got a paper cup, dug it in the ice machine's bin and helped himself.

"Want one?"

"Naw. Still full from dinner." I was worried about passing gas in the booth later. Since we had all the doors shut to close off the noise of calling cues, the air became a bit stuffy because of the light's heat. The smells coming from Dick were, well, earthy. But I wasn't about to return the favor with sugar farts all through Act One.

"Jeezus Chrahst," Dan slurred it out. "It's the Jay-zus Kraahst Musical."

"I am so over these songs. 'On the Willow There,'" I squeaked.

"Ugh."

"The only part I really like is the opening part where there's all these philosophers—"

"I saw it. I came to dress rehearsal last week."

"All right. Whatever."

"You're right. It's the best part, with all the voices on top of each other."

"I forget what they call that."

"A round?"

"No, that's like that part in *Once Upon a Mattress*."

We both started singing. "We have an opening for a princess, for a genuine *bona fide* prin-cess..."

Arthur McCabe, the director, appeared at the counter. Dan and I felt like criminals for a moment, then relaxed. The candy wasn't out yet or we probably would have copped some of that.

"A scotch and soda, rocks!" Arthur joked, smacking his palm on the counter. He was a tall man with a full beard and a bit of a gut. His eyes sparkled as if he was a grown leprechaun. I think he was my first hero. Sure, the other guys were hunky sex symbols of a sort. But Arthur McCabe was the first man I knew who seemed to constantly say, "Damn, I am so lucky to do this for a living!"

"Comin' right up, Mistah McCabe, suh!" Dan fell into it easily, miming serving up a drink. Actually he was quoting himself from the previous summer, when he'd played the son in *A Thousand Clowns* to Arthur's lead. I didn't get that part. Dan did. I was too young, they said.

Not that I'm bitter.

I was still uneasy joking like that with adults like Dan did. I get the same feeling when I'm on a set full of straight techies, and they start talking about pro basketball.

Mostly I listened and asked questions. I didn't get drinking jokes, either. Why did these people all drink and do okay, but my mother made such a big deal about not drinking, like it was an accomplishment?

"Are you boys allowed back there?" Dad appeared, concerned, as always, with protocol.

"It's okay, Dad."

Mom stayed behind, talking to Arthur's wife, Marsha. I guess they were best friends. Marsha McCabe was Dutch-descended, from some great old farm family that settled in Brookside about a hundred years ago. I forget how she met Arthur. They were a terrific couple, how I wished my parents were—younger, more attractive, energetic. Arthur and Marsha, always together. They fit in. It seemed no matter what my mom did, she was an outsider. None of us Grozniaks were born in Brookside, and people there had a way of reminding us of that, often.

Arthur calmed Dad's worries about his potentially delinquent spawn and offered everyone a soda. No takers. Dan sipped his.

"You can run the concession stand tonight if you like," Arthur joked to Dan. We both took it as a condescending insult, as if we were playing Store with plastic produce. Arthur rarely did that, but sometimes we couldn't get away from the fact that we were just a couple of college teacher's brats who treated the whole campus like it was our playground.

"No thanks," Dan said as he ducked under the counter. I followed.

There was an awkward moment, as if someone was waiting for a reason to continue this conversation or start a new one. My dad sort of sighed, as if it didn't matter. It's amazing how people think kids don't notice these things.

Then Dad said, "How about you take us up to the lighting booth?"

"What?"

"To see what you do."

Them? Enter the Lair of Light? Mere mortals? Just one whiff and all would be revealed. "You'll see it," I stuttered. "Just watch the lights."

"Stanley." My dad issued a warning, then shifted gears. "Maybe Dan would like to."

"I've been there a hundred times." Dan rolled his eyes, as if he was talking to an idiot. He gulped Pepsi, then shook his ice, as if to clear away the aimless conversation. For a moment, Dan was somewhat on my side. He glanced at me from behind the rim of his soda cup.

"I gotta go," I said. "Enjoy the show."

"We'll see you after," Mom called out, making me cringe. Did that mean I had to go home with them, too?

I slunk off, losing them. Maybe Dan had wanted to come with me just to get away from our parents. They always talked oddly in public, different, as if they were onstage. Oh well, Dan could take care of himself.

Passing Fran, the ticket taker, a frumpy girl who usually got the smallest of roles, I went to the door beyond the house entrance, a back hallway where row upon row of shelved unused lighting instruments and racks of gels, frames, and cables. Piping ran along the length of the tiny hallway like the underdeck of a battleship. I banged my hand a few times along the pipe, as if to mark it. This is *my* space. I'm not a kid here. I'm not a kid.

The lighting storeroom ended at off-stage left, next to the tie-offs for batons. Since *Godspell's* set was only a wire storm fence, all the curtains had been pulled up into the fly space to create the "stark, modern" look of the show's "contemporary take on religious themes."

The raised curtain meant that unless I walked outside to a back entrance, I couldn't go back to the scene shop, where beyond that, the dressing rooms were. I wanted to wish everyone in the cast, "Break a leg." Actually, I just wanted to see Lance Holtzer, among the other men in the cast, but that would have to wait.

I stepped lightly on the metal stairs that led up to the side costume storage room. I didn't want audience members to hear the sounds behind the scenes. *Crew members should be invisible and silent.*

The light to the costume storage room was off, and I knew it could be seen from onstage, so I used my night vision, and reached out to feel sleeve after sleeve, each touch recalling entire productions I'd seen or worked on. A brocaded gown with puffed elbows, satiny and cool: *Once Upon a Mattress.* A Victorian dress with lace at the cuffs: *Life With Father.*

Across them, the men's rack. Leathery plastic chest shields with straps as skirts: uniforms for guards in *A Funny Thing Happened on the Way to the Forum.* A huge purple robe with stars and moons: Merlin in *Cinderella.* Sometimes I'd try them on, but most times I'd just touch them, feel the fabric, the traces of sweat, see the stains of makeup around collars. I was enthralled by the history waiting there in the archive. I became lost, pressing velvet kingly garb against my face, trying on Russian soldier boots, peeking into drawers to marvel at giant fake jewels.

Through the wall, I heard someone in the audience laugh and was brought back. I hiked up the metal ladder to the catwalk in the upper section of wall and stepped into blackness.

As my eyes adjusted, the catwalk loomed ahead, offering the view from directly above the house. So many times I'd walked along here with my crescent wrench tied to my denim cutoffs' belt loop to keep it from falling through the acoustic ceiling tiles into the seats below.

I could have dropped spitballs on Dan if he was seated below me, but I knew better. This was the place where I didn't have to think about behaving. Goofing off up here could get a guy killed. I had to respect that, the creepy quivering in my legs just from looking down. What if I did fall to my death? Would that not be dramatic?

I walked to the middle of the front grid where the center walkway led back over the house to the light booth. I stepped lightly, thinking of the Lon Chaney *Phantom of the Opera*, how he, in his ugliness, lived in the guts of a theater. Not a bad life.

When I popped through the little door and down the ladder to the booth, Dick was at the control panel.

"Hey, bud," he said, grinning with his headset slung around his neck. We high-fived as I landed, me pretending the contact was ever so casual, when every touch meant mountains. "Where ya been?"

"Family night," I muttered, going to my side of the booth to the spot, breathing in the scent of the booth, the captured sweat smell of Thorson, vintage '76. My attraction to Dick zinged through my body, meeting between my legs. My voice cracked as I whispered, "Uh, I don't wanna test this with people in the house."

"S'okay. Just plug her in and try it on the wall in here."

I'd never thought of that. I did as Dick said. The spotlight's glow flooded our small room. It was working fine. Everything was fine up there. I slid the cover over the lamp, kept the motor running, and swiveled the spot to point stageward.

"Yer mom and dad watchin' the show?"

"Yeah, and Dan."

"Oh yeah? How is he? Haven't seen him around."

"Fine. Wants to make another movie. It's really stupid—"

Dick raised his hand to quiet me and pulled his headset to his ears. Someone was cueing him. "Five minutes."

I nodded.

"Hey, wyncha get the door and the window."

I obeyed, left my post and closed the regular-sized door that led down below to the house. I was about to cross behind Dick to the front window when he said, "Ah, ah, ah."

I stopped. He was pointing above and in front of him to the half-sized door up to the catwalk where I'd entered. Dick was such a perfectionist.

I hiked up the three rungs, ascending high enough to lean over the top rung to reach for the door. At that moment, I realized my shorts were riding up. My butt was facing him, and he was quite possibly looking at me. I waited a moment, pretending I couldn't reach the door, and leaned back, then closer, arching my butt up. For flourish, I grunted, once.

I finally "caught" the door. I closed it softly, then backed down the ladder, giving Dick plenty of time to look away or watch me descend. As I got to the floor, my erection pressed out uncomfortably, but I didn't adjust it. Dick wasn't looking at me.

Did I know what I was doing? Yes.

Did he know what I was doing? Probably.

But more important was the question that clung as thick as the air of that little room; Did he like what I was doing?

The cue from the house manager came through the headset.

Dick slowly dimmed the house lights. The sound of people folding programs and settling into their seats fluttered upward through the house. I put on the thick gloves that kept my hands from burning and flicked on the spotlight, keeping the coverlet over the beam. The whirring hum filled the booth. Bright light from inside the gun-shaped instrument bled out

from the air slots. Dick completed dimming the house lights with his right
hand, completing the first cue of every show.

From somewhere in that sea of heads, I could feel my brother turning
back to watch me, waiting for me to fumble or succeed.

The beginning of *Godspell* is strange.

The students who played the disciples first appeared in darkness, sitting on stools and clicking on overhead lamps as they sang the parts of
different philosophers. Since they turned the lights on themselves, these
weren't considered lighting cues.

"Wherefore, oh man of Athens, I say to-oo you..."

I silently sang along, watching my favorite part, whose words would
soon be drowned out by the religious fervor and clownish joy to follow.
The solos built on top of each other in musical confusion, a carpet of
theories, the overhead lamps flicking on and off in a frenzy. I could have
become distracted, but I knew my first cue was coming up. Like a con-
ductor, Dick glanced at me silently and raised his left arm for Cue #2. I
pointed the spotlight toward the back of the house.

The familiar trumpet sound, blasted out by Scott Disch, who played
John the Baptist, stirred murmurs of surprise from the audience. He cut
them to silence with his second blast.

Dick pointed at me and dropped his arm. Cue #2. I flicked the coverlet open, hitting Scott dead on as he stood in the back of the house,
causing all heads to turn.

"Pree-ee-ee-pare ye the way of the Lord. Pree-ee-ee-pare ye the way of
the Looord!"

The rest, as they say, is the gospel truth.

I prepared for all my cues in Lance's solos, breathing slowly and making sure not to jiggle an inch, so I wouldn't ruin the holiness of his singing.
Lance wasn't a great singer, but his curly blond hair fit the poster's require-
ments for a shaggy mop-head as Jesus. When he sang, he opened his throat
to pure honesty with very little vibrato, just big notes open as hayfields.

Lance even deflected a bit of community controversy when the leader
of one of the Baptist churches tried to get himself some publicity by at-
tempting to organize a boycott of *Godspell*. Reverend Fat Head decried "the
blasphemy of portraying Our Lord Jesus as a clown." Lance, in response,
was quoted in the *Brookside Gazette* as being a Young Christian Athlete,
proud to represent a modern retelling of the world's greatest story. I still
admired Lance, but figured he couldn't be a homo if he was a Christian.

Despite the fumbled boycott, or maybe because of it, the show sold out every night. It was a small town, after all, live theater being a rare commodity, as was air conditioning.

In between Lance's numbers, Dick and I whispered in the booth, making inside jokes about each line and music cue.

"Dick," I'd whisper, calling it like a pet, hoping he might let it out.

"What?"

I nudged toward the stage as Patricia Rosenzweig feebly strained out that night's 'On the Willow.' "Is she flat or what?"

"Her tits?"

"No, her singing."

"Beats me."

Beats you, Dick. Dick, what beats you? I muttered low word-plays, my hands sweaty under the asbestos gloves, the heat of the spotlight inducing rivulets of sweat. My groin was hot and damp. Sometimes I'd secretly take off my underpants beforehand so I could feel myself get hard in the dark, knowing he might see.

I didn't feel so much in awe of Dick in here, but more like his buddy, ready to do anything he wished, ready to take whatever command he gave. He taught me, as a director, to find the light and give actors tips. I could feel the artificial warmth of a 500-watt Fresnel and almost smell that cramped booth.

Every night we surveyed the domain from on high.

My spotlight burned with heat, the windows closed to cut the hum. Dick always said he hated hearing the buzz when the lights changed, one of those little touches of perfectionism that influenced me and made me love him and men like him.

Shows ran for two weeks, and the "pick-up," the half-assed, low-tech Wednesday night rehearsal before the closing weekend, was always a bit out-of-hand. Actually, the joke was for cast members to try to mess each other up as much as possible by entering in funny costumes or saying lines way too fast. It became a sort of competition.

The previous summer, the couple who'd starred in *The Owl and the Pussycat* switched roles and said each other's lines hyper-fast. People tried to mess them up, running onstage with toilet bowls and lampshades on their heads, but no one could keep up with their perfect Chaplin version of the play. It was as if the script had congealed between them, and nothing could interfere. They later married and now live in Akron.

The night of our sloppy *Godspell* pick-up rehearsal, Joy Compton, the woman in the cast who sang "Turn Back, Oh Man," started the second act from the back of the house as usual. She did the bump-and-grind like a stripper as she traipsed through the aisles and flirted with the increasingly bald-headed director, Arthur McCabe. I followed her patiently, but occasionally decided to have my fun, pulling the spotlight away from her. She ran along to catch up. Dick and I both giggled, but I cut it short after a few moments. I was already learning not to milk a joke.

During the musical break between verses, where Joy usually improvised with audience members like a stand-up comic, she outdid every gag of the night, if not the summer. She whirled around to face the lighting booth, squinted up into my spotlight, held up her hands as if holding a prize bass and shouted, "I hear Dick's got one *this big*!!"

Up in the booth, Dick fell to the floor in convulsive laughter. I stood laughing over him, my spot dropping down to the floor, waiting for the proof to pop out. I aimed the spot on Dick as he stood, and while all the cast members hooted and applauded, Dick stood and bowed at the window like Eva Peron. A few people chanted, "Show it! Show it!"

He didn't.

I hate to think he would have done it if I hadn't been there beside him. He glanced beyond the spotlight like a stag caught in headlights, the spotlight burning on him, making him glow like a human meteor. He knew that unlike the joking shouting cast members below, I really, honestly wanted to see it. And so, he balked.

The cast party was that Saturday.

All the jokes fluttered just a bit over my head, like a cloud, but I got some of them as they fell down. Other college students patted my head like a mascot or pulled me aside for patronizing lectures on the harsh cruelty of a life in the theatre. My parents often left me in the care of these college kids, knowing somehow that what I wanted to happen wouldn't.

Lance left early, about the time I started to smell something funny burning in one of the bedrooms.

At one point, while I downed another soda in the kitchen, Dick entered the kitchen and saw me all alone. "Uh, do you want a beer?" he whispered.

I gave him a conspiratorial glance. "Yeah."

"You've had one before."

"Sure," I said, trying to be cool, but I had.

He clipped two bottles from the fridge and led me out to the backyard. It was one of the cast member's apartments, by a small football field, a place I'd never noticed for its beauty. A row of trees lined the open field where we'd once played touch football at a cast party. That day I'd felt like a real boy, sweaty and muddy. I'd fallen to the ground, tackling Dick and mashing my face against his hips.

Dick gave me my beer under the dark night, and we leaned against a tree.

I kept my eyes down, afraid of what I wanted to do.

"So, what Joy said ..." I joked.

"Yeah, pretty funny. God, I was so embarrassed."

"Is it true?"

"What?"

"Is it true?"

His eyes had glowed in all sorts of light, under every color of gels, but I'd never seen him shine like that, admiring my desperate bravery.

"You really want to know?" he muttered.

"For years."

"Wow."

"I mean, I don't know how to ... like say it ..."

"Listen. I could get in a lotta lotta lotta lotta trouble."

"I won't tell," I promised, even then pleased enough to know he had even considered the possibility.

It reminded me of the joke I'd overheard in the dressing room or the scene shop. Dick and one of the actors said it before noticing me nearby: 'Women for duty, men for pleasure, but boys for ecstasy.'

"Dick?" I whispered.

"I'm sorry, Stan."

He gulped down his beer in one swallow.

I could not stop staring at him, pleading.

"How about just a kiss?" he said.

I grinned.

He did, after looking around to assure our privacy. His beard tickled my face, his wet, cool lips surrounded by his own personal forest. We didn't talk much, but I think he said some good things, how good it would all be, later, but I wanted later now.

"You comin' in tomorrow?" he said, after a pause the size of a passing blimp.

"What for? There's no set."

"The lights."

"Oh. Oh, okay."

Sunday was as I'd hoped. No one else was there, all hung over, no doubt.

Dick was already there when I arrived at ten the next morning. I felt like I was late, although we were both early. The theater was abandoned, bereft of people, naked. I love an empty theater. It's full of all the possibilities in the world.

Dick had the scaffolding all set up three high and was tossing gels off the sides into a pile on the stage floor. The *Godspell* fence was rolled up in the back of the shop to make room for the incoming, half-built set of *The Star Spangled Girl*. There wasn't an inch of it our hands hadn't touched.

"Hey," I called up.

"Listen, I'm gonna take 'em off the baton. You take 'em down, okay?"

I monkeyed up and down with ease, each time crawling back up to grab a heavy instrument, then jockey down one-handed. It was quietly thrilling. I considered falling on purpose just to feel him cradle me in his arms as I babbled under the seizure of a concussion. I settled for feeling his concerned glances hover each time I descended.

He had worn the same cut-off jeans, the edges a whiskered tease, but he had omitted the jock strap this time. Every time I reached up, he stood over me long enough to show it, just peeking out of one leg under the frayed ring of denim, the rounded tip of it. Another time, a bulbous testicle. It was like he was testing me, making sure I still wanted it.

This is how I would like to have lost my virginity.

We did it in the light booth. Maybe it was because I was so small then, but it seemed I could have cracked my jaw open and still not had room for his erection. I couldn't touch it all at once, even with both hands, and I'd never be able to lick up all it spit out for me, my body too small to contain the breath surging into me as his tongue slithered over my teeth.

I think that's why I cried.

I knew my body was too small to contain so much passion and heat. I think I understand why he pulled away in shock upon seeing my face coated in his sperm, as if it were an accident. He hurried to wipe it off, when I really wanted it to congeal on my skin. I think I know why he waited until the show was over to do this with me, just before some trip that led to a move to a wife to some city I forgot a long time ago.

When he suggested we go wash up, I said no. I left the Lair, stunned after his last kiss, the scent of his sweat and sperm surrounding me through the chilled lobby and out into the humid blast of my own Independence Day. I didn't go home, just hiked it to the woods, to keep smelling the

cracking remnants of him, feeling my skin heal from the chafed scrapes his
russet beard and chest hair left on my body.

This is what happened.

Dick saw me watching his cock peek out from his jeans. He smirked.

When we broke for lunch, I pretended to go home. Instead, I waited
for him to leave, closed the main proscenium curtain as I'd done a hundred times, the simple cord hand over hand, and stood in the spot where
I saw Dick's dick. Performing for no one, I silently jerked off where I'd
stood, letting the sperm fall from the pipes of the scaffolding to the stage
floor. I was so afraid of getting caught, I'd almost come too fast to feel
the orgasm. I smeared the globs into the stage floor with my worn-out
Converse sneakers and went home to have a peanut butter and banana
sandwich.

My mother was thankfully in the basement tackling a mountain of
laundry. I ate silently, without greeting her. Before leaving, I dug in her
purse, stole what would be my first cigarette, and smoked it on the way
to the theater.

He was back up on the scaffold when I returned. My stain had already
dried.

We went back to work.

There weren't any kid parts in *The Star Spangled Girl*, nor spotlights to
run. I'd already built the set with Dick and a few other guys. I didn't work
on that show. In fact, I almost gave up on the whole summer. My feelings
for Dick were too overwhelming. I vowed never to return, but then my
mother tried coaxing me into auditioning for *Gypsy* as a Newsboy.

"It'll be fun," she said.

Fun. I knew what would have been fun.

I said I wasn't interested, and I retreated to the bedroom to blast some
Styx until Dan came into our room and announced he was going to audition, and he bet he could get a better part than me.

"The newsboy parts are all the same," I sputtered. We'd both watched
the Rosalind Russell version enough times on TV to sing all the parts.
That was one of my few concessions to camp.

"So, I bet I do better than you."

"You will not."

I knew what he was doing. He couldn't ask me not to quit, so he
turned it into a dare.

I took it.

9. explain TV birth

I sleep late, trying to ignore Mom's sounds below. Dad is off at the college, teaching a new crop of bright and cynical freshmen how to square roots.

Before breakfast, I peek into what was our bedroom closet. Our films are stuffed away behind plastic hanging boxes of Mom's clothes: *Metropolis, Phantom of the Opera, The Lost World,* some Laurel and Hardy shorts, and the little reels of our movies, those not lost by Dan's abrupt Chicago move. I want to watch them all, to disappear into basement darkness.

Instead, I shower and dress, go downstairs, eat, and chat with Mom. She'll ask me how Barry is, as if we're still together. I can't tell her we didn't really have a fight. I just got tired of hearing phrases like "not giving exclusive energy," and "processing grieving," and "like butt-ah." Okay, I still like the last one. But trying to explain to her I'm now possibly in love with the same man I fell in love with here, more than twenty years ago, might not sit well with either parent.

I have to connect my PowerBook to Mom's Performa, if I can weed through her pile of notes and kitten-in-a-bag Post-Its and Kitty Face stamp kits. Her real cat, Valentino, a small tuxedo breed, predictably jumps onto the desk and pads across the keyboard, until I place him in my lap.

I've got to work.

The tribute to Arthur McCabe is due to take place Saturday night. I've got two days to finish my little speech. Mom is very excited about the whole event, telling me it will be at The Inn. The last time I'd been there was my graduation dinner. It was not pretty.

I remember going there once, back in the dark days when she would declare herself free of the kitchen for the night, even though she wasn't free of the bottle. I remember her arguing about her salad being too "wet."

She asks me if I brought a nice suit, and if I didn't, we could go shopping at the mall beyond Akron. The mall is named Lazarus. After age thirty, no shred of irony escapes me.

"No, Ma, I brought one, an Armani. I don't think they have those at the mall."

"Well, all right. I was just asking."

I lighten up. "Maybe I can get a tie at Chess King."

"If you want to."

But she doesn't get the joke. Just the mention of Chess King to some thirty-something L.A. ex-Midwesterner, and I get loud laughs of remembrance: the flared cuffed pants, the polyester shirts, the green corduroy jacket I bought for my first semi-formal at Brookside Middle School.

Mom lights up another cigarette, and I make some comment that doesn't please her. I understand about the harping. I let it go. Smoking is an unpleasant topic, particularly for those who do in the presence of those who don't. It's something distasteful that's better left not discussed, like politics, autoerotic asphyxiation, or Andrew Sullivan.

I go for a walk down Claremont, the main street off our town. It's autumn, near Halloween. Cleveland Indians logos pop up everywhere, the locals hoping their team might have regained their near win back at the 1996 World Series.

Homes of grand and small proportions sit comfortably on lawns picked clean of debris. The leaves are stuffed in sagging plastic bags printed with leering jack-o'-lanterns.

When I get home, the newspaper reporter has left a phone message. Mom has scrawled the name and number down, handing it to me as if it were important. I call back and tell the interviewer to meet me outside the theater that afternoon.

"Who else is going to be there?" I ask her, the names hovering in the air around me.

"Oh, um a lot of professors. Students from the old days."

I can't bring up their names, or she'll see right through me. Lance? Probably. Dick Thorson? Please. Just to see him again, to know he's gotten fat or tired or isn't as gloriously handsome as I recall.

I've got four hours to kill. Mom is already getting antsy, what with another full-size adult lumbering around her house.

I go outside and rake leaves. By the time I'm done, my arms and shoulders ache. I'm damp under the sweatshirt I pulled out of the closet to wear. The moisture on my face dries in the cool air. The rake has made the fleshy apex between my thumbs and first fingers grow blisters. I drop the rake and rip off the bubbled skin, tossing the tiny flakes of flesh onto the long pile I've shoved along the curb. The exposed pink layer of the blisters sting against the cold air. I lick them.

My whole life and career is all about losing men and then finding them. Have I said that before? Sorry, I hate quoting myself.

This is what I long to tell the perky interviewer from the local paper. Katsuo, my post-production producer for *Reel to Real*, has a publicist arranging these things for me. I'm supposed to be polite to Chet Miller of the *Brookside Gazette*. Brookside High School Class of '96. Maybe I'll spill it to the cub, watch him squirm.

I've been waiting for him outside the lobby of the Brookside College Theatre for a good ten minutes. It's funny how time and cold weather don't effect me anymore.

As he approaches, I can tell he's too handsome and too young, like those *In Touch* centerfolds that get me hot and bothered until I notice they were born the year I finished high school.

We stand outside the theatre. He mentions a photographer who's supposed to show up, but he's so eager, he starts asking questions.

"What's it like being back after all these years?" His freckles and sandy blond hair overwhelm me.

"Brings back a lot of memories."

I don't tell him everything. I tell him nothing. He eats it up. He is an open page, unimpressionable, post-Reagan Youth. Aberzombie. He is still forming his nostalgia. My gaydar is on ultra-high.

"Have you seen any shows here recently?" I ask.

"Uh, actually, a few."

"Hmm. Which ones?"

"They did *Little Mary Sunshine*."

"Again?"

"Scuse me?"

"Let's go in. See if the theater's open."

"Are you sure that's okay?"

I smile. There isn't a room in that theater I haven't sniffed out, hammered on or spewed upon. "Sure it's okay. We can scope out a good photo op. You did say you wanted a picture?"

"Oh, yeah. He should be here, actually." Chet looks up and down the street. No arrivals.

"C'mon." I am making him nervous. I love it.

Maybe I'll take him up to the catwalk.

That afternoon, after omitting a few pivotal events, but enough to finish the interview with Chet, he seems satisfied with his G-rated version of me safely recorded in his microcassette. He'd blushed crimson each time I said the word 'gay.' He says he'll call if he has any more questions, one of which seems probable: "Could you please fuck me?"

When I return home, I report to Mother, then politely ask to borrow her car.

I drive slowly through town, examining it for changes and architectural fatalities.

I pass Brookside Park, with its abandoned pool and men's locker room, now locked up. I someday hope to dedicate a shrine of some sort to this place, the joyful arena of so many summer visions, where the entire town's men, all changing, all wet, all older or dead, or gone, once passed before me. IN MEMORIAM OF STAN GROZNIAK'S FIRST SIGHTING OF AN ERECT PENIS OTHER THAN HIS OWN.

I drive on, passing through black gates like those featured in the Grozniak brothers' *Jekyll and Hyde*. I park Mom's car on a small road in the local cemetery and visit the grave of Baby June.

The wind is thick with decay. Green pachysandras pleasantly adorn her headstone. I don't cry. We just talk.

10. yet we urge the bare boy to sleep

"We're taking June and leaving soon to star her in a show!"

"Cut!!"

Another stop. The other kids, all the younger versions of the Newsboys, lounged away the endless rehearsals in the green room, playing doctor or other games in the scene shop, getting into trouble. I sat front row center, taking notes, watching the most beautiful man in the world, Lance Holtzer, dance in rehearsal sweat shorts, a flimsy T-shirt, and, for rehearsal purposes, an incongruous top hat and a cane.

Arthur McCabe hiked himself up on the stage, had a mini-conference with the choreographer while stroking his beard, and then something was redone. I wasn't paying attention.

Throughout the break, Lance sat down on the stage rim, looking down at me with his shorts riding up, his spread legs merely arm's reach ahead and above. His thighs resembled blond-dusted hills, undulating as he innocently swung his feet back and forth, two muscled metronomes. His eyes glimmered, his grin as dopey as the farm boy he played.

"Hey, Stan Din. You havin' fun?"

"Yeah," I smiled, squirming in my seat, charmed by Lance's smile, the sparkle of his eyes, and the light sheen of sweat making his T-shirt cling to his chest in a translucent way that made me ponder the function of male nipples.

"Jus' sittin' here watchin' us?"

"Yeah."

"You wanna understudy me? You're my little Tulsa."

"Sure."

"Well, come on then." He hopped off the stage, jumped down, scooped me up, a boy bundle of giggles, and carried me up the aisle out into the lobby, where we snuck sodas from the closed concession stand. Then he taught me all the steps from his solo, "All I Need Now Is the Girl." Others came by every now and then, making fun, but I didn't even see them. I was watching Lance's feet, step for step. I wanted to be Lance. I wanted to marry Lance.

I'd felt a separation from the other kids in *Gypsy,* a sophistication. I knew more. I'd done more. Up in the light booth, Dick Thorson knew

me as if we had had that imagined affair. Out in the house, Arthur the
director had seen my films and called them wonderful. Dan and I could
pick out the light gels by number. That place was my summer camp, my
bar mitzvah, my manhood ritual, my Cub Scouts, my secret handshake.

Before curtain, cast members held hands in a huge circle, Arthur giving us broad cheerleading notes about our performance. The college kids
gave each other knowing smirks, the young ones dizzy imitations of the
glances. Then we spread out to a larger circle, where we held hands again,
and Jo Ellen Stringer, who played Louise, led us in "the Pulse."

She gripped the hand to her left, then the person next to him, and
around the circle. I squeezed Lance's hand until his fingers blushed red,
then released him, only to feel another pulse from the woman to my right.
The grips moved faster and faster, until people began to giggle from the
energy, as if our circle might whirl its way up through the ceiling and take
flight.

Every once in a while, you realize you are living through the most
precious moments. I had one of those then, and I watched those college
kids all have theirs. Lance was only twenty-one to my fourteen. That seven
years would seem negligible today, but then, it was a chasm. Nothing
brought us together. Nothing, that is, but a musical about a stripper.

During practices and performances of *Gypsy,* I became known as a
bit stuck-up. While other kids swarmed in from every local ballet and fire
baton studio for the Uncle Jocko scene, I was already known there. I was
a regular. Dan and I had our name on almost every flat.

This superiority didn't make me any friends my age, not that I wanted
them. The other newsboys were geeks. Dan began to hate every performance when he realized he couldn't dance. He dropped his gun almost
every night during the military section. The only pleasure he got was from
sneaking backstage with the other boys to watch Jo Ellen Stringer strip
four times between her quick-change finale numbers as Miss Gypsy Rose
Lee.

I, of course, had other interests. During intermission, I quietly slipped
up the catwalk and watched the entire second act from above. If I couldn't
sit in the Lair of Light with Dick Thorson, at least I could ascend to his
level in my own dusty lair.

Sitting on the steel grate, sometimes not moving for the entire hour
and a half, I sat watching the curtains part, the sets float in and out, the
actors move about below me. I felt the heat of the lights, heard their me-
chanical hum, watched gels slowly melt against the top hats and frames
of the lights.

When the senior who played Mama Rose finished belting out her big deranged aria, I crept down the catwalk ladder. During the prolonged applause, I emerged in line backstage a minute before curtain call, and bowed with the other kids, smiling for the sea of darkness and fluttering hands. They saw me as just one of those cute little kids. I saw myself looking down on myself, just another puppet.

During the run of the show, the stage manager put up a chart on the wall of the scene shop next to the two dressing rooms. Everyone had a little box to check for every last rehearsal and performance. Several actors had become creative, filling in the boxes with little drawings and cartoons. I did the same.

A *New Yorker* cartoon was taped to the door beside the chart. Two circus seals are sitting beside their stands, one with a ball on his nose, while the other says, "Actually, what I really want to do is direct."

I followed Lance around, asking him what he thought the character of Tulsa was like, ignoring the fact that musical theater characters usually didn't have highly developed personalities, just choral parts and a few good lines. Nevertheless, I felt like I bonded with Lance. I cut my hair short like his, combing it in a feeble attempt to imitate his curly blond front lock that jutted from his crew cut.

Every night, during the famous Newsboy scene, the strobe lights flashed, the music blaring, the newsstand whirling and twirling with flags and sparklers. The theatricality was so simple, yet each night it thrilled me. We'd dance, Baby June hoofing away, then shuffle, shuffle and move as the older boys snuck up behind us. One by one, we became them, or they became us, and the years whooshed by. We handed off our youth to them like a fresh-off-the-presses *Daily News* baton.

We became known as Tulsa One and Tulsa Two, but he called me Stand-In, or Stan Din. I think the nickname had something to do with always standing nearby whenever he had to make a costume change.

At rehearsals, Lance wore sandals, I wore sandals. He wore cutoff denim shorts, I cut my only pair of jeans, much to the consternation of my mother.

"You have plenty of shorts. Why did you have to cut your best pair of jeans?" she sighed.

She didn't understand. I was shadowing Lance, whose azure eyes were one thing I couldn't imitate, my browns dull in comparison. With Dick Thorson, I felt that I had failed somehow, so I threw myself into devotion. Lance was full tilt worship.

I stole glances at Lance as I watched him become Tulsa, whose cinematic version gave birth to my cravings and appreciation of the male ass. As he shucked off one pair of pants after another, night after night, me carefully timing my trips to the dressing room to coincide with this glorious evening miracle, his snug white jockey shorts displayed a thick round bulge.

Maybe he talked to Dick Thorson. Maybe he fucked him, I didn't know. There was a whole world of adult activity going on I couldn't translate. Half of them were drunks, a few closeted, more depressive, one a serial shoplifter. Who knew? All I knew was I wanted to see a naked man, particularly the ones I loved.

Lance, like Dick, but in a different way, must have decided to allow a moment of benevolence. We were alone in the dressing room, with only the tinny sound of the stage monitor piping in conversation from the Mister Gransinger scene. Lance gave a sly glance at me, winked, and pulled down his underpants. He gave his dick a few tugs and turned away to display his furry ass before changing into his street clothes for his "All I Need is the Girl" number.

Before he left, he made an unusual comment that, for the life of me, escapes memory.

Let us choose to recall it as something encouraging.

ACT II

"Despite Hollywood's embrace of the B genres, exploitation movies are still treated in many quarters as somewhat déclassé. Watching is like eating a quart of ice cream while standing over the kitchen sink: You know you aren't the only one doing it, but that doesn't mean you necessarily want to discuss it in mixed company."
— Maitland McDonagh, *Filmmaking on the Fringe:*
The Good, the Bad, and the Deviant Directors

"Grozniak's trilogy subverts the genre of exploitation films in that the hero is considered the sex object, and desired by the villains. It is his female sidekick, the revolving-door-cast Christie, who is always his savior. His neo-phallic symbolism is both campy and lightly homoerotic, giving him the tightrope status of both gay underground and exploitation director, a position which may explain his virtual disappearance from the filmmaking scene."
— excerpt from a 1992 *Film Threat* review of
The Manipulator, I, II, and III

11. feel the **secrecy** of produce

I don't love Barry Goldstein because he's a redhead, but it kept me coming back. He also has the capacity to really listen, like remembering my birthday. He doesn't need to know that he reminds me of the G.I. Joe doll, or Dick Thorson, or Uncle Sean, or Bill Douglas if he'd put on a few pounds.

These pieces of memories came to me in different positions when Barry and I made love, particularly at the height of the passion, before the um, riot thing. More on that later. Now, let's talk about love and passion.

Spring 1990-something. Barry's Ace Award-winning teleplay about incest was still a work in progress, being processed in his therapy writer's group, I'm not sure. He hadn't brought it up. I hadn't brought mine up. Funny how we were attracted to each other anyway. Maybe our mutual dysfunctionality had a way of presenting itself in some intangible way. Maybe everybody is dysfunctional.

I used to feel guilty that my surges of passion for Barry were sometimes based on the way the light hit his back, making him look like someone else from my past. Sometimes I'd want to kiss him with a different taste, just after a bit of food or with beer, anything but that same Tom's Fennel Toothpaste that was simply Barry. He always came to me clean and fresh, too soapy. I told him once I liked it when he didn't bathe after working out, and he couldn't understand it. I always felt randy in the morning because it was the only time he smelled real.

"I rented some movies," Barry said. He'd called me to ask what I was doing for my birthday.

I was sitting in front of the TV with some cheddar cheese popcorn, and some favorites from Woo Video; *Forbidden Planet, Dawn of the Dead,* and *HorseHung Hispanics* for after the popcorn. I lied and told him I was working.

"What kind did you rent?" I asked.

"A comedy and a heavy one. What are you up for?"

"Whaddaya got?"

"*Bringing up Baby* and a bootleg of *Looking for Mr. Goodbar.*"

"Cary and Mister Brooks. You're a master of mix." And a master of insight. I'd never told him about my little experience with Dan when we went to see that movie in high school. Does fucking a guy actually some-times lead to getting into his brain?

He looks just like—

Shut up.

Do you wanna leave?

Since I figured I'd return my videos to work the next day, I brought them and my overnight stuff, not at all being presumptuous. I tooled over to Barry's after one last cigarette. Barry hated it when I smoked, even outside. It was a little battle, trying to cut down by putting myself in the company of non-smokers, which is just about everybody with any smarts.

We'd eaten dinner and had wine. I pissed. I began singing loudly in the bathroom. "I can't give you anything but love, baby..."

"I take it that means you want the comedy."

I strolled back into the hall. "Well, let's just fast forward to the Richard Gere and Tom Berenger parts."

While scanning through the favorite scene, he got more guacamole. I glanced at the shelf, then slid the low door back to look over titles of his tapes, films he'd worked on and junk shows he'd grabbed on the VCR to file away some handsome actor or stunning woman to cast later.

On the end, though, in the dark edge, away from the fresh porno and review tapes, was a trio of cassettes still in their flashy clamshell boxes with the smirking face of their star, Rick Dacker. *The Manipulator* trilogy. My movies. He'd paid retail.

"Aw, Barry. I didn't know you cared."

12. use ugly UFO s beyond their necromancy

Let's cut back to 1978.

I am not dragging out the drama of my deflowering, which happened in 1976. I just want to explain who Ricky is, and was, and *The Manipulator*. Don't worry. We'll get to the dirt.

After our family fell apart and put itself back together again, Dan and I changed. Tired of making little movies in the backyard with cardboard cutouts and the neighborhood kids who couldn't stand still for a half minute even if we paid them, my brother and I became collectors.

Blackhawk Films catalogs made me ache and pine come payday at my lowly job in a Denny's more than a gun rack to an NRA father. I bought the classics, the oddities, and also kept subscriptions to *Scream,* "the monthly magazine of Terror and Sci Fi."

Several articles featured the infamous Guy LeDrac, Editor-Publisher of *Scream,* and proprietor of the Scream Archives, "a library of horrology." LeDrac's small mansion was decorated with kitsch from the eras of horror, sci fi, and monster filmmaking, complete with glass-encased robot models from *Forbidden Planet* and *Lost in Space,* masks galore, and photos, photos, photos. It took me two years of subscribing to figure out the guy ran the magazine pretty much to hype his Los Angeles house and to do the horror circuit. He'd be at all the conventions I never braved to ask for transport to, except when he came to a mall in Akron.

It was my first faraway trip since I'd received my driver's license. My mom forced a map and her AAA card on me just in case, and I was off to seek my hidden hero.

After perusing the temptations of bins, photos, films, posters, and memorabilia, I found my way to the Guy LeDrac autograph booth and listened to other pimply diehard fans extol his visionary virtues.

As I approached the table half an hour later, it occurred to me that what Guy LeDrac was giving my sixteen-year-old frame was not a look of mere friendliness. I was getting cruised. I suddenly felt cocky. That, or I wanted to chat away my boner.

I bragged that I, too, was a collector. "Even have a copy of *Metropolis.*"

"Oh, Fritz's best," LeDrac agreed, as if we were longtime neighboring vintners comparing a claret. He had removed his gaze from the contents of my jeans and made eye contact through his thick eyeglasses. He wasn't exactly wrinkled, but definitely mature, and his attempts at horizontally shifting his departing hair were less than flattering. Still, he was an icon worthy of adulation.

"If you ever come to L.A., I'll show you my autographed poster from *Metropolis*. Quite a find."

"Really?" I overreacted.

I reluctantly asked for an autograph, since by then we were good friends. The old man really seemed to like me, and kept his hand on my shoulder the whole time I told him I wanted to become a film director and would like to look him up when I moved.

Seven years later, when I actually did move, I had one friend to live with. Guy was my only other contact. So, I made the best of things quickly and visited him, unannounced. He was in sweat pants and a Niners T-shirt. He'd been doing aerobics.

It would have been less embarrassing to see him parading around nude, because anything so healthy in that set of gloom seemed incongruous.

I remember Guy chatting amiably and showing me his robots, and his masks and his capes and other clutter, and all the while getting a quiet thrill, knowing that I, the adored, the young, the beautiful Polish-Irish kid, was the one in control. With merely a word, the old queen would drop to his knees and know the meaning of spunk.

But I didn't. I wanted to see the poster of *Metropolis,* the landmark of my introduction into corruption, my welcome wagon in fluttering black and white.

It hung above his immense fireplace. I gaped. I wanted him to give it to me. I considered dropping my pants for it. I would have, but instead I merely gazed.

The soulless metallic face looked outward beyond an emerald green backdrop. The black slits where eyes should have been beseeched, sought out warmth that would only come by fire. She was the incarnate of all that mechanism required, the lustful desires of men pushing forth, into industry, into profit, into power. She was the real It Girl before Madonna resuscitated her imagery. The metallic bust of all inhuman and sexily inhumane glistened in Deco decadence. Her name was Hel.

"Would you ever sell that?" I asked.

"Oh no, not unless I was absolutely desperate. Or met the right buyer," he said.

"Something tells me I'd never have enough money for that."

"Not all transactions involve money." His eyes glimmered.

I ended up meeting with Guy LeDrac again in 1987, before I'd moved to Santa Monica and discovered that "young" and "fresh" were terms only applicable to the boys who sold their wares on the Santa Monica Boulevard Loop, or in magazines and movies worth a quarter a minute, or in the video store where I managed to land a job after two burger joints in a week.

With steady income and the budget to keep the car maintained, plus an extra shipment of a few suits Mom shipped after a family friend had died, I finally got the nerve to ask Guy to read one of my scripts.

I was still hanging the possibility of sexual gratification over him like the oft-mentioned carrot by playing the "new young thing," whatever pose that was then. He called back two weeks later and said he liked the script. A lot. He sent it to Roger Corman, who produced *The Manipulator*, which ended up paying my rent for a year. I bought a few other things after the sequel. Pretty good for a flick that took only a hundred-twenty grand to make.

In production, Corman said he was only slightly impressed with the script, but after mentioning my name to an old friend of his, the old friend being "Santa," he told Corman I was the guy who decorated Mr. A-List's Halloween party a la *The House of Usher*. Then he called me.

See, sometimes things work like that out here, boomerang-style. You never know when you're networking.

Basically, the plot of *The Manipulator* was, to quote my less than coherent, yet favorite, review, "... amusingly parodic, if not blatantly derivative."

Our hero, Professor Parker Parrish, is a young and handsome mythology professor at a small Southern California college. Parrish moonlights as a government agent, catching dastardly bad guys who plan to take over the world, or whatever parts they can get their hands on.

Through a farcical eavesdropping nighttime classroom session in which Christie Crystal, the sparkle-eyed student of the Manipulator, overhears the plans of our hero, the two engage on an adventure to stop the mad Herr Boering from distilling his psychotic Frenzy Juice into the L.A. water reservoir with the help of his half-dozen muscle thug zombies, played by a crew of Venice Beach pump boys in too much blue body paint.

Parrish ends up tied and roped *Wild Wild West*-style no less than three times, the final climax of the film involving his engaging in a knockdown wrestling match with a muscled thug in a knee-high river. While the audience gets a pleasant show of Parrish's parts bulging under wet chinos, with Christie held at gunpoint by Herr Boering, then finally elbowing him into submission, the two save the city and join forces in bed. Before consummating their love, however, Parrish falls asleep.

Stupid, inane, and a hell of a good time. The cast provided a lot of ad-libs that stuck.

The Manipulator achieved a world premiere in a small L.A. art house on the brink of bankruptcy, an event a pot brownie and a bottle of champagne helped eradicate from my memory. It then enjoyed a successful run at drive-ins through the South, and eventually jumped to video. It's also supposed to be popular in some art houses in Taiwan, where they call it *Fast-Talking Action Guy*.

I caught it on the Sci-Fi channel once. At least it wasn't considered bad enough for *Mystery Science Theater 3000* to rake it over the coals.

My star made *The Manipulator* great. Without him, it would have totally flopped. Before becoming the Manipulator, Gerard Kulozik's stage name was so bland I forgot it, one of those interchangeable Chet Johnson kind of names.

But that face, oh dear God, Gerard's face—a jutting jaw this side of self-parody, a grin made from demon spit, and a glimmer in his eyes that read baseball, hot dogs, and oral sex with anyone. He also had just enough chest hair and muscles to make even a straight man hard.

The day after his audition, which had quickly turned into a date, I convinced Gerard Kulozik to use a campy sexy name, just for this film. "That way, if it's a total flop, which I think it will be, you can forget about it."

It wasn't. He didn't, and Rick Dacker was born.

I also learned how to make a star out of a guy who couldn't remember his lines every day but could make up an even better one if needed.

My trusty costume designer, Jorge, whom you've met, made sure that Rick Dacker's shirt was either torn or torn off for most of the film, for he had the body to go with it.

What he didn't plan, exactly, was how tight Rick's pants could appear, especially while wet.

Before filming the majority of scenes in humid Georgia, I gathered the crew for an action scene from the beginning, set in a recently flooded warehouse. It was cheap and the actors were easy to find at a local gym, a hunky near-*Powertool*-muscled quartet of thugs Ricky would single-handedly defeat.

After a few hours of fight rehearsal, the guys plowed through the first volley, water splashing about. We couldn't afford duplicate costumes, so we had to shoot sequentially as they became muddier.

During a break—there were no trailers, just a table of food by the warehouse door, and a rented porta-potty outside—I followed Ricky off for a soda, and noticed the contents of his khaki action pants.

"You're, uh, sportin' some there, dude."

"Oh, yeah." Ricky flopped open the button fly to reveal his thickened penis and cock ring. "Special effects. They won't know what hit 'em." He slipped his prize back under wraps.

"Until it's on video."

"Which will make you a million." He smiled and ate half a sandwich in one bite.

I didn't realize until later how Ricky was daring the world to see him, showing himself off but defying all as well.

I did catch on through filming, accentuating shots of him tied up, glistening, and the occasional crotch shot mid-fight scene. Maybe the deliberate, sexy camp of it is why it grew a cult following.

What would he now think of the fan websites and pages of screen-shots and animated gifs of his package bobbing about mid-tussle? Would he be honored? Amused? Probably.

Despite the fact that the movie didn't make that million, it didn't cost much either, and I got a green light for a sequel. Ricky and I wrote it at my house in three nights, him improvising with me as I played all the other characters. We'd already thought up the third during filming of the second. It was like a fever, interrupted only by food, pot, and sex.

Each time we got a little more money, more cast members and more toys. Each time his pants seemed to bulge in all the right places. And in each film I made sure to include him getting wet or shirtless, usually both. What made the trilogy work was our constant state of the ridiculous. With almost no money, we had to play with language, puns, and innuendo.

Example:

In part two, *The Manipulator II: Revenge is Best Served Cold,* Christie and Professor Parrish both hang from their feet over a steaming vat of boiling wax (a set leftover from *Indiana Jones,* believe it or not. My favorite project was re-writing scenes around existing sets and props. I was Ed Wood *sans* cashmere).

This is the scene where I blatantly borrowed from Fritz Lang's *Metropolis.* There's a shot where we wanted to recreate the feel of standing in a building while it's collapsing. Fritz had a lot of exploding walls and those scared children running around, but for one shot, he just swings a camera at the actors. It's hanging on a rope. It's just one shot, but it works.

Well, I thanked Fritz for five minutes, by hanging the camera while shooting Parrish and Christie, hanging upside down above the vat. They are to be made into statues by Ronald Blep, a crazed hyperrealist sculptor driven insane after being spurned for a series of NEA grants for not being ethnic enough.

                        CHRISTIE:
              Oh, Parker, what'll we do?

                        PARRISH:
        After Blep's death, increase in market value.
        I can just see us being wheeled in at Sotheby's.
              "What am I bid for this lovely—"

                        CHRISTIE:
              Oh, Parker, be serious.

                        PARRISH:
        If there's one thing I'm serious about,
                  my dear, it's fine art.

But my indulgence grew to concern the executives of what had once been a funky studio in a small office that became a subsidiary of an international corporation. The people who controlled my work no longer had any connection to my work, nor did they at all "get it."

Example: In the 1989 third series, *The Manipulator III: Brunch of the Living Dead*, evil mortician Cade Avers unleashes a secret formaldehyde potion to bring back exceptionally annoying dead people. The only way to kill them, of course, is to behead them. Prof. Parrish and Christie III (we could never get the same woman to replay the role, so it became a sort of Darren Stephens thing) are forced to hire Zen Wang, a mercenary Korean weapons designer who specializes in airborne limb-chopping mini-missiles, only to have his idea stolen by an American competitor who makes a bundle selling it on an infomercial as a weed-whacker. The only problem with Zen Wang was that everybody cheered for him when he killed his competitor. He became the favorite villain of the trilogy. Anybody cheers the death of an infomercialist.

At the final post-climactic moment, Wang's eventual death, much gore and splatter and flying corpse limbs later, Parrish, in a state of complete exhaustion, coated in blood, tosses aside the last functional weapon and says, "Christina, no more hired Wangers."

Ow. I will admit that the entire film's plot was based on that simple pun, uttered by Gerard/Parrish/Rick one wine-slurred night when he wasn't sure which one of himself he liked to be, and I still wasn't sure which one of them he really was, until he stayed well after everybody else left and ended up in my bed. I liked to growl at Rick after that time, "Damn, we coulda fucked in Georgia when we did the swamp scene. That's a federal offense down there!"

All that time lost.

The Manipulator started knocking around a few cult film circuits by the third go around, which we banged out in three successive years. What is the term for the one after a sequel? Overkill?

Manipulator night enjoyed a brief camp Halloween quality into early 1990. Ricky and I enjoyed attending a few of the cons and events. Our favorite was staying with Dan and his wife Gloria when we attended the screenings at the Roxie in San Francisco.

My brother finally seemed okay with my being a relative of some renown, and Gloria was a great host. They were still childless then, and we were being encouraging, since they weren't the only ones who wanted to see the Grozniak-Mikuria name live on. Gloria is Russo-Slavic. Her grandparents escaped one of those now not-Soviet tundra lands and migrated to New York.

What with Ricky flirting with Gloria all the time, and me and Dan getting along terrifically as long as we were joking about old times or playing some new games, it was a wonderful trip. I love San Francisco the way Dorothy loves the Scarecrow. If it only had a brain.

Evenings included me boinking Ricky in the guest room, among other places. We learned how to do "silent sex" for the first time. It was the longest, slowest ... anyway, we had fun. We had to keep quiet. I didn't want—well, let's just say I learned how to be quiet around Dan.

We did do one three-way, and that was our one night at a sex club where we lied and told Dan and Gloria we were going out to the wine country for a night.

Dan didn't understand how we could stay up so late and still be perky in the morning.

"Coffee," I'd say, after having Ricky finger-fuck me in front of a dozen leather-clad admirers. One of them was one of my favorites, a Falcon model, I forget his name. Chase Chandler? Foster Grants?

The next morning, Dan had to go off to work. Gloria was between projects and kindly gave us a tour of Vulcan Pass.

On all our walks, either Ricky and I held hands, or we hugged her from either side like some sort of cheerful billboard. We took her to a few places she hadn't been, which was great. I mean just neighborhoods.

I remember the three of us up at the top of one of those windy little hills, an ocean breeze slapping our backs, the sprawled downtown of San Francisco before us like Oz with a five o'clock shadow. The perfect little houses with perfect little window boxes were beginning to have their effect.

"Always wanted to live on a street that was really just a staircase," Ricky said.

"Well, the traffic sure is quieter."

"You wanna move here with me?"

He said it. Ricky said it there. Gloria still remembers.

Neither of us remembers why I said, "Sure," but never took him up on it. I like to think Ricky would have wanted to keep seeing me.

After struggling to get other work, he did a few commercials in between surviving the fan attacks in parking lots and at Hugo's, as well as a few sex clubs and bars. If only he could have manipulated his way out of all those opportunistic infections.

I have a photo of Ricky at our last wrap party at somebody's pool. He's wearing nothing but water and a pair of Kelly green Speedos. The photo shows almost everything, the body of life. I remember Jorge blurting one of my favorite Bette Davis lines as Ricky disappeared with a stunt gal, for a change of pace, on his arm.

"There goes the good time had by all."

Ricky was adventurous in so many ways. He did all his own stunts.

Having never made more than a few commercials once he started losing all that muscle, Gerard Kulozik made money in other ways, keeping that part pretty well hidden from his friends.

We used to talk about doing a fourth *Manipulator,* and I often half-joked with Dan about developing a video game version, but the ideas always fizzled out.

I still imagine sleeping with Ricky. Sometimes my memory requires a viewing of the quaint tape I have of him, with every outtake I ever captured of him on film, including a few dick shots of his censored nude scenes. Rick didn't seem to care who saw him. I guess he also didn't care who did him.

Wait, that's cruel.

His sense of the bizarre led our love life. We'd do it in all sorts of positions and scenes. He kept wanting to tape them. I relented a few times. We went through piles of rubbers. At some point, though, he said he wanted to stop fucking, that we could do more amusing things.

Some of our bondage games meshed with his athletic endeavors. We'd giggle through an hour or so of him being suspended to a tree while I smacked him. We'd gone out to the Santa Monica Mountains to find a private spot for a John Rechy tribute. He did pull-ups while I yanked him off and peed on him. It was like a sexual version of an action movie, the way Ricky always dared me to go farther. I could have settled for merely loving him in the old-fashioned way, but to him sex was for fun, for pushing boundaries.

Once, before he cut me off, saying it was too scary when actually he was more scared of how sick he was getting, he barked at me once that all I really wanted was just sex.

"Sure," I said, "when I meet my hero, I want to fuck him." He got it. He was my hero. I made him a hero three times.

But one of the great moments of our sex life was how Ricky got down to the bone of my sexual past, as if it unlocked the key to me. After I told him about some of my early teen sexual images, including the Big Chuck and Hoolihan days, he called to arrange a special night. Ricky invited me over, and when I arrived, I was shocked and thrilled to find a small Italian midget he'd found.

The guy was really handsome, and hung for his size, but the way Ricky had tried to recreate my fantasy was impeccable. He'd even bought a red nightshirt, and let me watch while the little person, named Tony, fished around under Ricky's nightie, and pulled out a ten-inch link of Polish sausage. Tony licked it, sucked on it, and after the three of us had done each other in several positions to a repeating tape of Peggy Lee's version of "Is That All There Is?", I figured there was nothing Ricky couldn't do for me.

Except stay alive.

The bastard died the day after the Oscars in 1992, the only time I actually attended.

Damn Ricky. Always upstaging.

Here's an honest question: Have you ever caught yourself jacking off to a sexy dead friend, crying and beating off simultaneously?

No?

Sorry I asked.

13. government conspiracy is elaborate on breast size

The people who owned *The Manipulator* didn't shaft me. The company that bought the people who owned *The Manipulator* shafted me. Or was it the company that bought that company?

Whoever it was, I didn't get anything more than little checks in the mail good enough for an annual trip to Ikea. I wasn't making much off of the video rights, so I scrimped and borrowed the money for my fourth screenplay. In dire economic straits, I re-shot half a comedy that will not be mentioned, whose original director got canned after spiraling off into a cocaine binge. It's the one without my name on it, but it paid another year's rent.

After that, I made *Boy Nation,* a serio-critique of body worship with footage of the AB101 riots that ended up with its own postcard series inspired by Philip Dimitri Galas. If you don't know who he was, or at least who his sister Diamanda is, find out.

Boy Nation was born from an argument at a party. Some activists and their poser imitators were hot on the outing trail that *OutWeek* reblazed. I actually enjoyed watching the Oscars where Queer Nation protested. It gave the usually boring proceedings an edge it's never seen. I'm not against outing. I just don't do it myself, or to myself. I just assume everyone knows I'm gay, or to paraphrase Harvey Fierstein, I assume everyone's gay until they prove they're straight.

But the lines weren't so blurry at gay parties. Certainly there was a relaxed attitude when some of the host's videos included graphic or anti-het sentiments. This was a film preview party, short video dramatic, whatever.

A multiple-pierced "activist" at a rather enjoyable low rent post-Awards party in Venice got me at a vulnerably drunken point in the evening where I merely wanted to get laid, least of all by him, so in a moment of self-parody, I hauled out the impressive titles, music videos, commercials, and oh yes, *The Manipulator.* He sort of gasped in what I thought would be followed by coos of adulation for its campy edge. Instead, he railed about its lack of positive gay role models.

"It's a fucking farce," I tried to explain. "Every one of them was more ridiculous than the last one."

"That is the point."

"No, there is no point. They were pointless movies. Half the fucking cast and crew were queer."

"Including Rick Dacker?"

"Yes, including Rick Dacker."

"Then why doesn't he come out?"

"Because he died of AIDS, you little fuck-faced poser. And if it would bring him back, I would gladly kill you now, because he was more of a fighter than you will ever be." I considered throwing my drink or spitting, but I just walked away.

By the time I got in the Dart, I was no longer drunk. By the time I got home, I was still seething. I hate to admit it, but the roots of *Boy Nation*, which is known as a "queer" film, was really a reactionary montage parody of the whole Queer Nation culture. The AB101 riot footage was a lucky accident. I had the camera batteries charged after a little dusk surf punk VoyeurVision shooting along the coast.

When Jorge called and said, "There's a thousand homos in the streets and they are all fabulous! We gotta go!" I obeyed. I was mad. It was time to stop bawling and start throwing rocks.

Boy Nation was not meant to lionize the now geriatric "Activist Community," which at this point, is ... I'm not gonna get into it. I'll leave that analytical critique for queens with doctoral theses to excrete. *Boy Nation* was about anger and the reaction to anger, the style of radical chic, the appeal of posing as terrorists, the Weimar Era of our culture. The days of rage and glorious screaming in the streets were doomed. We'd finally been backed so flat against the wall by the Reagan-Bush reich that we had to fight back. But all that remains is the costume, the fashion. ACT UP Ken. Barney Frank Soap on a Rope. Civil Diss Dildo mail order catalogs. Freedom Cock Rings™.

I'd pretty much cut my ties with horrordom by dealing with queerness in a way that at the time was shockingly blunt and got a lot of attention, despite my clumsiness with sound and script. It looked good, anyway, and it got in the major gay film festivals. I got to see San Francisco and New York again and be the toast of the town. Well, maybe the crouton.

After a short period of being one of the darlings of alternative cinema slapped into archly gay-positive magazine articles alongside Gregg Araki, Jenny Livingston, and Todd Haynes, I pretty much got schmoozed and boozed out, but not to twelve-step proportions. I'm too cheap to be an addict. I just took whatever came along, never asking where they got it or begging for more. I never befriended a dealer, although I went to plenty of parties where beepers were as common as baseball caps.

It was around this time, when some of my younger assistants were bouncing their schedules around ACT UP demonstrations while others were moving their schedules around clinic appointments, that I got a healthy royalty for the video version of *Boy Nation*. It had pretty much worn out its video festival popularity, but it had made it into the catalog of a few gay videos, next to those innocuous Greenwood Cooper tapes of semi-erect men frolicking on beaches and in swimming pools. Nude Volleyball. I imagined thousands of homos around the country making copies of my favorite, and it felt good to know they were all breaking the law and getting their own copy, even if I wasn't getting the twenty-cent royalty.

Yes, my first great sell-out was about radicalism. Go figure.

I had bills to pay, and my father the math teacher was still adding up the yield increase on a second mortgage, and still paying off my and Dan's college education, thank you very much, at the rate of...

Anyway, the point is, I needed money. The video's a box next to Greenwood Cooper's *Naked Young Running Men, Series 3*.

I am a shower curtain. I did softcore gayrotica under an assumed name. Who hasn't?

Something about film and its ephemeral quality always leaves me hungry. Knowing a copy of it exists in thousands of video nook shelves in bedrooms and living rooms with a Joan Crawford movie poster on the wall, or next to a copy of *Desperate Living*, gives me comfort, no matter if it's stupid. I know I will exist at least fifty years beyond my death, depending on the tape quality.

During this slack period, with only that ghost-directed comedy that went straight to video and Shall Never Be Mentioned since my name is not on it, and the softcore skin flick, I made *Keemoe*.

I was at a point in my career where those overweight film critics tell the public what directors like me should be doing—more "successful" pictures, more general interest, a dark comedy, perhaps. Something with my "Lynchian dark edge." God praise any critic who can use an adjective that isn't also a pronoun.

But no. In a high moment of failed career suicide, I began taping bits of TV stuff in a mad frenzy, channel surfing, seeking out content. Then I disguised my portable Hi8 video camera in a gym bag and walked up and down the halls of hospitals.

You see, people were very busy dying at the time. Ricky had already died. So had Baby June and about a hundred others I never got a last name from. Where did you all go, you beautiful young people? Ye Gods are so cruel I could storm Olympus in three leaps and smack y'all upside the head.

I guess it had to ricochet off a few walls for it to really hit me. I put it aside.

Almost a year into managing Mister Woo's Video, I settled into just sinking my teeth into the nightly fun of two free tapes a night. Although several HIV tests revealed negative results, I'd settled into a post-sex phase. My dual themes, my double headers. Musical, Porno. Comedy, Porno. Action, Porno. For a change of pace, I watched straight, bi, kink. I bought obscure titles for Mister Woo's inventory, assuring him that the Mardi Gras stripper collection, and the entire Dirk Yates Marine Solo Library would surely find a large audience. I was right.

Then one night, when I'd seen a touching film by Mister Schlesinger that made me cry, I was inspired and went back into my own stuff.

Death needed a hero to conquer it.

For sexy queer intrigue, I tossed in just the face shots of porn star Jason Daw's best-selling tape, *Pozitivities,* in which he sucked and fucked his way across the country, dispensing condoms and lube like a Pied Piper of safe sex, and at video's end, came out as HIV-positive.

After getting the rights to borrow shots from *Pozitivities* and a pleasant donation from one of the porn company's producers, a guy named Geoff, with a vaguely sincere offer to direct a film for them sometime in the future, I completed shooting *Keemoe.*

In a post-production process that lasted months, I slurred together these stolen images, added a hateful score of bumping, screeching and beeping sounds, combined with some monologues by a local poet and composer who has since died, and made *Keemoe.* For the credits, I got the rights to use a Front Line Assembly song that rocks.

At the time, of course, I didn't know this was my way of grieving, my way of making room for the awful feelings about Ricky's death, among many others. I couldn't find any words that weren't trite when discussing AIDS, and in the midst of the epidemic, I dared to make a video about sex and AIDS without mentioning the word.

The press was miffed, disappointed, and after the third unflattering Jarman-esque comparison, I did manage to get an *Advocate* interview at least, where I was quoted as saying I used Jason Daw as a heroic figure, not an erotic one.

A week after the publication of that interview, among the small slew of congratulatory phone messages, I got a call from Jason Daw himself, asking me to dinner.

Boomerangs. Throw enough out there, and one'll eventually hit you in the head.

14. report: an unknown visitor from lake poltergeist saw thousands stare in wonder as drunk unicorns chanted tales near Area 51.

I met a handsome young guy once. Asked him if he was Polish or what. He had crow-black hair and a unibrow above a stubby nose that made me think Slavic.

"Dunno," he said.

I asked his name. He said a name. Monroe, Feldon. Something Saxon. I forget. He had no idea where his grandparents were born.

At that moment, he struck me as a most unattractive man, disinterested in his history, trail-less, bloodless.

Blood is sexy. Immigration stories are sexy. They are about survival, movement, shifting in planetary communities. Every man is the composite of all of his race(s), which makes him precious, even more so if he's gay, since he is the end of the line. He is his own extinction. That, in me, stirs desire, the desire to experience, to touch, to taste the frailty of lineage, and yes, maybe capture it somehow, either through my own body or a camera.

At Ricky's funeral, I heard his full name for the first time spoken by someone else.

He was a glorious mix: half Czech, with one quarter Jewish and Italian. Wow. What a fun reunion that would have been, if only more of his relatives had shown up, had cared. If only he hadn't felt forced to cut them off. What an adventure it took, what a trail of tears to get to the body and soul that was him.

I sometimes write letters to a cousin of his who did come to his funeral. She, too, likes to dig up roots. Every time she finds another factoid about their clan, she sends it to me, knowing it's like continuing a conversation with Ricky, moving on, learning more, still keeping up the love.

I expressed my grief through smoking, eating, and sex. You put it together. I did things with guys in places I'd never imagined. I peed from a moving Jeep. I hung out with marvelous dear friends who never asked my last name.

Long, tangy, immense, I sought men who were how I imagined Dick Thorson might have tasted. I put photos of Ricky on the floor, impaling myself with produce. I wanted it to be better the next time. I wanted to feel that again, to choke for love. I needed somebody to fuck the life back into me.

So when a man with the magnitude of Jason Daw called, I listened. The thirty-two-year-old Australian porn star was so removed from L.A. life that his occasional visits were mere hissing word-of-mouth babble at cocktail parties. He was a rumor. I never thought of him as someone you could also talk to. He was that rare creature that had ascended a porn career into float king admiration, like Rex Chandler, like Steve Kelso or Nick Chase, the Colt model who became mayor of West Hollywood.

Jason Daw had the smooth heroism of an Eastwood, with a touch of Magic Johnson's fallen heroism, the accent of Paul Hogan, the humor of early Eric Bana, and a cock which when erect could accommodate a party of four.

"Yeah, there'll be about a dozen folks, y'know. Quueah friends. Bring a guest, if you like."

I would have liked, but I figured you don't invite a buddy to your very own tribunal. I thought he was gonna lay into me. What else could his purpose be? There'd be other men to meet, probably no women. That would give it a more predatory air. I had to go.

In New York, in Ohio, and almost anywhere else, social situations were a daily occurrence. Meeting new people was a dizzy, wonderful flood. In L.A., with so much time spent driving, and since I do not "gym," I'm left to whoever decides to stay in touch after a film. L.A. parties were/are/ will ever be more formal, especially an informal party. In their guest lists, of course, it was formalized courtship, a dating and networking service. Spin the Bottle was now Ride the Rolodex.

At this time, Barry hadn't allowed me to define our relationship. I wasn't "his." I had to go shopping, meet somebody who could shift me, distract me. Jason fit that bill.

"What time?" I asked, amused by the cordiality of chatting with someone whom I'd never met, but whose ejaculations I had memorized like straight men recall Super Bowl touchdowns.

"Oh, we'll be hangin' out by the pool fir the aftahnoon, then grill some free-range chicken. I thank that's so funny."

"What?"

"The fect thet yew Americans pey extra to have a fahm chicken that gets to run around." He was talking in a faux-campy way that comforted me. It said, *Sure I could fuck you until you passed out, but I'm just a regular guy.*

"Well, exercise is good for the muscles," I joked, "whether you're building them or eating them."

We both laughed at the remark out of a sort of awkwardness, the sudden stupidity of our being strangers preparing our first meeting with such common theatricality. We were two very different sorts of queens, but we each constructed an equally dramatic meeting deserving of our place, and for that I had to respect him, even if he was just an overpaid prison-stock porno whore who was hung like a horse.

Once I established that we did actually think about the issue of having sex with other people, the thing with Barry and I became more casual, or perhaps it aired out. It slightly crushed him when I mentioned once how my best orgasms and ejaculations were usually partnered with a video or magazine, and not him.

"You mean our sex isn't good?"

"No, no no, it's not that. It's just, I get ... tantric. I can get up in the middle of a rock hard, on the verge boner, and go have a cigarette, or eat or pee without having to worry about insulting someone, or you."

"Well, if you have to pee, you should say so."

"That's not the point," I said. This was over the phone. Why are we always more blunt to each other over the phone? To make up for the distance?

I tried to explain my love of film and video and the capturing of guys gone by or guys to be, but he's a writer, so I'm not sure he understood it, "the image, the pure starkness of a body captured. You know, the whole Dorian Gray thing."

"Yeah," he said. *You're rejecting me.*

"Once I made a montage of a porn actor, from the last cheesy, can't-get-anything-better tape, then backwards to the very first, blurry eight millimeter loop he ever made. Ever. *Martin Amis at the Adonis.* He was eighteen. Do you see how special that is?"

"I suppose," Barry said. "You know, I think there's a twelve-step group for people who, you know might be addicted—"

"Don't use that word with me. My images are not an addiction. They're an obsession."

"Okay."

"Look, my mom is the last in a line of full-tilt alcoholics. All the kids my age in the Irish side are straight, happy, and not beating their kids. I call that an improvement. When was the last time you even saw a six-pack in my fridge? If it weren't for porn, I'd be out fucking and sucking in a park, and probably dead from AIDS or a mugging by now. Porn saves lives!"

"Okay." Barry was shutting down. He knew better than to argue with me. We shifted to 'I was just kidding' mode. He understood, I thought, when I'd explained the fascinating feeling of relief, comfort, of 'I knew it all along' I got when some of those beautiful models, like Bill Cable, the cover guy for *Playgirl's* November 1974, later appeared it *Rip Colt's Private Collection* with a beard and the name Stoner. Like Rock Pamplin, the Playgirl Man of the Year in 1970-something, who turned up later in a Colt photo spread and then even later in the escort ads in the back of *Frontiers,* and, somewhere along the line, on a box of Anbesol.

Ecstasy, gentlemen. I give you pure ecstasy. That is the feeling of finally, after twenty years of wondering and hankering and worshipping, discovering the light and truth of your pagan gods. Ladies, gentlemen, others. My message is simple. Taste your idols.

Maybe they were just models, straight, gay, who cares. I just knew, when I put the pieces of my little collection together, that I wasn't barking up the wrong trees, that I was attracted to men who, had I been older or gayer, I would have seen anyway, since every last one of them was probably gay.

"Okay, okay." Barry relented. "So, who are you having sex with tonight?"

"What?"

"What are you watching?"

I laughed. He laughed. But then I realized he meant it, so I told him. "Ed Dinakos."

"Oh, I think I saw him at the gym last month."

"I hope not. He's dead."

"Oh." Then Barry asked me in a roundabout way if I could make a tape for him sometime, a sort of greatest hits. I declined. "Porn is a very subjective thing. I'm sure you wouldn't like my taste."

"Of course I like your taste, you Polack weasel. We're making a movie together, remember?"

"Oh, that's right, you Jew lumberjack. I forgot."

15. be ever the **brain friend**

In November of 1995, a Showtime executive expressed "enthusiastic interest" in Barry's pitch for what I was calling *Ball in the Family,* and Barry
had taken to bringing his PowerBook to my place to work on the script. It
was an inconvenience of technology, with one advantage. I cooked.

"So, do you want to go to Edmund's party?" he asked as we finished
our bowls of shrimp tortellini with puttanesca sauce.

"I don't know," I sort of moaned.

"A little too much veneer for you, post-grunge meister?"

"You got me there, Bear."

Edmund Martin, a graceful queen of bygone character role years, had
gone into producing after his hit TV show, *The Captain's Kids,* and made
an even more graceful exit after seven years on the top of the Nielsen
ratings. The tale of an erudite widower becoming the guardian of two
irascible tots charmed the nation, despite his subverted "single" status.
Widower was a very handy way of portraying an older gay dad, but of
course that was never mentioned.

The Captain's Kids has become a bit of a gay favorite, despite, or due
to its guises. You can see snippets in any gay bar with a creative VJ. Since
then, Edmund pulled back from acting, only to appear on bogus awards
shows or voice-overing a host of tasteful mustard and tasteful car commercials, his sturdy baritone bearing the resonant comfort of class and
secuuurity.

As *The Captain's Kids* circulated in syndication, two of the children
from the show began lives of crime, one robbing an erotic video store, the
other spontaneously combusting in a freebase mushroom cloud. Edmund
Martin had kept clear of them, raking in a tidy residual sum. He branched
off into projects where his increasing girth would not be captured on
screen. He produced TV movies with a lot of car chases and intimate
love affairs between older women and studly young men, played by studly
young actors who only years previous were rumored to have been gogo
boys at certain nightclubs. The TV movies Edmund produced were trash,
but they scooped up ratings like the Danielle Steele mini-series they glaringly imitated.

Edmund Martin was a success.

Thus our quandary as Barry washed the dishes and I paced outside under the moonshade of my patio. The invitation had a purpose; a pre-audition. Neither of us were close to Edmund, although Barry had script-doctored one TV movie for him. Should we go to seek help, or merely play the crafty independents, getting by on the skin of our union cards? Moreover, would Edmund be willing to produce such a work, thereby exposing himself to a potential "close association" with a "gay" project?

This was gonna be work.

"It's only up the hill," Barry said, as he dried his hands on a dishtowel, as if Brentwood was just a little skip across the fence. "If we don't like it, we can just come home."

"Whose home?" I asked, but I was already walking into the bedroom to pick out a shirt.

Barry's logic wouldn't soothe me. Parties were all or nothing. The host must be greeted, lauded and introduced, then re-chatted, and then, some-where, if you're lucky, a private audience could be had. And only then would there evolve a true pairing, a promise of phone calls never kept or returned deliberately when one is out, tossing the voicemail ball back into one's own court along with the other deflated and soggy pile of missed serves.

Well, none of that applied. He volleyed first.

"I want to talk to you about your project," Edmund purred as he personally took me to the bar, getting Barry and me a drink only minutes after we arrived. "I've got to greet. The herd is arriving at a strangely punc-tual rate. But don't disappear." I hadn't seen him since some film festival, maybe five years back. Then, like the second meeting, Edmund's abrupt-ness surprised me.

I didn't have time to ask him which project. I'd spread some hints about another gay film, but it was probably Barry's incest TV movie. I'd also heard Edmund had a personal interest in casting. Was that how he got his sex, renting the actors? Did he have a tax-deductible account to pull that cash from? What did they call it, the Edmund Pud Fund?

"Well, news faxes fast." Barry plucked an ice cube from his drink and savored it. I liked when he did sexy little things like that in public. It was our way of having our cocks aimed at each other in an oblivious crowd.

Edmund's home pushed against the usual L.A. decor. He preferred comfort over style, collecting rugs and furniture more fitting of an English second home in "Injuh." Most of his guests cooed and admired the arti-facts. Others were more absorbed in themselves or their various controlled substances discreetly consumed offstage.

I was sipping and whispering with Barry when two men walked up. One said, "Barry, you look great!" a bit too loud. They hugged, and Too-Loud's friend/whatever and I shared a look, then suddenly veered our eyes away.

I hunted down Edmund after giving a passing glance and finger graze on Barry's butt. It seemed I was next.

I enjoyed the way Edmund cheerily dismissed a guest, who sauntered off in search of alcohol or another networking contact. He caught my eye, and I excused myself from Barry and his two … contacts.

"Having a good time, Stanley?" Edmund offered a plate of something shiny on crackers.

"Oh. Always. This is … great. Is this meat-derived?"

I blathered on for a bit, two glasses of champagne making even an indoor ashtray seem fabulous. Edmund nibbled with me, waiting, then got to the subject at hand.

"I understand Barry's almost finished his script."

"Yes."

"Difficult topic. One hopes to avoid too much melodrama."

"Yes."

"Particularly with the questioning youth market today," he smirked. "You want to direct this, I take it?"

"Yes, sir."

"And you have directed features."

I didn't know if that was a question or his knowledge. What I did was, by mentioning my work, reintroduce it, like an old friend who's entered the room, obviously forgotten your name, so you do the intros. "*The Manipulator* trilogy taught me how to get it in on time. My other work taught me how to, how to, make art, I guess. I hope to combine the two with this project."

"Hmm." Edmund seemed impressed, if not amused. "Still, it's a touchy theme."

"Yes, well, with a spotty past, I believe, cinematically."

Edmund flipped into a camp voice, gasping in a scarily good impersonation of Elizabeth Taylor. "You haven't heard the worst of it yet! I loved it, every awful moment of it I loved!"

"What's that from?"

"*Butterfield 8.*"

"I must see it again."

"Oh, don't bother," Edmund scowled as he guided me back into the main room, our business done for the moment. "I just performed the only good scene."

A week later, he ended up inviting me to dinner. He was having "just a few folks over," meaning a more select crowd. I didn't doubt a few would-be executive creative consultant producers were on the list. Then he said, "Oh, I'll call Barry, too. You don't mind, do you?"

"Of course not. This is work, but play, right?"

"You're getting back into it, aren't you, Stanley?"

"Yes, sir."

"You'll have a good time. It'll be nice."

It was. I had a good time, even got an actor lined up for an audition as the father. Or did I get the actor they always wanted pitched at me?

Some more phone tag ensued with trying to hook up with Barry, who screamed innocence, saying that he really didn't know about this until Edmund called, and no, he'd lied when he said he was free, and had to cancel something else. He showed up much later.

The thing was, the Dodge Dart was taking the day off. When I called Edmund to please forgive my lateness, he popped off with less than a moment's notice, "Oh, well, I'll send my car around." I made the obligatory protests, until he squared me off with, "Stanley, you're the youngest smartest puppy at this shindig. You think I'd pass up having you?"

There followed a brief off-phone argument in Spanish, until Javier, Edmund's "assistant," came to the phone and took my address and directions quite cheerfully.

During the ride, Javier continued to be cheerful. So was I. I'd landed in the Emerald City, finally. And I thought I was living in it.

My sacrifice for the free ride was arriving early so Javier could get dressed for serving dinner.

"I'm in love," I said.

"Who?"

I nodded.

"Oh, Javier. Yes, he is gorgeous."

I kept waiting for the "but," as in "but he's a thief," or "but he's straight," or even, "but he's illegal, convicted/sexually dysfunctional." Apparently there was no "but."

While I scraped ginger for a sauce Edmund was making, he added up the figures of the potential Showtime advance I could get, if I was interested, and if he was interested. "Let me talk to a few people. And I'm definitely serious about this, Stanley."

"Great."

"What?"

"I was thinking about a day when I was a kid and would have wanted to be exactly where I am now."

"That's good."

"But then—"

"Oh, our childhoods are always much better remembered than lived." Edmund wiped his hands on his apron. "Mine was a completely bottled life until after the War."

He told me stories, then asked about mine. I told him of my early gay experiences, feelings. "There were always guys I had crushes on, but they were never the guys I knew were gay. Like the costume designer for *Waiting For Godot*. Raymond Kriskind used to fuss over my wings every night. I played the messenger boy, and he'd decided to go literal. I remember complaining once that they didn't really work, I meant flap, and Raymond, in his husky yet effeminate way of assured queenliness that terrified me at the time, said, 'They're not supposed to flap. This is Beckett. It's a sad show.'"

Edmund broke me out of my reverie with laughter, then the topic of skirts led to something about Hawaiian men.

"If you're still drinking, there's stuff in the kitchen."

"What did you say about Hawaiian men?" I was distracted, realizing that was another time I sort of blurted out the facts, the incest thing, and got a mere acknowledging nod from Edmund.

"Hawaiian pot, my boy. That's outside."

"Oh my," I cooed. "This is an old-fashioned party."

"Yes, and all the folks in recovery have the cappuccino machine. So, this film, this is a close project for you and Barry?" Edmund said, beaming, as if he were approving the marriage I would not enter.

"Yes. It's not right for a theatrical, you know, it's got more—"

"Yes, I've read it."

"Oh."

"Not just a treatment. I read it."

"Oh. Thanks. I mean, Barry thanks you." Mr. Goldstone had just got us into Mister Gransinger's. Mama Rose was not gonna fuck it up this time.

"It's time we pushed the boundaries again. I tell you, Stanley, after my *Out* interview, I have been getting so-o-o popular again."

"Really?" I asked, pretending I knew about the article I would later have to read before our next meeting. At the same time I was burning mad I hadn't been called to be included in yet another "gay Hollywood" article. I looked good in my promo photos, not gay, as much as maybe the missing band member from the Pixies. Not looking gay confused some of the style dictators of gay media.

Not that I'm bitter.

I liked Edmund. He was a vestige of old Hollywood. That's why I did my homework. But then I stumbled. "I always figured you as a Reagan kind of guy."

"Really?"

"Well, you had Nancy on your show—"

"Let me tell you about the Reagans," Edmund said. His face fell, his hand on my shoulder, ushered away from the drawer, where he extracted a knife, and began to chop an onion, proceeding, in *mezzo sotto voce*, as the onion became raped of its skin: "I moved into L.A. in the fifties. Got dumped here after Korea and the Air Force made me gay, and I will thank the U.S. military for that to the day I die. I worked my way up here, literally, from the mailroom. That man, Ronald Reagan, turned in my boss. He turned in more homos and Socialists and talented people than you or I could ever betray. He was a monster who thought I was his friend, so I didn't end up in the bin like better, greater actors. John Garfield. Writers, directors. You think you know. Don't get me wrong, I saw that activist short you did, and that is what sold me on this, Stanley, not Barry's script. You're angry, Mister Grozniak. You're still mad at the world for letting you get wounded. I think you can make a great movie, and I think I can produce it and if those motherfucking shits out on my porch don't like it, we'll tell them to fuck off, but first we'll take their gay children and their straight money with us."

Tears sprang out of my eyes.

I felt swept up, elated, as if I had finally seen behind that little green curtain Oz kept telling me to pay no attention to.

"Well, allow me to serve drinks in your honor. What'll it be, sir?"

"Crack the merlot."

I poured. We clinked. I watched the sunset glimmer through my glass. I looked back to the half dozen or so folk of his I had yet to meet, yet to charm, which I had already, conspiratorially, fucked. To paraphrase Fitzgerald, I saw a green light.

I went home with Barry, who thankfully showed up before all reserves of my chat fuel ran out. Both of us were eroticized enough by the cumulative flirts and smirks from the party to grope each other in the car ride home. We fumbled to his living room sofa, pulling off our clothes like teenagers with the parents out of town. I thought of telling him about my impending *soir a chez* Jason Daw, just to spice things up. Talking about a porn star could be as sexy as watching one. But with my mouth around Barry's cock and him gasping and petting my head, I realized Jason was going to be another part of me that had nothing to do with Barry. I should take advantage of that. I tried not to feel bad, all the while getting sexier as I pretended I was as hung as Jason, as powerful as Edmund. I flashed on an image of Edmund watching from a discreet *Masterpiece Theatre* chair as Caravaggio painted my being stabbed by Jason's spear of an erection.

Okay, so it was over the top.

I waddled to the bedroom, pants around my ankles. As the come dribbled to cool puddles on our opposing bellies, we fumbled our faces away from each other's groins and stood. I hate when that happens, when our fluids push us apart. It was a rush job. I'm not sure why, perhaps just the party's contagious power that clung to us.

"Thanks for feeding me, again," I said as we munched leftover pizza in the kitchen. I'd finally taken my pants off. Barry started making funny rhymes, Coco Chanel or something. I popped in with a "Co-co-copulate." He countered with "co-co-habitate," with which I parried with "Co-codependent."

"Any grants coming in soon?" he asked.

"AFA. Four grand. Plus the Frameline completion fund, eighteen hundred, but that's all going back into *Keemoe.*"

"Why?"

"You still haven't paid the poet."

"You mean his estate," which was his surviving lover, known in some circles as the White Widow. A stunning former surf punk-now-bodybuilder, registered nurse and surviving lover of four men. Nursed them all to death, they say, when they're feeling especially wicked.

Of course, I don't say things like that.

Morning burned through my eyes. Barry still lay sleeping beside me. I looked over his shoulders at his nightstand. 8:34. I could have slept, or I could have nudged my face down between his legs for a good morning blowjob, but I got up.

I hadn't brought cigarettes with me, and tried my best to ignore the urge, the need to light up first thing to re-engage my nicotine groove. But then I remembered something another friend had said when he just stopped smoking one day. "It's like any other urge," he said. "It comes to you, and then it passes." I passed.

I stepped into Barry's workroom. His computer sat centered on a long, white table. A lot of books were neatly ordered on a shelf, grouped by category: fiction, poetry, filmmaking, technical manuals, writing guides. Several had little Post-its peeking out of the tops. I opened a few to see what inspirational points he'd found. I sat down to open one, but then a book beside his computer caught my eye. *Overcoming Abuse: An Incest Survivor's Handbook.* It was a large green paperback. Inside were chapters on different topics, with little lined passages, worksheets. Several were filled out in Barry's handwriting.

I put it back before reading anything. It felt wrong to pry into it. But more than that, I didn't want to deal with it, not just his secrets, but my own.

I drank some juice from the carton. He came in wearing wrinkled boxer shorts. "You're up early." He rubbed his stomach.

"Yeah. Yeah."

"So, you have plans today?"

I looked up from his desk and flashed on some teacher's remarks twenty years ago. I'd been drawing again, in the middle of Math class.

"Working with you on that script."

"Work? You think it needs work?" He was only half joking. I took the copy that sat on his desk. How long had he worked on it, struggled with it, shared it, then gone home and licked its wounds?

"It's ... Shit, we haven't even had breakfast yet and you're asking for crits."

"Well, let's have breakfast then."

One thing we always agreed on was food. I chopped scallions while Barry put on coffee. There weren't any carrots to make juice, but that was okay. Regular old cartoned orange juice would do.

"So, what needs work, in your opinion?" Barry wasn't about to quit. He was so cute, in just his shorts, cooking away for me, chubby, hairy, a cowlick giving him that boy look.

"It's not that it needs work," I said. "It's fine as is, for what you want to do. I just—" How was I going to put it? It was so Made-for-TV. It rang all the bells of a middle of the road, realistic drama with matching pain reliever commercials, the kind I had long ago abandoned. "It's classic realism." That sounded like a simultaneous compliment and dig.

"Classic Realism? Like Classic Coke?"

"Not exactly. It's ... well, I don't know if, and don't get all upset, but I don't know if I'm the right guy for that kind of material. I've ... I'm post-realism. Reality sucks."

"*Reality Bytes.*"

"Right. Oh, that reminds me. Can we get Steve Zahn to play the uncle?"

"So you're not into just telling a story anymore. You've gotta deconstruct it, or do something like what you did with *Boy Nation*?"

"Not necessarily. It's just ... viewers are more hip. They understand a world chopped up, mixed, jump-cut. They get that. And to tell the story of a fifteen-year-old kid—"

"Eighteen."

"When did that get changed?"

"When The Captain said the ship that hopes to sail through a gay love scene would at least get out of the harbor if the cabin boy was of legal age in the state of California."

"Oh."

"So, anyway, we were talking realism?"

The eggs were done. Barry got plates. I picked the toast out of his Deco toaster and buttered it. For a moment, I felt like Lucy Ricardo, plotting revenge before Ricky got home from the club.

"Yeah, well, it's not just that. Who are we talking to? What's our audience? Mature folks who want a palatable, slow-paced drama, or frustrated young queer kids on the verge of exploding because it's the end of the century and they might die if they have sex?"

Barry plopped the eggs on the plates like fried carcasses. He was mad, but he wasn't going to show it. "I just want to tell the truth."

"Yeah, but film lies, Bear."

I remembered a picture I wanted to take on that vacation with Barry where he fucked me on that mountaintop. I was standing by one of those along-the-straight-people-trail Parks Department exhibits, a tree trunk five feet high, sliced open like a Cenozoic salami, with different points of history pointed out on a plastic screen (Alexander the Great, Jesus, Washington crossing the Delaware). I'd wanted Barry to take a picture of me pointing to different rings. I would later have redone the points in history as points in my life, each epoch, each ring, named after a lousy movie, with *Losin' It* being the first.

But Barry didn't take the picture. I forget why.

"Let's eat," Barry called out.

We sat, but I continued. "Film lies. It distorts light to make a picture that doesn't exist."

"So? A fairy tale is a lie, but it has truth."

"But, you're trying to tell a fairy it's real tail."

Barry sighed, then jumped up. He'd forgotten the coffee.

"Okay, Hans Christian, but can we just eat before we blow the whole script apart?"

17. smearing summer/ want power fast

The house where Jason Daw temporarily lived, up in the hills, Moorish, surrounded by porticos and giant plants, had been an ideal setting for Falcon Video's *Spanish Succulents*, my host informed me.

Things had been arranged in a state of disarray to show how lived-in it looked. The owner, a director friend of Jason's, was in Bosnia, seeking new pornographic talent amid the rubble.

"What's next on your agenda?" I said with all the flair of a *Laugh-in* guest star sidling up to a western bar set, guns just too low. I was a bit fried after the previous night's power party at Edmund's and then Barry's grumpy breakfast. I had all the lines from last night that worked. I could still use them.

Jason had endeared himself beyond my faux-assurance. He dropped a big arm around my shoulder. "I dunno. Thought about sim travelin,' see America and all."

It was so nice to be able to look at just his face, since he was clothed, and not at the monstrously beautiful penis that featured prominently in his videos. His demeanor was delicate, with glimmering blue eyes, a short hair crop, a rather plain yet sleek nose, and thin, constantly grinning lips that couldn't wait to break into a smile if you'd just say something everso slightly funny.

He led me out to the back yard to a small pool, where five, no, eight young, nearly identical gorgeous guys stood around in shorts and sleeveless shirts sipping drinks. I was introduced. There were too many Brads. I shook their hands, nodded to those too far away to shake hands with. I wasn't concerned about the awkwardness of making chitchat with the winner of an Adult Video News Award for Best Bottom Scene. They seemed like guys whose image I might have beat off to, but couldn't remember, porn starlets of a lower, more generic order. I saw the look in their eyes. *You're not beautiful. What are you doing here?* And, from the smarter ones, *What can you do for me?*

Jason and I sat down in Adirondack chairs that would have paid three months of my rent. He convinced me to doff my shirt and shoes. I pretended to ignore the evaluative glances from the Brads. I pulled down my shorts, having worn a pair of not-too-small swim trunks underneath. I felt pale and paunchy, pec-less. I tried to ignore a pimple on my shoulder that was due for a popping.

Jason used the big flat arm of the chair to extract some pot from a little Altoids tin, then damped it into a small pipe. He lit it, puffed, then handed it over. I felt the bit of his lip spit on the pipe touch my dry lips. I started to get an erection. After I passed it back to him, I pulled my knees up to hide the dent in my trunks, then thought it preposterous to hide a boner from a guy who used them for work.

"Yeah. I like to jump back," I said, about my own wanderlust, "Get a reality check, go to gay prides in the 'burbs, make little videos."

I thought I felt more of Jason's spit on the pipe. I thought of college bong hits, passing joints mouth to mouth with gorgeous dorm buddies I only saw naked in the showers. It was the closest thing to sex as I ever got with them. Most of them.

"I love it," I said. "Sacto's gay pride was like a big picnic. Families and stuff, you know?"

"What's Sacto?" Jason asked.

"Sacramento."

His suddenly-reddened eyes registered a boyish confusion.

"The state capitol."

Nothing.

"Of California."

We both burst into laughter. Some other stud came along and took the bowl, saying we'd had enough, and in the interests of security, he should take this away from us. Then he lit up himself.

Jason scanned the stud. I wondered if he'd fucked him yet or if he was going to fuck him that night. "Well, I don't even have me werk visa renewed, girline. How'm I sposed to know your geography!"

Jason leaned over his chair, extracted something from a pile of stuff, and lit up a cigarette. I'd left mine at home, thinking I'd be shooed out the door for the offense. It was with great relief that he offered me one, a Marlboro Light. I hated them, but it was a cigarette. As we smoked, others gave us glances that said more. *Smoking is evil, but pot's okay.* It gave us a space, two addicts, two criminals enjoying their crimes against the body.

The conversation drifted to what Jason jokingly called his "competition." I mentioned a few old favorites, but then got off on a tangent about the old films transferred to video, Falcon's San Francisco earlies, with charmingly historic scenes of Polk Street and the Golden Gate Bridge; the early Jack Wranglers, with all the strip show movie palace sleaze of pre-fascist Guiliani Times Square, how they documented the days when you had to go to such a place to see filmed sex. Jason gave me a quizzical stare, then said, "Guess I'll have to bone up on my predecease-ors, as it were."

"Well, it's not just that they're old, although, you know it has an archival quality, like the feeling you get when you sneak into the library and find a book on ancient Greek art and there's a vase with some discus thrower with a boner being rubbed down by a little serving boy."

"Huh." Jason wasn't getting it, or getting it but hadn't experienced it. Maybe I was just talking too fast. It's a problem with highage. Usually my mind zooms to Speedy Gonzalez proportions while everybody else is off on a cloud.

Jason said, "So, you don't like the new stuff, but you liked it enough to use my video in yours."

"Well, that was making a comment about now, about ... AIDS and the relationship with sex. I mean, it's not that I don't like new stuff. It's just ... video is so cold, and these directors of porn just focus on the oil-derrick shots, the—"

"Plumbing shots."

We laughed.

"Yeah. See, for me, the sexual thrill is what isn't shown; it's the anticipation—what you have to peek around to see. It's who's doing what to whom. Is your favorite guy gonna get fucked? Where's he gonna do it? What's he wearing? You know what I hate?"

"What?" He leaned forward with faux-excitement. I stopped a second, realizing I was deconstructing his line of work the same way asshole wannabes sometimes did to me at parties and clubs.

"I'm sorry, I'm being too much."

"No, no, whaddayou hate?"

"Well, aside from the usual things like gay Republicans and foam packing peanuts, I hate it in a video when the guys are in some uniform and then, once they have sex, they get totally naked. They don't even leave their boots on. Then they're just—" I almost gestured to the other guys around and in the pool, but stopped myself, "—hired studs. I mean, I love that one where you're in a tent with Steve Rogers—"

"*Boot Camp.*"

"Yeah, and you're both in military gear and you never get quite naked."

Jason nodded his head. "Accessories make the woman."

That and our giggles shut me up for a while, until I reached the real point, saying how warm film is, how it creates depth. "It feels good to the eye," I said. "You know? It's light coming at you, not emissions."

"Yeah."

"It helps you lose the camera."

"Yeah."

"Well, it'd be nice to use film, but it's so expensive."

"Yeah."

"Of course, hidden camera videos, now that's where video is perfect, because the camera is an erotic tool—"

"Oh, now you're getting off on a whole 'nuther thing, girl," Jason yapped, standing and affecting a Black southern accent and hip-jutting pose that, with the Australian twang, didn't work in a hilarious way. "I think yo brain is too fulla movies!"

He grabbed my arm, pulled me to standing, hauled me over his enormous shoulders and threw me into the pool with him. When we rose from the depths, the Brads had skittered away from the splash. Their eyes betrayed a calm envy. *Why is Jason paying so much attention to that chubby one? Why him and not me?*

They didn't know I was being courted.

It was smart of them to have Jason ask me first. He'd made it sound like an adventure and enticed me with all the sexual potential of it, the possibility of "having a go at life," as he said.

Once I was revved up, a few beers in my gut, and the smell of barbecued chicken and shrimp clouding the backyard, it seemed so easy when Geoff, one of Jason's "people," a muscle hunk who managed to stay behind the camera, put the proposal in clearer terms. His nipples bothered me. He'd obviously "worked" on them until they stood out like radio knobs.

Geoff first brought it up like it was just a lark, something that popped into his head. "Why don't you make a movie for us?"

I snorted back outright laughter at Geoff's attempt, his open-faced crass showmanship. I kind of admired him then. "Look girl, put it to me clear."

Geoff's grin dropped like glass.

"We're going to do a desert porn video, and we want you to direct it," Geoff said.

"But—"

"You don't have to use your real name."

"Oh."

Then it began to burn in, the image of me romping about hotel rooms, like an ACT UP demo road trip recast by William Higgins, and I would also be getting paid.

I considered my emerging career and my impending deal with Edmund to do the serious movie about incest, and how it all swung on my "making it" or not, in someone's terms, possibly Edmund's terms, or Barry's, or according to some invisible network creature who slithered from party to party like a wily Cronenberg creation, and got people into other people's beds for nothing more than a half-promised deal and the erotic attraction of power.

I thought about respectability, and its potential, and its responsibility. What if the TV movie deal went sour? What was next? Nothing.

What if I went mainstream, and then it got out that I made a porno? The thought that it could blow my career up in smoke was almost as exciting as what I really wanted, which was to spend many nights with Jason Daw's erect penis lodged in either end of me and his boyish face hovering over my anything.

"Which airline are we flying?" I asked Geoff. "I want mileage."

That betrayed my cheap nature, but I re-established some honor when he said, "We want lots of desert, very Herb Ritts."

My glare assured the severity of his *faux pas.* "If you want Herb Ritts, then get Herb Ritts."

"Oh, I'm sorry if I—"

"Better yet, pay me what you would have given Herb Ritts, and I'll give you even more."

He nodded.

"We good?"

Again. I held out my hand. Surprised at first, he shook it.

I patted him on his too-tanned shoulder and dove back into the pool.

18. honey, her skin hair and car heaved no alchemy

"If I could live my life over again," Jorge sipped his second Calistoga with a dramatic pause borrowed from a Barbara Stanwyck film, "I'd be exhausted."

We'd both escaped the preliminary meeting—my third, his first—for the TV movie with little emotional damage. An agreement had yet to be made. I was still auditioning. We were meeting Barry at MJ's on Hyperion. It was gogo night. I would not be swayed elsewhere. I needed to blow off steam.

In our meetings, the executives had been so formal. It was as if they were the purveyors of taste and control and had to check us barbarian artists at the gate for weapons. They were right, of course.

I sipped a screwdriver, desperately craving a double espresso instead. But it was already nine-thirty.

Jorge was hopefully going to be the costume designer. He simply loved doing boring American clothes. Banality fascinated him, like the bedrooms of some men he dated.

"Look," I said, "if they don't bite, someone else will."

The dancers hadn't started yet, so Jorge changed the subject back to work. "How are you gonna do a porn video and a TV feature at the same time?"

"Not at the same time," I said, sloshing the dregs of my drink in a swirl. Jorge promised not to utter a word of it to Barry. "They agreed to wait until after I finish the movie before we make the video. That is, if we get the Showtime deal."

"You're crazy," Jorge said. He knew from crazy. He'd been born in Rio.

"It'll be a working vacation. You should come, do sets for me."

"Sets? You said it's in the desert."

"Do costumes. Fluff. Come with us. We'll do fantasy scenes, a ritual on a mountain."

"*Rapa Nudie?*"

"Sure, why not?"

"What's a matter? You think Jason Daw's dong needs four hands?"

I grinned and sipped.

Barry called Jorge, saying he was on his way. I did not cell, nor was I celled. I had one phone, at home. Sometimes, when I left the seven-year-old machine off, people thought I'd been in a fatal accident.

But Jorge's was convenient this time. Good news about the TV movie, we hoped. Showtime was supposed to make a formal go the day before. They were late. We had to get drunk or laid, or both.

"He looks hot," I said of a guy in the bar, meaning, he looks like he poses in front of a mirror three hours a day trying to look hot. A sculpted thing posed under a pin spot by the bar. His transplants were showing.

"Him?" Jorge cringed. "Oh, don't bother."

"Why not?"

"He's into boys."

"Been shopping at Rounds?" I joked.

"Looking for me?" Barry mocked the bar ad as he joined us.

"Have you ever been there?" Barry, Jorge and I kissed hellos.

"Me?" Jorge asked as he and Barry hugged.

"No. Little Miss Grunge Queen here." Barry nodded at me with a joking dismissive quality I realized I never liked.

"The one in New York?" Jorge asked.

"Yeah."

"Actually, yes."

"And?" Barry and I blurted.

"And what?"

"Did you make a sale?" Barry asked.

"Well..." Jorge teased.

"Well?"

"Just once, on a dare, with some friends."

"Did they do it, too?"

"Yes, and we all called each other later that night and got together and ended up eating and drinking all our money away in a sushi bar."

"You could always go back to the biz."

"You must be joking. I am no spring chicken."

"Your words," I blurted. "You ain't even a bucket of wings."

"Bitch!" We laughed loud and hard.

Silence. We realized Barry was beaming for some other reason than our just being in a gay bar being so gay.

The man had news.

"Well?" I shouted.

"Houston, we have a go."

"Whoo, *Fuck Yer Uncle* goes prime time!" I hugged Barry and Jorge.
All the queens eyed us, wondering which commercial one of us had bagged
that they hadn't.

"Contract session's in three days."

His hoot made all heads turn, even the bartender's, but I didn't care.
We had done it.

"This calls for something special," Barry said.

"Such as?"

"Sham-puhs, Sweetie! I'm buying." Jorge went to the bar, leaning in
just enough to let his cantaloupe ass show its perfection.

"Are we together tonight?" Barry murmured to me later as the bubbly
hit. Jorge's beauty always threatened him.

Are we together tonight. Simple as that. Barry had a way of confining
even joyful times like that into manageable events. He wanted to prepare
for bracketing any potential binge. You know why I usually say yes to him?

That answer requires an aside.

Remember when you watched people on the news getting their skulls
crushed, over and over, black men and white men and burning Shoe Worlds
and flames as high as the helicopters? You remember. Forgive me for omitting this section of my life from this autobiography. You've seen that movie.

You want to know what little me, who wasn't shooting a camera that
night, you want to know what I did? Well, think about my friends at the
time, who included Barry and Jorge and some other *Manipulator* people
you'll never meet, who moved, who died, who were lost at sea, crashed on
the Sirens' rocks.

Anyway, that night, those nights, until it was over, some bad things
happened before I got out of it all, and Barry saved me. I stayed in the
highest topographically safe place, Casa Goldstein. As I left my Santa
Monica home, my neighbor lady said she'd be keeping an eye open. She
had a gun.

Anyway, that's why I defer to Barry, other than the beauty of his body;
the trust factor.

"What about Jorge?" Barry asked.

Across the bar, Jorge flirted with a guy in Portuguese. I could tell by
the way he carried himself. "I think he found somebody." We'd been at the
bar for a while. Were Barry and I going home, about to cast a three- or
four-way? Or just to go home and sleep?

"Oh." Barry said. "I guess so."

"Besides," I sighed. "We've both done him, haven't we?" Barry feigned
shock. "A three-way would be redundant."

He waited, let that simmer, then came to a proposition. "Come with me."

"But there'll be gogo boys." I nodded toward the empty stage.

"Come with me."

"Where?"

"A swim."

"Oh? You grew a pool?" I asked.

"No, I'm house-sitting."

"Where is he?"

"How did you know it was a he?"

"Where is he?"

"Seychelles. He's a—"

"Don't tell me. I don't want to know."

"Whatever."

"Better yet, I'll guess just from the paintings and the music. Or the awards, which will be on the mantle, No, he's in music. There'll be discs on a wall."

"Champagne?" Barry said in a way that implied impending sex.

"I'll get another bottle of champagne from the bar."

"It'd be cheaper at the Quiki Mart on Pico."

"I told you, I don't go by Pico."

We fluttered through intros with the studlet Jorge had met, then gave us the visual okay-to-leave-me signals. Jorge was a little suspicious with strange boys. You would be too if you'd been bashed twice, robbed and stabbed by a hustler before your third anniversary in L.A.

We zoomed across town, into Beverly Hills and to the secluded home of our mysterious host. His invisible presence became the third.

We swam and drank, and then Barry turned off the pool light so the neighbors couldn't see the way we swam laps, first innocently crossing each other in the middle, then swirling by. But then Barry swam under as I passed over and grazed my torso with his hand, then again we passed and swirled about like dolphins. I kept my mouth open and caught his cock for a moment. We kept at it for a while, then cuddled under and surfaced midway somewhere, toes barely pointing on the floor of the pool to keep our heads up. He finally got his tongue down inside my mouth as a police helicopter's searchlight whisked through some nearby poplars before moving on in search of that night's O.J. Menendez.

It was sexy, not so much him as the taste of chlorine, the thieving thrill of sex in someone else's home. It reminded me of swim team boys, changing room glances, but elevated. *Blade Runner*. King Riots Margarine ™. It was one of those moments when you remember that you are in California, but with a tourist's sense of amazement.

In bed, a candle's shadow dancing across the strange ceiling, I decided to tell Barry about Jason Daw's project, how it wasn't going to be just another porno video. "I want to make it so good I would want to use my real name as director, like Bruce LaBruce."

At first he laughed, and so did I. I thought he might ask later, then he did. "Do they need a writer?" I knew it meant *Can I go with you?*

"No, doll," I said. "I believe Jon E. Quest is an auteur."

"Who?"

"My nom de porn. He's got *hauteur*."

"Oh, my god. You're already sold. You're going."

"Maybe not to their desert, but yes."

"Besides, if it ever got out, it'd just be more publicity. Naughty, but good."

"Nice."

"What?"

"Nothing." Then I said, "Naughty but nice."

"That's a lousy title."

"Make me a good one."

"*Desert Forms?*"

I groaned. "No."

"*Suck, Suck, Sweet Charlie?*"

"I am going to bed now."

"*Hard Wars?*"

"I am sound asleep."

"*The Miss Fits?*"

We settled in, let the crickets soften the night, the distance humming with the cattle of the highway, and the far echoing sirens all simmering.

"*All About Steve?*"

That's when I had to spank that butt.

Later, we finally slept. It was never fully dark in the room. It was neither his space nor mine. I never asked whose house it was. We could have dreamt it. I lay watching him sleep, hearing his breath, trying to block the stream of hopes that trailed outward from my insides, the thens, and what-ifs of him, my home, us together as old men, feeding a dog, adopting Guatemalan twins.

The candle sputtered. I got up and wet two fingers, strangling the flame.

Darkness can be a clean space. Lying in bed with few shadows to discern, it's easy to think of nothing, relax the mind to a blank. But like a raccoon or owl, the eyes focus on the murky gray, a blurry photo, grainy little bursts of light, the VCR, the digital clock, the phone machine, the lighted coal of another last cigarette. Darkness should be a place where the mind can also be empty, like being at sea. My mind can never dismiss the little lights, the little landmarks that refuse to go away.

That last night of the riots, after some really strange and horrible things happened, none of which I dared to capture on tape, I called Barry and ran to him when the fear spread all the way to Santa Monica. My neighbors had begun to guard their lawns with night lamps and guns. Barry's home felt safe.

I put aside those dark memories and crept out of whoever's bed it was. Barry pretended to be asleep while I fished in my jeans for the pack, padded barefoot and naked out on the deck. I stood outside this anonymous millionaire's home, flicking ashes on his anonymous millionaire deck, the coal of the cigarette lighting my skin, my chunky body, my arm hairs, my fingers.

Gramma smoked right to the end. I was gonna make a video about her, but she kept pushing it off, and then when she got sick, everybody said it would be morbid. Actually not everybody. Just Mom. And Dad. And Dan.

The question I would have asked first in the video I never made of Gramma, would be, "How did you get out of Poland?"

She would smile and say, "Like my car. Dodge. Dart."

At least I would show Gramma driving it. Now? Now maybe they all wish I had. I don't know. I don't know Gramma's story. Nobody does, anymore.

I've seen the documents, though. My father's sister keeps them. She's the archivist. I have to get to know her better.

I have the documents she has. She made copies. On it, a woman and a man have been naturalized as American citizens. On the paper, Smyrsomething and Gladys Gryczyniec have become Stanislav and Gladys Grozniak.

They became less Polish and more phonetic. Something in me thought making a film about our family would heal that, with lots of photos. Maybe that's why I haven't made it yet. I'm waiting for the day I can put my wedding picture in there too.

19. he **disappears** in **streaks** of **faith** and **mist**

Closing a shoot, the post-production depression, the loss of Ricky, that was the reason I wanted to do the TV movie and the porn flick. Something inane to back up all this "work." I wasn't gonna let grief get me so far down I even gave up surfing. That happened.

I needed an update and stuff with Jason, more the stuff than the update, for the enthusiasm to get rolling. I had an idea I was going to be able to do both these projects.

I was telling Jason I needed a leitmotif, but the term, like Sacto, eluded him.

"Lite-motif, um, how do I say it in English?"

"Oh, that's right, you are English too, sort of."

"Cut it, girline, you're gettin' close."

"Sorry. Anyway, it's an image. An image that can serve as the kind of thematic rudder. Rudder. That reminds me, I want to recreate a scene from *Another Country* for an opener of a love scene. Have you seen that?"

"You know, you're very sexy when you talk crazy."

"I'm tawking cwazy?"

"Are you sure you can deal with jumping from one production to another?"

"Nothing coffee can't handle."

"I can get other things if you need 'em."

"No thank you, Mister Daw, sir," I said, actually a bit worried about the implication of Jason's proximity to drugs. "Don't go for the pills. Yucky karma. Besides, you shouldn't do those drugs. Bad for your system. Renal failure."

"Scuse me?"

"Did you know that eighty percent of any drug is excreted?"

"So I should get into water sports to enjoy the full value of my drugs?"

"*Chaque'un a sons gout.* But no, actually, you should watch out for your kidneys."

"Mmm. Point taken, doctor. Should I say director? That is, do you think you can handle wrangling a herd of roided-out homos with big dicks and bigger inferiority complexes?"

"Please, after recreating the domestic hell of the happy family, it'll be a relief."

"Of sorts."

"Hmmm?"

"I take it you'd like to sample the talent?"

"Um, well. Yeah!"

Our laughter masked something else, my edginess, my fighting falling for this funny guy, this totem of sexuality, this video deity, this Fag de Siècle. Was I just following his sway, as so many others had for handsome men, for men facing death, for men with, literally, dicks of death?

Sure I was, and he was going to save me from the gorge of post-production depression. Maybe I could do another project after the porn shoot wrapped, maybe I'd just finally find one project after another. I could become a directorial James Dean, burn and burn, leaving a trial of unedited shots and rescribbled storyboards in my wake. Anything to avoid becoming a two-time has-been.

Been there. Shaved that.

20. that flying girl dragon rose bitter- ly up my night sky

I and my brother. I love the way that sounds. He and I implies so much less. I and my brother were not always friends. We were like two countries with aligning borders, holding a constant, yet at any moment revocable, truce.

Winters in Ohio had begun their late '70s assault but had backed off. Streets were encrusted with gritty snow and the remnants of too much salt.

It was my fifteenth winter, well after it all. Carrot, Dick, Lance, Sean, Godot, everybody.

Dan and I drove to the mall to see a movie, *Looking For Mr. Goodbar.* We heard it was about New York.

I guess it was why I only visited there and then moved to L.A.

Richard Gere's performance gave me a renewed love of jock straps. Dan kept nudging me, elbowing me, joking. "Do you think he's cute?"

Seeing the red-haired man who played one of Diane Keaton's many nut job lovers, Dan said, "He looks just like—"

"Shut up," I muttered. It wasn't particularly pleasant to see a sort of older Dorian Gray version of my Uncle Sean, neurotic, no doubt like he was that summer. My buffer brain turns him more hunky with each stroll back there. Can you blame me?

"Do you wanna go?" Dan said, sympathetic then.

"No, I wanna see the rest."

My intuitions had proven true, showing me not only a young Richard Gere cavorting in a jock strap and a glow in the dark knife, followed by a twisted yet gay Tom Berenger in drag. More than worth the admission for a mid-winter, mid-Ohio mall movie.

Yet afterward, I remember arguing with Dan about driving, and the depiction of crazy fags on film, to the point where I grabbed the steering wheel, and we nearly drove into a lamppost in the mall parking lot. I think he hated me a little forever after that day. Hated me or feared me.

I switched allegiances to the gang of theater kids I ran with. We came to be known as the Dead Cat Society. The name comes from a *Monty Python* episode. One of our crew, a girl I mistook for a lesbian, who is now a print artist happily married in Texas, was the only one of our crew to have the then-exotic VCR, in Betamax, no less. We often overindulged on sodas and pizzas with late night viewings of *Saturday Night Live* and *Monty Python* episodes. We memorized every sketch, from "the dead parrot" to the "point-ted stick," as if they were gospel.

Among them was the fellow whose talent on a telly show was flinging his cat Tiddles into a bucket. Somehow this joke got mixed in with the unfortunate flattening of our hostess's cat by a neighbor's car. We all had a burial for the poor creature that ended in stifled laughter, thus the birth of the Dead Cat Society. You can even see it in my listing in the Brookside *Prism*.

STAN GROZNIAK
Speech Team, Photo Club,
AV Club, Drama Club,
National Honor Society,
Adv. Art Placement, D.C.S.

If you really want to find my legacy to Brookside High School, though, you'll find it on the lower right hand corner of every page of every textbook I was handed for the years 1974-8. I made cartoons. Flip books, the old way. I got to stay for detention filing books in the library when they were discovered. I told them they'd be valuable someday. They laughed.

Among my other extracurricular activities was feigning heterosexuality with my childhood costar. Baby June was the only straight girl in the DCS. We fake dated through my junior and senior years.

The first time I actually spoke to Baby June was after a few days into rehearsals of *Gypsy*.

It was another air-conditioned afternoon. Lance and the older chorus boys hadn't been called in that day, and there wasn't anything technical to play with, since the set hadn't been built yet. Dick Thorson had given me a lot of space. We met in the halls and aisles of the theater like ex-lovers, which we were at the time, somewhat.

I sometimes hid out in the green room, a smaller octagonally-shaped area that sometimes served as a performance space for experimental works like Samuel Beckett one-acts and other great works of theatrical art doomed to small box office failure.

Through the run of *Gypsy*, it served as a mere playpen, a sort of night version of daycare for all the teens and tots that composed the crowded Uncle Jocko scene in Act I.

Unfortunately, all those kids had to hang around for the next two and a half hours to show up and take their bows at curtain. As strict as my rigors of theatrical protocol remain, I was quite willing to see that rule forsaken. The kids were pests. Dan and I escaped to the costume shop, hidden storage spaces, anywhere away from them.

But some nights I stuck it out in the nursery. I settled myself down on the floor to read the local paper, *The Brookside Gazette*. My perusing of Gerald Ford's latest stumble was interrupted by a pair of thin legs that split apart in front of my newspaper like a collapsing lawn chair.

"Bet you can't do that," a girl chirped. She was Baby June, our little star.

"No, I can't." I admitted. "Bet you can't tell a Leko from a Fresnel."

"What?" She continued to stretch herself over the shreds of my newspaper.

"Are you paper-trained too, or should I find you a box to pee in?"

She didn't talk to me for days after that.

This is how girls like Baby June flirted. They poked me. They threw things at me. They called me names. If I hadn't already known I was gay, I would have switched just to avoid the abuse.

I guess I was cute then. I guess I'm cute now, just thicker. All I thought was that I was skinny and fat at the same time. My hair was due to be cut short only for *Gypsy*, to give us that 1920s look. All I remember is wanting to look like Lance Holtzer or Dick Thorson. If they got haircuts, I got haircuts. When I came to dress rehearsal sporting my new brush cut, Lance was the first to rub my head for luck.

Jump forward to 1979, near the beginning of my senior year. Still twirling batons and doing splits, only on football fields, Baby June rose quickly to the ranks of popularity when she made the Brookside High Twirlerettes, quite an achievement for a sophomore. The only thing she needed to further her status was a manageable boyfriend.

After seven years of just "Hi" in the halls during the intervals in junior high when we occupied the same building, she asked me out. She was actually quite healthy-looking by then. Annual trips to her grandparents' home in Orlando had given her a burnished post-holiday glow. She always wore a small gold crucifix, only exposed on certain days when the girls in the school seemed to secretly agree that they would bend the dictums of the dress code and wear culottes, those neo-shorts dresses I always, deep down inside, thought were fabulous.

I remember making out with thinned, burnished Baby June, and pretending to be a heterosexual, played by Rock Pamplin, star of my latest

Playgirl heist, or Tom Selleck, or a picture of Tom Selleck over the Rock Pamplin.

I remember Baby June not minding when I didn't touch her too much. I remember her liking when I did, and when I cooled down graciously, knowing a better time awaited me at home. I recall scooping her tiny crucifix between my lips as I licked just the tops of her breasts. I never disrobed her. She never saw my erections that popped up during our post-date make-out sessions in the electronically reclining seat of my dad's Cordova with rich Corinthian leather.

Twenty dates and one year later, we were supposed to go to the prom.

Actually, I got as far as driving Dad's car to her house, hoping to get the picture-taking thing over with, but then I broke up crying and told her I couldn't take her to the prom because I was gay.

I guess she didn't believe me or understood but still needed a date, since she'd already bought the dress. I even got a tie to match, yellow like corn butter. Saffron, I don't know. It matched her hair.

We did the prom thing.

We kissed goodnight.

I never saw her again.

Move forward to her dying of cancer while I was in L.A., me afraid, and conveniently too broke to go home.

Hearing that she had died, I ended up going out, wanting to lose myself in booze or sex, anything. I ended up at the Tattered Page, a used book and magazine shop I'd visited back in my broke days. I'd bought a few vintage *Mandates* with the cash I had handy. This time I had a credit card. I piled up quite a sum, but the best, the finest, made all the others useless in comparison. I found *it.*

The first one.

Playgirl. March 1974. The cover shows a strangely wall-eyed man, mustache, head surrounded by brown fur, accessorized by an eyes-closed blonde woman with garish '70s hair and rings, and glitter fingernail polish only accentuating the man's disregard.

I waited to get home to really savor the imagery, the fascination I had with finding this treasure again. Someone once said, if you can't relive your childhood, buy it.

I plopped the magazine on my bed, then put on some appropriate music, one of my mixes: KC and the Sunshine Band, Peaches and Herb, Boston.

I lit a bowl, waited for the tingles to seep through my body, and then had a date with a magazine. It would be better than the most graphic video, more of a get-off than the biggest studly new gay mag model, because it was the seed, the essence of my affair with erotica and sexuality that can be captured.

The centerfold, Bill Douglas, "works as a lifeguard, which fulfills his need to work outdoors." The pages of photos: him sitting on a log, one foot in the river, naked, his skin muscled, lightly furry, ochre; him sitting up amid tree limbs, smiling, his hand out, smirking, Not yet, Don't take a picture now; him standing on a log, his torso and legs bronzed and coated in a dust of mossy hair, his mane slightly damp. He is like a bear or lion.

And the four-pager, the centerfold, surrounded by trees, his cock now at its largest, both in swelling and almost actual size on the page. The page fold creases right at the tip of his cock. I pressed it flat, worrying about finger marks. It was then that I saw the difference, the problem. He was physically beautiful, but more importantly, he was looking away, not interested in me.

I continued tugging myself toward the hard-earned rediscovery orgasm, all the while anticipating the obligatory after-solo sex cigarette. I was more looking forward to having done with this image than doing it. I kept clutching my cock, knowing what I'd discovered after all these years, how disinterest from a man had become my aphrodisiac.

After that night, I realized that somewhere in a cedar chest is a photo of me and Baby June, gussied up in classic '70s mode, smiling for other people.

I realized that while most other people have pictures from every moment of their lives together, I have a huge empty space where pictures of all my lovers should be. You know, like that Wall of Fame, or Shame, depending on your values.

It's a photo shop in WeHo. On the inside of a glass wall, hundreds of hunky shirtless guys pose at street fairs and Gay Prides. Selected by the photographer, they appear as supposed icons for our generation, our desires, when actually all they are is one shaved, pumped, primped, prissy muscle-bound body type, and other attempts to approach it.

Screw that. I am proud of the beauty of every guy I touched, and most of them are nothing like that. They shine from within, or, as Jorge once said, "Don't ever fuck nobody you wouldn't be proud to greet in daylight."

I made a gallon of coffee and began to make a list. I tried to remember every man I ever came over, under, on or in. And then, by dawn, nine her time, I called my mother and asked her to send some kind of subdued flower arrangement for Baby June's funeral.

21. may a puppy impregnate your goddess

December, 1995. After talking and lunching and schmoozing and flirting, I finally got to read the revisions of the damn TV movie script. The nausea-inducing working title was *A Family Matter*. That was shot down, happily, when I explained that a two-letter difference would not deter an angry mob of Urkel fans. I wanted to call it *Uncle Up My Bum*. Barry didn't think that was funny.

> KARL:
> "But wouldn't it be great to have someone to show you, I mean literally show you how to do these things?"
>
> JOE:
> "What kinda things?"
>
> KARL:
> "If you...if the kid knows he's gay, he oughtta have a mentor. I mean, nobody helps a man come out, really."

"Hey, Barry? What do you think of this?"

Barry looked up from his desk. "What page are you on?"

"Um, where the kid is saying, 'Nobody helps a guy come out.' How do you think GLAAD would read that?"

Barry sighed. "Don't worry about them. We'll buy a table at their cheesy awards show. That'll shut 'em up."

I grinned, happy again to have such a fuck buddy pal for a business partner. "Okay, but do you think it's true?"

Barry sighed again. I loved this guy, but he had a twenty-page production budget to do for the Robeson Fund in two days.

"I don't know. I think it's sort of true. I mean, there's no welcome wagon, one poet said. What about the Greeks and the Spartans?"

"That was a forced social code," I said. "That was economics. They had no choice. A young kid in Greece got fucked because an older man owned him." No response. "I'm talking, what if a guy was there to show him? I mean, what is wrong with a man showing a young kid how a dick ejaculates when the kid is biologically able to do it?"

"That's not right. It should be between boys."

"Sorry, I wasn't a Boy Scout. Never had the protocol down. I couldn't even tie knots if they weren't attached to a theater curtain."

Barry chuckled as he rolled over to me.

"Besides, who's to say what's not right?" I said. "Until I was in junior high school, I thought guys pissed into women to get them pregnant. When they hauled all the boys in our class over to the health room to watch those fuddy-duddy movies, I had no idea how it happened. And forget even asking about gay sex. You ask one question about that, and you're pegged forever. You think that's right?"

"You learn," he said.

"But I didn't. I didn't know it was okay to jack off with a buddy and go on and do other things, so I hung out with my little clique of theatre fags. I wanted desperately to play football, but I knew deep down inside I was different. There was sex going on between guys, but I was robbed of the camaraderie because I thought since I liked guys I couldn't be a part of that. Don't you see how easy it would be, if a football coach could just drop his jock strap and show guys what a man's hard-on looks like? To let them feel it, see him come?"

"You sound like a porno magazine."

"We all had to start somewhere, baby."

"Now, now." He shook his finger. There was no need to bring up Barry's amusing literary past. I won't, except to hint of a certain publication whose editors often bought *The Erotic Tales of Jack Steel.*

"But why do all those porno magazines put all those daddy stories in?" I persisted, despite Barry's look. "Because guys want that, and if we can get beyond that daddy/son stuff, men can grow into more mature relationships beyond role-playing."

"You're talking about a world that does not exist. Our entire culture is based on role-playing."

"Not now," I countered. "Not anymore. Not for me, at least."

Barry paused. "I had a friend in grade school who told me he took showers with his dad. No sex, just showers and stuff. Once in while. It was okay. He got a good look at his dad's dick and told me he realized, 'Wow, someday I'm gonna have hair and big balls and I'll be a man.' The mystery was wiped away for him. He was very well-adjusted to sex as a young guy."

Barry's words made it sound damn normal, not at all specious. Not a trace of Boy Scout priest coach scandal attached itself to his explanation. It was cleansed. Pure. Simple.

"So what happened to him?"

"He runs a gay plumbing service."

Barry ended up on top of me as we chuckled, us rolling on the very nice carpet, knocking over the very nice objects in his very nice home, until I had him in a very nice Nelson and got him to say Uncle, and that's how we got the title, which later got rejected by the Suits.

We both felt happy about that, heaving and blushing, us laying on the floor like Alan Bates and Oliver Reed. Thank you, Larry, for writing it, oh yes, and thanks for that little ACT UP thing. Thank you, Ken Russell, for directing, Thank you, Leonard Maltin for your succinct capsule review: "Fine adaptation ... really impressive, as is memorable nude wrestling scene." Thank you HBO, all ten times you broadcast it. That was before we had video in Brookside, other than the black and white reel-to-reel contraptions I mastered in junior high school as an AV geek.

We got up and separated, pulled our shirts completely off, since he'd half-ripped mine, a look I liked, but it seemed we had to cool down in the shower, then on the lawn. I felt a primal serenity. I'd faced off aesthetically against my mate without losing his love. I wanted to fuck later that night, long and slow.

Then Barry said, out of nowhere, "So, what are you doing for Christmas?"

22. will love **spray discover**ness here?

College was chunky guys and skinny guys and furry guys and smooth guys.

College was that Dr. Seuss book, *Dogs and More Dogs*, only with guys.

College was wild stuff. Parties until dawn with Talking Heads and the B52s shaking the walls, movies for late hangers-on, delicate worship of an intimate nature for whoever was handsome enough to be invited to stay. The advantage of being an AV geek is that you get access to all the toys.

Dan and I occasionally lived together in Columbus. A few of our apartments were 'rat-trap-no-heat-behind-a-nightclub' hellholes, but oh, the films we made. Gloriously stupid.

I got one dance major I fucked for most of 1984 to choreograph this big dance piece, and we snuck onto the football field at night with the lights on, and Dan and I each ran around with video cameras. We dubbed it later to Philip Glass's *Koyaniskaatsi*.

We also helped out other majors with more narrative sense, or sets. One guy let me make his sets. I was getting college credit for things I already learned from Dick Thorson. That degree would have been a breeze.

And the sex. Oh, the sex. I swear, Ohio grows homosexuals like cornfields. Just grows 'em. I think those times when Dan wasn't finding the right girl and I was just rutting like a buck, Dan got jealous. I think that's why I moved out. I think that's why I dropped out, too. Just went to L.A. Yeah, right. That's what happened.

Then Dan graduated and after a brief foray to Chicago, wound up in San Francisco designing animated games for a Silicon Valley computer company.

Ever since he graduated from college, Dan and I had been trading off taking trips home for Christmas. The house had shrunk to a size too small for both our egos.

To accommodate the size, and my parents' own emotional time warp, we usually retrofitted ourselves to twelve-year-olds, especially after the usual holiday imbibing. We began fighting and bickering about old grievances with the ease of putting on old leather boxing gloves, and we often traded off taking early exits to the airport.

By the early '90s, I'd skipped turns for the last two years. Phone conversations with Dan turned sweet, almost flirtatious. His new job as the head idea guy at the animation company was booming, and I was alternating between temp prop jobs, a music video, and vast cesspools of unemployment. Dan offered to pay for my plane flight. I politely declined while considering how I could have turned the ticket into a cash refund.

But even better, that year, 1991, I had Ricky, my Manipulator. His last few friends that weren't dead or off on shoots had decided to throw a Christmas party at his house, since he wasn't very mobile in those days. I felt more embarrassed that I hadn't seen him in over two months. Funny how I seemed to find time for him when I was working. Not having a job took up all my time.

Ricky's AIDS gave me the out, and for that I was thankful in a twisted way. It might not have been his last Christmas, but with the gathering that was prepared, it seemed everybody thought it would be.

"But this is *your* family," Dan said on the phone, giving me the fuse to go ballistic. I told him about my other family, my chosen family.

He got it, but dismissed it. So in his honor, I dumped the biological family and spent Christmas at Ricky's. Yes, his last one. Everyone brought ornaments. I brought two Ken dolls in white gowns and wings. I impaled one on the top branch and suspended the other from the ceiling with some fishing line.

"Looks like one's going to heaven," someone said.

There was one of those party pauses where nobody knows what to say. I blushed, felt awful. I'd done my job too well. I was too accurate.

"Given the alternatives, Heaven sounds good to me," Ricky blurted.

Everybody laughed, and the noise dissolved into joking comments. Ricky smiled at me, forgiving, and I hugged his bony frame, holding back tears.

How was I to explain this to Dan, who was busy trying to breed, whose closest death was our grandmother? He didn't even attend her funeral. Who was he, this guy who used to be my best friend, who now lived in the city where I should be living, in a house with Ricky on a street that's a staircase, like he wanted?

With these past holidays clotting up my head, I decided once again to stay in LA. I've done it ever since.

Christmas with Barry years later was wonderful. He called two other Jewish friends, and three of their friends, orphaned for the holidays.

We ate Chinese food, rented movies, and played a camp version of the "Hi, Bob" game but with *Valley of the Dolls*. Every time somebody drank, we drank or puffed. Barry even had candy pills for us to take.

Back at his house, we all played non-Christian music but drank spiked eggnog. I hit on a game.

"Loneliest holiday." I pointed.

Karla Gold, Barry's third cousin through a gay marriage, and an excellent production manager, said, "Hanukkah. My junior year. I came out on the phone a week before, and my parents wouldn't let me come home because they were having guests."

Mutual oohs and ughs. It was somebody else's turn.

"My twenty-first birthday." As Mitchell told his story, I saw him that young, the same hopeful look in his eyes. "I went to a bar, then another bar, then a sex club, and nobody would touch me."

"You? That's crazy."

Mitchell returned my gaze in a way that warmed me. I swear everybody in the room saw us suddenly become totally attracted to each other. Then Mitchell asked me, and I immediately went into subterfuge/court jester mode.

"The Christmas I accidentally burned all the holiday checks with the wrapping paper!"

"You burned wrapping paper?"

"Sure, the fireplace was handy."

I began to wonder how different my family really was from others.

I turned away. "Barry, you got one?"

He returned from the kitchen with more popcorn and sat. "Well, this doesn't qualify, but I'm telling it anyway. It's my house and if you're bored, you can leave."

Laughter, flying popcorn. Barry waited, cushioned himself in, like he was telling a bedtime tale. "I was at the commissary. It must have been just a few days before Christmas, um, five years ago? I was still working on something for Universal."

"Those *Married With Children* episodes?" Karla asked.

"Probably." He shivered. "Anyway, I'm sitting there having lunch, when I see this middle-aged guy who looks like some kid I knew, or some surfer I picked up, sitting having lunch with some old guy I also thought I knew, you know, an actor. And they're just chatting away like old friends, and nobody is looking at them, because some other famous person, I dunno, Danny Glover or somebody is over at a more visible table."

"Who was it?" Karla asked.

"I don't know." Barry waved it off.

"No, the old guy and the other guy." Karla tried to explain.

"You're not gonna believe this," he said.

"Come on." Mitchell urged him.

"Bill Mumy."

"Who?" Faces beamed recognition or confusion.

"The kid on *Lost in Space.* "

"Oh, my god."

"But wait, wait. Wait." Barry shouted, trying to reign in the nostalgia attack. "The old guy was Doctor Smith."

"Jonathan Frid?"

"No, silly. Jonathan Frid was in *Dark Shadows.*"

"From the show?"

"Doctor Smith and Will Robinson were having lunch!!"

"Well, they finally landed back on earth."

"Did you go up to them and say anything?" Mitchell asked.

"It was too much," Barry sighed. "I couldn't. It was just so touching. I don't even remember eating. I just sat there stealing glances at them. I missed some meeting because I just wanted to watch them, see these guys getting together. I thought maybe this is something they do every Christmas. I don't know. It was so ... touching, how people who worked on something so long ago could stay friends. That is what I guess you guys are talking about, Christmas spirit."

Everybody just sat back, not making crass comments or jokes, since Barry's eyes were getting bleary. And then I thought about Ricky, bony and weak, and some odd little creak emitted from the back of my throat as I stifled a sob.

"There was always a monster behind the rocks."

"What?" I wiped away tears. Barry handed me a napkin.

"*Lost in Space,*" Mitchell said. "You'd think they would have figured it out. Just stay away from the rocks."

"Those totally fake wonderful rocks," Karla added.

One by one, we recounted our favorite episodes; when Penny gets turned to gold, the two-part episode with the world behind the mirrors, when the beautiful green space lady floats out the window singing, "Doctor Smiiiith." It made me hungry for the show, the innocence, the simplicity of having a monster get zapped away before the show's end.

I thought about the two former actors just getting together every year, the sweetness of it, and wondered if I'd ever be able to do that, have work that made people friends, made them remember, kept them connected.

I knew when Barry wasn't talking, he was looking at me, silently saying, *Will you do that for me? Will you be there for lunch when we're old?*

But I wasn't looking back at him. I couldn't promise that some monster wasn't going to zap me, or Don Robinson would show up in the nick of time in his Mylar space suit. I couldn't. There were just too many rocks.

23. so **who** will **find** how to love

Gypsy closed, after three sold-out weeks that Bicentennial summer, extended one week due to popular demand. The college president even came back from 'summering' at Kennebunk to see it. Yes, *that* Kennebunk. Brookside's got roots to Washington, deep, dark, dank roots by way of those fraternal organizations. You know the ones. Funny hats, secret handshakes, skulls and bones. All the town leaders are a part of the vast rightwing conspiracy. My barber was. Reagan came to our town. Creepy. The high school principal, all real estate developers. *Invasion of the Body Snatchers*, the original.

The TV spewed crisp video images of giddy Americans celebrating a birthday. Our country was two hundred years old, but practically a teen-ager by European standards, and acting just like one, bursting with pride, gushing with self-importance, screaming, hooting, and yelling in celebration of itself.

President Ford, looking like a somber, grown-up Charlie Brown, cut ribbons, clanged bells, and made proclamations. The TV ran on all day and nobody watched. The living room was empty, the nearby side porch door wide open. Look, look, New York Harbor is alive and kicking. Ships spew celebratory fountains of water, flags wave, the Statue of Liberty is awash in floodlights, a perfect bride of Godzilla.

Dad stood tending the coals in the barbecue, a round fire-engine-red metal thing that resembled an alien cartoon craft. I thought for a brief moment about roasting marshmallows. But that delicacy had grown stale, the too-sweet treat ensuring a headachy sugar rush. Kid pleasures were gone. Kid pleasures were stupid.

Mom was hidden in her bedroom, suddenly needing to change again after Dan's comment about her blouse being too loud.

"Where are all your friends?" my brother teased, passing by as I absently gazed at the drawn-out TV coverage of the New York Harbor Tall Ships gala. La di da, ships and boats waving their sails.

"Fuck you," I muttered to Dan as he escaped to the outside through the porch screen door. He knew damn well I hadn't invited any friends because I didn't *have* any friends. Sure, at one time I had a few, but they were for school. Nobody visited at our house anymore for silent movies. That was dumb. That was for kids.

When I was twelve, inviting a guy to sleepover was as simple as asking. No tension, no horrible icky pain, wondering if my room is cool enough, wondering where he'll sleep, even thinking about where he might sleep, whoever he might be.

The "he's" used to be Brian Simms and Gary Wheatcraft and Billy Thompson, but something happened between junior high and high school, some larval transition that made a boy into a young man. Sure, it happened to me. Biologically, I mean, but some code in the shell casing didn't get crossed in the process. Brian suddenly became a football jock, running around the high school practice grounds in a jersey and shoulder pads. Gary disappeared to a summer home in Florida with his aunt. And Billy? Well, he was a bigger fag than me, and no way was I gonna share a bedroom with him. I knew what I was turning into and he was closer to it.

So, I was left to wait for the adults, the big people, like Lance, to show up. I'd grown up with them, at all the college functions and parties, the summer theater where my mom sewed costumes, my dad hung out with the other profs and the guys tossed me about and made jokes, sometimes patronizing, other times understanding, most times just amazing.

The guys. It took me a long time to realize they were only students a few years older, but they had big bodies and beards and mustaches and hairy legs and muscles. They drank beer and smoked cigarettes.

But not Lance Holtzer. Not Tulsa.

The year of the bicentennial, the year of our lawn party, with burgers on the grill and Grand Funk's "Locomotion" on the radio, Lance was in the garage bumping with me. Lance and me.

He was Tulsa. I was Tulsa.

Every night, behind that little cutout newsstand, Lance helped me rush from my newsboy costume into my sailor's uniform, and every night he patted my ass, and the least I could do was help him, too.

You're gonna tell me somebody recruited me? You're gonna tell me somebody abused me? That Lance dancing wasn't me dancing ten years later? You're gonna tell me I didn't know what I wanted, even when I fol- lowed him to the dressing room, when he knew he couldn't shake me. You're gonna tell me that closing night, before that mad change from the farm boy section to the Broadway finale, as I waited to hand him his cane, him shucking off those overalls and pulling on those black pants, that he didn't forget to wear undershorts for anyone but me? Maybe that's all I needed then, to see a young man, who showed me the future was warm and full of love and sex and good stuff? Besides, he had great legs.

I spent days cleaning and pruning our expansive lawn in preparation for my family's barbecue. Our mysterious backyard, with its droopy Weeping Willow and dozens of other smaller trees, became as sculpted and precious as a Japanese tea garden. The wide side yard became an open playing field for volleyball. I'd mowed it myself, even under the dreaded pear tree, where the rotting fruit, fallen and razed neatly in half, attracted bees. I picked up the pear remnants and tossed them into the mulch pile by the farthest, darkest corner of the back yard.

The side yard also had a small crabapple tree, our neighborhood gang had used as a hideout for afternoon game of Jonny Quest when we were small. No grass grew under its squat limbs. The dead earth was cool under the stubby troll of a tree, a lost character from an edited forest scene in *The Wizard of Oz*.

Our own lawn never approached such perfection, for we had wider, open, more amusing lives, and the state of things were like them: overgrown and lopsided in design, but amusing and colorful.

I set up our volleyball net on the side lawn, got out a ball, and looked around. All was in readiness. The birdbath was clean, the cuttings piled away in the mulch dump, and the porch open and inviting. Our barbecue lay open, two bags of coals hunched beside it. I saw my mother's face in the kitchen, rinsing her hands over the sink by the window. I felt as if it were all my home, and they my personal guests. I was a duke and his groundskeeper in one chubby little body.

Arthur and his wife, Lance, Dick, Jo Ellen and her boyfriend, and dozens or so other cast members and their families showed up, walking and enjoying the freshly cut lawn I'd trimmed and cropped for their pleasure. But it was all really for Lance. I wanted him to be so captivated that he'd visit, and become compelled by its beauty. And mine.

It was soon trampled by his lust, or posed lust, as I later learned, for a student actress with a nasal giggle that could break glass.

Sure, I danced with Lance in the garage. But later, he strolled under the willow limbs that I'd trimmed just so, his arm around some girl. Well, she could have him. I had plenty of time.

Ducking into my parents' bedroom, I peeked out at the cluster of people on the lawn. The patch of porch light yawned out onto the dark grass. A gnat flew by my ear, sneaking past to get in the house.

The screen door to the balcony closed, I flicked the television on. The blue glow filled the room, endless news reports of the day's activities in New York harbor. I thought of the ships and felt a rush of desire as cameras caught shots of French, Belgian, Brazilian sailors.

Twenty years later, I would listen to an older gay friend's theory that AIDS began in New York on July Fourth 1976, with thousands of worldly sailors fucking thousands of willing homosexual men. Patient Zero was not one airline steward, but the international naval forces, he would say.

I don't know about that, but even then I felt it. Something loomed. The pictures of hand-holding leather men and drag queens on TV and in magazines was somehow going to be interrupted. I longed to dive into that picture world as easily as Mary Poppins and Bert hopped into that sidewalk chalk landscape. I wanted it quick, before the rains came.

Seeing the deluge of sailors, I felt a pang of dread, of knowing something was happening. Don't call it premonition or foresight, or anything, just call it gut burn. I knew something was wrong, and that the future of a little faggy boy was not going to be right with the world.

Before the last of our party guests had departed, I stole one of my mother's cigarettes and a lighter, then secretly strolled into the little jungle of our back yard, my mother's plants weaving a tiny enclave under the willow. I walked silently over the freshly mown lawn that I had nipped that day, my bare feet wet in the spot where I saw Lance kiss a girl. He was supposed to kiss me. It wouldn't have hurt anyone. It would be like kissing himself, the way kids practice French kissing on their arms. Harmless. Sweet.

It was a summer of locusts. I could hear them singing in the trees. Let's choose to remember them here. Let us call it Sound Cue #126, before the fade to black. A few of the drunken party guests sat on the porch. I lit my mother's stolen cigarette and sucked it into my young, still clean lungs.

Cue the audio of locusts chirping. Pan back to see a wisp of smoke rise above a chunky boy, pacing under a tree where he had hoped and planned his first kiss. Hold the shot as he places himself where they had been, as he looks up and caresses his own neck under the summer moonlight.

ACT III

24. show the vampire my drawings

In August, 1976, on a full moon weekend, Uncle Sean O'Leary, my mother's brother, arrived only days after *Gypsy* closed.

As fast as I began planning ways to see him naked, other questions lingered. Why hadn't he shown up to see Dan and my last theatrical efforts for the summer? Why hadn't he wanted to be there then, to meet my parents' friends? Was he the one who went to prison? Was he so aware of his pariah status that he waited until our busy summer didn't interfere with his plans? How did he know there would be such a lonely place between my being an all-singing, all-dancing star and just another dweeb come the first day of school? How did he catch me when others failed?

Mom put him up on the sofa in the basement, the place I'd already imagined having sex with him and other men. How convenient.

Uncle Sean kept me rapt with his and Mom's stories of Pittsburgh slum youth, being delinquents, and getting beaten by their father, the grandfather who died before I was born, the grandfather who was only home long enough to pose for one picture. They brought out photo albums.

A few nervous days later, the scent of his Old Spice brought my showers a new flavor and gave me the inspiration to jerk off a lot quicker.

The days were full of talk, mostly, listening to my mother and her brother. Although many of their conversations were more mature and sophisticated, and a lot of words and ideas passed over me like birds, I remember the conversation getting around to sex. Maybe they were discussing Kinsey, I don't know. Just that he said that worn phrase about "everyone being basically bisexual," he glanced at me, half-grinning.

Uncle Sean soon became interested in his sister's son's activities. He wanted to get a tour of our room, the masks, the toys, the books. I showed him my voluminous collection of *Scream* magazines. He sat on my bed, leafing through one after another while I rattled on about this film or another, how I'd seen that one a lot, how the Hammer Films were much more grotesque than the classic version of Dracula. He put aside the copy of *Scream* he'd been pretending to read, leaned over the pile of magazines and said, "You know Stan, the last time I was here, you were a lot younger then, but you gave me the sweetest goodnight kiss."

I sprouted the fastest erection ever, uncomfortably hard before his lips even met mine. He'd still not shaved that day, or perhaps his beard just forced itself out quickly. Tiny bristles surrounding his wet lips, then back to his chin, by then a wet pinecone, as I was almost drooling.

The pile of magazines spilled over my bed, which bent so low from the weight of him. Him, on my bed, providing my second real male kiss.

I remember standing, watching him kneel down to pick up the strewn magazines, then glance at my crotch, the obvious tenting. I felt powerful, despite quivering, standing above him, his wonder, his anticipation. It was going to happen. This is why he came here. He wants me. A man wants me.

Uncle Sean said he wanted to see the movies Dan and I made, but I said Dan would want to be there too, since he liked to watch them.

Uncle Sean said to pick a movie anyway.

I thought I'd drag it out, so I picked a four-reeler.

Metropolis.

He waited a long time, possibly the second reel, before making his move. But even before that, I felt the heat of his intention. I smelled the scent of him, that sailor's cologne emanating from him.

We sat in chairs, the projector back behind us on the old AV stand my father retrieved from the college when they got new screens. On the sheet on the basement wall, Maria the saint was gesticulating in her German way, looking heavenward in that dark, candlelit cavern where she preached to the downtrodden workers. For a soundtrack, I had put on some Kraftwerk.

The only thing I remember wondering, where was my father? It was summer. He wasn't teaching then. Dan? Not with his girlfriend of the summer. Her impending move to college helped them break up a bit sooner than expected. Mom? Shopping? Picking up dry cleaning? Something that utterly banal? It was as if they all sensed the inevitable, and they cleared the space the way forest animals duck for cover moments before a hurricane.

I had to appreciate Uncle Sean's sense of timing. At the moment of Hel's unveiling, when Doctor Rotwang displays his robotic beauty, his hand found my thigh.

He took so incredibly long to get my cock out, almost an entire reel, in fact. I sat still, my gaze locked on the screen. Black and white Germans rushed in and out of closing doors. The rich young industrialist's son met his father in the enormous office atop the great city. Fluttering flying machines whirred over the spirals of the futurist city like fat dragonflies.

He finally got it out, caressing it like a delicate glass sculpture. He leaned down and surrounded me in his wetness. His beard grazed my soft belly. My hips rode up as I clenched my buttocks, burrowing up into him. This was it. This was what Lance and Dick could not, would not do for me. This is why he came. He came for me, and I was about to come on him.

"You got a big cock for a little guy."

"Thanks."

The reel ended, flooding us in white light. I stood. But as I replaced the next reel, not bothering to rewind the previous one, Sean followed me, his hands on my pants while I fingered the projector's delicate insides. I remember not letting him continue until the movie started again. I forget what coincided with his ministrations. I remember we stood, facing the screen, standing, him reaching around from behind me. His scent surrounded me, him holding me, tugging it slowly, sensing the closeness, holding off the way I'd already learned to do on special days in the woods.

"Are you okay?"

"Yeah."

Sean led me to the sofa and laid me down. I wanted to watch the movie, but gave up. His head loomed over my crotch, his red crewcut was silver in the light, bobbing up and down, then burrowing between my legs as he pulled my jeans lower.

He stood and dropped his pants. I sat forward, not looking up to see the back of his head silhouetted by the projector light. I had him in my mouth. He wasn't completely hard. I wondered why he was doing this if he hadn't been excited by me. My only worry was, doesn't he like me?

Then, I didn't care. I wanted a man, if not completely him, but this man was here. I touched his lanky muscled arms, licked in places that made him wince, ticklish, rubbed my face over his short hair, and licked his stubbled chin like a dog. I refused to be a toy and made him mine instead. Until his smell became mine.

I stopped again and looped the last reel, determined to push the entire film through, as if setting a limit on our time together.

"You oughtta learn how to fuck a guy," he whispered.

"Oh, um. Wait." I crept upstairs, worrying about my mother, anyone arriving home, I didn't bother to go upstairs to the bathroom to find some lotion. My cock would not go down.

Instead, I went to the kitchen cabinet and grabbed a bottle of corn oil.

He was sitting on the sofa, waiting, his pants hiked back up. I set the bottle down after pouring a dab onto my hand. He chuckled.

"All natural," I said. He leaned forward, put his mouth around my cock. I stood, knees quivering, rubbing his head slowly, touching his ears as I watched his cheeks bulge out. That's me inside him. I'm inside his body. He pulled away when I got close. I gasped slightly, his spit growing cool against the basement air. We both watched my cock throb, bouncing once.

He shucked his pants down again and lay on the sofa. "Wait. Give me some of that." I handed him the bottle. He stuck his finger in the opening, turned the bottle almost upside down, and extracted his finger, then fiddled around between his scrawny buttocks as if he were wiping away shit. I thought how much more I would have wanted someone else, a guy more built, with better legs and a worthy butt. But they didn't happen.

In a manner Sean may have thought too practiced, I pulled my shorts off, but kept my sneakers on. The cement floor was too cold for bare feet. I'd tried that.

I straddled him, parking my shiny cock at the bony spot above his ass where his tailbone protruded.

"Be careful," he said.

I nudged. He backed up, then stopped, putting a hand back to stop me. But I didn't. I burrowed in, feeling a mix of heat and flesh and shit, or guts. It wasn't what I'd expected. It wasn't comfortable at first, but once I figured an angle to slide into him slowly, I felt it, clutching his shoulders and thrusting.

He kept having to rearrange himself, and my knees ached, but I shoved in and retracted, breathing through my mouth to avoid the combined smells of basement mold and heating oil.

"Stop, stop." He pulled himself away, but I was too close. It was one of those orgasms that doesn't feel tingly and warm and wonderful, but simply liquid release, my body merely a channel for a flood.

It went everywhere, on him, on the sofa. I wanted to aim upward to hit the screen, splatter one of those anguished Germans, but my knees buckled again, and I fell back on the sofa while he collected himself.

Then he did something I didn't want. He stood and placed his half hard cock in front of me. I didn't look up at it. I muttered something. I think I'd like to remember him being considerate for finishing himself off. I wanted to finish watching the movie, which we did, after washing up over at the other end of the basement at the sink beside the washing machine. We sat back down at the two chairs, and I caught him up on the plot as if nothing happened and said, "This is my favorite scene."

Hel emerged from a sort of beaded giant clam, and tuxedoed men gawked and leered. Eyes watched in exaggerated glances of lasciviousness, while the actress Bridgette Helm performed her strange, reckless dance.

Years later, leafing through an old copy of *Christopher Street* I would buy for the image of Hel, Quentin Crisp describes in his review, "The Most Erotic Movie Ever Made," this era of film, when "stars had the power to wound the imagination beyond repair." He describes Miss Helm, in her decadent dance, as resembling "a large spider that had been dipped in melted sugar."

The underground city had flooded, the children had been saved, and Hel, disguised as Maria, stood roped atop a bonfire, madly laughing, knowing they were just burning an image of her. It was over in the movie, over to the mob, but as in all horror movies, the monster never really died.

"Watch this," I said, as the false Maria melted, burned, and turned back into the metallic robot. She was beautiful and tragic. The gesticulating workers bugged their eyes. Sean and I laughed. We really laughed.

I said, "Ya got a cigarette?"

I must have shifted my hips sideways like kids do, not realizing they suddenly resemble classic Caravaggios or old film actors. Here, in this darkness with Hel watching, I found a man who could not take his eyes and hands off my body. I looked over at my mother's abandoned sewing machine and wondered if this is how clothes feel when they're finally sewn together.

25. watch delicate energy return smelling ly

Taking a ride with my parents the next day, I wondered if they knew, and if they might calmly, coldly shoot us by the side of the highway, leaving our soiled corpses behind some abandoned one-room school. I wasn't feeling talky, but I secretly crept my hand across the back seat just to touch him. Uncle Sean's fingers caught mine, brushing them like damp cigars. Did my parents mean to speak to us, to get us alone? Dump him or me in an alley? I wondered what was going on.

Nothing, it seemed.

Later, washing dishes after dinner, he kept looking back over a chair in the living room. From the chair he could tilt his head and watch me scrub over the sink. He made my every move feel sexy.

"Did he make a pass at you?"

The question came out as simply as if she were asking if I mowed the lawn. I was on my way upstairs, the day after, or was it that very day? Whenever it was, it wasn't long afterward. I must have been obviously changed, thrilled with the secret of it, zinging around the house, avoiding any look, any talk, waiting for another chance to offer it again.

"What?"

"Did he touch you? Make a pass at you?"

Pass? He made a goddamn touchdown. We won the Super Bowl. "No."

"Are you sure? Your brother told me he tried it with—"

"Yeah, I'm so sure!"

I raced up to my room, lay on my bed, and, if I remember correctly, stayed there for three days. Sometime during my retreat, Uncle Sean left us.

It wasn't what he did. It wasn't what I did. It was that we didn't get away with it.

It was the crush, the horror of knowing he wanted Dan, too. He was just there to toy with us, to try to ruin us, to damage us. Try it on Dan? Didn't he know that Dan liked girls? Wasn't that obvious?

That is what I prefer to think made me so upset that, with my hair greasy and my stomach growling from hunger pangs, I refused to get out of bed, except to use the bathroom. Mom and Dad came to me, Dan was surly, avoiding the room at all costs, only slipping in silently to go to bed. Why didn't he say anything, because he obviously knew I had taken Sean up on the offer? I was the guilty one.

I didn't have a girlfriend to fuck. I didn't have the advantage of heterosexual privilege. I didn't have a choice in casting.

"How come a girl's cunt stinks?"

The boys in my freshman high school class were taken in a herd across town to the basement of the town's only Catholic school. We were shown a scratchy and worn film about sex, featuring a corny medical narrator. It didn't show any sex, just boys and girls holding hands and a biologically accurate yet completely laughable animated side view of a man's penis getting hard. It got me hard. Guys laughed. To this day I thank the diocese.

Afterward, we were allowed to ask questions. I held mine, since any question I wanted to ask involved a different cast. How come I wanna kiss boys? How do you butt-fuck and not make it hurt? Why did his come not taste as good as mine? Why the hell didn't you show me this film earlier?

One boy had no problem asking questions. Curt Bronmeyer was known for his tasteless humor.

"How come a girl's cunt stinks?"

The room broke into roars of laughter. Even my doctor had problems keeping a straight face. After the laughter subsided, he explained about bodily odors, but it didn't quell the giggling and guffaws. Somebody asked about getting girls pregnant, and if you could get them pregnant again while they were already pregnant.

I sat nervous, waiting for someone like Curt to ask something horrifying. *How come some guys are fags?* Funny, nobody brought up the topic.

I didn't do any theatre at school that year. I didn't make films. Dan and I were strangers. There were long silences when he was home. Weekends, he wasn't home. He'd found another girlfriend, Rita Clinger. She lived in Red Haw, far enough away that he had an excuse to return home later and later. They dated for more than a year.

Mom started making dinner later, or not at all. She started "not feeling well." She stopped shopping, or would come home with twice as many groceries as usual. Fourteen packages of Yoplait in every flavor. Three kinds of cereal. Canned goods, potatoes, and, for the first time, frozen dinners. It was as if she was preparing us, stocking up for the collapse to come. Dinner wasn't served at the table. We ate in separate chairs in the living room, at different times.

Dan stayed home one evening and even ate dinner with us. After our parents went to bed, and I showed no interest in the remote, he got to asking why everything was so fucked up.

"It's because you all hate me. You hate me!" I seethed.

Dan waited but didn't respond at first. Then he said, "Come here. I wanna show you something."

We walked downstairs. I heard him stop halfway down, waiting for me to follow.

He kept going past the living room into the kitchen and down the basement stairs. *Ah, I see. He wants to rub my face in it, so to speak.*

But he led me past the scene of my crime on to the washer and dryer and the sink. After fishing around, Dan found a small Tupperware container, the kind for soup or juice. A red fluid sloshed about inside. He opened it, held it before me.

I smelled the sour odor of wine. Wine in Tupperware. "What is this?"

"You dolt. She's drinking again."

"Oh, shit."

"Why do you think she had that 'accident?' Why do you think she's acting so weird? Why do you think we're so embarrassed when she's running off at the mouth? Why do you think I've been staying away every fucking minute I can?"

I looked around the room for an answer behind the piles of laundry and boxes of Cheer. "I thought it was me."

Dan hissed and shook his head. He was about to toss it in the sink. "Don't!" I said. "She'll find out."

Dan held it, took a sip, as if he thought it would be a great gesture to drink it, if only he didn't hate the stuff.

"That's the point," he said as he poured it down the drain. I leaned in to the sink. The red wine bled on a discarded fabric softener sheet. I turned on the water to wash away the evidence and wring out the Downy, which had become a wet clump, like a piece of gut. I dropped it in the trash.

"She'll think she already drank it," I half-laughed. Dan appreciated the joke, but didn't laugh.

"I wish she would just..."

"What?"

"I don't know."

We left the basement. I said I had to go somewhere.

"I gotta get a car," Dan said.

I imagined us going off to Hollywood. Dan & Stan Grozniak. Big names on a big screen. Everybody would know how to spell it by then. Dan & Stan Grozniak present...

Present what?

When Dan passed me in the halls through our last year together in high school, we merely raised our eyebrows in a silent acknowledgment, prisoners doing time, counting days.

Dan started driving to school, having borrowed money from Dad to buy a used Camaro. He'd successfully argued he needed the car for a job he was getting at a Stuckey's off I-71. It was where he'd met Rita Klinger. I was glad to help him. It meant I had the bedroom all to myself a lot more often. "Hell, move in with her," I muttered, out of range of Dad.

Dan got a four to midnight shift. Dad had argued about his homework, but Dan said he had study hall and weekends for that. "Besides, all the senior courses are Mickey Mouse. Our movies are getting me into Ohio State, Dad, not my grades."

That shut him up for a while. He must have been insulted that neither of us even considered going to Brookside College. As a faculty member, Dad could have gotten us free tuition, but that was useless without a film department. The real, unspoken point was that neither of us thought to stay home. Not anymore.

When he realized our filmmaking wasn't just a hobby, he just stopped complimenting us. He seemed let down we didn't pick something practical, like business or economics as a major.

That winter, Dan and I drove to school every morning in his half-paid-for muffler-glugging Camaro. It needed a paint job, but it felt great to arrive at school and have a space in the parking lot. It gave me fewer obligations to have to speak to anyone else.

When we locked our doors and headed in every morning, parting ways inside the school to our separate lockers, I always felt a small rip inside myself. Dan and I must have looked cool to others. Kids without close brothers must have thought we had some deep, admirable connection. They'd seen our movies. We were, I'm told, popular.

But we knew, or I knew, it was a pose. We were so hurt inside. Our sense of family had been ruined by another member of our family.

I began to be an "unmotivated student," sullen in class, not raising my hand. I got bigger. I spent weekends going out driving around with one guy at a time from high school. Drinking, hinting, smoking pot, hinting. Strike zone.

My father eventually got my mother back into Alcoholics Anonymous meetings and therapy. We had to drive into Akron Thursday nights for Mom, with a family session afterward. While she had her session, Dad took Dan and I to dinner: Arthur Treacher's, Arby's, or the new fast food place called Wendy's. I hated how the meat hung out of the sides of the buns, the way the too-thick shakes froze my throat, the way Dan dipped his French fries into little paper cups full of catsup, then mayonnaise, pulling the French fry up, showing its swirl of white and red goo. I hate that sneaking fast food makes me feel good, that the smell of grease is comforting, as is the resultant gut.

Dan resented missing a night of work for what he thought was a waste of time, and he seemed determined to make the nights as annoying as possible. While we waited for Mom's hour to be up, the three of us ate, saying next to nothing, gazing off to the salad bar for an answer.

We would return to the box-like office, the "Professional Building." Dan and I mocked the logo on the cream brick wall exterior, repeating the name like snooty academics.

In the shrink's office, Mom usually looked like he'd been beating her around, her eyes all red, a small pile of tissues clustered beside her. The shrink asked everybody questions about how we felt. Dad said things, sometimes choking up, but holding back. He'd still kept his tie on from a day of teaching.

Dan grunted a few things, usually: "She just needs to stop drinking," or "It's not anybody's fault." The shrink would nod his head, then turn to me, but I wasn't willing to talk about things with Dan present. I could re-script it with Dan or my parents, but not with them all in the same room. They each required different vocabularies.

I hated my own private Saturday sessions. Dad drove me, then graded papers in the car while he waited. Mostly I just mumbled words and cried, repeating my story, telling some guy with a beard how awful it was, lying, telling him bits and pieces, him telling me it was okay to be gay. That was the only thing that saved me. I remember going to someone else first, but when I told my parents the white-haired guy told me I should get a *Playboy* and try masturbating with it, I never saw him again.

I did try it, though, but ended up finishing off while looking at a picture of a lumberjack type in an ad for Camel cigarettes. The lumberjack sat on a log by a river. He wore jeans, boots and a flannel shirt. A Saint Bernard puppy sat in his lap. There had been some guy on TV talking about subliminal advertising that year, and it didn't take me long to see that the puppy's paw, which dangled from between the guy's legs, looked like a foot-long cock. In other ads, he's displaying a basket of similar pro-portions. I don't make this stuff up. It's in the fucking ad. Jorge has them all, framed.

27. contact rod & research alien miracles together

Because we'd made films together and shown a few at school to wild acclaim, we were paired. Guys who befriended Dan were by default my friends, even though he was a senior.

Post-Sean, that changed abruptly.

But one of Dan's friends, an older guy from his job, ended up spending a few nights with us when his girlfriend kicked him out. I don't recall the exact logistics, except I suddenly found myself glued to the TV with him as my company, his bed ready in the basement, Dan and the parents were asleep upstairs, and, well, conversations and late nights usually having the same results no matter their gender, I ended up getting to know Dan's friend better than he ever would.

It would have helped if Dan's friend hadn't been so eager to compliment my technique to Dan a week later. Arguing over that was the last time Dan would ever try to hit me. It was a fight we carefully arranged to exclude parental supervision. I shook him off, then stopped off in the basement for some clean socks and a sleeping bag and stayed in the woods all night. Good thing it was spring.

After that, I just crossed Dan off and cut the line for weeks at a time. I resented his pressured rush toward popularity and scholarships based on our reel. He was taller and older. He was firstborn. He had a car and a girlfriend and a job. He paved the way and left successive teachers curiously wondering about the glowing talents of his younger, chubbier kin. Would I measure up? Why wasn't I more like Dan?

But when he saw me, defiant in a flash, he knew something odd had taken hold of me, obviously queer, more than the obvious lack of athletic capability and my devotion to theater.

A few days later, he blurted out that I was "weird." I'd already gone through a few shrinks in the post-Sean phase. Of course I was weird. That much was obvious, and he was a snotty teacher's pet yet cool stoner dude. You bet I'm weird, Doofus.

His muttered "You're weird" did not go without punishment. We fought. I hit him first that last time, Cain-like, and pounded on his skull. His screams ricocheted in the house and around the neighborhood.

Astonishment and horror, then things were settled. I vowed I would never speak to him, let alone apologize, nor would I go to school that day. My father sputtered demands, my mother, still blitzed on some medication, cajoled and offered.

"It'll be all right, he forgives you," Mom said, spokesperson for the house. I didn't believe a word of it.

A flood of tears later, huddled in a corner of the dining room, a shelf of Funk & Wagnalls pressing into my back, I calmed down enough to consider going to school late. Dan had departed, driven to school to plot some future away from me. He was off the list.

Dinners together were reduced to weekends or holidays. We grazed separately, from gallon pots of sauce or soup or stew. We scooped our plates full, unfolded tray tables and sat watching TV from opposite ends of the living room. The kitchen, once the hearth and center of our evening chats and jokes, had been reduced to a filling station.

I dove into a few school projects; well, every school project available: designing the set for a play and half of the junior prom, pictures for the yearbook, rock concerts, and parties with stacks of albums and beer and friendly guys who didn't know or care who I lusted for. That was simultaneously relaxing and frustrating. But I needed to be away from my family, and it helped.

Around the time my dad was trying to be a nice guy about the family stuff, I was flunking math. Pretty embarrassing for the son of a college math teacher.

"What makes you think you have a venereal disease?"

This was also the time I went out to do some more sexual proving. I got the clap, from a girl.

I was really drunk at the time.

The doctor was not friendly; in fact, he was hostile. He didn't like having to inspect the penis of a sixteen-year-old boy who was telling him what the symptoms were. I hated having to drop my shorts as much as he did looking at me.

"There's a ... dripping."

"Discharge?"

"Yeah. And my underwear smells funny."

"Well, you shouldn't be sticking your nose down there in the first place."

I stood while he bent over me, examining my dick like unworthy bait.

"Who was the woman you had sex with?" he asked.

The Woman? You mean, prone slut whose name I never remembered? "Uh, it was at a party. I didn't know her."

"What was her name?"

"Uh…" Think of someone, anyone. How about that girl on the volleyball team? "Jan." I was still wondering why I never got to see the other guys do her.

He brought a device from the table, something a dentist would use to pry off a chip of plaque. He seemed to take a slight pleasure in jabbing the metal rod inside my penis. I jumped back, only making it worse, almost backed into a corner. He dabbed the device onto a Petri dish and closed it. While walking out, he said I could get dressed and wait.

The tests came back negative, but I knew better. I was going to go insane just like Rudolph Valentino, but nobody was coming to *my* funeral.

I was still trying to remember why I'd had sex with her. There were a lot of people at the party, then only some, then pairs, then I was so drunk I allowed myself to be shoved into a room with her. Peer pressure almost turned me straight. But nobody I knew talked about it, or whether they got sick as well.

Senior class commenced, along with a barrage of *Welcome To Brookside Senior High* banners.

I made friends via rock concert T-shirts. I talked. I wasn't a total geek. Then one day, Brian Jenkins, sitting next to me, suddenly became a new pal, when he said a nasty joke about the clap. He must have liked how I laughed so hard.

He dared me to loosen the screws of my favorite English teacher's chair, me, the A student about to become a hood. I smoked Camels with Brian, absorbing his pornographic details of recent encounters. He'd been the first that night.

Everyone else I knew had some equal or bigger problem, or enough of one to distract me from my own. We'd be away soon, stumbling elsewhere into adulthood.

28. beat to ghostly voidful dreamous crypts

Arthur and Marilyn McCabe and their two daughters, Christine and Carla, came over for one of our frequent Sunday roast beef dinners, which had been postponed through the dreadful months. Sundays always tasted of roast beef or ham, something that made me sleepy. I dreaded finishing my homework as much as the prospect of facing the other kids at school whom I grew to have less in common with every day.

Dan and I also had to manage the kids' hyper excitement, at least until we could get them revved up enough to bump into something. That usually put an exclamatory note to the end of the evening. Christine bawled better. Carla was more wistful. She usually fell asleep on the couch or got lost reading books.

I won't get into Arthur's kids, except to say that they were like most other professors' kids: precocious, loud or somber, brilliant, beautiful. It was at one of these Sundays when Mom was still not getting dinners right, but trying. The girls had run outside to play in a pile of leaves I'd raked for them.

Arthur brought up the winter play the college was producing. They always did dramas during the cold months. Arthur talked about the play with some excitement. My parents were already acting oddly, as if they'd heard him run this by them beforehand, but were pretending to hear it for the first time. I wasn't listening too clearly.

It was something about a couple of guys who wait around for some guy. Arthur needed a boy to play the messenger, who keeps telling them they have wait. The kid who played the boy would get to wear wings.

I looked at Dan.

"Don't look at me," he muttered, his mouth full of food. "I got a job."

He wouldn't even dare me.

Arthur wasn't even asking if I would audition. I already had it if I wanted it. "There are only two scenes, so you'd have plenty of time to do your homework in the green room."

The play sounded really depressing.

I couldn't wait.

There was never a joking pick-up rehearsal. Dick Thorson was long gone. A few students and crew members made nice with the high school kid. The show ran for one week, in February.

The theater was half-filled on a good night; okay, a few dozen people if we were lucky. It was winter. It was Beckett. There certainly weren't any dancing cows or quick-change farmboys in this show. People didn't get it, and if they did, they didn't like what they got.

Instead of waiting in the green room, I remember sitting offstage in a big dusty armchair, my wings carefully splayed out on either arm. My peasant boy costume made me feel impoverished. I was so tired and the show seemed so repetitive, I had to be cued by the stage manager, some other college kid who paid no attention to me. He'd signal me, I'd remember my cue, then comb my wings out, go onstage, tell the men Godot wasn't coming, and they had to come back again another day. Then I did the same thing in Act Two, except the actor playing Estragon yelled at me, shook my shoulders, nearly brought me to tears. He was very convincing. That or he was pissed off that night of the show, when I figured out how to make the wings work.

Always upstaging.

"They hung a guy out a window, for just a second. This other guy flies the Confederate flag when he gets drunk. This other one's scoopin' pot on a tray, and this other guy's bong catches the tie-dye ceiling art on fire. The fire alarm went off, and we evacuated the dorm like ants in a hill crushed by a foot. Among the parking lot refugees were two rather large athletes of your type who were both wet from showering. I should introduce you when you visit."

Dan told me stories from Ohio State, wrote mad letters home, and generally raved about the atrocities of what he called the Kafka Ant Hill, a looming duo of spires worthy of a Tolkien book cover. These were the madhouses known as freshmen dorms. Thus he wrote me in the letter I've just found in the midst of my attempt at cleaning my parents' attic.

Aside from Dan's letters and dating Baby June, the banalities of school overwhelmed me. My senior year in high school passed uneventfully. I now had a right to be a zombie, but was already tiring of the pose. I was on to other places. Morning announcements. Assemblies. Pep rallies. Pencils. I remember bursting out laughing for no reason when I stood in line at the cafeteria and received a tray of applesauce, creamed corn, and a Brookside School district specialty, hot dogs wrapped in a buttered slice of white bread with a sliver of cheese. The concoction was baked, greasy, and held together with toothpicks like food origami. They called them Wiener Winks.

Wiener Winks.

The winter Dan returned from college, it snowed two feet.

We walked to the local theater on a freezing January night when neither of our parents' cars would start. We walked two miles to see *2001: A Space Odyssey* at midnight, knowing no one else would be there to desecrate it with a sound. The projectionist, a hulking yet pleasant man we called Baby Huey behind his back showed us the huge reels lying sideways, rewinding, spooling in the massive film. He also took us down to the storage room of the theater to see the piles of photos and movie posters, telling us to take as many as we could carry out. We puffed home in a daze, dropping a few lesser ones along the way.

We dealt in sales and collected, but we grew tired of it after a few months. It was the making of the thing that we loved, the creating and watching movies, over and again: That's a matte. That's backlit. That's looped. That's a hand-held. We conquered the mystery of film, since we'd already conquered the mystery of theatre. We never lost our joy of watching, but having discovered some secrets, we could enjoy it even more. No one loves fine embroidery more than a crone with withered fingers.

Post-carrot, Post-Uncle Sean, Post-Alateen, our little movies grew just a touch darker in tone. We did a nasty, abrupt version of an Isaac Asimov short story, "The Burning Man," ten years before a Nevada desert version became a pagan tourist attraction.

The animated short I remember best was a series of clay sculptures that just kept eating each other, melting, transforming one into the other, until all that was left was a pool of blended clay. I was seventeen by then. Dan was off to Ohio State and wanted to have a few more films under his belt. He came home on weekends, inspired by screenings of *THX-1138* and *Alexander Nevsky*.

The locations were better in our part of Ohio, but the talent left much to be desired. I was supposed to follow Dan to Columbus, after which we would conquer the Ohio State University Film Department, and, subsequently Hollywood. Dan had to make one more film, something impressive to take with him back to college, and it took a lot of coaxing for me to even think about it.

We decided to do a moody live action piece. Somehow Dan had made peace with me. It brought me back to working with him and exploring the darker edges of our vision.

This was when I'd once again befriended Baby June, and that friendship somehow got around to dating, or my pose of dating. She seemed eager to go along with it. I think she knew it was a farce the whole time. She didn't seem to mind. I think it was just our way of trying to relive our *Gypsy* days together.

When I told her Dan wanted to make another movie, she said she'd like to help.

We shot a few action scenes with another guy in it, Brad something, a theater major from OSU. He was an incredibly cute pal of Dan's, but he flaked out after Dan brought him home one weekend. It seemed Brad was questioning his sexuality, and when the truth came, in the form of me, my mouth, to be specific, he had to go home to think things over.

I guess we shouldn't have put him in the basement.

The remainder of the unfinished film starred the teen Baby June. Mom tells me she watches the video transfer a lot. We were in our Hammer Films stage when, faced with a film without a monster or co-star, we simply made a short with Baby June as a girl in a nightgown being chased. There were several grand old houses due for demolition on a stately block in our town. It was one of those streets where you could almost hear hoof clops on the wide avenue. The homes were all Victorian, with huge porches and terraces, some even with side carriage entrances.

One of these homes was due for a razing. Disheartened as we were by the complete lack of historical pride Brookside's town fathers took, my brother and I decided on plunder as apt tribute.

After pilfering every extractable brass doorknob, chandelier, and fixture, we returned to capture the way sunlight slatted on rotting walls, the clouds of dust, the immense and perilous staircase. The weeds were overgrown and, when we snuck in, it seemed obvious why the building had to come down. Floors were rotting, walls peeling. It was perfect.

Except we couldn't film at night. We had one light bright enough, and it had to attach to the top of the primitive GAF Super8 camera, a box meant for capturing wedding cake slices and baby steps. It was not the appropriate equipment for a gothic melodrama, but we had nothing else.

Baby June played the part of a pining poet girl stuck in this place. There were supposed to be other actors. There was supposed to be a plot, but we just went out one day with six three-minute rolls of Super8 and started shooting. Baby June changed into a nightgown. I had an old Amish boy coat I'd bought for five dollars at a farm auction in Jeromesville.

We added a few wispy shreds from an old set of drapes we found in the attic, and she wandered, in white, through the halls of this lumbering mansion, peering out of doorways and running down halls, while I brooded and toiled in the basement among a pile of old chairs. In some places, the winter snow had bled in small drifts through broken windows. It was brilliant. We would project it while playing "Josette's Theme," that twinkling music box melody from *Dark Shadows*.

What stopped the production short was our star taking a fall and cutting her bare foot on a board. We had to go to the next-door neighbor's to get my dad to come pick us up and take her to the hospital, where she had to get five tetanus shots in the stomach. Her parents went ballistic, but they calmed down when we showed them the footage.

Seventeen, standing in the middle of Randy Nicoplous's living room, Randy Nicopolous, the handsomest athlete in school, and nice, too. Greek.

Seventeen. I'm dancing with Baby June to "Sweet Emotion" by Aerosmith. We have been an item for months. I danced slow with Baby June, who smiled as she felt my erection dent her thigh, stirred not by her presence, but the warm smells of being in Randy Nicopolous's living room. I distract it by dancing with Baby June, hip swaying, bell-bottomed, Love's Baby Soft turning to pure sweat as Joe Perry's guitar churned the air into desire, and all the cool kids in my high school are watching. They thought it was love. I knew it for what it was, a mere show, a reunion, Travolta and Cher, maybe, but inside it feels like Shields and Yarnell do Reno.

She stood up for me. She let me get by pretending, acting. She said she didn't mind.

The movie was shelved, but we still have Baby June's only cinematic debut and swan song. There are parts of it in *Keemoe,* what I call "The Wandering Girl," the section one critic called "superfluous."

30. knife d by a fright light ET bumped

In August 1980, Cousin Mike and my Aunt May came to stay for a few weeks. I was no longer into science fiction movies and TV. Artaud, Brecht, and the Theatre of Cruelty became my secret thesis.

Little Cousin Mike was a distraction of titanic proportions, a sort of Shrinky Dink version of Popeye. He fought. He was from "Piss-bar." He expressed his anger and fear by hitting trees and marauding the neighborhood kids. Four years after his father boinked me, his mom dumped him off in Brookside for a month.

This time, he got to sleep in the basement.

It had been renovated into a den, with a fake Tiffany lamp and even a pool table Dad bought from a garage sale. Most of the time things were stored on it, but sometimes we used it. Despite the fix up, though, the basement remained clammy and moldy. Some things stayed, like that old sofa.

Could there have been a way for it to be okay? Is there a way for a boy to lose it in a good way? How many people have a wonderful first time? When asked about mine, I simply skip to my second time with Brad, or was it the third, a wonderful sexy sperm-shooting love fest with a lanky mustached college boy in my tiny single dorm room bed at Ohio State? My night with Doug Cantarella, which has been publicly re-classified as the first time, or Dan's wayward buddy, or the Drive-In with Todd and his coming attraction. I felt like forgetting family plots, or kicking them.

My mom's sister forgot her first try. After a clumsy first marriage that didn't work, she just left. Erased the tape, left only a few pictures. She didn't tell us about it until I was sixteen and she wasn't drinking anymore. We're allowed to make mistakes and cross them out.

It's only recently that I think of what it felt like for my mom. What if my brother had seduced my kid? Wouldn't I want to kill him?

Playing with Mike at the town pool gave me a wonderful chance to show off my parenting skills, which were negligible, especially when Mike's fear of immersion led to squawking and more fumblings with his water wings.

Off on the lawn behind us, kids my age and older were tanning. Among them was Kurt, a high school varsity swimming jock I'd only seen pictures of in the local newspaper. He seemed to notice me looking at him, or fumbling with Mike, and he smiled at me. I nodded a shrug, quietly thrilled.

Having recovered from his trauma at my trying to teach him to swim in three feet of water, Mike splashed for a few minutes, declared himself bored, and retreated to annoy my mother.

I sat along the edge, my feet dabbling at the water. Then Kurt walked by, saw me, and smiled again. "He's a real handful!"

As he headed for the locker room, I nearly jumped to follow him, but waited, prayed, whispered to myself as I followed.

With only a few men at other ends of the locker room, or in the shower, Kurt stood at a far bench. He seemed to have slowed, waiting. I passed him and turned back as he pulled down his swimsuit, leaving the untanned parts open, stepped out of his shorts, and grinned for a moment.

I stood, looking away from him nonchalantly and shucked down my Speedos. He watched as my already stiffening dick popped out.

And at that moment, little Mike came racing up between us.

Kurt abruptly turned away, stuffing himself into his shorts.

Mike turned to me, babbling some complaint in kidspeak. Then he stopped and stared at my dick.

I should have turned away, put something on, but I was darting glances at Kurt, trying to explain ... okay, *and* catch a glimpse of his butt.

And then, in a moment before fumbling for my shorts, I looked back at Mike and thought, Well, this is it. The dick that your father sucked, kid.

I suddenly understood how my uncle felt when he fondled my faunlike frame. I knew how they all felt, him and every sick daddy and abusive mommy and monstrous older brother and naughty uncle and crazed aunt and nasty granddaddy and twisted babysitter and horny neighbor and fucked up trucker felt when faced with such a simple victim.

Gramma take me home. Gramma take me home.

Once we were in the driveway, I abandoned mom's car with Mike in it. I raced upstairs, took a towel from the hall closet, closed the bathroom door, turned on the shower and jacked the come out in a minute, trying to forget Kurt's stare and focus on his untanned portions. He never spoke to me again all summer, and then he went away to college, which explains why the movies starring my young cousin took on a certain sadistic theme, thus necessitating the stunt-trashing of my Danny O'Day doll.

31. to capture the mother aura his ship was under him

For Christmas 1995, Dan and Gloria begged off an Ohio visit until after the holiday, having promised a trip to see her parents instead. It was my turn to visit in time for the actual day. Barry's TV movie was rolling along in pre-production and the desert porn epic remained a mere possibility.

But what clinched my decision to make the porn epic had nothing to do with Jason Daw's charm, or my battle with the imminent post-production blues after the TV movie would wrap by late spring. What convinced me was a strange discovery in my parents' attic.

Whenever I returned home, the idea of my father helping to attack any projects—lawn leaves, the garage, the basement—did not appeal to him. He made good short lists, though.

Even in his retirement, my father found yet more puzzles. Projects diverted him. The moving of objects and the exercise involved had become less appealing to him. Screen doors, grout, and making shelves used to interest him. We had dozens of shelves. At least I could shovel snow.

Our quality time was spent with me talking about my work while he fiddled with a clock, or on my mother's computer, playing online chess with an old college friend in Helsinki. We were discussing economics as a reason for my imminent success, not so much artistry. Dad was very proud of the upcoming TV movie because of the larger fee. I countered with my youthful ability to economize, as I had with my *Manipulator* trilogy.

"You're good when you're paying for it, right?"

"Yes."

"A movie, your average movie, I mean, like this last one is, what did you say? A hundred-twenty—"

"Yeah."

"Minutes, and how many scenes?"

"Well, it depends, but a minute a page."

"There. Pure math. Get paid more for less, divide it up and think how long it took you to get this made—"

"Well, no."

"But you're getting what you worked for. You shouldn't have to go back to cheap little movies."

"Well, I like making cheap little movies, too."

"Suit yourself."

"That way, I still own them."

He was saying, *See? You made a nice movie and you are a success.*

I tried to show him I agreed.

Behind puppets in plastic bags, assorted puzzle pieces, Christmas or-nament boxes, and about twenty more boxes archiving our family, I put the attic into a kind of order. "One of these things is not like the other," I sang in my head, recalling *Sesame Street*'s indoctrination. Valentino, then barely more than a kitten, joined me out of curiosity, but then pounced about between boxes in a futile hunt for an unseen mouse.

But I'd already started extracting items and placing them in a growing pile by the landing of the stairs. I'd decided to finally start taking things back to L.A. I finally realized I had my own home, and I was gonna stay there. UPS would make a bundle off me.

Among the slowly filling boxes were my complete collection of *Scream* magazines, my marionettes, a few choice vintage Nixon-era *Life* maga-zines, ancient books, movie posters, T-shirts, crumbling plaster sculptures.

I kept thinking, where the hell will I put these things? But I felt like I was saving them. Some synapse of senility might strike my parents any day. Mom joked of setting it all on fire like Roseanne Barr in *SheDevil* once too often for my comfort, and she's still smoking.

I found a 1968 Montgomery Ward Christmas catalog. The latest goldmine. In it, my G.I. Joe Apollo capsule retailed at a mere $8.98.

Under yearbooks and old files, some really ancient bills and cashed checks from the 1960s traced our move from Pittsburgh to Brookside. Telephone bill: seven dollars. Prescriptions; four dollars, Hawkins Market; twenty-seven dollars. I could almost remember the days, Mom and I trooping out to the car with four or five bags full of food, assisted by some gangly yet cute grocery boy who I prayed would only look at me while I tried to help him stuff the groceries in the car.

And then I saw a check, written out to Sean O'Leary. Twenty dollars. I scanned through the years, flipping through them, seeing my mother's handwriting grow wilder. Her handwriting on the check was all over the place. How could the bank have read it? Sean O'Leary. Fifty dollars. The date was March 12, 1977.

After it happened.

"How's the excavation going?" she called up as I trundled down the stairs to the living room.

"Great," I said.

My mother was watching TV and reading a book at the same time. This I knew because my attempts to change the channel were met with protest. I consented to watch with her, wondering, if I switched books, would she notice that, too?

I thought I shouldn't bring it up. I countered that I should. It was a safe time, with nobody else home, like it had been that afternoon, when the flickering of the projector covered the basement sounds.

"Mom?"

"Yes?" She put down her book, as if I was about to ask something simple. What's for dinner? Can I borrow the car?

"Can we talk?"

As I scooted closer to her on the sofa, she took the remote, turned the TV off and gave me the sort of look I faced when I came home, high on the booze and pot of guys I loved in high school.

She rearranged herself, dug into her purse, and fished out a cigarette. She lit up and moved the ashtray on the coffee table closer to me, equidistant, like a diplomat singing over the official pen.

"I don't smoke any more," I said.

"Oh. Good for you."

"So. How's your brother . . . these days?"

After a long pause, and a drag, smoke curled up to the ceiling, then back down.

Some time after she waded through excuses, apologies and other evasions, I had an address in a small town twenty miles from Phoenix, Arizona.

My little desert epic was going to have an interesting side trip, and on someone else's dime.

32. convince a frantic witch to cry see her devil fall. scream it must

It was one of those special flipover years, Clinton being reelected. Barry and I were apart, not dating then, and not a lot of fun to be around each other. It was about the movie, of course. I was nervous. He was anxious but acting indifferent. Pretending to be professional forced us to be that way. I could not believe he was sleeping soundly, not considering re-writes into the dawn, because I sure was, in the arms of another man.

"Why do you surf?" Dave, a week-long fling, asked.

"It's easy," I said. "And warm and wet, and I like to swim."

"That's it?"

"No. Actually I could just swim with the fins, like a seal. It's just being part of the earth, floating."

Dave swam, too, but in a pool. A lot. He had the lats to prove it.

I rested easy, having convinced Dave of a lot of impromptu reciprocity. More important, I'd secured a pre-fucked date for New Year's Eve.

I had just made it into a less than amusing gossip column in one of those pocket-sized gay nightlife miniature magazines. The photo caption's quip was not nice, but the photo was.

"You didn't see it?" Jorge shrieked over the phone. He read it to me over the phone, a full week after the New Year's nightclub party which, I recall, culminated in me, swimmer Dave (who I had been seeing for a few weeks) and about three other guys on a well-lit dance floor, going at it in about four different positions.

Arriving at my door half an hour later, Dave in his shorts in the kitchen, with a stack of magazines, Jorge clipped the pages, covering the fridge with dozens of pictures of me with my shorts tugged down below my cheeks, which were being grabbed by some glorious stud whose name escaped me. Dave couldn't recall either, but took a few souvenir copies before leaving.

"You're proud of it, aren't you?" Barry asked when he'd called later. Jorge couldn't resist spreading the gossip.

"Dude."

"What?"

"Look, Bear. Yes, I'm proud of it. Let's use it. They're all gonna be looking at me, this first-time director, with no experience—"

"You're not a first-time anything."

"They might as well enjoy my butt."

"This is your seventh or eighth film? Come on."

"Those don't count."

"Yes, they do. *The Manipulators* were features. They made money. They were good."

"They were jokes." I was spitting on Ricky's grave. I'd say it hurt, but he liked that sort of thing, the naughty boy.

"What about the gay ones?" Barry again defended my reputation. I felt a bit of remorse, my only claim to fame at the moment being a nice photo of my butt.

"Shorts, impulses, messy little collages, self-indulgent—"

"Why do you always sell yourself short, Stan? When are you gonna get a DBA and start writing off the things you're allowed? When are you going to realize that you are a success, and you also have a hot ass?"

"Okay," I said, feigning consent, but let it soak in later.

Why brag? See, I didn't have the advantage of all Barry's years of therapy and carefully measured career moves.

Everything I did was an accident, an impulse, the fortune of other people's whims or availability. Even the TV movie was only because of him.

Barry warmed me back into moving forward on the movie over a therapy session disguised as an expensive candlelit dinner.

He'd chosen another small place whose name escapes me, filled with more Hollywood lore than a Kenneth Anger book. I felt the legacy daring me, sneering, perhaps.

"I just see myself as this idiot captain," I said, "and they're all gonna be these veteran actors and techies who know twice as much as I do. I keep seeing them jumping ship."

"They're not gonna jump ship. They're gonna be under contract."

"Oh, forced. Perfect."

"Will you just—"

"Enough okay? Let's just forget about it and go out."

"You sure? You seem to be acting out some sexual ... whatever."

"Look, I went out with Jorge, and we had a good time. I was drunk with male beauty. Dave is just for fun."

"You can't keep avoiding the root of your self-destruction through cheap anonymous—"

"What, what? The root of self-destruction? Are we off on another of your Louise Hay Rides?"

Barry held his breath, then hissed out an exhale, glaring at me. He was so ugly when he was upset. "You have to deal with your incest experience."

"I do, Barry. Every time I suck a cock, I get better and better."

We left the restaurant. I felt the urge to dart outside ahead of him, having spotted a lone smoker. Just one, I could bum. I held back.

"I'm going to go home," Barry said as we drove east toward Silver Lake. "If you want me to drop you anywhere—"

"No, just home. Thanks."

Let me back up from that downer to how I ended up butt-first in one of those gay mini rags.

"*Ola regine.* Hello, you queens—." I hung up without leaving Jorge a message and paged him instead. He called back.

We went to Mayan and bought drinks, Jorge yet another Calistoga, me a rum and Coke. Since he was driving, I was allowed. I'd called Dave, who said he might show up. I left my smokes in Jorge's car, knowing it would be impossible to smoke comfortably in the club. I didn't bother, tried to think of other things, or nothing, as I surveyed the gradually unfolding parade of the pectorally blessed. I began to play a game with myself, the Flirting Game. Just make eye contact, smile a bit. The club consumed us.

We danced, Jorge bobbing his head about in search of other conquests. I was happy to finally be breaking a sweat. My ears were already ringing, my sides were beginning to ache, but I didn't care.

The video projection screen in the club had mixed music videos, but mostly just unconnected images, my favorite kind, where you, the viewer, were the glue. You put it together.

Another drink and more wandering with Jorge amidst the faces and bodies of men, their glistening chests, T-shirts hanging from the backs of shorts and jeans like tails, began to meld as one herd of sexual heated creatures. None of them resembled Barry. Five of them recognized me. One of them was named Dave, who'd finally arrived.

We found a place off the center of the dance floor with room, but then a favorite beat came on, only a few years old, but already elevated into the ranks of greats, as if every year of gay life had become its own epoch. Addressing the herd of us, the mass of us, the boys, her flock, She sang, She Who Rules, Madonna Veronica Ciccone on a Fritz Lang movie set.

"Don't go for second best..." The video screen loomed over us. Men danced strangely, all heads twisted toward it in one direction or another.

On the screen, Madonna clutched her crotch while sporting a deco suit, standing atop a huge platform built as a replica of the machinery in *Metropolis,* a Deco/Mayan monstrosity of steps leading up, up.

In the original film, that set piece transforms to the mouth of Moloch, the eater of souls or some such German myth. Madonna had turned it inside out, making it a font of joy, release, and abandon, dancing in a city where forty-five people died over a gang of cops who beat up a black man. Dancing in a city where lies were turned into gold. Dancing, my epiphany took me back to a basement screening of that film, that metropolis, and I vowed to sweat off any remaining guilt or hate about any of it.

Jorge and Dave seemed a bit surprised by my sudden burst of energy, but I didn't care. I was dancing for her, the Goddess, the Whore of Babylon, Hel, the robot queen, the maker of dreams, the killer of spirits, the giver of life, She Who Will Be Obeyed.

Or not.

Shaking it off via my hips, we just danced. I saw myself in the mirror in a sea of men and laughed. Pointing Jorge's attention toward our reflections, I shouted, "Mama! I'm pretty! I'm a pretty girl!"

"Sing out, Louise!" he called back, before twirling around yet again.

Anyway, it was around that time that the other guys joined me and the fourway-grinding led to pants being lowered. Because of that rather nice butt shot, I was heralded in the lower circles of gaydom, for a while. It's not pretty being easy.

33. many **soar** but she sings sweetly

After the 'butt of fame' shots were put away, a party invite on my ever-changing Santa Monica fridge door showed a gorgeous muscle man, his arms cradling a heart. Behind his shoulders, a pair of feathered white wings crested outward. I glanced at it as I held the phone on one shoulder while foraging for breakfast.

Jason Daw called, at nine in the morning. I did not lie and say I hadn't been asleep. I told him it was the loveliest wake-up call a guy could receive.

"So, there's a uniform party next week I'm supposed to perform at. You wanna go with?"

"Am I your date?" I asked.

Swimmer Dave had since paddled off to other shores.

"Well, we might accumulate a few more. You can pick 'em."

"Are you dressing up?" I asked, pouring the last of the juice into a glass.

"Of course. Although, military's not kinky for me."

"Really?"

"Not aftah two years in it, sweetie." He'd been in the Australian Army.

"Then what is?"

"Surfers. Been lookin' for seabait."

"Found any?"

"They all want to boink a movie star, but I like the ones who don't know me."

"You mean the straight ones, or the gay ones that don't watch porn?"

"Does naiveté turn you on?" Jason asked.

"No, neither does ignorance," I said.

"What does?"

"That's personal."

"Sweetie, we have to discuss our plot synopsis, our scenario, as it were." Jason snarled "scenario" like he was picking the word out of his teeth.

"Oh, I dunno. Overalls, followed by tight black pants, white shirts and top hats. There's a cow in there somewhere, too."

"Huh. Now, that's kinky."

If not specific.

Jason and I mulled over other tired porn scenes we'd seen too much of. I found myself clutching my dick, charmed by the relaxed queeniness of his voice, imagining him naked in bed too, or by the pool. Any place with enough ample parking for his weaponry. He rambled on a bit about guys shaving the backs of their necks, how he liked that immensely.

"One of the most beautiful and vulnerable parts of the male anatomy," I panted. "I'd like to start with a close-up of the back of your neck, pulling back to show you standing before an infinite desert highway."

"Like a beer commercial," he said.

"A beer commercial that drinks the whole six-pack."

"Ah. What are you eating?"

"Nothing you'd like," I said. "Um, this may be personal, but are you in the program?"

"Huh?"

"No, that's right. You drink."

"Right. But if I'm gonna be pouring stuff all over meself, I want a shower in my trailer."

"Who said anything about a trailer?"

"Don't worry. That's Geoff's job."

I wondered what else Geoff of the worked nipples could provide.

Jason rang off, but I still felt horny. I called Barry.

After a few phone message apologies, we, or I, made up as friends. We had to. There were contracts to sign for my other project.

It would be nice if other guys figured out how to keep people around after you make them mad but you want them back, so I'll very subtly try to offer some advice. I told him a funny story.

I told him I didn't feel like I was rejecting the gay community. In fact, I felt it was rejecting me. After all, I had proposed that safe sex video, to do it for free, but they didn't go for the concept at The AIDS Foundation.

I had drawings made, and cutouts with big Batman style Whammo, Super Spirograph signage. This would appear on a Kenner ad for Sit 'n' Spin with shots of guys and gals riding on a Dildo-a-Gogo. The slogan, in cheerful letters: "Go Fuck Yourself!"

Maybe I should have made it boring or clichéd, like the winged muscle boy club invite on my fridge.

Anyway, Barry liked the descriptions. I got him to laugh. But it was true. "I really wanted to do that!" and Barry kept laughing.

When he calmed down, he said, "What you're saying is, we're going to have to spend a lot more time together, so we might as well be friends."

"No, I'm just saying that I wanted to say, 'Go fuck yourself.'"

"Bitch."

Shifting gears, we did spend time together. I spent it at his, since his script was on his computer, plus storyboard space on his living room wall. Barry's space made me feel comfortable. Funny how that wealth thing relaxes one.

All over the living room floor and on the walls, I shifted storyboards like tiles. In one, I had the back shot of the Kid opening the door to his bedroom, except it's shot low, and you see the form of his uncle sleeping in his bed. Should he close the door, I wondered. No, too ominous. He should leave the door open. We should see him get undressed. No, that happens off camera. Just him climbing into bed. No, just approaching it, and his uncle waking and smiling. Fade out.

"What's that?" Barry said, coming in from the kitchen for another munch session between our blocks. We'd have little discussions over the screenplay, then my eyes would get tired, or I'd get tired of piddling over words the actors would move around anyway.

"The actors. Shit." I dropped the picture, went to my backpack for my calendar. I was supposed to appear at my rent-a-office at the studio to meet my new secretary. I figured she was just a network spy, but the office thing was going to come in handy. What name actor would have a meeting in Santa Monica? It all had to be formal, slotted in on their budget, couchless.

"Stan?"

"Yeah. Sorry. I just remembered something."

"What scene is this?" He was smiling, but it had that, *Son, who made these crayon marks on the wall?* tone.

"When they make the whoopee," I said, raising my eyebrows like a Marx brother.

Barry refused so much as a grin. "But I had the uncle leading him into the bedroom."

"Yeah, well, I figured the uncle doesn't need to wake up from his nap after everybody else in the house is gone. He should be there, waiting."

"But that's different."

"I'm sorry. I wanted to ask about that."

"But it's not the same."

"How is it not the same? We could put the convincing dialogue before it."

"But you're making the kid go in."

"Yeah."

"But that changes the intention."

He caught me red-handed. "Not really."

"You're making him want it."

"He does want it."

"No, he doesn't. Not totally."

"Oh, so this is about rape?"

"No, but it looks like we're advocating it."

"Look, the people who hate it are still gonna hate it, no matter how we portray it. They are still gonna get barrels of letters from the fundies. I just think he's still manipulated by the uncle. His just being there is manipulative, luring him. Think of it as, like, mind control."

"Mind control."

"It's a visual moment, Bear, full of tension. It ends Act One perfectly. It's Dorothy going through the door of her house from black and white to color."

Barry sighed and set down the picture. "I hate it when you're right."

"Sorry."

He smiled, started to go back into the kitchen. Then I heard, from out there, him saying, "For a guy who never had kids, you sure know a lot about them."

We moved on, but I was so close to saying, make it about love, man, or I am out that door and not coming back.

34. rob water; weak knife all red. none cry

Having also been invited to the uniform party with Jason Daw and other performers, Jorge called. I knew he'd want a wingman for that. But I wouldn't be able to bear being Jason's second banana. Hanging out with Jason had become a rudely humbling experience. Every moment was spent in his shadow, half-listening to the same adulatory comments from others, the bold and eventually rude flirtations. I needed a posse. But then Jorge added an earlier dinner party to the schedule.

"How's the cast list?"

"Oh, you know, Trisha, Ben, Marcus, the old gang and all their new friends, I suppose."

In other words, the Gerard Kulozik Memorial Wing. The room would be full of Ricky and old *Manipulator* stories. "I think I'm gonna pass on that one."

"You sure?"

"Yeah. They just think I'm no more than what I was when I left them, and I don't want that."

"Whoah."

"No offense, dear. It's just that you're one of few people in my life who've made it to the next act."

"I should feel honored?" he quipped.

"Better that than burdened."

"You know, Stan, it's okay to miss him."

"I know," I said, coolly. "I remember once, if I may *share* now ..."

"Oh, by all means."

"Thank you. Well, I remember once, when none of our old pals you just mentioned were available, Ricky asked me for a ride to go for a check-up at the hospital. He had Giardia."

"The parasite?"

"I said it sounded like a Republican Senator."

"You cad."

"I asked how he got it, and he said it's from rimming and somehow the jokes were about rimming senators and the day just fell apart from there. We laughed all the way to the hospital."

Jorge laughed with me, and we sighed and let some silence kick in. I figured I couldn't blame Ricky's other friends for leaving, moving apart.

"You know, if you can't forgive them or forget them, you might as well eat their food."

"Can you pick me up? You know how I hate driving home alone."

Jorge knew I'd think it was because he was the only person who knew what had happened that one night when I didn't get home. I told it to someone else, but she didn't know it.

What is it like to burn years later, to be a survivor? Why the panic attack when a helicopter passes too low and you're in someone else's home, even while in the arms of your sort of ex-boyfriend business partner?

I will tell it the way I told the baby, the daughter of my brother, as she lay in my arms one night in San Francisco, after it was all over. Two years old, yet to witness the footage on the news, yet to ask why.

"Once there was a man named Woo," I told the child. "He sold all his possessions to leave a place called North Vietnam, where there was violence and much evilness in the streets, and he brought his family to America. He opened a video store in the City of Angels. It was not a success, until one day a pair of boys came to work for him, first Jorgerismo, then Stanleyoski. The two boys showed Mister Woo many ways to attract all sorts of people, particularly men who like movies about men. The boys showed Mister Woo that with discreetly designed sections, videos for grown-ups could be rented and even sold as well as videos for kiddies and families.

"Things went very well for the boys and Mister Woo. They all had fun sharing images of people doing fun things like blowing up trucks and recreating new creatures out of sewn-up bodies. It was entertaining.

"But one day, an image of a man getting beaten by police got a lot of people upset. Things like this had been happening for a very long time, but because it was seen, by everyone, many, many times, everybody who pretended it didn't happen couldn't pretend anymore.

"When the policemen who beat the man were not punished, people were angry everywhere. When it started, luckily Jorgerismo was making more images somewhere else, but Stanleyoski showed up for work, a little nervous. So was Mister Woo, who brought all his brothers and cousins to come and defend the store and the videos.

"Unlike the adventure tales he made into films, Stanleyoski was not a warrior, but he took his position with Mister Woo's family, because he liked his job. This was before he ran off to the safety of Barry Bear. Things got very scary as night turned to huge walls of flame and no electricity and gunshots and trucks full of soldiers. People in the darkness tried to rob Mister Woo, and Mister Woo got down from the roof, which everyone, including his worker Stanleyoski, told him not to do.

"Once there was a man named Woo. He opened a video store. He had to spend some time in the hospital, because he'd been beaten by a man in the darkness. That man did not get away alive. When the police came, a long time later, none of the Woos or their workers remembered who the man with the hole in his head was or how he got there."

35. be sure an outer vision is essential

"Can the roller rink music."

"Certainly."

The funeral director whisked off into a back room of the converted mansion in Recita. Ricky's parents were weeping in the viewing room, awaiting the entourage of guests who'd driven from the church to finally lay to rest the boy who got away.

Gerard Kulozik
A Remembrance
January 18, 1958 — March 24, 1992

I didn't know which I hated more; the font, the bad grammar, or the nagging suspicion that the word "remembrance" was invented by a marketing executive at Hallmark.

I had banged that guy's ass for three years, shared mountains and rivers, naked on ecstasy. I drank that guy's everything for a while, and lived. And who were these people at this funeral? I only knew a handful.

Janice, Jorge, and I huddled in a corner, craving sunglasses. Three of Gerard/Ricky/Parker's surviving boyfriends came to me, shaking hands, offering hugs. They were all really nice guys, all gorgeous.

My command to the wispy funeral director didn't seem at all out of place. I was an up and coming director known for his attention to detail, so there was no reason why I shouldn't use those same skills at Ricky's funeral.

The taped organ music was beyond cliché. It made the funeral a farce. I enjoyed the creeping silence. It forced others to equal it, talk in whispers, hear the creak of wood under their feet, under the carpet.

I sat in a chair I would have fawned over under any other situation. Terry, Ricky's surviving boyfriend number three, sat beside me. He was stunning in a suit, even though he seemed out of place in one, like me. I started sobbing, and he held me a while. I think I wanted to stay in his arms a long time. That's what made me cry even more, envying the sliver of romantic longing his beautiful ex-boyfriends had for him even then, with his body only a few feet away.

Then I started inviting them to a few one-on-one after-wakes at my house, private events for the real widowers. I made copies of all Ricky's private stuff, gave it to them, had a few, held a few. We don't see each other a lot. It hurts too much when all you have in common is someone who isn't there anymore.

36. by my leave   trace one mad chain

Cousin,

Remember when we were little
and we used to play games together?
I just have one question...
Why did I always have to be It?

Happy Birthday anyway!

Love, Mike

The card read from my cousin, but I knew it might really be from his mother, my aunt in Pittsburgh. I scanned the signature for authenticity. Maybe Mike had at least signed it, but she bought it. She would think of that, and wouldn't consider the implication. Aunt May, like my mother, kept a stack of cards for every occasion and never forgot a birthday, while I forgot to tell most people of a new address even months after moving. Most of my generation is like that, full of the sin of postal rudeness. Always find time to fax your memo to a modem car phone message center, but an actual card to relatives? Um, gee, I'm so busy. Gotta go do laundry.

But I wanted to call back soon, because my cousin had dropped a note in the card. I could tell it was his handwriting. Maybe he'd put it in himself. Maybe his mom knew that in the note, he mentioned that he wanted to visit L.A.

"Is he gay?"

That's the first question that pops up when a guest like Barry, Jorge, or an overnight *amour* asks when they see the picture wall. It's along the back wall in the living room. For the longest time I tried not to show my past in my home, but after years of doing it for other people's lives and the fictive lives of their films, I saw a blank wall that needed its shrine.

Pictures of me as a kid, my brother, his wife, a healthy Baby June in high school, and my parents fill the upper wall. Off to the side are the relatives, all set in a loose family tree. Over to one side is a picture of Sean

holding an infant Mike, and one of Mike in college. He's too damn handsome. All the Irish blood finally made someone worthwhile.

A straight-edge former punk, now airline rep with a string of beautiful girlfriends, Mike's is the face that compels my friends to question his
sexuality, usually followed by, "You must introduce me."

Should a guest comment on the dark, angular good looks of my uncle,
I've always resisted the possible response, "Yeah, and he gives great head!"
Instead, I say he died. I change the cause from one gruesome accident to
another: three car pile-up, boating accident, random urban shooting.

Well, Mike, all grown up, was coming to L.A., and when I called him,
we joked about what we'd do. I promised not to mention his brief film
career under the hands of The Brothers Grozniak.

In one action thriller, we took little Mike, then seven, on an adventure, in which he parachuted from a cliff and burned to death in a truck
crash. Of course, what actually fell off the roof was a battered Danny
O'Day ventriloquist dummy.

My brother and I took an interest in action pics during the time our
young cousin visited. Using Mike as our victim/leading man, we engaged
him in a series of intrepid trips, where he was taunted by monsters while
strolling through a forest, or, in our best scene, chased to the sunroof off
my parents' bedroom by a ghost and forced to jump off the balcony.

Of course, we substituted my Danny O' Day doll for Mike for the
fall, and it came to be our favorite film. Since the resemblance between
a skinny brunette ventriloquist dummy and our chubby cousin was so
ludicrous, it was our own private joke, having predated the absurd style of
Monty Python's Flying Circus years before it would hit our shores via PBS.

Why did he always have to die? Had I already been seduced by his
father? Did I understand the odd feelings I had for him then? I remember
enjoying their time out, except when Mike spilled a bowl full of cereal on
the living room carpet or when he rode on my lap and gave me a hard-on,
never realizing what he was doing. How easy it would have been to play
out the family curse.

But that's what the movie we were working on was all about, wasn't it?
To stop the course, to undo the chain of pain? Wasn't it?

It doesn't take a child psychiatrist to figure out what we were processing during that action-adventure phase, but Mike survived. He also
survived an abusive dad, a recovering alcoholic mother who dated some
other men for a while, and moving back to Pittsburgh after the collapse of
his family. The straight edge qualities of his punk days seemed to help him

continue to shake off life's burdens as easily as a good stage dive, even after his musical tastes moved on.

"As long as you don't want to break into show business, you're welcome in my home," I said, long distance. "So, you comin' through town?"

"Yes, actually."

"Well, I won't be home much until after March. Should be wrapped by then, but um, about a month of post-production."

"Well, I won't be flying out until April."

"Cool. You're welcome to stay at my place," I said, immediately wondering what that would turn into. I wanted to swallow my words, but he was family. I could always just go over to Barry's. If that burned out by the time Mike got there, maybe back to Jorge. What was I thinking? I had to convince one of these guys to love me. I would introduce them to Mike.

"So, you gonna stay, what, a week or so? See the sights? I won't do Universal Studios. You know that."

"No, cuz, that's okay. I just need a little crash pad for a few days before my trek. On my way to Hong Kong."

"Hong Kong?"

"Yeah, I got a bunch a miles from work, and well, there's Hawaii, too, but eventually Hong Kong." I imagined him in bliss, surrounded by tiny Asian women, his apparent preference.

"Take some pictures for me while you're there," I said, thinking of my picture wall. I needed a photo of him that wasn't so damn compelling.

"Actually, I was hoping I could stay with you a few days and see L.A. again."

I thought about Mike's arrival, and of course it brought back memories, like the ones I was busy constructing for a TV screen. It was distracting, so I went out.

I visited cafés along Santa Monica Boulevard in West Hollywood. Being alone, not taking a meeting. It was nice.

I stopped in a magazine store and picked up a copy of *Details*. There was supposed to be some admiring yet irreverent capsule review of *Boy Nation,* then released on video, written by an old acquaintance I never slept with but should have.

There was a collection of zines and arts journals, so I grabbed one that included a few familiar queer names. I also picked up a *Newsweek,* since there was a cover story on gays. Oh, boy.

I drove home, trying not to dramatize the passing scenery into an underlay for opening credits. But I couldn't help it. The L.A. streets curve too well, the ride is too smooth. It begs an eye.

"Film is how I interpret the world, my Rorschach," I was quoted as saying once too often. I don't need an analyst, like Barry once suggested. Not when I have an archive.

Early January, 1996. Saturday night, a week before pre-production officially began. They were going to give me an office, an environment that had become foreign to me.

I decided to celebrate my last days in a 'boxers and noon shower' lifestyle. I planned a solo evening, without Barry, Jorge or anybody.

I prepared the toys, the music, the lights, the weed, and then lined up my visuals for the evening, spread out, magazine-size canapés. It's like sorting negatives.

Ricky knew I like to save things. Years after the *Manipulator* days, he'd sometimes come over for dinner and go through the blooper version of the trilogy. Good nostalgia requires copious and haphazard documentation.

Before he got too sick to care, Ricky'd started giving me things: personal garage sale items, photos, scrapbooks. I am his unofficial archivist. It doesn't take a fascinating subject. That's the archivist's duty, to maintain an obsession, or at least an interest.

Ricky gave me things he knew his mom and dad wouldn't appreciate, after he'd…well, you know.

His circuit party photos, his List, a stuffed photo album and scribbled description book of most of his sexual conquests, and his Speedo collection. None of the swimwear was his.

I have negatives of trips Ricky and I took to San Francisco, others he took to Hawaii and France, with others now dead or misplaced. In the negatives, pale blue bikini men pose under skies the color of dried blood. I am hesitant to get them printed. After that, I'll know more people who knew him. And what will I do when I recognize their faces? Seek them out in cafes, have reunions, a semblance of chitchat based on the coals of a dead man's fire? Or will I ignore them, pretend no knowledge? I don't like sorting negatives.

One that I did have reprinted though, is from his cousin's baptism. He looks terrific in a suit, holding a month-old baby. He would have been a great dad.

Of course, life is full of would-have-beens, like Bruce Trzcinski, Cub Scout crossing guard back in grade school. I fall in love again with boys I should have kissed a long time ago. Not that I could have saved Ricky, or Bruce, who also died of AIDS but never left Ohio. Now Bruce is just a series of yearbook photos, a shift from cherub to boy to stoner to military to MIA.

Who would it be tonight? Just Ricky? Would I manage to get off and bleed from my dick without leaking from my eyes? Sometimes, porn isn't about finding a fantasy, but forgetting the loss of the fantasies that have come true.

I stripped off my clothes, showered, put on a bathrobe, and purveyed my evening's slightly interactive entertainment.

Before I got my fingers greasy, I got a call from Barry.

"I just wanted to let you know something I've been withholding."

"Oh." It was going to be one of those conversations.

Barry started as usual, bluntly. "I had a relationship with my brother for years. He was gay. He died of AIDS."

"Whoa."

"Yeah, well, you said you thought the screenplay was conflicted. I worked very hard at making it not my story, and you seemed really okay with yours, I mean, which is why I thought to make it an uncle. You know this is your story."

"Yeah, so? I got others. You wanna talk?"

He did. I listened.

Half an hour later, I said, "So, you're okay?"

"Okay."

"Okay."

"Well, I just want to be at a place of peace with you, Stan."

"Well, you are. I mean, don't expect me to be like totally in tune with you at work, though."

"You wanna come over?"

"No, I don't."

"Oh." And then it went on downhill, in a soft-spoken, see you in a few days thing, and well, what was I supposed to do, just run at the flick of a neurosis? I had plans. Why do "alone" plans always have to be dropped?

I smoked a bowl, dove into my mags and memories, and got lost, knowing somewhere in it, an idea, an image, a visual theme for this mon-stah TV movie would pop up, and be the needle for Barry's thread.

Barry fucked his brother? Huh.

I tried to sexualize, eroticize the image, the context, for my own plea-sure. It had too much baggage, so I returned to my magazines.

But while rifling through that night's visuals, I ran across a cologne card insert in *Newsweek*. The smell of it stuck. Even as I tossed it to the floor, the scent of that ad clung to my sheets and fingers. As I reached under my bed for the alphabetically filed porn pile to whip up a night's fantasy, the sex memories took over.

The real ones were always harder to get off with, because the emotions and heartache followed. Jeff Stryker and Lex Baldwin carry no memory. They're mute as posts and just as thick and fuckable. Void of location, tension, or risk, they stand, prongs glistening and jutting from their groins. No, they're not it.

It's that scent. The smell wouldn't go away. I went back into the living room to retrieve the *Newsweek,* and sniffed myself hard.

Cloying, falsely butch, almost sweet and tangy like sap, yet rubbery and cheap, it was the odor of hair tonic, sweaty locker rooms, and truck drivers.

It was the smell of him, my Uncle Sean.

A scent patch of Old Spice.

That night became a sort of olfucktory experience. Having sorted images and a video with men similar to him, I yanked out that experience, for the first time, in a sort of multimedia nasal sex therapy session.

38. dress **pyramids** to **delirious** beauty

As the first of Showtime's 1996 New Directors series, a few suits toured me around their palm tree-laden "campus" and then showed me my "office." After making introductions, they left me with my new "assistant," Katsuo Matamora. She basically ran my life from that moment on. Sorry about the quotation abuse, but nothing about this situation seemed mine, because it wasn't.

Katsuo was about five feet tall, with powerfully serene black eyes and short black hair straight out of a Pantene shampoo commercial. She liked to smile at a few of her own comments, as if showing me she was just kidding. Parked on her desk was a huge round wheel of cards the size of a Goodyear tire. This came to be known as the Power Rolodex.

Katsuo knew simply everyone in the film industry, and a few other industries as well. I wanted to ask why she didn't just start her own company, but she didn't give me time. She also wanted a project with which to reorganize it into a database system, which, when merged with mine, she would provide on disk for my own post-production mailing needs.

"We've already set up an appointment calendar for preliminary auditions," Katsuo said, checking through a list as she sat in my new office, which had extraordinarily bland prints on the wall. I tried to make the desk and chair feel comfortable, but I still felt like Imposter Man.

"Are those actors already filtered through the executives and the casting people here?" I asked.

"Yes."

I looked around my neat little office, unable to tell if the large plant in the corner was real. I made a mental note to check for listening devices.

"Can we get around that?"

"You want to get some of your friends in?"

"An open call."

"Do you need to insulate your house with headshots?"

"No," I smiled. "I just want to get some fresher faces, you know?" I wasn't sure why, but I didn't want TV faces. I wanted faces people could believe were the characters, not faces they associated with bathroom cleansers.

Katsuo sighed for comic effect. "Okay, but we gotta go through their channels first. They've already got some lined up who've worked with them before. The kid part's first. Then the parents."

"Oh, great."

"I'll help you with that stuff, too."

"You mean you'll attend the auditions?"

"Sure, if you want."

"Yes, I want."

Katsuo screwed up her face. "You making fun?"

"No. Sorry."

"Seriously, anything else you need?"

"Um, you got any of those Madonna headphones for the phone?"

She smirked before leaving. "Bottom right hand drawer. And no, you don't get a cell."

The tension dropped. I was in capable hands.

I had started watching a lot of television, sorting through faces, taking down notes to figure out if I could find some actors worth using. I wasn't going to go through reels or agent pitches. I wanted some new faces, good actors, people who'd done their homework.

Somewhere in the middle of all this and a leftover pizza dinner, and too many cans of soda, I saw a shampoo commercial. The actor, whose thick hair and muscled arms sold their product, looked familiar. Could that have been someone I knew? His face remained obscured by close-ups of his hair. I recall making a note about the brand, then in the midst of that night's distracted scribblings and storyboard shufflings, I forgot to see about tracking down the ad company that might have helped me find that handsome face.

Casting through Showtime went through a sieve-like process that usually ended up with me sitting in a silent, climate-controlled office, with people I sort of remembered selling cars and cooking oils. Some of them were great, especially the kid, Brendan Ivers, who I cast after only a few minutes. I was hoping for a sixteen-year-old Jason/Jeremy London and I got him. Barry and the producer and the network person and Katsuo were all just grinning so much after he left. Kids can do that when you don't have to deal with them every day.

Barry said to Katsuo something about being relieved to have cast the kid's role, and one of the suits said something about being glad not to have to cast a pet, that their agents were worse. The joke wasn't funny, but others laughed.

"What's that?" Barry asked. I flashed back to that summer in *Gypsy*, where the cast was mostly dogs and kids.

"'Never work with dogs or kids.' That wasn't Gypsy Rose Lee."

"W. C. Fields," said the suit, whose name, I re-remembered, was Alan.

The process continued over two days. Faces, chats, every fifteen minutes. More coffee? No, thanks. Bla. It was doing okay, I guess, but it wasn't going to get the leads. I wasn't going to find the uncle.

A week after Katsuo placed a small ad in *Variety,* four stuffed mailbags arrived. After dumping them in my office, she said, "Don't expect me to sort these." I had to drag them out to the parking lot to the Dart's trunk like bodies.

Home again with some very old Bowie on the CD player, I began to sort.

Men to the left, Women to the right. Kids in the middle, just in case. Then old men, old women. Then cute men, cute women. Wife-type women, then not-psychotically cute kids, then really cute men, then … wait.

Lance Holtzer.

Now an adult. Ruddy, a man, but still, it was him.

I checked his resumé. Yes, he was the shampoo guy. And yes, "B.F.A. in Theatre, Brookside College 1976."

Lance Holtzer.

Tulsa.

I still had another two bags to go through, but I called Katsuo's voice-mail at the studio and gave her his number.

This was the reason I had come this far. He was the only reason for any of this success. I was determined not to fuck it up.

I wanted to call Barry, anyone, to celebrate, to scream, to shout with joy.

But then I calmed down, realizing the implications of letting Barry know why I had to have Lance cast.

No. It had to be my secret. Maybe he wouldn't recognize me. Maybe I could keep the secret all to myself.

And maybe I could suddenly turn straight and father six kids. Yeah, right.

I settled with screaming for joy and playing the CD of the original cast recording of *Gypsy* at full blast.

I prayed. Please, God… please, Ethel… until I see him, do not let him get hit by a bus. Or worse, get a series.

When I got in the next morning, late again, Katsuo was finishing up a grid to input cast info: addresses, phone 'n' fax, birthdays. I had to thank the very muted gray walls of the studio. She was worth every cent of their money.

"Called Lance Holtzer first, like you asked." Katsuo smiled. "We can put him in next week at one-thirty."

"Can we bump that to tomorrow's group?"

She rolled her eyes, then made a deal. "You get to pick the bumpee."

I agreed, took my mail after Katsuo stopped me on my way into the office. She said, "He's probably the one, right? The gay uncle?"

I smiled as if she'd caught me stealing bagels again. "What makes you say that?"

That night I stayed up late, a sectioned-off script splayed across the kitchen table. I thought I would get something done, but all I ended up doing was staring at Lance's headshot, then going outside to smoke another cigarette under my tattered awning made from that twenty-year-old piece of muslin scenery.

My neighbor stepped outside, perhaps to water her plants. I ducked behind the flat, cupped the glow of the cigarette in my hand. I was hiding. It was my little space for smoking, hiding from the OJ helicopters, the Tobacco Police.

The possibility of having Lance back in my life made me nervous, queasy, hopeful. I thought I might fix things, redo what went wrong.

If it had been him that first time, how different might I be now?

So, why did I fall apart because it was the wrong person? Or just that there was someone to do it? I was getting a chance to be with Lance. All those years of filming had reached a point. Once again, I was "It."

I had asked for a bulletin board wall in my office. I got it, plus a thousand pins, for storyboarding. It was like planning a battle in space. I got more toys and things to make me want to go to the office. Then people started bringing me stuff along with lists and charts. They started bringing little gifts. It was a way of softening me up to agree with whatever concessions they were offering for my approval.

I looked around at the dinosaurs and action figures it was rumored I collected. I didn't want Lance to think of me as still a kid. I thought of swiping the dolls away.

Why was I so nervous? Why such pretense, making sure Katsuo never told Lance my name until the last minute? Why was I sponging the plant as if I were due a room inspection from a drill sergeant?

"He's here," she said as she popped her head in the door.

"Okay," I said.

"Bring him in?"

"I said okay!"

"All right." She gave me a look that said, *like you're the one auditioning?*

His face was still a cherub's, but like the man said, time is a thief and gravity's a vandal.

"Hi."

"Hi, Lance, glad you could make it." We shook hands.

"I didn't get your name. Um, Katsa? Katsi wouldn't tell me."

"Katsuo. And I'm sorry, I didn't want to scare you. Yet."

"Huh?"

"I'm Stan Grozniak."

At first, nothing registered, then his smile twisted sort of sideways until his mouth hung open. His eyes sharpened as he stared, looking for the fourteen-year-old boy inside my chubby face. I saw Lance dig into my eyes and just remember stuff. Newsboy songs from another life, the kid whose sailor pants he yanked up behind a flat every night for three glorious weeks.

We were still shaking hands when he said, "Stan Grozniak? *The* Stan Grozniak? From Brookside?"

"None other."

"Oh my god. Jesus fuckin' Christ."

"I guess you're no longer a bible thumper."

He burst into laughter, came closer, and we hugged. He patted my back in a very friendly way.

"I can't believe it."

"Neither can I. I called my assistant the second I got your headshot."

I do remember pulling away a bit too soon from our hug. It wasn't a purely sexual energy, but more as if The Muse had entered me. All of a sudden, no matter what might happen between us, I really wanted to make this a good film.

It reminded me of some other artist friends, one a painter who said he found the man of his dreams by painting him first.

"So, you just wanted to see if I was still alive?" Lance chuckled.

"No, no. I want you to read for a part. I got a movie."

"Of course ya do, Stan Din. I'm jus' jokin.'"

Yeah, a joke, just playing, like when you cradled me in your arms and patted my butt. "Sit down, sit down."

"Thanks."

I noticed the dark tanned nape of Lance's neck. He surfed or got outside a lot. He looked like Jan-Michael Vincent if he'd taken care of himself. He looked like Apollo's stepson. He looked like...

Don't get me started.

As I sat behind the desk, I joked about my newly installed mess, and Lance gave me some gossip about other auditions, his life, then asked about my life. We each had that down to fifty words. You have to around here. But I wanted to move, be professional, doncha know.

I handed him a section of the script, his scene with his sister. "I want you to read for one of the leads in a Showtime movie I'm directing."

"Didn't you do *Boy Nation*?"

"Yeah. I also did a trilogy called *The Manipulator*. J'ever meet an actor named Rick Dacker?"

"No. I never saw those."

"Anyway..."

"Oh, see, I never even thought of putting it together. I'm sorry ... I, I'm just—"

"I know. It's pretty weird, isn't it?"

I was quivering. I wanted a cigarette, but the nearest smoking facility was in Redondo. I tried to focus on my goals, my fears. Lance was still so goddamn handsome, only now we were both men. I wanted to be on even terms, but in the back of my head, I thought, he's got a promise to keep.

"So, um, what's the film about?"

"Well," I said. "It's a family story, and you're the brother of this kid's mother. And you and the kid have an affair of sorts."

Lance's face fell. I really saw the years since that closing night party seep into the room. The gap. The time.

"Oh, a gay role."

"Yeah. One of two. There's also a lesbian friend, but it's only alluded to."

"But I would play the heavy."

I leaned back, trying to be honest, or at least trying to remember what I was telling at the time, and the possibility of further changing the intonation of Barry's script to please this gentleman, who was also one of my childhood heroes and gods.

"I would say, think more *For a Lost Soldier*. Totally sympathetic."

"But it'll still get grilled because this is for, what, HBO?"

"Showtime."

"Oh."

"One broadcast?"

"With repeats and two-year option for rebroadcast, after which video rights, shared, will be optioned. My agent wants to buy them out, but he wants to wait. You get points on that."

"Whoa."

"Sorry, Lance. It's just the good coffee here, and the fact that I will move heaven and earth to work with you again. Is that a problem?"

"No, it's just ... I don't know if I'm ready for a role like this."

"I understand. It's, uh, a pretty heavy story, but we have ways of making even family strife entertaining."

"It sounds like it might be a problem. But damn, I need the work."

I understood Lance's problem, the impossibility of getting farther while having a GAY attachment. How would this play in Idaho? Why don't I just make more off-the-cuff art pieces like *Boy Nation*? Send 'em off to Europe, or even Taiwan, where I can do a *Manipulator* circuit and sell Rick Dacker/Parker Parrish action figures. They love me in Taiwan, I swear.

"Well, um, things have really come a long way you know, since, I dunno, Reagan."

"Yeah, sure," Lance said with a shrug. "Everybody's gay these days, er, out at least."

"You wanna give it a shot?"

"Sure."

I grabbed the scene I wanted from the script. "I'll let you prepare, or whatever, then Katsuo will read the other parts. You're gonna have to do this again with some other people, the producer, some executive suits."

"Oh, that's okay."

"Okay, well, um, I'll just ..." I went for the door. "Go get some water, and we'll be back."

I stepped outside. Katsuo was on the phone but gave me a wide grin. When I came back from the kitchen area, I waited for her to finish her call and wrangle a suit, since there had to be company reps present, then I took them in. We sat. Lance stood.

He read beautifully. Just a sweet trace of his Southern accent slipped in, like a bit of honey in lemonade. I was already planning the script changes to make it a semi-Southern family. Anything to get him hired, to get my hero to be in my little Mexican puppet show.

I thanked Katsuo and she excused herself. The suit shook Lance's hand and left.

On our way out, I said, "I'm gonna fight with them to get you in."

"Why?"

"I just want to see you working, see a bit of Then mixed in with Now. It works for this project."

"You also want to make what you want to have happened happen, right?"

I stuttered a moment. "Isn't that what art's all about?"

"Look," Lance looked to the door, turning back to speak softly. "I'd rather this not be how we met up again. But if you remember, I told you once I'd wait until you were older."

"Well, I haven't been carded in a bar for quite a few years, so I guess it's okay now."

"Well, good."

"But, um… don't tell people how we know each other … yet."

"You think it might be done up the wrong way?"

"Maybe. I'm more concerned about you than my friends."

"Why? I should think they'd find it kinda romanic." He said it that way, without the t.

"Roman-ic." I mimicked.

"I'm sorry, I always get my accent back when I'm relaxin'."

"I didn't mean to tease," I said, still smiling, happy I had. "I really, really miss it. Your voice, you know, a voice like that."

"Wahl Ghhooo-oo-leee!" Gomer Pyle. "Ahl tawk all ya lawk."

Fortunately, he stopped after that. I also told him to not let it creep him out while we were shooting.

"Huh, whatever you say, mister director."

"Please."

"Well, you are the director."

"Yes, and the monkey will be buried at midnight, Miss Desmond."

After he left, I stood silently, ignoring the damp sweat under my arms and down my back. I longed to rip off my shirt and dance, whirl into a dervish of joy.

I'd found Tulsa.

A Brief History of the Midway Drive-In Theater

After the Native Americans were slaughtered, and before the great glacier that shaped the basin known as Northern Ohio pushed its way through what is now the no-man's land between Brookside and two smaller cities, the piece of real estate that came to be the setting of the MidWay Drive-In Theatre was a chunk of not very successful farm land owned by German settlers by the name of Schronk. There were a few houses built on it in the 1910s, when a land boom led to more rural development around Brookside. However, in excessively rainy seasons, the land, located near the Penawka River, frequently flooded.

The rather boggy land was sold again in the early 1950s, when a man with a vision, Harry Walbrook, decided to build a drive-in movie theatre. Various town elders grumbled protests, claiming it would crumble the morals of the community.

Fortunately, Mister Walbrook's property was located between Brookside and the nearby township of Mifflin, so the town elders couldn't say much anyway.

Mister Walbrook decided to call his Drive-In Theater the Midway, since it was midway between the two towns. He was eventually honored for providing new construction business in two counties. The design of the theatre was a tribute to the Deco era, with gargantuan curves framing the forty-foot marquee on the back of the immense screen built of wood and steel. Mister Walbrook had his structure painted an emerald green, and the screen painted three times in titanium white "for maximum viewing pleasure," he was quoted as saying.

In order to get people used to the concept of watching a film in their cars, Walbrook allowed free admission the first week of opening on a June weekend of 1955, where fireworks were shown between a double feature of an Yvonne DeCarlo film, *Flame of the Islands*, and what was billed in the *Brookside Gazette* as the Family Classic, *The Wizard of Oz*.

The popularity of the Midway Drive-In was such that Mister Walbrook continued booming business through the autumn of that year, culminating in the showing of a less than cheery film that the Brookside Downtown Cinema refused to screen, citing it as immoral. It was a called *Rebel Without a Cause*.

Mister Walbrook continued his run of quality films, including, as the 1960s changed even rural culture, many occasionally progressive films, such as *Little Murders*, and *Getting Straight*, as an Elliot Gould double feature.

Many of Brookside's young parents, starved for culture with children to raise, let their kids enjoy themselves on the swing set and jungle gym that were installed on the grassy yard at the base of the immense screen. The swing set was dismantled though, after a series of accidents that occurred, specifically between two boys, brothers, who were admitted to Brookside Hospital in their pajamas. One had been released with a minor concussion and the other with a sprained wrist.

Following Mister Walbrook's death in the 1972, the Midway Theatre fell into a state of decline, due mostly to inept management by Walbrook's son, Denny Walbrook, who was often detained at the county jail for providing alcohol to minor girls whom he entertained in his private booth behind the snack stand.

Faced with the financial burden of police payoffs and divorce proceedings, hounded by alimony and child support payments, Denny Walbrook's desperate measures to gain audiences included an all-night festival of all five *Planet of the Apes* movies. A number of teenagers were detained for consumption of alcohol, specifically one group that called itself the Dead Cat Society. They were found drinking alcoholic beverages in the back cab of a truck owned by a Todd Hess.

In 1977, there followed a period of closure, until the destitute Walbrook sold the Drive-In and the land for $15,000 cash. The subsequent owner, Clifford Chelton, owned two other theatres in the Northern Ohio area, and proceeded to reap a tidy sum by altering the content of his Drive-Ins to adult films.

In 1978, the Brookside Police, rumored to have been taking payoffs to keep from closing the Drive-In, decided to do a check for minors. Among the almost twenty juveniles detained were a Stanley Grozniak, 17, of Brookside, and Todd Hess, 19, also of Brookside. The two boys were charged with indecent exposure and lewd conduct, but the charges were dropped. Todd Hess served thirty days in Brookside County Jail for possession of marijuana.

The Midway Drive-In closed in 1983, lay dormant for eleven years. Somewhere in the middle of that time period, a number of vandalisms occurred, including the theft of three lenses, a few moldy posters, several projector reels, and over fifty-seven portable speakers made by the Projected Sound Company of Plainfield, Indiana.

ACT IV

"You're nobody
'til everybody in this town
thinks you're a bastard."
—Elvis Costello, "This Town"

"Each man delights in the work that suits him best."
—Homer, *The Odyssey*

40. Shaman winter mystery cooking for Bigfoot:

juice bones in chocolate fluff ing
group part of spring garden Ouija petals
water them
place sausage behind objects
and manipulate finger apparatus
incubate in combustion demon circles
fiddle above repulsive fire
boil
heat & eat

```
Say Uncle - synopsis/Barry's draft 1
```

(need: Mom family character names revised to Southern-sounding)

Say Uncle is a family drama about how a Midwestern family deals with their oldest son's incest experience.

When Ken becomes affectionate with him, the boy is shocked. Although he does have strong desires for the man, he doesn't know how to act on them.

The mother's family is from ~~Southern California~~, very conservative, and her gay brother, a sort of drifter, arrives at their home between journeys in the Far East. He fascinates Mother's young son, whose questioning sexuality has Father disturbed, trying to make him do more masculine things like playing basketball.

Uncle tells Kid stories. They go out together, but Mother warns her son about Uncle, saying he's gay, to which the son blurts, "~~Yeah, well, so am I, which is why I like him.~~"

The parents get upset when they think the two have made love. They get separated, but the boy begs parents to let him stay.

Then, on a day when Uncle'll be leaving, Kid sneaks into his room, where they make love.

Uncle goes away ~~and writes a few letters to Kid~~.

The family recovers from the discovery, the father ~~beats~~ scolds the son, but later apologizes.

The family comes to an uneasy truce, and goes to a therapy session together. Then (what? Act III not dev.)

Say Uncle - synopsis/Stan & Barry's draft 2

From the first scene, we are made aware that the family's oldest son, Brandon, is harboring deep problems.

His parents, however, are clueless. All seems well as Marcia, the boy's mother, keeps the family busy helping out as they prepare for a Labor Day weekend visit from her brother, Matthew.

Marcia's family is from Southern Tennessee, very conservative. When Marcia's brother Matthew comes to visit after his tour in the Air Force, Brandon is confused about his mixed feelings for his uncle, whom he romanticized from pictures and letters sent as a child. They work out together, and Brandon becomes embarrassed by their close contact.

Matthew's attempts to talk to Marcia about her son being gay are thwarted when Marcia's husband, Ron, overhears the conversation. Tension develops between the two men.

Through a strange sort of agreement, Marcia finds the time to leave Matthew and Brandon alone for an afternoon. Brandon waits for his family to leave and goes to Matthew's bedroom, where they make love.

After Matthew leaves, Brandon seems better adjusted. The tension of Ron's disapproval looms, though, particularly when he asks his son to do work in their garage, only to find him smoking pot.

He becomes grounded, tries to run away, but when he tries to contact Matthew, his uncle tells him to go home and work it out.

Brandon does, and is seen talking to Brett, a boy from his school who is rumored to be gay. ~~They go to the prom together and live happily ever after with bunnies and chipmunks and birdies and~~

Jan 15, 1996
1937: Margaret O'Brien is born

Favorite Christmas Gift from my new production crew: a Hollywood calendar from Janice, the production manager, with daily birthdays of movie magic celebrities. We love Janice.

When the location gal took Barry, me, Janice, and Eric Liu, the director of photography, to see the house, we'd already seen photos, but driving into the neighborhood made me feel as if we were actually moving in, which we were, in a way.

Janice Constantine made the loveliest grids.

She was my assistant producer for *Say Uncle*, the TV movie I thought I would live to cherish but which nearly killed my spirit. She'd also been my production manager on *Manipulator III*. I felt secure in her printouts, her sense of time, of seeing a calendar as blocks to be eaten like cheese, sliced delicately and savored.

Janice was as efficient as her hair was crazed, like Gilda Radner on a frazzled day or Hildebrant brothers ringlets when she found time to style it. I could stare at her grids, and her gloriously hennaed ringlets for hours. They gave me the secure illusion the film could be made on time and on budget, and with her cheerfulness, even in the midst of a bloodbath.

Janice is part of the rumor about me being bisexual. I think it's cool. Gay guys who wanna fuck me give me this angry look sometimes, those that believe the crap about me inning myself. I heard about it, let it ride, then waited until just before the *Say Uncle* opening. What do you think that picture of me at the *OutFest* party smacking Lance a big wet one was all about?

I had to re-out myself. We have to do these things again and again.

Janice still has the clippings on her fridge. Since she's a line producer, she doesn't get many upfront perks. Although she only spoke of men with curt half-jokes, she's straight, not that she wouldn't have made a good lesbian. I told her that once, and she laughed. I think she liked giving herself an air of sexual orientation mystery, since all the men around her were determined to remind everyone else of their desires with every comment.

Only after getting her masters in Behavioral Studies did Janice realize she loved crunching numbers and schedules and making things work, like operas.

For example, there was a scene in Barry's draft of the script that involved dozens of extras, students, teachers, and cars. Janice had it marked with a Post-it, one of many pages, before even signing with us. She'd suggested a simple dual scene with Brandon's character and another student, a sympathetic girl who wants to date him, but knows she can't. The cluttered original scene was reduced to one small hallway in our rented school, with a few extras shuffling by out of focus. With that one suggestion, Janice would end up saving us about twelve thousand dollars. As she'd said, "Moviemaking is a balance of creativity, budget limitations, and logistics."

"*Manipulator* was different," she'd warned me, and I knew. It had been a party.

Nevertheless, I was really glad Janice decided to join my team again. When she'd signed her contract at a lunch someone else paid for, Janice and I got to know each other again. It was fun and serious, schedule stuff, and we got a lot done. When Janice had her first meeting with Katsuo, they told me bluntly that they were pretty much going to talk about me and how to make me work best, so I was dismissed.

After they'd colluded on the best way to deal with what was fast becoming their little bro, we set about finding a home.

Oh, and a Suit from the studio came. Janice's ex-sister-in-law met us there.

Barry drove. So did Malcolm Washburn, our director of photography. When the Suit heard Barry had a four-runner, and he was thinking of buying one, he jokingly demanded to ride with us.

Janice and I sat in the back, like kids.

The budget had limited us to a hundred-mile radius. We wanted mid-middle class, but after turning down the thrice-lived *Donna Reed/Outer Limits/Wonder Years* neighborhood, we had to hunt.

Janice's ex-sister-in-law is in real estate, so she saved the location manager a lot of time.

We like Janice.

"Am I the sister you never had?" she had said earlier that day as we sat before her computer, composing shooting schedules, comparing drive times between the last of three potential home set locations while scarfing down the remnants of her homemade sesame noodles.

This was a reminder from the last *Manipulator* shoot in 1989. Janice liked to smoke indoors. With her, I did, too. We shared. Janice smoked her cigarettes like joints, savoring them after a good conversational point or while a spreadsheet was printing, the needed smoke for another idea cooking in her mind.

"No, I never had a sister." I'd said, thinking about Baby June, wondering how long I could stretch the truth before I re-altered it for comfort's sake.

"Oh, sorry."

"But you're a good replacement."

I was high on the blossoms of California tropical plants and working with an old friend. The house hunt was in full gear.

"So, how do you feel about working on a project like this, Janice?"

"Huh? Oh, it's great."

"No, I don't need cheerleading, yet. Try it when I'm being knocked down like Joe Montana on a rainy football field."

"Huh?"

"What do you think of the content?"

"Oh." She stopped, cut off by the arrival of Barry and the Suit. We were moving out.

Wind swept us as we rode. In a gesture that has become part of our secret language over the years, she pulled her flickering hair once more under a baseball cap with the efficiency of any minor leaguer, then merely darted her eyes toward the back of the Suit's head, leering, asking, *So, what do you think? Homo? Asshole?*

I dismissed her glance. Even if he was queer, I wasn't interested. She should get to know him, that is if he would just shut up already from talking cars with Barry.

"I had a little experience myself," she said. I waited until I remembered her habit of pausing discussions until later, after she'd thought of the best response. We were talking about The Thing, incest, the film's theme.

"I dealt with it, and I think this project might help others. It's going to be very difficult to make it entertaining, to keep people watching. But it's something that needs to be said."

"Let's just hope they don't turn the channel."

"Or beat their kids."

"Or fuck their kids."

"Oh, you're awful."

Our laughter distracted the Tonka truck talk up front. The guys smiled. Barry called out, "You guys having fun?"

"Always," I answered, taking in Barry's glare from the rearview mirror. I knew what it meant. Behave. The executive is among us.

A solid white classic American post-colonial with a brief front porch, big windows with blue shutters, an expansive backyard and neat garage, the house sat comfortably amid a block of homes the location gal said had also been used for films. She'd even mentioned them. It came furnished, for which we would have to pay extra, plus the cost of paying for the family to get out of the house for a month.

"They're going to Europe," the location gal said.

"How wonderful," I piped up in a slightly insincere way. Sure they were going to Europe. Wouldn't you, if you were getting ten thousand dollars a week to leave home?

The house wasn't exactly what we wanted, but the other ones available were too nice. This one was a bit worn around the edges. It had the look and feel of a perfect middle class white family with a few skeletons in the closet, the appropriate setting for an Ozzie and Harriet nightmare.

Marla Shoener, the set decorator, arrived later, brought a camera and took copious notes. We made jokes about Ethan Allen and Williams Sonoma as we made up a dream shopping list. She knew all the best rental places. "Oh, honey, it's perfect," we joked while Barry looked askance. I felt sympatico with Marla, having arranged many a set in my younger days. I felt a pang of sadness after leaving the place. "I can't wait to make this the unhappiest place on the block," I joked.

"It has a happy ending," Barry reminded me, making sure the Suit heard.

"A hopeful ending, not a happy one," I corrected. "Happy endings are sunsets and basketball players lifted on shoulders of cheering crowds. Hopeful is tearful hugs and wiping eyes. That's yours."

"Okay, whatever."

He left me upstairs with Malcolm. I helped him take measurements for the tight shots required for a set without a detachable fourth wall. We poked into the bedrooms as the location gal made coffee down in the kitchen.

Something was bugging Barry, but I wasn't going to argue with him like fighting brothers in our new home.

What sold me on the place was the boy's room; a simple bed, some posters of REM and Nirvana on the wall. The bookshelf had just one trophy. The rest was packed away in boxes stuffed into a small closet. It was as if the son knew strangers were on their way in, and he'd closed himself off except for these few decorative items.

Maybe it was just the smell, the warmth, small things I knew wouldn't translate to film, but I could see our teen actor Brendan sitting in this room, lying on this bed, going through the emotions and events of Barry's story, my story. Malcolm stepped into the room delicately and leaned down, grazing his hand along the bedspread as if petting a jittery lamb.

He purred. "Perfect."

I agreed.

The invasion commenced on the Ides of January, in the Year of Our Lord 1996.

We'd taken over a small motel ten minutes from the house. It's amazing how a highway can slice a town into two such different zones. Happy green leaves north, and strip mall-o-rama south. I forget how many affairs hopped hotel rooms. I can't keep track.

Cables trailed up and down doorways like washed up snakes. Men installed things, moving furniture to accommodate more cables and angles from the shot list I thought I had set in stone in pre-production meetings, but which seemed to get less and less clear as angles began to not work, or sunlight refused to obey.

I was trying to make the equipment as invisible as possible to get the first shot out of the way; a very long rove through the house, where the camera follows Brendan from walking home through what would be the opening credits, walking up the sidewalk to give a great view of the house, going in the front door, passing through the kitchen to grab a snack, finding no one home, going upstairs to his bedroom and flopping down on the bed, where he sits a few moments, then inexplicably bursts into tears.

It was tough enough for Brendan to start off like that, to act assured and relaxed, do about seven different things, then just burst into tears over what seems to the viewer to have no cause. Of course it *is* something. It's what starts off the whole film. It's what will keep the viewer watching, wondering what is wrong. What will happen?

I'd rarely concerned myself with such devices in my work, because all my previous viewers had either paid to see it in a theatre or at home. This time, they would have an option, dozens of options. That's why Barry's script intrigued me. He knew hooks.

But since the shot moved, we had to light the whole house. I'd jokingly argued with Malcolm about the modern cliché of opening rove shots. He rattled off a dozen films I'd seen and not seen that started with such a shot, including a Blaxploitation movie his father worked on. Filmmaking was a family thing for him.

"But it works," he'd said as he agreed to hire the Steadicam operator back in pre-production. But SteadiCam guys charged over a thousand a day, and if I wanted my money's worth I needed to arrange all the shots in a row. That messed up my hopes to keep shots in some semblance of theatrical order, at least in acts.

We'd wanted a SteadiCam shot for the scene where Brendan gets chased by his father for getting stoned in the garage, but that took place months after the first scene. I'd wanted Brendan to start off healthy-looking and lose weight from depression. The shots wouldn't match.

He and Jorge came to the agreement that we could shoot the running shot without close-ups, plus they could get extra large clothes and just sallow up his face a bit with makeup. The shot also had to be done that day, both of them, because the entire cast and crew wanted January 28 off for some ridiculous thing called the Super Bowl.

All this dodging and adjusting and planning for one frigging shot! Brendan wasn't the only one who'd be in tears.

We went for a dual set-up, having the inside lit properly, with the garage and Dad on standby. The only thing we'd have to do was take the outside reflectors off the exterior windows and the "running down the driveway" shot would work.

This all took five days.

We didn't get a take worth saving until Saturday, January 27.

Here are the characters. Each of the following is a block on the board. Gain two points for every alternative move forward:

  * In a rehearsal
  * Brendan/the Kid comes to the set stoned. (Back two steps)
  * Lance/the Uncle is being strange, but not stoned. (Lose a turn) Makes a comment about my smoking. I quit for the day.
  * Exec/Prod-Writer's cell phone dies (Two points for you)
  * Barry, the Exec/Prod-Writer and you out to dinner. The network pays. (Five points)
  * Lance comes by. He is with another man (Lose a turn).
  * Talk with Barry about Lance. Explain our mutual history. Make up and vow to at least get along, then decide to go home and fuck like dogs...

Jan 27
1921: Donna Reed

...until Barry asks, mid-thrust, "Ja fuck him yet?"

"No." I scowled.

"Will ya?"

"I don't know."

Barry waited. "Well, then, can I fuck him?"

I rolled over and got up to sit on his chest. He needed to be smacked around. I'd allowed him to think he was wooing me back to his arms and home and bed, but it wasn't working for me.

"No!" I shouted.

"Why not?"

I gave up my horse ride. Barry heaved beneath my legs and relaxed his ribcage. "He's different."

"He's an actor. What do you expect?"

"I just—hell, it's been too long."

"He's not positive, is he?"

"No." I actually didn't know. I lost my boner and peeled off him.

"Not that I should worry. I think you know what the rules are."

"And I think you know what the rules are, too." We had realized one day, or rather over the course of a few weeks into our fuck buddy relationship, that we would not be exclusive, but we wouldn't make a big deal about our outside endeavors, except if they ended up especially juicy and worthy of gossip.

But Lance wasn't like that. I'd never slept with my performers before. I'd always hated the tangled itchiness of sex with co-workers, except, of course, my Manipulator, the cocky and suave Ricky, God rest his sexy soul.

I made a point of seeing non-industry people. That's why Barry was special, and I didn't want to fuck it up. Barry did his own thing. His writing stuff kept him in his world, away from today. His only interest in culture started with the remote, the difficult to acquire, the secret fact lost in journals of gay historians and academics.

He worshipped dead Hollywood. Living Hollywood was a bright and silly backdrop to him, and I liked his air of superiority and benign amusement at my TV tales. He admired my spotty career, and that made his company utterly relaxing. Our collaboration was as easy as the early days with my brother. We just barreled through it, pretending we didn't care what anyone thought.

"So, you were both newsboys?"

"We were both Tulsa."

"Oh." Then he got it, the distance, the relativity. "Oooh. Tell me about it."

"Barry, I'm tired. Let's just sleep."

"Tell me about it."

I thought of providing an edited version, then gave in. I shared it all, every dressing room epiphany. He never really looked at Lance the same way after that.

Jan 28 (Super Bowl Sunday)
1934: Alan Alda

Barry was at his computer when I woke up. I went into the kitchen naked, hoping he'd find me and perhaps ravage me. He didn't. I put on my shorts and made coffee.

One of the things that bugged me about Barry was how he always wanted to share his work with his writer's group. I thought, why not just cut off your own arm for the sharks instead of swimming in the water?

What he got out of it were critiques that basically left he and I shifting story ideas. A bit more of my experience came into it, and then we'd share it, and try to find what remained the same between us. Little things ended up being pared away for the sake of story, plot movement.

Barry got a lot of flack from his group, but he has a novel or three sitting in that filing cabinet he keeps closed but not locked, and I would hate to think I never might have gotten a chance to have so much fun just doing something because I loved it because some committee-think dismissed my impulsive creative choices.

During shooting of *The Manipulator II*, we added a boat chase simply because one of the grips knew a guy who owned a boat and acted, and it worked and nobody got hurt and we all had lobster that night by a campfire near a lake in some park the location guy found. I remember the lobster. The caterer got two marriage proposals that night. I think Ricky and I flirted with moving in together. That night we ran off, our fingers coated in corn and lobster butter, and wanked each other off behind a rock while everybody else was by the campfire. This would be what Barry calls a meander from the storyline. This would be what I call one of the precious jewels of my romantic necklace.

Segue insert: summer camp scene in *Addams Family Values*: blonde girl about to be burned at the stake by Wednesday (Christina Ricci).
CUT TO: *Metropolis*. Hel, outside a church, burning at the stake.

Jan 30
1931: Gene Hackman

The loft was comfortably airy, yet drafty enough to remind me of an empty theatre stage. Even though we'd already completed the opening shot, I begged Janice for a read-through, with only crew heads watching, cast sitting at tables, or walking around if they liked. I wanted everyone to get a sense of flow, and bring a raw line interpretation. I wanted to form a company. There were grumbles, and union things had to be squared away, but it got done. We did a reading. People had already done some homework. I could tell.

The read-through really worked. I wish it could have been a play, too. I wish I could have done all I wanted to do for these people. I wish a lot.

"Okay," I said when the script person read Fade to Black. Roll Credits, and the crew clapped! After it subsided, I said to everyone, "Well, I'm hoping you'll all be around when we cast the musical version."

With that, a few folks began to kick up heels, and others laughed, and others ducked out for a cigarette. "Mom," Penelope Laughlin, a fine actress with a lot of soap experience, and "Dad," Dennis Haley, who had quite a few musicals and a Ford Ranger commercial among his credits, made plans to do scenes together. The kid, Brendan, shook my hand and sort of flirted, I couldn't tell then. Lance disappeared after saying he'd call, and others talked and made plans for dates before the next shoot day. Barry went off with Edmund and then I left, too.

Basically, we'd all signed on to be a family for a while. But we were also at work. We would immerse ourselves in each other. We would become what each of us complained about when we got home to our lovers and spouses and roommates and cats and hopefully, somebody, if not a long distance friend. Who would these people talk to when they talked about me?

Feb 1
1901: Clark Gable

"It seems everyone is an incest survivor."

"The TV is glutted with the talk. *Sally-Jesse, Oprah*."

"They've got five channels in the console room at the editing facility in Culver City. I sit there at lunch some days, just to give me something to shake my head at."

Eric Liu, the editor, his assistant, Steve, and a post audio guy and I were smoking and eating, and drinking beers. We were getting to like each other. We had to, for the duration. The suits were already inspecting the first week's dailies.

The suits had suggestions. The edit team had suggestions.

I was keeping my cool.

I listened to them talk about It, their little events, their versions of It. Eric said he had circle jerks with all four of his brothers, two of whom are gay, but he still prefers women. It only made me want him more.

Why do I look back on those times as a void where I wanted to be seduced by older men? Why is not getting seduced traumatic? Maybe I'll start a twelve-step group, Survivors of Incest Who Really Wanted It.

Sure, it's a bad thing. I should be lucky Daddy never abused me and Mommy never forced me to feel her up, or brother never shoved his big old ugly dick in me, but I wanted something, surely. I knew what the neighbor boy had when he pissed in the creek and saw me watching. What harm would it have done if he'd let me touch it? What was all the fuss about, besides the book sales?

I could spend days without Barry and know it's okay. Whine "Fuck me, Daddy" and know it wasn't him, but the sound of it fit our script sometimes. That was a comfort. He didn't want to see me when I got in a slump, or just go off on some wild project. He didn't want to "manage a relationship," his words. And we've talked about my uncle and all that happened.

I didn't think I needed therapy. He didn't push it, another achievement. But put one or two together, and it all locks back in. It was only with the availability of that magazine that smelled of him, that I finally realized it was only cheap Old Spice, and I could jerk my dick into a furtive frenzy and not feel guilty, not feel dirty, not feel tainted or as cheap as the cologne. I could just get off and get it over with.

Feb 10
1929: Charles Laughton marries Elsa Lanchester

Jorge and I were set to meet with Edmund and a few others to screen the rough first half. It was being edited as I shot. It made me nervous. I think it was supposed to make me scared.

Barry was late. Edmund wanted to talk about things, he said, basically see if we had our act together. Edmund was actually not in yet, either, but he called from his car phone. Jorge and I were served up nicely by his houseman, Bippy, or Beppe, who was replacing Romano, who was away somewhere, I forget. We lounged indoors.

We were spying framed photographs of Edmund as a very swank young Navy boy, circa WWII. Arm in arm, with three different guys, he was a picture of handsomeness. I couldn't wait to hear the tragic stories of all the boys.

"This guy I slept with," I leaned into Jorge's ear, "kept his sailor cap on." Jorge and I could talk about sex the way chefs discuss sauce recipes. The subject we were supposed to discuss was costumes for the movie to go with the publicity shots. I wanted to maintain an army of conspirators in my work.

"You did a sailor recently?" Jorge asked.

"Naw. It was years ago. Uniform night at some club."

"Why do you never name these clubs and go with me?"

"Because it'd be like taking your sister to a hockey game."

Jorge hissed. "So?"

"So, as we got into it, I let him go in the bathroom while I... got ready."

"Yes, enough about you. Did he get in the shower clothed or something pseudo-*Nine and a Half Minutes?*"

"Better. He came out smelling like a sailor."

"Did he have a fish under his arm?"

"No, man, he was wearin' Old Spice."

"Which takes you back?"

"To..." I almost told him. "...that commercial."

"Ah, yes, the *GQ* model in the P-coat. Gordon Merrick book cover model, too."

"Jeez, how do you remember this stuff?"

"Devotion to beauty carries a lot of baggage."

"He must have searched down under the sink for it, but he knew."

"What? Your equal taste for a decades-old marketing scheme? That's why you're now in television, darling."

"And you are playing the Orpheum Circuit?"

"The what?"

Sometimes my humor was just too specific.

I listened to Jorge's comments and retorts, giving him fodder for his wit. We settled in to watch the sky grow dark.

How did he know about the Old Spice? He was one of those Mennen Speed Stick guys who wraps the towel on just a moment before you can see it. He was the hunky dentist brushing his teeth. You know the one. Even Ethan Greene the comic character fell in love with him. So did I when I met his creator. But anyway, Lance made a great deal of money being the handsome guy in a series of very popular shampoo commercials.

He still has great hair.

Feb 16-17
1926: John Schlesinger 1934: Alan Bates

A two-day break while we waited for the seasonal change of the yard. Fake leaves don't come cheap out of season.

Lance and Brendan and I met up to discuss the scenes between them. Brendan was late to the rehearsal space.

I made a joke about his shampoo commercial. Lance told me about guys wanting to have sex with him in a shower. "That must have gotten boring."

"Actually, the hardest part was the mirror thing," Lance said.

"Huh?"

"I don't like to watch myself."

"Really?"

"Nope. Don't even watch my movies or reel more'n once a year or so."

"Huh. But you still like acting?"

"Oh, yeah. Shows'd be nice, but this is better money. I'm just lucky I look better onscreen."

"You're right."

Lance appreciated my understanding of a cold hard truth. Some faces look awful through a camera lens. Some can be fixed up, but other faces shine, no matter how small the part. Meg Tilly. Cary Grant. Jake Andrews.

Lance decided to cut my hair. "That shaggy look is over, Stan-Din. Get something that shows off your skull."

So Lance cut my hair. I invited him over. He brought clippers and scissors, even a little tent-like apron. He only asked that I not smoke while he was there. I complied.

Even though I'd spent hours housecleaning before he arrived, it still felt shabby as he politely surveyed my home.

"So, this is the famous Rick Dacker," he said as he looked at the framed poster for *The Manipulator*. The artwork had always pleased me, deliberately retro, Ricky's shirt torn open just so. "I wanted to tell you; before we started shooting, I rented all three; really fun stuff."

"Thanks. Was."

"Beg pardon?"

"He died in 1992."

"I'm sorry. Was he your boyfriend?"

"I wouldn't use that term, exactly. Muse, obsession, freaky sex partner. Ghost."

"Hmm. Tough shoes to fill."

"Are you applying for the position?"

"I'll take the first two, for now." He smiled, taking control. "Let's set up in the kitchen; easier to wipe up the clippings."

With the apron wrapped around my neck, once he started rubbing the back of my head with the humming clippers, my skin tingled.

"*Magst du dieses gefuhl?*"

"What?" I spun around. He gently pushed my head back in place.

"I studied German at Brookside. Didn't I tell you? 'You like the feeling?' he repeated in English. I nodded. "Just relax, then. I'll take my time."

Under the apron, I clutched myself.

"Tell me a story."

I told Lance a story.

Vinnie Manini ran the small barbershop only five blocks from our house. I cut through back streets to get to the converted house on Claremont, Brookside's main drag. I always arrived a little early, hanging up my coat and patting the pocket to make sure I had the right amount of money. Dad taught me how to tip at a young age. I'd leaf through the tattered magazines, soak in the manly sticky scent of tonics and hair spray while watching the men hover over their customers in their collared tunics.

Climbing up into the chair, resting my feet on the metal grill, I luxuriated as Vinnie put me in the gown, then wrapped my neck in the snug bib of some mysterious papery fabric. His combing and ministrations tingled my scalp, the high soft slicing whisking around my ears.

I don't know if it was true, but Vinnie seemed to take an extra long time with my hair, despite my abrupt instructions of the usual—shorter on the sides and the back. I'd get a tingle of another sort as he leaned in close, pressing his crotch against the chair seat, precariously close to my hands clutching the padded arms.

It wasn't until I was about fifteen that I got bold and asked for an occasional real short do, especially in summer months. He'd get the clippers set and begin on my sides, gently turning my ears over to dodge the teeth of the razor. The humming and clipping gave me chills as I grew a warm erection in my pants, safely disguised under the cloth that caught my dead locks.

I'd been thinking about Vinnie and his close attention to my hair, how he smiled warm and slow, making chitchat with me or another man about some football team or the weather. As he was about to change from scissors to clippers, I edged my hands over the arm of the chair and let them hang lower, holding the sides. Vinnie edged close, perhaps expecting the arm, then feeling my hand there, pulled back a second, expecting me to replace my arm, perhaps.

I didn't. He pressed back again, staying close. The soft bulge between his legs against the back of my hand grew stiff. I wanted to turn my hand and hold it, clutch it, but he gave it another slight rub, then switched sides to give my other hand a feel of him. My dick throbbed under the sheet. Vinnie finished and shaved the back of my head. Warm lather soothed my neck, but I stayed hard.

He finished and unwrapped the neck cloth, then carefully pulled away the dressing gown, revealing the obvious bump of my erection. I think he glanced at it. I stood, suddenly flushed and proud, almost showing it off, my hard-on in my pants. An old man looked up from his magazine, never once raising his eyes above my belt.

Was this where they did it? Did those long haircuts on those near bald men actually take so long because they were jacking off the barber?

I paid Vinnie, who seemed to make sure to touch my hand as he took the money. Then I bid farewell and trotted off in the afternoon day, my newly bared scalp tingling under the breeze, my twisted little questions clouding the contents between my ears.

If I wanted more, suspected more from Vinnie, what was I to do? Ask for a home permanent? I mean, how does a boy tell his barber he wants to see him alone, feel more than a grab from a barber chair? It simply wasn't possible. I merely got more haircuts and said nothing.

"Did that really happen?"

"Not exactly."

"Why do you make up stories like that?"

"Because the real ones are sad."

After the haircut and the story, Lance and I had dinner, another night when I was determined not to hit on him. It would be up to him. I was flattering him, telling him how he could determine what was going to happen next in his career. I admitted that it would be wise to find a straight role, fast.

"Yeah, fame, like Sonny Curtis."

"Who?"

"You see?" Lance said. He said a lot after a glass of wine. He could cut my hair any time, though. I kept rubbing it like it was some other guy's scalp. I felt sexy. Just knowing I could make out with him, at any moment, thrilled me. I had to hold off, and I enjoyed flirting. It seemed he did, too.

"What?"

"You know him," Lance said. "You know his heart, from one song that is such a part of your life, and your memories."

"Okay, what song?"

"One that makes you hopeful and sad at the same time, makes you think of bell-bottom hip-huggers and wide black belts and Herbal Essence..."

"Sing it. Who?"

"I'm giving you hints."

"Sing it."

"Love is all around..."

I drew a blank until Lance sang, "No need to waste it."

Lance mimed tossing a hat in the air.

Sonny Curtis, composer of the *Mary Tyler Moore* show theme song. Celebrity mixed with obscurity. We were each little bits of pop culture, known only to thousands. I had my hits, sub-genre-specific as they were. My PSAs for Los Angeles Animal Shelters, AIDS non-profits, a local PBS affiliate opening sequence for a kids show. Nobody who'd never see my reel knew those were mine.

Lance had shampoo.

Feb 21
1925: Sam Peckinpah

With all exterior shots done, leaves were stuffed back into bags for use somewhere else on some other fictional lawn.

I showed one of the grips my Hollywood Birthdays calendar. He looked at today and quoted the director: "It's *how* you blow up a bridge."

Well, the house had not been blown up yet, but we'd knocked quite a few dents in the walls, scraped the floors and generally trashed the joint. Included in the budget, of course, were repairs. A few guys on the team were actually dishing up redecorating hints to leave for the lady of the house. At lunch, we joked about wrapping the house in a big bow for the returning owners, a cross between TAG activists and Christo. That led to Janice talking about working with Christo. Her now ex-husband, another international artist of renown in the '70s, had worked with crushed cars. I wondered how much mileage art like that could get these days. "They'd probably need to add real crash victims," somebody joked. Nobody laughed.

Feb 27
1932: Elizabeth Taylor

Note: meeting with the suits TOMORROW!

Janice would call a lot, at odd hours, clacking away on her Mac from wherever, the studio or at home. It was a chess game, with us as the pawns. We were redoing the budget to make it work before we got checkmated.

Forty-five scenes, most in the house. But even so, it could have been maddening. Who was where, what was going next? How much time would it take?

In the *Manipulators,* there were so few people. We all just hung around. Of course, the extra scenes were done last, because by then the actors all had a few friends eager to make a few hundred. Imagine Troma, but smart.

This film, however, had to be tighter. These people were professionals, and it was their money. I kept waiting for an earthquake to mess things up.

Feb 28
1910: Vincent Minnelli

Shooting the confrontation scene with Mom (Penelope) and Uncle (Lance).

Meeting with the suits.

The Suits were impressed by the Product, but they had a question. They said the rough cut was very "interesting."

I asked Barry what that meant.

"It means he wants to know why he's not seeing a master, two close-ups and a reaction on every shot."

"Tell him I'm not George Eastman, nor indecisive, and on this time-line and budget they're lucky to have me, the fuckers."

"Don't get all upset."

"I'm not upset."

"Then you're high."

"Was high."

"How long ago?"

"What is this, twelve-step phone-in?"

"Look, I'm just concerned for you. You don't drive stoned, do you?"

I recalled once procuring a hit from a guy on the Ventura Freeway. It wasn't like I stopped traffic, veered lanes, and parked it mid-lane, but it was a bit silly. I liked smoking with him in his car, me and him, the high-way beside us grazing the back of our necks with harsh wind. We were obdurate stumps, refusing to advance. He'd asked me what I did. I told him I was a director.

"I was in a few movies," he said. He named them. I'd seen them, but didn't remember him. It would have been a closer proximity to providence if he had.

Instead, he mentioned the first time he used a camera in college to take pictures of girls. He feigned horniness at the mention of girls. I considered the pose of sex, then felt CHiPs men approaching, and retreated to later construct my version of events.

March 1
1954: Ron Howard

I was peeved. I like that word, peeved. Barry's script keeps getting in the way of my movie.

I did not want to shoot these scenes. They were around the dining room table, with the mother and the son. Barry had seen it as this roving camera round table, a moving thing, I thought it would be just too Coen brothers, I don't know, just obvious, not right for the rest of the look. But I couldn't say, "I want it to look like *An American Family*, like hidden camera, but framed better, reality, nothing virtual about it."

But I didn't say that.

So I smoked, then shot it his way just to shut him up.

It sucked, but we still kept it.

I was accruing points for good behavior, deferring to him. Later, I'll cash in on these for the big change.

I went home with him. When I wanted to smoke, he kept kicking me out of his house to pace around on his back yard. A few times he came out with me. He said I was smoking a lot.

"Look, it's my first feature in a long time. There are no guns and jokes to hide behind this time. This thing's a lot of pressure. It's... this is a big responsibility."

"Yeah, and you're fucking it up."

"No, I'm not."

"Just play by their rules."

"Yeah, but I don't have to drink their coffee, chit chat, be nice to every single person on the set."

"Look, I got a clue for you. This is not gonna be like those college party film days. You can't get away with that."

"I know. A lot of suits are watching us." Most of the suits, however, had their eyes elsewhere, since Showtime was at the time a subsidiary of Bla Bla Corp, which was about to be bought by HugeCo, which was about to possibly merge with Rupert Murdoch's monster. We were supposed to ignore all that and just make a little movie about a boy who fucks his mother's brother.

"Ya wanna know what it's gonna be like?" Barry said.

"No."

"Here's a clue. How many Teamsters does it take to screw in a light bulb?"

"What?"

"How many Teamsters does it take to screw in a light bulb?"

"I don't know. How many?"

"Nine. You gotta problem wit' dat?"

Brendan/Son would be smoochin' with Lance/Uncle in a bedroom while those nine guys stood around by their trucks eating donuts.

"Hey, Bear?"

"Yeah?" Barry was looking at me, as if from a distance at a guy he'd just realized he liked.

"You know those monologues Brendan's gonna overdub?"

"Yeah?"

I didn't say anything.

"You wanna cut them."

"No. No. I just ... Whose story is it?"

"Well, his, of course. Even though we pitched it to Showtime as the mother's story, which is why we have to extend all those Concerned Mom at the Window shots, if you don't mind. Penelope looks really good with those motherly glances."

"Yeah, yeah, yeah. But, Bear?"

"Yes?"

"How would a kid his age express himself, given the chance?"

"Well, by talking."

"Would he?"

Did I? Have I told people? Have I not tired of admitting it to guys, mostly dates, who react as if I had admitted to the Brinks robbery or an affair with Bruce Willis? Will we all ever get over our collective abused selves?

After he'd read the script, Jorge said, "Oh, honey, This ain't conflict. I had sex with all my cousins. Now, having all your grandma's relatives shot and dumped in a pit by Pinochet, then escaping Chile to Brazil; that's conflict."

I remembered someone, some party, some gay poolside banter, some underling of an agent's hairdressers, designer's dental technician, who was gay, they were all gay, but one of them dismissed the homophobia in Guns and Roses' lyrics, and some other queen snapped back with, "Yeah, but he was abused." Like he was allowed to be a jerk because of that. "That is no excuse to sing like a turkey at Thanksgiving," someone else responded. There were snaps all around, as I recall. Item dispensed with.

Mar 2
1919: Jennifer Jones

I didn't intentionally try to quit smoking. The shoot just helped it. I was so busy, not bringing a pack and not bumming made it easier. Plus hardly anyone smoked on the set except the Teamsters, and they were way back down the street from the house, their trucks hidden away. I focused my tension and energy toward filming, had an excuse to pace, to be nervous, to be irritating. And Janice kept giving me chewing gum and Tootsie Pops.

But although I'd quit before by simply pacing around my own home, it became easier during filming. I was so exhausted after a day, I didn't have time to go and get any. I just wanted to sleep.

Mar 4
1952: Ronald Reagan marries Nancy Davis

Homophobic comment by a gaffer today. He'd been giving us trouble to begin with. His boss agreed. I had him replaced, instantly. That felt good.

Had a talk with Lance by his trailer. I lit up, and he started off about how he would never date a man who smoked, never has. I got presumptuous and asked if that meant he wanted to go on a date with me.

"Look, I really would like to see you on a weekend maybe, off-hours, to just really get—"

"What, my butt?" I grinned.

"Eventually."

Twenty yards off, a PA was calling for me.

"Are we … is this … okay?"

"Stan-Din," he almost sang. "I wanna give you what you came for."

I felt queasy, sweaty, in total control, a little boy and a man. It was a moment. "Let's wait. After the shoot."

"Let's not."

"Okay."

Lance blinked and smiled. "That weren't tough."

I shrugged as I turned to the PA.

"Don't you want my address?" he whispered.

I waved him off to the set. "Katsuo probably has your entire family's addresses."

Put a Monkees 45 on your Close-n-Play. It's 1967 and Cindy Sharr is babysitting, letting Dan and I dance in the dining room while she grins at our energy and quietly knits in my dad's comfy chair. Later, after too many cookies, hyped on sugar, I throw a fit and overturn the coffee table, prompting my parents to bribe her with an extra ten if she'd only come back the next week.

What was once pain is now a distraction. What once bled is now a pink bump, a tiny scar on the skin. It hurts to go back, to dig in, but it's a purging, a cleansing, some sort of suburban Indian ritual handed down from the Native ghosts who once hunted on what became the golf course near our house. They show how. They whisper in the wind between the weeds and corn stalks, if you only listen.

That night, as we approached the inevitable taboo of a mid-shoot affair, Lance seemed comfortable, almost taking casual control as I fidgeted on his living room sofa. His home was clean, and sparsely yet tastefully decorated. Relieved to see several shelves of books, videos and music CDs, many of them musicals, it still felt too neat, absent of my own cluttered eccentricities.

After a brief dinner, he put on some appropriately romantic music, a mix of K.D. Lang, Sadé and other singers. We engaged in some slow, then intense, kissing, until he stood to peel off his shirt.

"No, wait. Slowly," I begged.

He understood. So many years ago, that simple little dressing room moment had sparked a thousand urges. I sat quietly, pleased as he consented to a slow striptease while the fourteen-year-old inside me hooted in victory.

Eventually, naked before me, he took my hand and led me to his bedroom.

I ran my hand through cornstalks, Lance's hair. I burrowed between furry thighs, the plains. Seeming to tire of my slow caresses, Lance rolled over, grabbed my dick and said, "I'm not made of glass."

"Sorry, it's just… all these years of wondering…"

"Wondering what?"

"What you taste like."

"Only one way to find out."

I planted myself back home between his mounds, and I was consumed by him as I consumed him, every lick and bite fulfilling the need from so many years before. We never got much of any full insertion, just humped each other, him atop me. Kissing and adoring his face got me off, just staring into his soothing eyes as we rutted slowly, each smooch erasing every year of regret.

I slept all night in his arms.

Mar 5
1905: Rex Harrison/Full Moon

It was so easy to laugh, to make Ohio jokes, to not think of smoking—well, to at least not smoke, since I knew he would disapprove. The next morning, in bed, he still looked young, the face of a forty-year-old man who rarely drank, never smoked, and rarely did drugs, not out of any force, or pressure, just out of taste.

Over breakfast, we got to talking about experiences like those in the TV movie. I told Lance everything, but without blaming him, even though I wanted to. I merely said, "after *Gypsy*."

Lance had more innocent experiences: jerk-off sessions with cousins, an abrupt forced blow job with a bible study partner who later disappeared. We shared some things, but the way he said them, they all seemed bucolic, innocent, hay-strewn.

"You mean you never had a bad sexual experience?" I asked.

"Naw; except one night when my cousin wanted to fuck me." Then he smiled, as if kidding, but I couldn't really tell. "And he was a big boy, too."

"My uncle hit on me while we watched *Metropolis*."

"The movie?"

"Yeah."

"So, watching it must be kind of, like, flight simulation for you. Why didn't you tell me?"

"Oh, no, it's not like that. I'm, it's not..."

"Is this why you wanted to do the movie?"

"No, I'm doing the movie because Barry's a good writer and it's a job, and... I don't know. I think I'm moving forward. People keep telling me this is a move forward, and the only perk I see is getting you out of my past and into my present."

"I mean that's a good thing."

"But you wanted me then."

"Of course I did," Lance said. "Wasn't it obvious?"

"But you were dating girls then."

"Yep, and almost engaged, until I split Brookside. My parents were really disappointed."

"And you forgot about me."

Lance shook his head, gulped the last of his coffee. "I tried to keep things friendly, 'cuz I knew. I mean, you didn't act gay, just... It was like you were ready to pounce on me but you didn't know how."

"I wish I had."

"No, but see, what woulda happened? You'da told someone and by now I'd be a parolee with a neck tattoo."

He was right. I would not have been able to keep such pleasure a secret.

"Well, hopefully you can bring some of that into your scenes with Brendan."

"What, like, show that I'm into him for real?"

"Something like that. The problem I'm having with Barry's script, and probably our producers, is deciding whether it's a good thing or a bad thing. And your performance needs to portray both."

"Oh, okay. Huh." He looked like I'd just asked him to fuck a cow, which to an ex-farm boy is not an unusual request.

Mar 7
1942: Michael Eisner

On the set, waiting, as usual, Brendan was listening to a band on his headphones.

"You like them?"

"Yeah, it's my motivation music."

"Really? Do you mind?" I reached for the headphones.

"Naw. Sure." I put them on, listened to the simple trash, a nice beat, listenable.

"What's the name?"

"Blood Ties."

I was a bit stunned. "The song?"

"No, the band. Actually they're some friends of mine. I like to think it's the music my character would listen to."

"Huh." I handed the cassette player back to Brendan. "Would your character like to make a music video?"

"Are you kidding?"

"I don't kid kids."

Mar 8
1921: Cyd Charisse

I had to get Barry's permission. I got it, thank goodness. The idea was Brendan's, anyway. What better way, at that blank point, that point where Brendan doesn't know what to do, what to say, than to escape into his world, pretend to have made his video. The coup would be that we'd have a tie-in video to send to MTV. The Suits loved that.

Katsuo seemed to take it well, immediately processing a marketing schedule. "You want the video done before the release date. It'll be messy, but if we treat the video as if Brendan is making a piece of promotional material, it'll work."

"Whatever," I told her. "As long as he doesn't have to join the Music Video Director's Guild."

Katsuo did not laugh, and I wondered if my joke were actually true. She started in about other problems. I decided we'd deal with it later, the music rights, the papers, the mess. First thing was to get Brendan a camera.

That boy was gonna save us all.

Mar 9
1940: Raul Julia

Some pieces from the script that got cut, then put back in:

```
                    KID:
            So, did you tell anyone?


                   UNCLE:
      Well, my parents were very understanding.


                    KID:
            Oh. I don't see how.


                    MOM:
          Did he make a pass at you?


                    KID:
            No.


                    MOM:
      I've asked him to leave. He'll be gone
   tonight. If your father found out, he would
            kill him. Do you understand?
```

I remember it.

Lying in bed, not eating, the sheets a tangled mess, oily skin and hair, refusing to get up. Days later, going downstairs, bawling as I heard my brother peeking up the stairs. They knew. They would know. They all knew. Fortunately, such stinky ennui doesn't translate to film. Instead, Brendan got to break a few windows.

Mar 11
1898: Dorothy Gish

Realization Blues #203

Talking with my co-producer and writer, and now, it would seem, ex-boyfriend.

Not pretty. Write this one later.

Mar 13
1953: Deborah Raffin

Exteriors; the AD supervised. I re-wrote scenes with Barry, and argued, and re-wrote. I longed to ask Lance to spend another night together. I didn't.

Mar 15
1964: Richard Burton marries Elizabeth Taylor

Barry and I ended up fucking in our hotel room that night. Rather, he let me fuck him. That wasn't often, not that I requested, or demanded it too often. We simply found so many other things to do.

I felt bad since I had to close my eyes and think I was fucking Lance's butt. Barry's ass felt like bait, a last resort for him. No way was he gonna let this happen again for a long time. He still didn't know how to get comfortably fucked.

But we were exhausted, having tried to dredge up a kinky sex scene that became merely perfunctory, then failed. It was over, sexually, between us, I realized. It wasn't as if Lance and I had established any formal relationship status. He had a few days off and had driven back to his house. My tumble with Barry had started as a stress relief and ended in my dick's failure.

I made a joke with Barry about doing a night at gay clubs; "recreate the famous nude scene," with a different film actor each week. I would have continued joking, but I felt guilty, got a glass of juice and disappeared outside the motel, hoping to find a sleepless cast member to offer a cigarette. No one. After a hazy last glance at the parking lot, I returned to hear Barry snoring lightly, my purr track for bedtime. I checked the alarm clock. We had a six-o-clock call.

Mar 16
1925: Jerry Lewis

By two in the morning, I still couldn't sleep. I took Barry's cell phone back outside. Dan had called days before, and I hadn't replied. I hadn't heard from Dan since before the shoot began. I had to get back to somebody else's reality.

"You up?"

"Actually, I was," he said. Between the phone jostling sounds, I could hear music. Tinkling glasses.

"You have guests?"

"Yes, but they're on the verge of realizing it's time to go, so I'll just ... there, I'm in the other room, and are you all right? I called three times."

"I'm sorry, but didn't Katsuo tell you?"

"Yeah, but I mean, you do have lunch breaks."

"Sorry. I'm really rolling on this, bro. I just got the last scene to shoot, and I am so psyched. You know, you know that feeling when we used to drop off like four rolls of Super8 at the film counter and cross our fingers and high five?"

"I seem to remember some elation, yes."

"You're stoned."

"Fried and frittered."

"How's the baby?"

"Asleep and soundproofed, baby monitor on high, though."

"What do you mean?"

"The thing, the walkie talkie."

"Oh."

"You turn the baby volume down and—"

"Oh, I see, so you're like spying on the kid already, huh?"

"No, it's ... that is so silly."

"Whatever. So, ask me how it's going."

"How's it going?"

"It's shit. It's all those awful After School Specials we used to laugh at. It's such—"

"Hey, man, look. Don't worry. Just finish this and move on to whatever else you wanna do next."

This from Mr. Mileage. He traveled to nearly every computer animation convention there was, and there were a lot of computer animation conventions in the last decade of the twentieth century, that is for damn sure.

"So, listen," I geared Dan up, not caring if it was appropriate, just that something Barry or Lance did or said, or the kid, Brendan, I don't know who, but I had to be blunt. "So, who was your first girl?"

"You mean that I...?"

"Yeah, that you..." I suddenly felt embarrassed thinking of it. The idea of Dan and some girl...ugh. I tried. It doesn't work. Weird thing. You'd think I would, but I don't.

"You saw how fucked up I was after Uncle Sean and I did the wild thing," I said.

"You were fairly unhinged, yes."

"Um, and I really appreciate you helping me chill out of it, when you could, you know, deal with..."

"Yeah, okay."

"But I hope you know how disappointing your first time can be, and..."

"Well, I didn't think that was your first time."

"Really?" I said.

"Yeah, what about that boy who, god, you don't remember? All he wanted to do was be tied up when we played Jonny Quest."

"Really? Which one?" I seemed to have blanked that out. Or was Dan fooling?

"Yeah, Ronnie somebody. Remember when we did that skit, or no, you weren't in it. But you kept watching us rehearse from up on the stairs, and I wanted you out of there, but you were telling us things, what to do, and it worked I guess, 'cause everybody liked it at school."

I remembered a picture of a picture of a picture. The alligator.

"Was there a sleeping bag shaped like an alligator?" I said.

"Well, yeah, it's still down there, for all I know."

"What is?"

"That sleeping bag. You got all out of shape 'cause we couldn't let you be in our talent show thing, 'cause you were still at the elementary school, and I was in junior high. And then Ronnie Best let you direct us, and Mom let you stay down with us and you shared the sleeping bag with him."

I won't say it all came back to me, but of course, neither does the theme from *Dark Shadows*. I'll say it was drawn for me, storyboarded by video bro, finalized, arranged by the Arranger, blessed by The Manipulator, strung by Mexican puppets, breathed in cookie milk sleep breath, two boys, Fire and Ice, wrapped inside the serpent.

"Who?" I asked.

"Ronnie Best."

"I slept with Ronnie Best in an alligator."

"Yeah. You don't remember? He tried it with me, and I told him to get lost. He and you were kissing and humping. Dude, I knew you were gay before you did."

The kiss. Ronnie Best. How could I have forgotten that?

"Thank you, bro. Thank you so much. I gotta go. I got a scene to rewrite."

"But Stan, it's only three o'clock. Let's talk at least until my guests get the message that I want my wife before she passes out."

"No, really, I gotta go. I'll call ya when we wrap. I got like a seven-day window."

"You mean a week."

"Thank you. I'm still trapped in an Excel spreadsheet."

"I understand, bro. Whatever. You take care."

"I will."

I turned the phone off, shoved it in my pocket, and walked back across the parking lot. Looking up, I said goodnight to the stars.

After the household generally had let the dust settle on the whole event, my Dad did inquire as to my well-being, as if all he were up for was a sort of wrap-it-up and move-it-along summary. He asked if I felt okay about myself.

I did not say yes. I remember saying I was "experimenting." A couple other guys said it like that.

"Well, actually, many boys go through a period where they are close with their—"

"Dad." I didn't even want to go there.

"So," he said. "I just want to let you know I want you to be a little more careful when you experiment."

"Yeah, well, I'm pretty sure I've already ... confirmed the hypothesis."

We smiled, like, it won't be such a mess next time, right? No more blowing up the house.

I stole this conversation from my life, scribbled it out that night, and gave it to Barry in the morning. He fixed it, gave the new daily sides to Brendan and Dennis, and we shot it. I shot it. One take. It was outside in the yard. No filters. The lighting guys set up one side buffer. But the actors just sat, unmoving. Sitting outside. Simple. Clean. Men being honest.

Mar 17
1964: Rob Lowe

We had a half-day of work scheduled. The other half, Dennis, the Dad in my cast, and a few crew guys, shot a PSA that got canned by an AIDS group with the straight director who thinks a father talking about gay stuff to his gay son is too much. The nerve of some people.

Oh, well. We can get lots of PSAs for other groups. We could get stars from everywhere to say it. Get all the queer ones. Dan Butler. He's always great.

Whatever. I was exhausted. Too exhausted for close-eyed sleep. I had to go home to my bed.

But first, I trolled the Dodge Dart down to a twenty-four-hour diner with a 1950s marquee. As I pulled up, people stared at Gramma's car like it was an alien spacecraft from *Time Tunnel*.

I had a big pile o' breakfast, gasoline coffee, then spooled cigarette smoke out my nose as I drove to my set of a home. I had five hours to drive back to somebody else's home, where I was going to break the law and film it.

Four more scenes to shoot, all around the sex scene. I've been whittling actors off, every day reducing the techies needed, trying to clear the set, while stirring up gossip.

Mar 19
1955: Bruce Willis / New Moon

Since Brendan was actually seventeen, we had a shooting schedule that worked around the youth labor laws. Still, I knew how it felt to be the center of everyone's attention. That was why I was happy to be doing interiors in the house. While the crew set up for the faked sun filter though the afternoon curtains, Brendan and I shot some hoops in the driveway while munching truck drivers watched, laughing. I'm lousy at basketball.

Somewhere between panting and wheezing, Pam Chester the Props Manager distracted me with a prop question, and I took a break with Brendan. He didn't sit in the grass, since his costume would get shot from behind. We were setting up for the last shot of Act One. *The* shot. The kid going into his bedroom to discover his uncle naked in his bed. I'd asked the AD to clear out everyone except the cameraman and Lance, whom I imagined sitting on the bed, under covers, sleeping probably, while they arranged lights around him.

"So, we got this shot, then a reverse of your face going upstairs, then we gotta get another one of you watching your mom and brother leave. You do a look upstairs, something nervous and unsure."

"Right, the scared young thing."

"What?"

"I just ... Stan, since we're almost done, do you mind?" He held the ball. "I've been ... I haven't said anything, since this is my first lead, well, whatever, and the video was so cool. I owe you for that, but don't you think this ought to be different?"

"What?"

He spat the ball down to the asphalt a few times.

"More, like, no big deal?" he said.

"Yeah, well, maybe doing this will help make that happen, help kids get over it if it happens to them."

"You really think so?"

I stood, took the ball, and tossed one in. "I don't know, but every time I see Martin Sheen or Hal Holbrook, I feel all gooey inside."

"Who?"

"*That Certain Summer.* Pretty much the first gay TV anything for my–" I couldn't say it. My generation. Brendan came of age amid Queer Nation, AIDS, Broadway shows about gays and drag queens. The revolution had been televised.

At his age, I had Paul Lynde and Charles Nelson Reilly.

"Whatever." Brendan took the ball and dribbled. "I just don't see it as my character's problem. It's everyone else's."

I smiled. "That's fine. You're right on target."

Brendan smiled. "Besides," he nudged me before dunking another shot. "Lance is pretty hot for an old guy."

Mar 20
1986: James Cagney dies / Vernal Equinox

Everybody had been scooted out of the house. I wanted synch sound. I wanted Dorothy in black and white you know is gonna turn to colors as soon as she steps outside.

I followed everybody out, trying to catch someone, anyone with a cigarette, far outside our home that we were about to abandon five days early and $13,000 under budget. Through the magic of Janice and her grids, we were about to move those funds to the J. Quest Co., Consultant, my freshly established DBA.

I didn't see anyone smoking inside, so I ducked out back of the house and found a gaffer puffing away on a Marlboro.

I returned to the upstairs set and sat on the bed, speaking softly to Lance, who was keeping his eyes closed, not moving, hoping to really capture sleepiness.

"Thought you quit," he mumbled from under the pillow.

He wasn't even facing me and he could smell it.

That was the last one, I knew. The last cigarette.

He chuckled under the sheet. I grazed my hand down the valley of his spine.

I closed the door as I left, looking down to Lloyd the Cameraman's crouched form.

"Ya got it?" I asked.

"On the kid and the door, then move in with him, right?"

"I thought you wanted me to keep the shot."

"No, I meant focus."

"Sorry. Yes."

Brendan waited in the hall.

"Okay. Just move in right before the door. Give Lloyd a moment to get a focus."

He did, then pulled back, tried it, and opened the door. Inside, Lance was a landscape of sheet and back muscles.

"Okay." Third time. Brendan pulled me aside. "I'm gonna do something in the same focal range, but different."

"Go for it."

Somebody must have told him. I don't know. Barry? But it couldn't have happened better. Even the redo we made after everybody clapped at the dailies didn't get it.

Brendan approached the door, his butt and legs in the shot. He made a little fist with his hand. I heard his knees creak as he crouched down, peeked through the keyhole, watched for the longest time. While my heart fluttered, I tried not to make a sound. I made a mental note to get a reverse of this genius improviser. Then Brendan stood, opening the door.

It wasn't until he walked closer, at the bed's side, that the camera saw the curve of Lance's butt. He'd pulled down the sheet.

Brendan stood, waiting for his presence to rouse Lance, who arched his head up, waited, then rolled over, reached out his hand. Brendan reached a hand forward, touching a part of Lance's belly we couldn't see. He brought his hands down to the mattress, push-up position, hovering over Lance. They were face to face, the boy's lower half twisted along the side of the bed, the sweats pulling up just right.

Their faces met, and they kissed. Brendan didn't move. They kept kissing. He was in control. He was directing with his movements, saying, this is where you fade to black.

Mar 23
1910: Akira Kurosawa

Wrap party. Barry's house. I decorated.

We celebrated. People took pictures. We ate, drank, danced, shared next job connections, goals. But even in all this, later that night, I overheard some of the usual common strange news, which led to a small heated discussion between two crew members. Some newspaper noted that seventy-nine percent of the businesses burned down in the King Riots had been Korean. Then, people started sharing their "Where were you?" stories. I looked at Barry. We left the room.

Outside, the night sky was thankfully helicopter-free. With Barry's arm over my shoulder, I felt content in a way I hadn't with *The Manipulator* trilogy, or my other work. With those films, wrapping was only part of the process. I had to work on so much more, scrounge, hire PR, beg for funding, fill out festival applications, self-promote. Of course, Ricky and his intensity wove through all that.

This time, it was like painting someone else's house. Once the ladders were taken down and the tarps folded, I would be outta there. I'd won my prize, and set my sights on learning how to be in love with Lance.

Mom once lied that Uncle Sean was probably in a mental hospital or a halfway house, possibly dead. It sounded more like one of the many Danielle Steele novels she secretly enjoyed. "I've read all the classics," she moaned of her college years. "Now it's recess."

After her full confession the previous Christmas, I pondered the Arizona address she'd given me. What should I do? Find him? That seemed fun. Arrange some kind of heartfelt reunion? No. Kill him? Why? For giving me what I wanted? Maybe just string him up for a few days and have some fun. Pissing in his mouth, fucking his ass raw with a nightstick. Nothing serious.

I sat on my bed, talking on the phone with my mom. *A Family Matter* (possibly to be retitled *Say Uncle*) wasn't done in post-production, but I was already making plans for afterward. The plans included a trip to the desert.

"You're not going to do anything rash, are you?" she asked from two thousand miles away.

"When have I ever done anything rash?"

"When you threw the coffee table at that babysitter?"

"I flipped it over, not at her."

"She was so nice, Cindy. She's got two kids now."

"Good for her. About Uncle Sean. I won't do anything. I just want to see him."

"When you broke all the windows in the garage."

"Ma, I was only fifteen."

"When you financed that film on my credit card."

"It made money."

"You're still my son."

"Well, your son wants to see how your brother is doing."

I finally added him to the Rolodex, one of two. But after I lodged him into the roll, and considered when or if I'd place a call, I got distracted and went to my old Rolodex, flipping through twice to pull out the dead ones. About thirty were definite.

I ended up on the carpeted floor, laying them out in a swirling row, then laying a strip of tape along it. I hung it up between the panes of one of the French doors between my dining room, which had become the screening room after I'd bought a wide-screen TV and new VCR. Around the edges of the ceiling, I'd hung tiny jalapeno lights. During the day it hung dark, but when I lit the outside porch and darkened the lights inside, backlit, the taped-together chain of cards became a glowing spine.

Morbid, perhaps, but it reminded me of my own spine. I found the strength to sit upright.

I waited about half an hour. That would be enough time for Mom to call Dan and spiel, blow off some steam, and then I could let Dan compare the two versions. We ricochet phone calls sometimes. I don't know why we don't conference it once in a while and yell at each other on speakerphone while watching TV or doing laundry.

But I talked to Dan about an hour later.

"Oh she's all worried now about having a screening at their house. Her neighbors want to see it with her."

"Oh, my god. Incest Cocktail Hour."

"Jeez."

"So, Dan."

"Yes, Stan."

"We're cool on this, okay? I did not cause Mom to get upset."

"Okay, we'll take that into consideration."

"You hoser."

Then Dan said, "So, you know he's still alive then."

"Yeah," I told him, then added, "For now."

"What?"

"Just joking."

A beep. Call waiting. It was Barry.

"I'm on with my brother."

"Oh. I'll call back. When's your cousin visiting?"

"I forget."

"Oh, I'm sorry, I wanted to—"

"It's okay."

"You wanna come over?"

"No, Bear, thanks, I—"

"What?"

"I have a guest." I lied.

"Oooh, smell her."

"Oh, come on."

"Is he nice?"

"Yes."

"Well, good. That's a step up from me."

"I'll see ya soon?"

"Okay."

I think he was disappointed I didn't tell him who it was.

Ten minutes later, Dan called me back, since I'd forgotten him.

After that, I left what had been my third unreturned call to Lance that week.

Then I invited Jorge over.

We talked over takeout Indian food while watching a screener Jorge had been given by a director who wanted to work with him. I burped while we watched.

"Agita," I said.

"You're still worried."

The press release announcing the wrap of our film had been leaked to a news source, which had been read by some conservative Ladies Fascist Watchdog club who inexplicably read *Variety*. Jorge told me not to worry about it.

"Controversy is good publicity," he said. I knew that. I also knew it was better to stir it up after the shit was in the can.

"Of course I'm worried," I said. "What am I supposed to not be worried about? I want to portray my community, if there is one, in a healthy light, and with this—"

"You know what you need? You need to get out. Get your mind off your boyhood fantasy."

"You mean Lance."

"He'll come around."

I was sporting a studio tan from the weeks of editing. My complexion was somewhere between caulking and bathtub mold.

"What? After all we've been through?"

"No, dummy." Jorge almost shouted over the phone. "We need to go out. I wanna give you a refresher on what this community is that you're so worried about offending."

"What?"

"I think they need some offending."

"Okay. Thanks for sharing. Now, where are we planning this social assault?"

"We're going to a few clubs."

"Fashionable clubs?"

"Yes."

"Oh, do I have to wear Gaultier to get fucked?"

"I don't wear Gaultier to fuck. I just go to fuck."

I laughed out loud.

"Besides," he said. "Before I take you home, I am keeping you on a very short chain." He picked out a shirt from my clothes, sporty butch club gear I hadn't worn in years. "Ah, this I like."

As we headed out, I had to set a rule with Jorge. "When I want to leave, or I'm being cornered by some dolt, we use a code phrase. That means we exit immediately."

"All right. What's the code?"

"'The hors d'oeuvres are fabulous.'"

And they were, a swirling mass of purple and green human popcorn, bouncing away under the beat.

I ended up in the VIP room with Jorge, who moved with a younger set than Barry, or certainly Edmund. I could hardly hear the introductions. A short man in black framed glasses introduced himself while I considered the possibility of making myself so drunk I wouldn't have to talk with anyone while thinking about Lance or Jason Daw, who hadn't called, or Barry or Brendan, who had, again.

"Walter Schmidt, with the *Film Review*."

I was supposed to be impressed, so I acted like I was.

"I hear you finished shooting."

"Yes."

"I look forward to seeing it. Will there be an advance screening?"

"Yes." He quizzed me for the PR company's name. I hesitated, then gave him Katsuo's number.

"A very intense subject, very delicate," he mused.

"What?"

"Incest, child abuse. Too bad you couldn't get Susan Sarandon as the mom. Would have lent even more sympathy."

"Yes, well, I think Penelope did a fine job. You're gonna love Brendan. And Lance. Everybody. It was great, a great cast." I was getting the hang of this.

"Very intense. Like the work of Kurt Cobain."

"Nirvana?"

"Why, yes, of course; a perfect example of untended child abuse victim. If only he'd found therapy."

"You think that was the reason? Not just easy access to heroin and guns?"

"Oh, one can't deny the intention of his music. No need for subtlety, even the lyrics. The album is, after all, called *Incesticide*."

"Yeah, too bad we couldn't get the rights to any of their songs. That bitch Courtney."

His jaw dropped.

"Joke."

"Well, I hope your film isn't."

"Are you doing some kind of treatise on it?" I said.

"My thesis, actually. Cultural Studies."

I excused myself.

"Jorge, what are we getting ourselves into?"

He was already a bit glassy-eyed from a swift cocktail.

"Well, my man, either an award-winning breakthrough in television history, or the worst career move in our sordid lives."

I finished my drink and nodded, my silent opinion being that I felt the latter more probable.

"Did you get anything to eat?" I asked.

"What?"

I said, quite clearly, "The hors d'oeuvres are fabulous."

We were quiet in the car, making little commentary on the evening, the guyish radio voice of John Corbett from *Northern Exposure* selling a car. I'd tried to get him to act in the film, all the time knowing I just wanted to get up his tree.

"Remember that show where he catapulted a piano?" Jorge asked.

"Yes."

"Remember what he said?"

"No. I suppose you're gonna tell me."

"Yes." Jorge said, turning to me in the middle of a very long red light on Doheny. "'It's not the thing you fling. It's the fling itself.'"

I considered it and didn't talk for a while, but then it just sort of fell out, like a sproinged piano. "I love Lance."

"Sounds like a thirteen-weeker with no option to renew."

"I'm serious."

"Really. The memory of Lance or Lance now?"

"Both."

"Not fair."

"To you?"

"No, to Barry."

"Barry's not—"

"Not Ricky?"

"Ricky's dead."

"Not to you. Nobody lives up to him, or whatever you want, so even Barry isn't good enough."

"Look, we aren't... We have to work together."

"So?"

"What about old couples? Don't they see the young newlyweds in each other's eyes? Aren't we allowed to think long-term? Why can't it be long-term with Barry, but with retroactive mileage?"

"Yeah, right. You're sounding like my mother. You're just—" Jorge's hands flew about, as if a bee was trapped in the car.

"Don't get all like this with me. You can tell me how to dress. Don't tell me who to love."

"Sorry. I just want you to be happy."

More silent streets. I flipped on some radio Red Hot Chili Peppers and felt better. I thought about our few nights together when he lived up on Olympic, the near-palazzo with a pool, the one up in the hills. That might work.

"I need a pool."

"Sorry. I don't have one."

"Right." Silence. "I guess that means I'm dropping you off at home."

"Yes." Jorge said. "You are."

We apologized, hugged and said, "See you soon," but I knew it. Jorge needed a break from me.

Jump back to senior year in high school. I was finally popular.

Crashing a summer party, swimming nearly nude and being admired by my friend, who casually glanced, yet couldn't stop glancing, from the table. They sipped their drinks as Nate Keyes and I flirted in the pool, swirling about like two dolphin pups in Jockey shorts. It was one of the few times in my teen years when I felt completely beautiful, at peace with myself and my queerness. Although Nate and I never said it, we knew then. We may have thought they all knew, too, but we didn't care.

By three in the morning, I had paced the back porch, edging for a cigarette, knowing the various nearby convenience stores would welcome my visit. It was pot, or lack of it, or the film, or the post-production panic. I had a phlegm hack that never went away. I'd always managed to cough it out in private before going out, but sometimes, it just gagged up when I laughed, and I'd be embarrassed.

Sometimes I think the zits on my back were not from exercising, or sheets, or cotton or anything, but my lungs trying to press the toxins out through my skin to warn me.

The next day I called Katsuo's voicemail, reminding her to see if we could get rights to use a Nirvana song. Surely she had David Geffen's yacht phone in her Rolodex.

Katsuo walked into the studio office. "It's that reporter from *Entertainment Weekly*. She says she's on deadline."

"Aren't we all."

I comfied myself in the chair, kicked my shoes off, and hit speakerphone.

Through the interview, I kept wondering how the writer got her voice to tread the fine line between aggression and flirtation, as if she'd worked very hard not to end all her sentences with a question? I doodled on a blank storyboard pad.

"You know, a few words with our star might be better for your magazine," I suggested, Lance's number at my fingertips.

"I want to get to the heart of the issue in your film," she said. "We really enjoyed it here."

"Oh, thank you." I leaned forward. My doodles became dolphins.

"I shouldn't have said that, but three of us wanted to watch it. Before we left the screening room, we got into this discussion about similar experiences. It seems each of us had some kind of abuse story to tell."

"Oh." Boxes grew around my dolphins.

"Is this where your inspiration for the story came from?"

I sighed, feeling myself soon dragged to some hand-holding circle in a community center in West Hollywood, being forced to *share*. I drew swirls that kept becoming claws on the boxes.

"Um, well, I collected lots of stories. Barry really contributed a lot to the story. I mean, he's the writer. Maybe you could interview him." I doodled a bridge to a blank spot.

"Oh, that's okay. I'm on deadline."

"Oh, you mean you didn't just use that to get me on the phone?"

She laughed lightly, awkwardly, and in that laughter I knew I was once again safe, having skirted the issue like a beachside cliff on Interstate 1.

"So, don't you think you'll get some complaints about that sex scene?"

"The love scene? I'd prefer you use the word love, just like for straight scenes."

"All right." A pause. I could hear the clack of her keyboard. "Where the boy kisses his uncle."

"We had to show that they made love."

My doodles had changed. The boxes grew dark.

"Made love. You think I should use that terminology?"

"I won't tell you how to do your job if you won't tell me how to do mine."

"Oops. Is this a touchy subject?"

"Touchy? Yes. I'm not really concerned about it upsetting some people. I didn't make it for them." I leaned back, dropped the pen.

"Who did you make it for?"

"Look, uh, this is getting weird, and I have to go."

"But I just want to—"

"You studied Wernar Erhard, didn't you?"

"What does that have to do with—"

"Scientology Lite?"

"That's not an appro—"

"Robotic interrogation comes in one flavor. That's all I have time for. Ciao!"

I hung up and stepped outside to Katsuo's desk. "I'm outta here."

"Homework." She thrust a cluster of messages into my hand. Why did I take them?

The Advocate. Eric in Post. Edmund.

Barry. Lance.

Cousin Mike; arriving Sat. three-ish. Will take shuttle.

43. a **holy zombie** is still bad

Question: Comet. Earthquake. Oscars.

Answer: Natural elements in our environment which occasionally alter the rotational axis of the earth, or leads participants of such events to believe as much.

My cousin Mike arrived in time for the Oscars. This was a very off-year, Oscarwise. Do you remember that time? 1996? Mel Gibson winning two awards for a movie that includes a homophobic murder, as well as more male asses in one shot than any gay porn film ever?

Can we say, "Conflicted?"

After we'd dropped off Mike's luggage, grabbed some food, and foraged for Oscar party-worthy garb, I tried to warn him about the crowd that would inhabit Edmund's party, given in his absence, since he would be at the actual awards show.

"This is Campology 560. You do not have the prerequisites, Bette Davis Film Biography, *Laugh-In* Closet Cases and the Alan Sues Eye-Whirl Training School. I have to warn you, Homology 101 you've got from me, but after that—"

"Don't worry about me," Mike said. "You just get high or drunk as long as I get to drive this home."

"Oh." I hadn't considered the possibility, but now, handing over the wheel and getting blasted kind of worked, with someone else in the driver's seat. Then I joked, "Home being...?"

"Oh, your home, of course."

"Ah," I was relieved, but then Mike took it farther. "For now."

We should have taken bets. I would have cleaned up.

I was the first one to say they were probably going to bring Christopher Reeve out in the wheelchair. I knew because somebody who is somebody's boyfriend of someone I trust just told it to me at a party, because his publicist is ... well, whatever. The event itself wasn't so sickening as the fact that I was so once again connected to the world of the gravely unimportant, the passage of celebrities and artists, their terrain, their paths, their approach, on top of the odd chance that we might see Edmund and Barry on television. It was all too fucking much, like a Nascar speedway after a three-month Greyhound bus trip.

The Oscars. Fuck that shit. "Gay Rights Disease," my ass.

I got plowed. Part of me felt envious of Barry, who was there as Edmund's guest, but inviting Lance, who said he had other plans. It was a free night, an extension of Jorge's crowd, and some of mine, but not the main players. Odd. I flirted with one guy too many.

"How ya doin'? Looks like you lost." I said of a hunk's ballot. He smiled. I kept thinking, This is where I might aim. This is aimable.

"Oh well," he smiled. "Guess I don't know Hollywood."

"Neither do I."

"What do you do?"

"I direct films."

I got him laughing. I got his number, too.

I remember pieces from my drunkenness, and these were all uttered that night on TV, just past the Ides of March; Kevin Spacey talking of thanking some guy, I forget his name, but he was "the manipulator, the guy who pulls the strings." The touching almost not-heard woman, a Holocaust survivor, who, in her thank-you speech, spoke of those many who perished, "who will never enjoy a boring evening at home."

Later, in the viewing room, screams and hoots echoed below me as some other favorite won an award. I recalled an anniversary.

"Kulozik," I muttered as I stood outside, in the yard, beyond the pool, beyond the camp, the champagne and fabulous hors d'oeuvres. "Kulozik."

I drove the Dart with Mike, who ended up more drunk than I was; so much for being straight-edge. I decided to show him "the view" from the Hollywood Hills. I was trying to show off how long I could go without a cigarette. We were discussing the Straight White Male's burden.

"So, what's all this stuff about patriarchy?" Mike said. "Are you in on this thing, or is it a no-gays policy?"

I love imported Easterners. It's like having a stand-up comic in your own home. In California, there's so much space between sentences.

"No, really." Mike was rolling. "I mean, I'm supposed to be a master of the race, running everything, making the world a worse place for minorities and women. I'm like, but what's in it for me? I don't feel like a patriarch."

Mike has finished school, I thought with amusement. He was still mulling over that which would soon prove useless, all that thinking.

I tried that, did the festival chat session, panels. Once, I found myself being verbally shot down by some willowy film theory doctoral student who was set on telling me what my use of symbols represented. I think I politely evaded the multi-syllabic question when I said, "It's so nice to meet someone who knows what I'm doing. Why don't you direct my next movie? I'll take a vacation." It least it got them laughing, and the geek sat down.

What I hated most was having to repeatedly get prodding questions about my degree, or lack of one. That burned.

I tried to convey this to Mike, but somewhere it fell apart. On impulse, I turned left and uphill.

"Where are we going?"

"You'll see."

I think there was some nicotine synapse thing. I expected to have the cigarette in the left hand, out the window, whenever the sun or moon was at that angle. You must remember that I'm writing this after I quit smoking, and to write about scenes where I was smoking, a lot, is kind of rough.

It wasn't like we were tense with each other. We were just bridging all the years of seeing each other, then not, for years, all according to the relationships our parents had, or rather, cut off, since Old Uncle Sean was still in alleged oblivion when Mike and I started talking independently of the mood swings of our moms.

We are like little bombsites, survivors of our parents' mutual turf wars. Why travel thousands of miles when you can argue over Friends and Family?

I parked at the crest of a small twisting road in Lake Hollywood Park along Canyon Drive. Shushing Mike to silence, we walked past private homes to a hidden path beside a forbidding gate that led us uphill to a dirt plateau next to more houses.

"Well, here it is." Above, us, the iconic letters were still lit.

"Wow."

I held out my hands like a benevolent wizard.

We stood silently for a few minutes.

"We should have brought a camera. We can't get closer?" Mike asked.

"Not without a long hike up and around behind it, and it's dark."

Still, the cool air sobered me up, which would make the trip downhill easier.

The glowing Hollywood sign shut him up for a while.

For a moment, while flipping the green and red duvet over the sofa, Mike's makeshift bed, the red under-throat looked like a mouth, and the bumpy green top the skin of an alligator. Where did I get that image? Was it some joke I'd made about the Peter Beard picture over my bed? I couldn't recall. It was like Déjà Vu Lite.

I bid him goodnight, then stepped outside to pretend to have a smoke while he channel-surfed, then retreated bedward.

The green and red duvet made me think of some other image, though. I looked to the small photo on my bed and shrugged. Of course, the photo: the famous photographer laying on the ground, writing in a journal, his lower torso in the mouth of a dead alligator.

Funny, because for a moment, I wondered how my imagination made that picture. See, that's where maybe a lot of analysis can solve problems, I guess. But for me, figuring it out was fun, too.

Cousin Mike used his mileage to also rent a car, thank goodness, so that kept him out and about, but he seemed to want me to entertain him, like my life was all poolside parties and glamorous openings.

Of course he didn't think that, but I almost felt guilty for not providing that so he wouldn't report home with a disappointing review. I could always keep the family at bay through a phone, without the visual disappointments of my actual life: a pile of papers and deals gone wrong, distributors in foreclosure, and projects shelved and re-shelved.

It was about Four A.M., Usually I end up having to pee about that time of the morning, especially if I've had a few. In between times, when I'm not on a shoot or working some stupid day job, I usually got to bed around one, then wake up to pee at five, sometimes dawn. I like those times, sometimes so much I just boil some Joe and stay up editing or storyboarding till I'm so jittery around ten I have to jack off and then sleep. I then wake up around noon, answering the calls that came in. It's a nice pattern, one of luxury, controlling my sleep and leisure to my best advantage. It's why I then work sixteen-hour days for weeks on end for a shoot.

Barry's analyst says that film people, along with having control problems, also love waves of behavior. Mood shifts of chaos and business followed by long fallow periods of little activity. Maybe he's right, but I'm not paying ninety bucks an hour to find out.

Since Mike was asleep on the sofa, though, I crept into my kitchen as if I were the guest. I sipped a glass of water and glanced out the window at Santa Monica's pre-dawn, a purple ink. I didn't want to wake Mike, so I didn't walk by through the living room to go outside.

Instead I hovered, looking down at his form, an elbow hanging out of the sheet, his knee at another angle. I had a crazed image of his little Popeye bowl of boy popping out, horror film morph style, into this lanky man. His head was back, his mouth half open, and he seemed more a boy than his chubby kidhood days, when his grumpy nature and baby belly made him seem more an old man. Was he as tough and well-adjusted as he seemed? Or did he have a few dark memories too, perhaps with his dad?

Then I realized, the last time I stood over him sleeping, was in the basement. It was the summer of our movie. He'd come to trust me as I led him on little adventures with family to the playground, and the pool. I could see how afraid he was of everything, how he sat in my father's lap with the quickness and familiarity of a cat, as if it were the only natural thing to do for the nearest dad facsimile.

But it had been an especially harrowing day for him. He'd tried to help me paint our porch and spilled an entire gallon of paint. I'd screamed at him, leaving him in tears. My mom tried to soothe things and get him away from me. He kept spilling things, knocking things down. At fifteen, you don't always make a great babysitter.

So, my mom took Mike across the street to play with another kid his age who lived across the street. He'd caused a scene there when he basically took over the poor kid's sandbox, a doe-eyed pup who'd never known such aggressive urban playground tactics. I even heard the bawling when he came home.

But Mike came to me. I thought he'd counted me off as enemy number one, but he came right up the porch, crying.

"They made fun of the way I tawked," he whined.

And then I understood his pain, being away from home, wondering if he ever would go home, or what that was, and having these little white bread kids think he was some freak for having a "Piss-barg" accent.

I took him up in my arms and told him, "Aw, they're all boring. They never seen big city kids like you." We went inside to get some cookies.

I often wondered if I'd tell Mike that someday when he was old enough to go out and get drunk with me. But he's not much of a drinker, God bless him.

Later in the morning, I heard Mike in the shower. I waited a polite few minutes for him to get dressed, and I entered the kitchen as he was cooking something.

"Omelets?" he said.

"With what?" I asked, sure that I didn't have eggs.

"Oh, I went to the store. That deli by the ocean."

"Jeez, did you bang a few waves too?"

"Huh?"

"Surf."

"No, but I'd really like to give that a try." He chopped a green pepper. "Not."

I decided to forsake a few hours sleep for some quality time.

"You're welcome to give it a try. I've got a wetsuit and a boogie board out back." They were fading away under the California sun from neglect. There had been a time between projects when I could spend most of the day in the ocean, bobbing, not going for waves as much as being in them. I hadn't been in the water in months.

"Is it difficult?"

"Floating around in the ocean? No. The hard part is leaving."

"Don't tell me you've been completely Californized."

"It's not a California thing. It's not a thing."

I thought when and if I should tell him about his father, but the comfort we had, the jokes about sex and the differences between our tastes, sprinkled with lots of regional slams, kept diffusing the confession.

"New York has everything," he bragged.

"Yeah, and everything's got a matching alarm," I countered.

"Like you don't have a crime rate?"

"At least our riots have some breathing room."

"You're gonna fall into the ocean one day."

"Better than getting blown up on the subway."

And in those squinted glances between guffaws, I ate his omelet, which was surprisingly good. He'd worked at the Marriott Hotel in Pittsburgh all through high school. By the time he graduated, he was the manager. They offered him a raise. He took a better job with the airline and has been there ever since.

I thought about ruining this morning with the bluntness of it, telling him about his father. Hell, I was about to tell half a million cable viewers about his father, in a way. But I stopped. I saw that he knew, recalled, and took account. There was no need to tell him. Blood knows without words. We have survived with minimal scar tissue.

Mike channel-surfed while I picked at the remnants of our chips. I'd submitted to watching *The Manipulator*, with my own in-person production commentary. Then we switched to TV.

After about half an hour, I saw Brendan's video on MTV. It was a great moment, the hip female VJ afterward saying, "That's the new video from Blood Ties, directed by, believe it or not, seventeen-year-old Brendan

George, an actor who stars in the Showtime film, *Say Uncle*, a film about ..." and then I saw her get uncomfortable, the poor, longhaired dear, "... family problems. Okay. Coming up tonight, *House of Style* with Cindy Crawford."

Mike dropped his pizza.

"Is that?"

"Yes."

"And you?"

"Yes."

My cousin leaped up as if I had just made the best jump shot in the NBA.

Seeing it. Seeing it rock, with Brendan's funny handhelds and zoomy zippy energetic cutting, all the rules I told him to break. It was a glorious mess. I had given birth to the auteur of the twenty-first century.

My phone rang.

"Brendan."

"Stan? How did you know it was me?"

"I'm slightly psychic."

"Ja see it?"

"It rocked, man."

"And the way she stuttered at the word?"

"It rocked, man."

"Thank you so much, man!"

"You did it, man."

"I love you, Stan! I owe you."

"No, you don't."

"Yes. Please. I wanna give you a big wet sloppy kiss. Lemme—"

"Don't go there, man."

Seventeen-year-old skin. Sure, he loved me. But what about after, when I had to face him not loving me? Just once more, and I would never love again. I wouldn't even ever *like* again.

"Okay. Sorry. Hey, man. A bunch of us are going to Swingers for food. Bask in my fortune. Wanna meet up?"

I imagined his posse of scenesters, goatees, smokers. I imagined their disappointment if I didn't show up, even more if I did.

"Um, mebbe. I got my cousin in town. See if he's up for it."

"Cool. We'll be there in about an hour. I'll see ya when I see ya."

"Okay. Brendan?"

"Yup."

"Buckle up."

"Okay, Uncle Stan."

I took Mike out to Swingers to meet Brendan and his gang. Mike drifted toward a comely female. Brendan and I huddled up. We got to talking about future projects. I couldn't tell if Brendan was authentically flirting, or doing what I so often had done, simply engaging a guy in some idea so you'll have the excuse to be together, since you're both too scared to simply say, "I wanna be with you."

In the middle of one of those late night phone calls that listed my spirits, even in the worst times, Gloria had put it simply when she told me why she married my brother. "He never lies. He may be wrong, or a boy when he wants, but he never lies. So many men lie."

Being a man, I couldn't agree less.

As he'd made a potential date with the Swingers gal, Mike was feeling pretty studly. He felt as I did early in my L.A. phase, surprised anyone would actually speak to me, until I figured out they were really after something, anything else.

I didn't want to burst Mike's bubble by explaining that the babe was an actress who probably had an itch for him only because he was the cousin of a director. I prayed I wouldn't have to get my number changed again.

"So, what's after Hong Kong?" I asked as we tooled back to Santa Monica in the Dodge Dart. Mike was planning another trip to Europe.

"Well, I like to start off in Paris, wherever I go. I think Prague, before it gets too Americanized."

I withheld my envy.

"You doing another movie? Another slice of gut-wrenching family drama?"

"No," I chuckled. "Actually, something very different."

"What?"

"Well, maybe, a porno movie."

"Really?" He laughed in way that said, *I hope you're joking.*

"Actually, it'll probably be sort of porno, y'know? One of those heavy R's that you only find at the video store, expecting hot action and not getting it. Only you'll get it, but not..."

I was stumbling. Truth is, I was still completely unaware of what to do, but sitting with Mike, some kind of picture was forming, a mix, a collage, like my hidden work, my private tapes.

"Isn't that a bit of a career reversal?"

"Maybe," I said. "I'm not gonna use my real name."

"Oh," Mike said, understanding. "Just for the money?"

No, it wasn't. "It's just something I have to get out of my system, and, well, the opportunity arose."

"So to speak," he smirked. "Not exactly something you'll be sending home."

"No."

We were both a bit antsy for amusement, and I wanted to continue playing tour guide. I wanted a cigarette, but said nothing. I turned back to West Hollywood, and took Mike to a mixed bar, telling him we'd go to a wilder club, but it wouldn't get rolling until midnight.

I hoped he'd see some famous people, have something to tell his friends about his "famous cousin's life." They were famous by my standards: Chi Chi LaRue, Tim Miller, Lance Loud, but I had to explain who they were, which lost the celebrity effect. It wasn't annoying. If he'd taken me to a Mets game, I would have had to ask about a Latino pitcher with a cute butt.

Amid some loud thrash music at a one night a week gay punk night, we sipped sodas as I enviously eyed the kids lighting up cigarettes. He shouted, "So when might you be surfing again?"

"Boogie boarding," I reminded him. I am still a grommet, a low life form on the wave food chain. "Tomorrow, if you like. I don't have an office to go to." That had been given out to some other up and comer, with Katsuo in the deal, no doubt. Shortly after the project's completion, I'd received a fat check from my agent. I was eager to spend.

I kept glancing at a pair of gogo boys on stands. One was half-dressed as a sailor and the other as a farm boy. His overalls kept showing the sides of his hips, one strap off the shoulder, the other in constant threat of being grabbed by the lower dancers.

"We have to go shopping first. I wanna get a new wetsuit."

"You don't have to do that for me," Mike said.

"I'm not. Mine has a big hole in the butt. You're wearing that one."

"Wait a minute. I'm not going out with my ass showing."

"Don't worry. I have some black Speedos you can wear under them. Besides, none of the surfers are gay. Well, most. And even the gay ones don't care. Everybody goes for themselves."

"Okay. As long as you don't let me drown."

"Hey, rule one. Once out there, you're on your own."

That summed up the conversation, but I took a mental note of something that burned into me with the unfocused thoughts of the porn video and the gogo boys.

Those farm boy overalls.

Call Jorge, I wrote on a napkin with a pen I borrowed from the bartender.

I got a simple basic black body suit, since I like to swim in winter. We piled it all into the car trunk and returned to the house, where we added the old stuff. Mike clutched the backpack, stuffed with rubber in shapes made to fit limbs and extremities. I parked the Dodge Dart. We changed in the parking lot, glaringly more obvious than others who had the benefit of bigger cars or vans to hide behind. I showed Mike the striptease-with-towel trick. It was fun.

By the time we were suited up and in the water, cool waves of salt water already slurping down my throat, I was happy. He was off somewhere, paddling about, then relaxing, getting into it. I felt half-seal, half-man, like a science project. The waves made a shifting blanket of salt and foam. I was in love with the planet again, even if it did have a slight reek of off-shore petroleum.

When we got back, the phone was blinking. Two messages: Jorge returning my call, Barry just to say hi. I called Jorge.

"Hey, girl."

"Are you finally succumbing once more to my Latin charm?"

"You bet, and your sense of taste. I want to talk costumes."

"For what?"

"Our little road movie."

"Who cares about clothes in a porn video?" He said he thought he'd been conceptualized out of the project. I reassured him that his talents were sorely needed, that we were going "icon shopping."

"Like what?"

"Oh, costume-wise, a sort of decade parade. A mixed combo."

"Such as?"

"Aldo Fellini," I said.

"Hmm?"

"The love child of Ray and Federico."

"Oh. Cool. Black and White?"

"The thirties scene, yeah."

"Oh, you're doing like, eras, filmically and ..."

"Whatever. I'm still scrambling for equipment. This is gonna be totally low budget again."

"But you're a cable TV director, on your way to success and mayonnaise commercials."

"Keep your claws in, dearie."

"All right," Jorge declared. "I would love to continue working with you, but only if I get some of those boys."

"Hey, I ain't pimpin'. They're guys. They have off hours."

"Terrific. I love the vision thing," he did George Bush with a Brazilian accent. It was an old joke whose origin eluded me.

"Really? Do you see it?"

"I do, my dear. Now, have we selected cast members?"

Jorge and I used to trade porno. We knew the boys. I hadn't heard from Jason or his peeps in weeks, but knew which corral to choose from.

"Yes, but no dating on the set. Get that over with beforehand."

"Awright, baby."

"We'll talk."

"Ciao."

I felt warmed, secured, not disconnected. I kept my friends working again. I was going to keep the machine rolling, the puppets dancing, my way. *Manipulator IV: Independents' Day.*

Even though he had the rental car, I let Mike have my car for his last day.

I leafed through some magazines, trying to put casting ideas together for the porno shoot. I almost wanked off once, but was still distracted. Knowing Mike might return at any moment took me back to my room-mate days. I put on a Ricky tape that night, the one where I loop a half hour alternating Adam Baldwin and Jake Andrews, Adam Baldwin, Jake Andrews. *My Bodyguard* and *Behind the Barn.* If you get it, you get it.

It took me a few days afterward to even consider it as a yenta move. I recall Mike telling me that in the course of my having my little chat with a few fey friends on Melrose I just had to chat with, Janice had propositioned him.

She and I had to work on some post-production paperwork, and since it was a weeknight, we might just have some dinner. Janice wouldn't even have time to boink Mike, but a night alone might be nice. And no, Barry's was not an option, nor Lance's yet.

Janice and I finished for the afternoon about the time Mike came back from a trip to wherever he went in Gramma's car.

I hit some music, and we headed out to the back yard for a late dinner under the moon. Janice got sidetracked by the family photo tree, which I guess wasn't posted before her last visit. Mike sipped a soda and made jokes about oceanic black mucous settling into our lungs. He actually made us laugh enough for me to hack a bit up.

When we went back inside, Mike darted into the bathroom. Janice perused the photos aligned on the wall. She scanned, smiling, asking, pointed to a few.

"So, which one..."

I smiled. Uncle Sean. Should have been played by Viggo Mortensen, before he got so damn famous, or Jet #4 from *West Side Story*. Third delinquent redhead on the left.

She said nothing except, "At least he was cute."

I smirked. Sure, we're healed. Thanks for sharing.

"But you and your brother never...?" She smiled, expectant.

"No, I and my brother never, nor did I and my cousin," I declared.

Then she kind of looked relieved, I don't know. And I said "What?" She explained that she thought my cousin looked straight, and I thought about that, and how I so often have to explain to people. Things. The Plot. Who didn't do it.

Mike took her out to dinner and, thankfully, didn't return until the next morning.

The day after Mike left, I had a weird dream from smoking a few pipefuls of pot after he was out of the house. Gramma was still alive and living in a shabby little apartment, and the walls fell away at one point, like in *The Time Machine*, and became a corroded slum, with old ads painted on tenement brick walls, and then it became a movie theatre, and while Gramma's bed sort of glowed like Edward G. Robinson's in *Soylent Green*, all these kids started pouring in. The weird thing was, then I was more into the movie, and my dream vision moved to full screen, which it does a lot. Anyway, in the movie, apparently some killer snuck up behind Bruce Lee, who was sitting in a barber chair in some neon fashion sci-fi district. The killer shushed the barber at gunpoint, then broke Bruce Lee's neck.

Cut to exterior shot in an alley, with Bruce Lee's psychic boyfriend, played by Mark Wahlberg, who stops chewing on éclair he's eating.

In my waking post-dream rewrites, I later wondered:

1. How a killer could sneak up on Bruce Lee while he was facing a mirror and sitting in a barber chair?

2. Would Marky Mark play anybody's psychic boyfriend, and hadn't I better consider recasting, and:

3. Why did I pay more attention to the movie than to my dying grandmother?

44. take lost year's chills built only by me

"But you see, to get past that shit you have to dig to the root."

"Just like dandelions," I said.

"Whoah."

Lance had finished his last looping session. His job was over, filmically. He seemed calm, ready, eager for the onslaught of publicity that would alter his life forever, possibly in a bad way.

"I'm sorry I didn't call you back," he said. "I just had to shut down after it all."

"I understand."

We had dinner at his home in Silver Lake. I felt nervous, since we had no risky frisson to excite us now that the filming was over, only the wide open possibility of merely dating.

Lance had done small roles in a few moderately successful films, but no great critical raves. He showed me his reel, a cut of his best scenes in a few teen beach romance stupidities, plus his two appearances on sitcoms as "the gay person" who pops in and out of the regulars' lives in thirty minutes, leaving Dad or Coach or whoever reaffirmed in his sexuality as soon as "the gay person" is out of the picture. Either he was too buffed and bleached for me to recognize him at the time, or I never saw the stuff.

My favorites, though, were the shampoo commercials. He was more burnished in those. He had a great face, but the cleft, the little divot most men crave to own or to lick, was what sold the product.

"That shampoo paid for the down payment on the house," Lance said.

And he had a nice bungalow, with a shared circular pool and poplar trees jutting up to hide the neighbor's house only a few yards away. I wanted to swim with Lance in the pool. Imagine Lance played by Barry Tubb, me played by…well, me. I didn't know if that was more a Jarman thing or a Kink Video thing.

We had drinks and walked by the pool. I still couldn't tell if he wanted to bed me again, or thought he had to bed me again as thanks. Lance's roommate, if you could call someone who lived on another floor a roommate, was not at home.

"Do you want to do more features?" I asked.

"Yeah, I guess. But for now, it's just TV. Except the 'gay guy' roles are getting slim, and the commercial thing is pretty much over now that I'm more known as gay."

"Being gay's the rent for me."

"Yeah, I guess it's as good as it gets. My parents tape all my shows. Force the neighbors to come over and watch. You know, that reminds me. When you were talking on set about my back story."

While not in the mood for work talk, I listened.

"Back when we were in *Gypsy*, I was curious about why a teenager would leave home to join a Vaudeville act. So I went to the library and read up on Tulsa the city. Did you know there was a huge attack on a Black community in 1921? A white mob killed hundreds of people."

"Wow. We never learned that in U.S. History."

"Right? So, I figured, even years later, it musta still been an awful place to live, so Tulsa woulda been happy to leave."

While I had only considered the less 'musical' aspects to our shared role as an adult, Lance's earnest perspective charmed me.

"Your performance was very convincing."

"Guess I've done pretty well for an ex-football jock with no talent."

"To have no talent is not enough."

He laughed. "Where'd you get that line?"

"You don't remember?"

"Huh?"

"*Gypsy*. Mazeppa."

"Oh, my god. You remember everything, doncha? When did you turn into a show queen?" He leaned in.

"When I met you."

The night was calm and clear. He sipped his drink and brought his face close to mine. I heard him gulp before he kissed me.

Tulsa kissed Tulsa.

We took off our clothes by the pool's edge, swimming and making out. Another helicopter passed far off over the hills, distant this time.

I never get used to the helicopters. I still fear them. I always think there's some guy lying at an intersection in a pool of his own blood, being beaten to death for no reason, other than rage and racism. That's the scariest part. No reason, except being there.

"Let's go inside."

"So, did you know you wanted me?"

"Sure," I said.

"But gosh. You were only fourteen."

"I know, but…" I wanted to tell him, blame him, say, if only you or Dick Thorson would have done it, then I wouldn't have done it with the bad guy. "I knew what I wanted."

"That's you now saying that. You weren't so sure then."

"Yes, I was."

"Naw. You see, you were a different person then. Different moods, different thoughts, even different cells." His hand spread over my chest. "You know, your whole body has been replaced since then."

"That sounds a bit Body Snatcher-ish."

"You know what I mean. The kid who loved strawberry ice cream now can't stand it, he likes … pickled artichoke hearts."

That's what I was, a pickled version of my boy self, soured. I said, "Wiener Winks."

"What?"

"Nothing, a stupid joke."

"Okay. By the way," he said as we walked back inside, "I'm negative."

"Yay. Me too."

"I was a lil shy last time, but we can go further."

"I may not be an actor anymore, but I do take direction."

We were doing vanilla, I guess you could call it, smoochy and all. I mean I was taking my damn time, thank you, but then he said, "You wanna get kinky?"

I grinned, having had my share of leather theatricality. But I didn't expect him to be so earnest. The whole thing seemed to clash with the decor. But I got into it.

He asked me to put on a military outfit, and he frankly looked pretty good on his hands and knees, his butt in the air while he licked my combat boots. I bent over and smacked his firm fuzzy butt.

Firmly clutching on to him under me, I scooted around and slid my cock in and out of him with a smooth stroke. Dog tags he'd given me dangled from my neck, and he reached up to suck on them. I wondered if the names were of anybody real, anybody who'd actually served time and gotten his body shot up, or were they just another prop?

I bent him over on his belly. His face was too handsome to be this rough. Looking at him just made me want kiss and lick, and that wasn't what either of us wanted then. Sliding back into his ass from behind, the rubber scrunched up a bit, but still held. I could continue the smacking and the pinching and the slamming and the nasty love.

He grunted, "Oh, yes, sir, fuck me. Fuck my ass."

"Little soldier likes bein' fucked by his sergeant, doesn't he?"

"Oh, yessir. I love it when you munfff…" I shoved his face into the pillow, letting him moan so only the bed sheets could understand. Sure I enjoyed it, but I would have settled for a little dance in a back alley with a guy in tight gray pants and a top hat. I'd pretty much worked out any relative eroticism by then.

I tossed the props off the bed, scooted around to nestle with him, face to crotch, and we suckled each other, slowly, then forcefully, until we burst into each other's mouths in an almost simultaneous bout of spurts that nearly made me levitate.

We lay in bed, holding on, still a bit sticky. He occasionally reached over and grazed his hand over my skin, making sure I was still there.

"When did you leave Brookside?"

"After college," he said. "I was born in Wooster, actually a farm outside of it. Didn't go back much for a while. Did summer stock, then some dumb jobs in Cleveland, traveled to Germany, then came back and did the U-Haul trek here with a friend."

"What's he do?"

"Not much. He's dead."

"Sorry."

"But we did okay, at first. We were so eager. I was working days. Nights too, sometimes."

"What work?"

"The usual. Waiting tables, temping. For a while I was a folder."

"A what?"

"A folder. I folded clothes at a J. Crew store. They liked having handsome guys wear their clothes in the store. I didn't have to sell anything, just be there, keep things looking nice."

"Sounds…"

"I know. Banal. People think I'm stupid 'cause I'm so utterly blond."

"I never thought you were stupid. I worshipped you."

"Thanks." Lance craned his head over and kissed me. We lay back, looking at his ceiling.

As we drifted off to that half-sleep state any couple feels the third or fourth night together, trying to ignore and enjoy the other's grunts and snorts and warm presence, I half-dreamed myself back to that time, that first taste of theater, when I learned that one sometimes had to pretend to be happy just to be happy.

45. but after languid music he screams

The editing session on *Say Uncle* was a bloodbath, with more sacrifices than a busload of Iphigenias.

Eric, the editor, and I were working, and Barry kept coming in and out, depending on his temper, then left us alone.

"Okay, have it your way," I told Eric over some issue. "But you know they'll never go for it."

"Stan, we have to give them something to cut, some extra fat for them to trim, or else they're gonna start slicing away the meat."

"Oh, you are one slick dog." I glanced at Eric. We'd banged out the final edit in Showtime's rented space. Three weeks. We liked it. It would sell. I should have asked for a higher share. Jason only got a thousand for a porn video. I was thinking about that, since we'd done up the budget at the same time I was editing the TV movie we had derisively called *Uncle Funkle, Cents and Incestibility,* and, Eric's favorite, *After School Spillage.*

I'd mentioned bailing on the porn video. Jason had left three messages. I had to call him.

Eric pulled himself away from his desk. "I suggest we stop for the night."

"You sure?"

"Yes. My girlfriend is waiting at home with a warmed-over dinner and a fresh bag of Colombian. Care to stop over?"

How could I refuse?

Eric talked about his other freelance jobs amid the expansive house tour of his place in the Valley. This was my third welcome into other homes that were much better than mine and owned by people who worked for me. Hey, wait a minute.

Eric asked what else I had coming up.

I mentioned, as a joke, the proposal that I do a porn video, "but smart."

He said, "Cutting it's boring, but it pays."

"You edit porn, too?"

"How do you think I paid for this house?" Our laughs echoed, but the immense living room was still homey, a hangar with a fireplace.

"You like living out here?"

"Of course. You should come out and visit more often."

"What made you make the big move?"

"I've lived in apartments and little houses off Melrose, and I got to the point where I missed some things really bad."

"Like what?"

"Hearing crickets before bed. Having a porch to sip wine on and watch the moths get caught in the screen door. Cutting the lawn. Having a yard where people can play volleyball and walk in their bare feet."

"You're a country boy at heart."

"The 'burbs," Eric murmured. "All the magic and terror of modern America lies in the 'burbs."

We puffed smoke and admired his comment, that and the distant helicopters behind the poplars. Another car chase, perhaps. We left the TV off. I chased the buzz with nicotine gum.

"What brought you here?" Eric asked me.

"The pools."

"Huh?"

"The pools. I never swam in so many different pools. I like it."

Eric gave me a glance, then drifted his gaze back to the small screen, as if he knew the glint at that moment would hit his eyes just then.

"Can I use your phone?" I said.

"Sure."

I stood, expecting to be led into the house. Stupid. Eric handed me his phone.

I dialed Jason and left a message with Eric's number. Before we even began another topic of conversation, the phone rang back.

Jason, of course.

"Come over," he said.

"Jase, I'm way over in the Valley."

"I'll wait."

"But—" It wasn't like Lance and I were boyfriends yet.

"Do nut say a wud. This may be your only chance to dew whatchew want with me, and for me to convince you to make this video with me. Now, just git up and politely tell whoevah yaw with that you rilly must go, because I am standing in the middle of an empty hass with a view o' half the fickin' wuld, a bowl of condomes at my very lahge feet, and my erect penis clutched in hand, waitin' to enter any available orifice in your budy. Am I cleah?"

"As an azure sky."

"Got a pen?"

As I politely left Eric and his girlfriend to do whatever they liked to do in their privacy, in the car, I kept the radio off as I glanced down again at the scribbled Brentwood address, muttering again and again, in Jason's Aussie accent, "Condomes. Condomes."

46. she played after some, like, paranormal apparition

"It's not that we don't want to use it, it's just that the material needs..."

"I know what you think it needs, Sal, and I am telling you it's going just as the screenplay says. We're being very sensitive to the issue."

"They're getting mass mailings."

"So, that's it."

"Well, in a word."

"Fundies."

"Whatever."

I had decided to communicate with Showtime through my representative. I was beginning to understand how annoying his voice truly was.

"They could sell it to another cable company in a day. They could chop it up and turn it into a hundred cat food commercials. You don't own it. You were a hired gun. You know that."

I was very irritable, possibly because sitting wasn't the most comfortable position, post-Jason. Why is so much hell always preceded by such brief heaven?

"Look in your contract."

"You look, Sal, because it's going to be in shreds if you neg out on me."

"Don't get in a fizzle, babe. Hold on a sec."

Call Waiting on his car phone. I hung up.

I called Barry.

"Look, you need to settle down," he said. "It's going to be okay."

"No, it's not. It's gonna be chewed up by some corporate fuck who lets focus groups rule his every fart. This is what I get for trying to go mainstream."

"You're not going to fail. You can't let yourself fail."

"Stop with that Louise Hayseed crap. That doesn't work with me."

"And what does?"

"You know what does? Pot does. And cigarettes, and cock and coffee and Jolt, and more coffee, and you know what? I think if you take all that away, if I just quit all of it, there won't be anything left but a little old man sitting in a room playing movies in his head, but not getting a fucking thing done!"

They wanted "the scene" to be re-cut. Eric was on to another project. Brendan was in Bali. Lance stuck to my side and pretended to be elsewhere, even though Edmund had politely suggested to Barry that all parties involved "make themselves available as soon as possible." He, of all people, playing bully.

They even had the right to haul in a guest director for reshoots. It was supposed to be out of my hands after a certain point. Tell that to your ripped out cinematic placenta.

There was huffing and puffing, testosterone in Armani suits making me nauseated and giddy at the same time, since HBO had bid on a buyout of unedited film. What they couldn't sell to anyone suddenly was a hot property and they seemed to want it again, but on their terms.

Edmund returned to my side, accepted Brendan's international return phone call of, "No fucking way! The waves here are like God. Use a computer graphic of me. Tell them I died surfing."

Edmund didn't tell them that, but as executive producer whose character had basically been the Suits' pop culture babysitter of sorts, his melodious old owl tones won them over.

In the middle of it all, Jason invited himself over with a call, saying he was in Santa Monica at a boring dinner party, and dessert looked bleak.

Jason Daw in my crib. I didn't know whether to clean up or make the place dirtier.

He filled my house like a huntsman in Snow White's dwarfish *pied-a-terre.*

A beer later and some near-fellatio, he quizzed me. "So, when are we going to do this, guy?"

"Do what?"

"Fuck me with your camera."

"After I finish this film."

"Thought it was done."

"Post, baby, post. It's not like your business. Lots of details. It's down to some legal shit I really can't bail on."

I was lying. It was done as far as I was concerned. I also hoped to jumpstart being boyfriends with Lance, and having a semi-naked porn actor standing in my living room didn't help.

"Well, I just wanted to get this thing done soon. Can't do all those positions very well while attached to an IV."

"How are you?"

"Congratulate me on my first OI."

I said nothing. This after I'd deep-throated him to choking and he'd fucked me from here to Calvin Klein's Eternity. He had worn a series of rubbers, but still. I contemplated getting another HIV test, but figured it would be better to get tested for every known STD after the porn shoot. I lied to myself that I wasn't actually cheating on Lance, since we hadn't decided what we were yet, and sex with Jason seemed like more of a perk with a business transaction.

"In the meantime, how 'bout rounding up a cast list," he said, with a bit of false bravura as we lay in my bed.

"Huh?"

"You know, pick the boys."

"I thought I was going to just get a stable, you know. Whoever works for your company."

"Listen, with the phone calls I been gettin', every whore in Babylon wants a shot."

"Well, okay then. I'll start shopping."

That night, I pulled my drawers open. My bed became a cluster pile of images. We chose men not only for our own taste, but their diversity, their looks, their size, and their ages. I wanted every homo to have a favorite, and all of them to be mine.

But after a few hours of pot-induced video priapism, we fell to another round of live action amid a pile of tapes. I realized I was trying to put them all together, line 'em up. Uncle Sean fucks Lance, who sucks Barry, who rims Jason, who fucks...

When I woke up a few hours later in the arms of my favorite porn star, as much clout as he had, I realized I was going to need some people on my side.

47. Illness Fatal to Photographer LYLE
by JOHNNY BOWEN

San Francisco LYLE FRISBY, noted physique photographer of Los Angeles who was known professionally as LYLE, died after a long illness. He had contacted pneumonia and then other complications developed which brought about his untimely death.

The passing of LYLE came as a great shock to his many close associates in the physique photography field. He was known as a true, sincere friend. LYLE's work, which appeared in physical culture magazines throughout the U.S. and Europe, including TOMORROW's MAN, commanded a wide following of admirers.

—obituary from the physique magazine
Tomorrow's Man, May 1957

For all his incredibly good taste, Jorge Oribe's apartment is a bit cluttered. He had stacks and piles and boxes of neat and amazing stuff. Every AMG magazine worth having. Two boxes of *After Darks*. Dolls, autographed magazines from old Hollywood days, muscle mags like *Vim*, every Colt, autographs and props, two Tom of Finland original prints, Deco photos from the actual Deco period, and family photo albums from Buenos Aires vacations with uncles holding him on their sepia shoulders under bright off-white beach landscapes.

Casa Larissa, a tiny apartment building perched on a quiet hill in Silver Lake, just off Santa Monica Boulevard, looked the part of old Hollywood. Demure French doors led out to a patio that faced the street. Jonquils and palms crowded around the building, giving it a submerged Southern quality.

"Shall we imbibe?" Jorge lifted a pipe.

"Mais, oui!"

We sat on an ancient yet comfy sofa. I flipped through a March 1960 *Motion Picture* magazine. Half a color photo of Elizabeth Taylor filled the cover. The headline read: *WHAT the Doctors Can't Tell LIZ about her Hidden Illness!* Inside, pictures and stories of Sterling Hayden on his infamous boat, a story and picture of Fabian covered in Hawaiian leis, the Brylcreem crooner; a story and picture of James Darren, still another full-page color picture of Tab Hunter in a bathing suit, his tanned legs glowing in perfectly buffed sunlight as he sits, a vision of studliness in a rocky cove. His story's headline read: *I've Made a Bride of Loneliness and She Is Lovely.*

The cascade of pictures combined with the smell of the rotting newsprint, plus the impact of the pot, swirled through my brain and body down to my groin. I wanted to dive into the magazine and fuck the past. Jorge had piles of this stuff, a maze of it, a treasure trove.

"Isn't that one fabulous? I found it yesterday."

"You bought it?"

"No, I bought it years ago. I just found it yesterday." His eyes glistened like a faun having found a new trick.

"It's making me horny."

"Mmmm."

Maybe Jorge thought I'd let him seduce me again. Maybe I'd just play the role of his idol while letting him do the same, or play whomever he wanted because he liked characters. He was a bit miffed I hadn't properly introduced him to Jason yet.

I noticed one wall filled with James Dean pictures. A *Giant* lobby card in French. An autographed *East of Eden* publicity still.

I was amazed, but more amazed that in all these years I'd known him, I'd only been to his apartment once a year. We were always meeting somewhere in between.

"You like the Mutant King, eh?" I said.

"I adore him. My only bow to necrophilia. When I heard about this apartment, I had a feeling, and then, two minutes into the apartment tour, the landlady says Jimmy lived here, and I was like, I don't care if he just spent the night. I'm moving in."

"J'ever hear about those nude pictures of him in a tree?"

"Not him, unfortunately. The myth is wrong. There are nude pictures of him, but that is not one of them."

"Oh, you are devoted, aren't you?"

He was silent, as if about to make a confession. Then he led me to his bedroom, opened a closet door, then turned back, pointing at me with absolute conviction. "You are sworn to secrecy."

I crossed my heart, which was beating in a new thump, not unlike my old *Playgirl* theft days, walking home in Brookside, the magazine under my shirt and stuck to my back with panic sweat.

He walked into the closet. I heard clicking, then a small door—no, a small safe—opening.

He returned holding a box, which he unlocked with a key. He patted the bed for me to sit with him. I carefully placed myself inches from the box. He removed a folder, leaned over into his night table and extracted a rubber glove, then said, "No, just wipe your hands. I can see you've got the fire. You deserve to touch them. They are reproductions, however."

I opened the box.

There he was, Jimmy, posed artfully, looking away, the man himself, king of angst, his docile penis nestled between his legs, innocent, half erect, clouded above by, surprisingly, blond hairs.

I had to close my mouth to stop the drool.

"Can I—"

"Nope. No copies. But, if you're nice, you may see them again sometime."

I held the photo. He took it, showed me another. And another. Other stars, still living, whose names I am sworn to never reveal. But the main event was Jimmy, of course. Always Jimmy.

I recovered as he led me out to the kitchen for a drink. For the first time in his company, I had no casual joke, no crude comment, no campy line. He had shown me his innermost treasure, his deepest devotion. I didn't even think to ask how much it cost him, until he said, "I've had offers to sell, but you know, I don't need that much money just yet. Haven't found the right house."

"You are brilliant."

"Obsession ain't just a peh-fume, baby."

I mentioned the infamous dance with the scissors that marked James Dean's Broadway performance in Gide's *The Immoralist*. Caked up in Arab makeup, the Hoosier was said to have stirred longings even in the straightest of male audience members' members.

"I heard there was a film of the play, but that must too be a myth." Jorge sighed, then laughed. "Am I twisted or what?"

"But elegantly so," I said. "Your selectivity is admirable. Me, I just grab."

"When you hunt for two rabbits, you get none."

"Who said that?"

"Jimmy Dean, Jimmy Dean."

I whirled from the drink, the image, wondering how long I could last before I begged Jorge for another showing. Then I realized that I had something to offer.

"I really want you to do the costumes for the porno. They have money. We're shooting in Phoenix."

"I told you, I'm in. If I get my own room."

"I expect there will be a lot of sex."

"Isn't that the point?"

"No, I mean, off the set, too."

"You bringing your new beau?"

"Lance? Oh my god, no."

"You telling him about it?"

"Not yet."

Jorge shrugged it off. "Torn between your boyhood crush and a porn star. Poor you."

His joke stuck in me as the cinematic bacchanal took shape. What would Lance think?

"You should also be in it," I said.

"And do what?"

"I see you as the muse, the bringer of fantasies. How about a dancing Arab boy?"

"Oh." Jorge panted as if his heart were being broken. "To put such a temptation before a poor boy is surely the seed of corruption."

"Who said that?" I asked.

"I did."

I laughed as he led me out of his shrine/bedroom and into the living. Then he turned to me and said, "No kidding, if I die, those go to you."

"Thank you, dear. But I'd rather kill you over a live man."

48. ask who lights a black storm

Like a distant relative or ex-boyfriend, *Uncle Up My Bum* aka *Say Uncle* had been reduced to phone conversations, nasty ones.

A monthly film mag wanted an interview. I forwarded those off on Katsuo to arrange with Lance, Brendan or other cast members. If Lance could face off against Ohio Christians in the '70s when he played Jesus, he could damn well handle Hollywood's worst. Besides, he needed the practice and the place to come out.

I don't like to knock reporters. They do produce the stuff that keeps us known. It can be a symbiotic relationship, like a rhino and those little birds that pick his earwax.

But I learned something during the years of my one-man road show of the indie circuit. It was like Madame Rose, her jalopy broken-down outside of town, she looking for an Elks pin. Find a brother. Flirt like mad with some local scribbler, whatever town the festival's in, and make sure to get some copy.

I learned to say the best stuff within the first ten minutes, because that's all some of those reporters can recall. A few listened a lot more. I had to stem the ego tide and remember sound bite technique.

But this wasn't a festival. This was one massive, national broadcast, and I was dealing, or actually avoiding, communications directors for national teleconglomorates, not hometown papers. I was out of the loop when, as they say, the fit had hit the shan.

There was the problem with the growing boycott by Concerned Ladies for Decency or some other pinched fascist temperance league. I faxed a response to an activist rep, and spoke to them through GLAAD, then let them sling a little mud.

Then there was a problem with the airdate. Some executive wanted to bump it to eleven p.m., because of its "delicate subject matter."

But as Brendan had recently snagged a one-time travel segment from a rave in Bali, and his band's music video had led to a contract with RCA, he himself was pulling a bit of a Jimmy Dean with his own mysterious absence and growing fame. Brendan's agent had become a rabid incredible hulk of opportunism.

There was a new, unconfirmed, offer of a distribution company offering to simply buy the thing off and sell it on video. I stood to make the same royalties, so by this point, I didn't care. I wanted to move on to my desert *National Pornographic* with Jason.

But with no launch, no air date for the kiddies, my audience had been deprived of an actual showing. I felt a career robbery on the menu.

Edmund gave me a call. Edmund saved it. Edmund steered it into the hands of GLAAD and editors of gay papers all over this great land.

"Smithers, release the hounds," he'd joked.

A week later, thanks to Katsuo's finding time between the post of this production and another project, she got copies of all the articles about the show in all those gay papers around the country, tabulated the readership and presented it to all the appropriate Suits as if it were merely tracking a target market, not her telling these jerks how to do their jobs, which is what she did. She sure did for me.

Showtime finally realized it had a hot property that got some good gossip and a bit of scandal. After a week of phone calls and meetings, lawyers and more lawyers, we had an airdate, and my agent Sal was crowing like he'd thought the whole thing up himself, the little bald fuck.

I got a call from Janice, who was calling just to see how I was doing, and to complain about the Showtime accountant geek wanting to look at the production day charts again. "He thinks the Teamsters are double-billing."

"He's probably right."

"Oh, I swear, if it weren't for his Hair Replacement patch just sewn in, I'd swear he's gay."

"Gay men do that, too."

"Yeah, but not in that style."

"Oh, darling, your rampant generalizations at my sexual tribe are demeaning. How dare you put the burden of good taste on all our waxed backs?"

She laughed, and I remembered how smart she was with those damn charts.

"So, what are you working on?" I said. "Got anything else planned?" I'd forgotten her update when I last saw her disappear into the night with my cousin, who, she discreetly informed me, was a rather fine lay.

"Um, some bites are out, but for now, I'm thinking about how to throw my salary into the endless repairs on this old house."

"Where is it you live?" I asked.

"Topanga. You've been there twice."

How embarrassing. Why didn't I know these people? "Oh, that's right. You own that."

"I work. A lot."

"Great. Um, Janice, do you want to work with me again and help me spend that little bonus from J. Quest Productions?"

"Sure."

"Do you like the desert?"

"Sure."

"Do you like men with muscles?"

"Sometimes."

"How 'bout next month?"

"What?"

I explained it to her. The idea of traveling around the desert and wherever else with a bunch of gay men on sexual overdrive didn't strike gold until I told her that at least three of them were bi.

"You know for sure?" she asked.

"My dear, I have documented evidence. Would you like to come over for a pre-production meeting and pick one out?"

49. as a **hot** day needs **rain**, as **wax** could fly

"I really wanna shoot on film."

"We don't have the money for that," Geoff said on the phone. "We don't have the crew, we don't—"

"Well, I'm planning on hiring a few friends to help out."

"Who?"

"A production…" I wanted to say manager, but somehow that term seemed to be Geoff's supposed turf, either that or Cock Wrangler. Penile Picker Upper Pez Dispenser. "…assistant." Janice would be insulted by the demeaning title, but this would be more of a working vacation for her. "And Jorge, my costume guy. You met him."

"Really?" I already felt his claws sharpening. Anyone named Jorge was his type.

That softened him up, but then he just started getting more contrary, and I realized I was going to have to do everything I could to make this guy feel important, which might even include shoving him in front of the camera. That or shoot scenes when he and the executive-producing Sugar Daddy were nowhere nearby. "Okay, okay, okay, just, just gimme June, okay?" I said. "I wanna be there for Gay Pride."

"In Phoenix?" Geoff asked.

"Yes. When else do you think we're gonna get extras?"

"Extras?"

"I want a real setting to counter the fantasy scenes. Can't you book some of the guys for a studio promotional event?"

"But we can't pay for extras."

"No, no, just the thrill of being there will be enough. Get 'em all to sign model releases, check ID, make sure none are cops. It's easy."

"Stan, I'm not really sure that our visions are aligned here."

I would have argued more, but the picture of the film, a *film*, not a video, was so clear. All the fights and mindfucks got me closer to redefining the porn film. I had already picked music, lines, situations. He was right. It had nothing to do with him.

I got Geoff back to earth by quizzing him about things he could handle, like the hotel, cables, filters.

I considering asking Geoff about him paying for my post-shoot rental of a single car, but that would have led to revealing my familial destination. Then I lied.

"I'm going to shoot some B-roll and take a little vacation after the shoot. I can pay for the extra car."

"Oh, you don't have to do that."

I appreciated Geoff's concern, but he had no idea what Janice the Grid Girl and I were planning on doing with his budget.

"I'm just gonna need to relax after all this," I said, preparing him to rehearse sympathy.

"Oh, believe me, I understand."

He understood what? Did he think I was going to play Casting Couch, take a few actors on the lam? I didn't want to crash his fantasy. Also, I'd already slept with our star twice.

"And the car. I need a four-wheel drive SUV."

"But we can take you around—"

"I know, but I need the freedom. If I get the impulse to do a scene, I wanna scout around." I really wanted time alone for my own little family tree hegira, but none of them had to know about that. "Oh, and I need the boys to meet with Jorge for costume fittings."

"Costumes? Is this gonna be another *Centurions of Rome?*"

"No, no, a little more Fellini-esque. *Reel to Real.* That's the working title." It came out of me like a lie, but the name was good. I was going to use it.

"Oh, that sounds hot."

I cringed at the word. Boiling water is hot. Weather is hot. People are not hot. "It will be. Trust me."

"Tell me more."

"You'll see." I gave him Jorge's number, hoping Jorge could be trusted to make all the men fill their roles in my landscape. I hoped he'd also take their inseams without too much damage to the talent.

Knowing Barry worked late, I called him around midnight.

"But where will you be? Can I contact you?"

"Phoenix. No."

"But we're in the middle of the publicity. What the hell are you gonna do about the other interviews?"

"You and Lance can take care of that. Brendan's coming back from his tour of Southeast Asia. They're doing a few club gigs with his band. Call Katsuo, tell her you want her to do some PR, celebrity guest lists, all the former junkie rock stars sitting by the phone."

"Honey, what I want has nothing to do with what'll happen with PR. I'm calling Sal."

I calmed him down, told him it would be all right.

"Don't forget to be back in town for the benefit screening."

"The *what*?" I asked.

"The benefit screening for GLAAD, in the middle of June. The Ides of June."

"Not exactly."

"Whatever. It's black tie. You bought a table."

"You mean Katsuo bought a table and will bill Showtime?"

"I did."

"Well, congratulate yourself and give her a raise." We laughed, but then he paused or sighed. I couldn't tell. I was losing his phone. Damn cellular.

"Where are you really going?" he asked. "A quick vacation? You can stay at my friend Ted's place in Palm Springs."

"I'm going to do the porno movie." Silence. "Parts of it."

"Now? You just finished—"

"I have to do this before I get all tired out."

"But, this is ridiculous."

"I need to do a little final research."

"Research? On a porn movie?"

"No, on our movie."

"Stan, honey, we're done."

He got that right. "I'm not."

He paused, shifted gears. "My house-sitting host wants to throw a little pre-screening party for us. I just want you to be there."

"Who's he inviting?"

"Just a few friends. It's really our party."

"Yeah, right, and his show."

"Guests of honor don't have to pay the caterer. Stan, you don't have to buy the chips and dip this time. You don't have to direct it."

"That's a plus."

"Plus, he's got that four-foot widescreen TV, if you remember."

"Gawd, I'll be sick. All those placating drunks passing by to praise me and eye salmon dip, especially after Brendan's shirtless scenes."

"It's not gonna be like that."

I sighed, let Barry's care sink through the whiny tone. This guy had been so good to me. It was gonna hurt like hell to break his heart. "I'd like to invite a few friends, too," I said.

"Oh?"

"Yeah. When is the torture session?"

"Stan, you can just duck out when the movie starts."

"Oh, as if. I gotta save that for this benefit screening."

"Christ."

"Don't get him involved."

The next day, since the porno shoot was as yet scriptless, I tried starting with words, then scrapped that and fished around for a single pipe hit of pot.

Storyboard pages covered my living room floor. I'd ripped out a whole pile of porno magazine pics of my hoped-for cast, and would hole-punch and bind them when I figured out the order, which could change. Boys in top hats all lined up, and then, as the camera dollies across, each one sets his top hat on the hook of his erect cock. Should I line them up by height or cock size? Skin tone? *The First Nudie Music Video.*

Hours later, Barry was at my door without calling first. Very dramatic for L.A.

"So, what is going on?" He was blunt.

"Um, I'm takin' off for a few weeks, days. I dunno. Avoiding post-production depression. I really want to do this movie. See? It's almost done."

Barry surveyed the floor collage of cocks, butts, and scribbled shot drafts. "Wow. You wanna eat?"

"Maybe." I got up to wipe the ink and glue off my hands, then remembered to kiss Barry. I pecked him, then paced to the kitchen. "Ya hungry? I was just gonna make some..." But my fridge scan revealed some scary remnants. "...take-out."

I turned. He was close to me. I realized I could still kiss him with my tongue. Being stoned and hungry and having spent all day making pictures of guys having sex, it seemed like a good idea to kiss Barry again, which would lead to pulling his shirt off, and dropping to the floor and finally doing that *9 1/2 Weeks* thing.

It was really Barry's move, his favorite form of creating tension. He'd do it before a screening, do it before a plane trip, heighten it by creating a deadline. This time, it was the imminent arrival of the delivery guy. I saw right through it, but sometimes, I liked it, too.

But you can't base a relationship on impulses.

I wanted to eat in front of the tube, but when the delivery guy arrived, I pulled my pants on as Barry ducked into the bathroom. When I returned, he started setting the table. A sit-down to the clatter of plates.

Face each other. Was this The Talk? Would he spurn me before I got the chance? That would be relieving.

"Well, I'm gonna get back to my storyboards," I said. "You wanna watch TV? Hang out? You can stay over, but we're not, like, back together or anything."

"Fine." he said. "I know I'm acting like a—"

"Look, let's just hang. Let's not therapize. Okay?"

We did, or our impression of it.

In bed, his hand kept grazing over at my butt, and I didn't respond. I kept having to think of someone else to get hard. I thought it sexually dishonest and couldn't explain. I had a Rolodex of sex fantasies stirring in my head. Kyle Payne as the sailor? Joe Andrews as the Farmboy? Who would Jason Daw be? Jason of Argonauts fame? How did he look in sandals?

Somewhere in the sexless night, Barry ended up on the other end of the bed. He was up and wearing only his boxer shorts when I rose.

"Breakfast?" he announced like a camp activities counselor.

"What? Cold Chinese?"

"We'll go out. Get dressed."

"Ugh."

We had a tortuous breakfast at Big Dan's, the scenester diner on Olympic. Thick coffee cup clatter interrupted vast eddies of silence stapled together by my cryptic comments aimed at discussing the "situation." Bleah. Worst eggs I ever ate. I wanted to leave, just to smoke a cigarette, but knew if I bought some in Barry's presence he'd start lecturing. I just wanted to be away, alone, puffing a bong on a verandah in my yard, then sleeping the day away with the phone disconnected.

"So, are we breaking up?" he asked.

"That came out of nowhere." I just looked at Barry, then out at the passing traffic on Olympic. Datsun. Bronco. Gardening truck with a cab full of Mexican day workers.

"Are we?" Barry asked again.

"I think we already did. We just didn't know it."

"Well, we have been busy."

Silence.

"Anything else?" the waitress asked, prompting a summary, a wrapping up, a wiping of napkins. We thanked her with a dual No Thank You.

"So, we can still go to the GLAAD benefit together, right?" he said.

"Yes."

"Who's gonna be at the table?"

I sighed. I knew he meant Lance. "Why don't you and Katsuo figure that out? It's definitely you, me, Edmund plus one, Lance, Brendan, if he's on this side of the planet, Katsuo, then some Showtime wogs, and … how many's that?"

Barry shrugged. "You're still directing, whether you like it or not."

I didn't think so. It just seemed so messy having all these people to think about. I wanted it to be a closed show.

I waited for Dan to call twice before returning his call. Letterman was on, so I knew it was him. Dan likes Letterman. I don't. Therein lies the quandary.

I imagined Dan holding the baby in his arms, because I could hear her. I remembered the smell of regurgitated Graham crackers. I like kids, I just don't like cleaning up after them.

He sounded a little tired. I was afraid of some bad news about the baby, some other piece of great misfortune or joy filtered out through his breezy cynical attitude. But then I heard her sort of chirp, and Gloria off in the background, being happy, and I began to hope for maybe a hint of an invite north. I needed a bit of San Francisco to fog up my life.

"I spent a day in Oslo. Had some reindeer steak."

"Dan, that's sick."

"They're like cows out here. They herd them."

"So, it's still gross."

"What, eating Rudolph?"

Split Screen: Norelco's cartoon Christmas show, with Santa sliding down a snow bank/Baryshnikov on PBS, in white tights.

"What were you doing in Oslo?"

"Shooting backdrops for the new *Galactic Guns* game."

"For the movie?"

"The sequel."

"When are they doing that?"

"Oh, it's shot."

"I can't keep up." I said. "I'm still renting *Twenty Million Miles to Earth*."

"Hey, we oughtta make a remake of that."

"Why not?" Static flooded our phones. "But it's still set in Rome."

"Definitely." More static. "It's not … Sorry, we're not connecting."

"No, it's just ... Hello? You shoulda sent me a postcard. You know I still collect stamps ..." I looked around my room. "... somewhere."

"You know I just go to hotel conference rooms and shake hands with a buncha boring guys with ponytails like me..."

I hmmed assent. Even he knew how boring straight guys could be.

Dan seemed relaxed, since Gloria was off somewhere and the stock exchange was up a few points. We talked about it at the mention of my third fat check. I was paid off to shut up. It wasn't gonna work. I wanted to spend it all like Brendan was doing, seeing the world. Dan brought me back. Dan helps me with this stuff.

But I needed his help somewhere else, with something altogether icky.

"So, Dan, you know what this TV movie comin' up is all about."

"Yeah..." He waited.

"And how, you know how Barry and I collaborate, you know we co-wrote this, but he helped direct too, but we like to say—"

"Yeah. The point, Stan."

"Well, there's not really a character like you. I mean it's an older sister, but you're her—and also another kid, who's really nice, this kid who makes friends with him when they get high."

"Stan, you think I'm gonna be upset with anything you do? I love your stuff, and I'm really sorry we don't get to make stuff together anymore."

"We could pitch *The Manipulator* video game to your new boss." I teased, hinted, pleaded.

"Well, I gotta redo the proposal."

"No problem."

"You sure you can get the rights?"

"I have an old friend."

"Really?"

"Yes, some of us do live long."

"I didn't say..."

"What?"

"You're making it sound, so, so, what? Separatist."

"Look, Dan, lemme ask what I need to really ask, and I think it'll take care of any questions about that stuff."

"Stan—"

"Hear me out, bro."

"Okay."

I held the phone away, knowing my volume was out of control. I said it.

"When Uncle Sean hit on us, you told him no, right?"

"Yeah."

"But did you know I did it? That I liked it?"

"Well, first of all, I knew you did it because I just knew. You weren't the only one who hid magazines in the attic."

We laughed. I coughed up a glob of phlegm.

"Man, why didn't you tell me that?" I asked. "Ever?"

"I didn't know much about it, either. Hell, I thought you told Mom you wanted him gone. You two coulda humped each other from here to daylight for all I cared, you know what I'm saying? Jeez, Stan, you really withhold, you know that? Me and Gloria just ... just, when you get that last paycheck? Just go, man. Go to Poland and find our roots. Go to France and fall in love. Just drive to the desert and drop acid."

"I am, but not acid."

"What, you mean, you're going on vacation?"

"Well, a working one."

"Oh."

"I'm doin' a porn video, Dan." I considered adding that I was no longer fucking Barry, and was alternately fucking Lance and a porn star, but I didn't. We do have boundaries.

"Like, 'bow, chicka bow wow' porn?"

"I think the music's changed a bit, but yeah."

Dan held off a chuckle, before I said, "But it'll be really artistic."

"Well, in that case..."

The conversation collapsed into laughter. We both had to hang up. Call Waiting.

Mike calling from Hong Kong. He wasn't paying for it. Neither was I. Something about access codes. I thanked my brother and said goodbye.

Note to Katsuo: Help me figure out how to do conference calling.

Mike was having a good time. I was crazed. I told him something touching or important, I forget what. Something about being welcome on the rebound.

Mike took that in. I remembered I had to call Jason about setting up our magical journey. I had to keep it going. *I will not crash. I will not crash.*

"So, I'm gonna go see him," I said.

"My dad," Mike guessed.

"Incarcerated authors for five hundred, Alex."

"You want me to come back early and go with you?"

"Naw. I think it's my scene," I said.

"Okay then. Can I at least send you a parting gift, like maybe a crossbow?"

50. touching child memory bar: last call

Autumn 1978 swept that summer of shows away into a scrap books. My parents suggested I get a job, since my creative needs became more costly, what with papers and paints, crayons and books, as well as subscriptions to *Scream*.

So, I got a job with the *Brookside Gazette* as a paperboy. I was to replace Jerry Morrison on his route. He lived a few blocks away, and every day after school, I went to his small house to learn how to fold papers and memorize the route.

I again realized how different our family was from others. Jerry's mother would barely greet us, and when she spoke to Jerry, it was more a complaint, telling him to hurry up or remembering some other chore as soon as he finished the paper route. I remember regretting missing episodes of *Match Game*. I wanted to hear Charles Nelson Reilly tell jokes. I remember seeing Jerry's room, once. Nothing on his walls suggested an identity.

Jerry's house smelled thick with a combination of starchy cooking and dog farts. Their house seemed crowded with junk, the walls bare except for a few cheap reproductions of forgettable landscapes, pictures I considered tacky even then, the subject of a running gag my brother and I referred to as "Starving Artist Sale" kitsch. Even at that age, our ultimate fear was to lack taste.

Jerry Morrison was one of those boys you never notice, their protean boy faces pale and meek. He had few, if any, social activities, and I only saw him to work on the paper route. I did acknowledge his presence from then on in the halls at school, snob that I was, but that was it. I wouldn't be surprised to find him still living in Brookside, with a wife, kids, and those damn bare walls.

I was a better singing and dancing paperboy than the real thing. When I decided to quit one horrid, rainy afternoon, the distribution manager sat in our living room and told me he had never had such a poor, incompetent paperboy in the time he'd worked there. My mother swiftly asked him to leave our house, and she canceled our subscription in a huff. We relied thereafter on the *Plain Dealer* and the Sunday *New York Times* for our print news, until the repetition of Dan and my numerous extracurricular activities being covered in the local paper compelled them to purchase it on the sly, at the market or the DeliMart.

I felt a keen satisfaction every time I got in that little newspaper, and somehow think my drive to achieve was in part fueled by those brief uncomplimentary words from the distribution manager. I could see him grit his teeth every time my beaming face appeared in the black and white photos, or my name was listed as the lead in the latest play, posed proudly with another scroll or academic plaque.

We were fighting back against this entire small town, fending off their slants and lowbrow comments about our otherness, our Polish name, and more core to my defensiveness, my veiled queerness. And like those other kids who went off to other cities to seek their careers, like Amy Deitz, who went on to become a *Star Search* spokesmodel, or Marty Stoller, who went on to become a low-level rodeo star, I hungered for the day when I would show them my path continued on while they merely thickened and grew deeper roots.

One joy I received from the paper route happened twice when I went to collect the dues. One customer brought a secret, delicious thrill to the route, and made that brief time worthwhile.

He was a young, unmarried instructor at Brookside College, Romanian, I think. I'd been collecting on Saturdays in the early afternoon. I went up to his door, rang the bell, and he opened it, wearing only a damp white towel, which clung to his waist. His black hair, thick on his head and fanning out over his broad muscled chest, sent a wave of fear and desire through me.

He had me stand in his hallway while he walked into his bedroom to write a check. As I tried not to stare at his body, I saw him in his room, leaning over a dresser, scribbling away to write a check, and his towel fell from his body all on its own. His thick dark penis dangled, and began to thicken.

He ripped the check out and handed it over, saying, "Here you go." I went in to receive it, and by the time I reached him, his cock jutted straight out from his thick, hairy patch of pubes. I must have been sweating profusely then, for I had no idea what to do, but I took the check, stole another glance at his groin, and rushed out to leave.

"Really?" Lance asked me. We were together the night before my trip south.

"No, not really."

I hadn't told it the way it happened. I haven't told anything the way it happened. I remember making it happen, but my memory of it is blended with a scene from *Big Guns*.

But by telling it to Lance, I got both of us aroused, and we played it out. It felt great, not just for the sex, but because Lance got into it. He was quite comfortable with role-playing, but I wondered if, like me, he was using it to cover up his true feelings.

On that day, as I stood between the last project and the new one, that equilibrium moment overcame me, like a kid atop a playground seesaw: dizzying, imperial, kind of like surfing. Somehow being with Lance kept me balanced.

The best time to approach a difficult subject is after terrific sex. One's listener is hopefully relaxed enough to face the truth.

"So, I have two things to say."

"Wow, okay, I like reviews." Lance rolled over, grabbed the sheet around his butt, which I pulled back down with a toe.

"Um, no. Not about that, although, yay, five stars. Um, I like you a lot and want to be a couple, like, just us."

"Oh."

"However…"

Lance smirked. "Optional threeways?"

I grinned in approval. He really was husband material.

"That, too, but I've been hired to direct a porno in Phoenix, and you can't go with me but I might probably have some sex of my own, but I love you so maybe you can go do something else to kind of get it out of your system, or—"

"Wait, you want me to slut it up so we're even?" Lance's mock rage perplexed me.

"Well, no, not if you—I'm just … there's this one guy, Jason, who I already made a movie of, or about, and he pretty much banged me into submission to direct a feature porno."

Lance tried to remain shocked but faltered like a blooper reel shot.

"What's so funny?"

He giggled. "How you snuck in 'I love you.'"

"Well, I do."

"Ow, wow, really going there." He sat up. "Have fun at your big bachelor party bacchanal," he said as he pulled me into a light kiss.

"You knew?"

"I knew."

"But…"

As he stood to go pee in the bathroom, the blond fuzz of his butt hit a slat of afternoon light at just the right angle.

"I'm Jorge's friend now, too, silly. And no, I don't want to be on a porn set ... again."

"Wait. What?"

Yep. Husband material.

But was I?

ACT V

Reel to Real

an erotic fantasia

treatment draft
J. Quest Productions

51.

Reel to Real is a tribute and a tongue-in-cheek parody of erotica but also an homage to the homoerotic aspects of mainstream cinema. Through the wonder of modern post-production technology, the history of modern film eras will be recalled through a series of romantic homoerotic scenes shot in a variety of styles: silent, wartime 1940s, Technicolor widescreen, verité foreign, and, finally, pre-millennial new age science fiction.

Loosely connected small duo scenes will be tied together through in a finale in the desert, where a mystical shaman conjures the various men from different eras for one last moonlit dance until dawn.

Reel to Real crosses boundaries between erotica and narrative film. *Reel to Real* takes risks as it eroticizes its performers while still humanizing them.

Soldiers on a Train

They're on a train headed home, two young soldiers together. I only need two crowd shots. For that, extras are easy to get. The terrific thing is, the boys all have some form of military clothes for starters. Jorge just fills them out with two trips to Army rentals, even fake guns.

The boys sit in their train chair, and we switch to studio for that. I want a look of romanticized artifice. We even have access to a rear projection screen with night scenes zooming by, very *Zentropa*.

For this scene, I really need two boys who can act, since one of them has to get so upset that he cries. I need a guy sensitive enough to make him cry and get him upset enough to deliver the lines. "It's just that, I'm never gonna see you again, and we're so far apart, after all we been through..."

A hug that turns into a kiss, then feigned sleep, then a trip to the men's room. A fumbled pants-down quickie, a lot like the bathroom airplane scene in *Rich and Famous* in terms of visuals, except this is black and white, 1940s-blurry, cocks jutting out of pants, famished bent-over knob slobs, passionate bone-crunching embraces, an interruption with a knock at the door, and a fiery blast into hands, onto the floor, tear-stained kisses, quick washing up, and a hasty exit with one soldier giving them a scant look. As the lovers exit, the braver of the two extracts a bottle. They go out, then he gives it to the suspicious guy. "Didn't wanna have to share it with the whole car. You understand."

"Sure," as he hands over the remains of the bottle. The other soldier goes in, but first looks as the other two return to their seats.

Cuddle, embrace, falling asleep, the face of the strong one, now him crying. "Truth is, it was the last time."

Cut to totally stolen scene from *Wings,* the men departing. It was so easy, it had to be done.

Campus Cubs

Etienne comics come to life in a musical number. The Coach leads off with a solo scene in his office, groping his crotch under the desk while he sings of the beauty of his team.

This is intercut with Technicolor 1950s, bright—all post-produced tonal changes—dance sequence, where the guys, like in the gym sequence from *Diamonds Are a Girl's Best Friend,* added *Best Little WhoreHouse in Texas* dance number, but they stay in their jockstraps, not getting dressed.

As the number builds, intercut scenes of an animated mascot, a la Gene Kelly/Jerry dance bit having sex with a player provide an amusing aside.

But the repeated chorus, a heavy house funk and very modern beat, closes with a mass all-singing, all-naked shower circle jerk.

In Boca da Lupe

A street in Rome, all shot in rear-projection screen with stock footage. A tourist and a *carabinieri* exchange glances. The tourist unfolds a map. The policeman offers assistance. The tourist takes him up on it. It is discreet. It is tense.

The two converse while figuring each other out, then find a quiet, cloistered part of a park to make love. A large nude statue stands nearby. They do not stop talking throughout. Subtitles in several languages appear below them. At one point, the Italian looks down at the subtitles, complains to the camera. The subtitles change.

In moody, arty shots of remove, we watch the two men do it standing against a tree, in a park. Beyond them, a statue of a naked Apollo grows erect. We observe the men from a distance, though the eyes of the statue. It is off-putting, yet intriguing.

After consummating their love, the two men pat the statue's ass for luck, walk off together, arms over shoulders. Cut back to the statue, still erect, and dripping. Maybe a nun, no, a priest can arrive and declare it a miracle.

Getting Experienced

Groovy 1970s scene, on a college campus. The flavor of this scene is very *Mod Squad* meets vintage Falcon, a hot three-way. A pair of guys pick each other up on the street. There is no dialogue, but a groovy soundtrack with lots of wawa guitar. The guys abruptly end up in an apartment. They smoke some dope. They take off their white bellbottom jeans and Qiana shirts as the groovy music builds. One of the guys lies back to have a psychedelic vision, which then dissolves to the desert finale.

Completion funds are sought for post-production facility rental, composer fees and audio production facilities rental. The vision of a cross-genre category of erotic yet artistically filmed stories, will have a wide festival appeal, induce ~~enough controversy to secure a video distribution interest, and overseas investment capabilities.~~

52. we gorgeous **occult persons** could **flood** an airbase

Have you ever had your favorite porn star sing you a Marc Almond song in the back seat of a rental car while driving toward a Phoenix sunrise?

Having already shot the studio scenes for *Reel to Real* on video with a lot of filmic special effects to be created later, I still had to plan the desert shoot for my own creative finale with two cameras, and their less than creative regular fuck scenes on video in various locales in Phoenix. We were under budget, and well, according to the shoot list, we needed some additional exteriors. Two days. That's all I had. That's all I needed.

Until we needed more. Then I was glad I'd received the third of three checks from *Uncle Fucker*. Ten grand of it was sunk into stocks. Three more to pay a few bills. Certified check, please. No, no credit cards.

Before departing, I read in the trades that the owners of the owners of *The Manipulator* trilogy had merged with some other Big Corp. Can't worry about that now! It's a working vacation!

I had four hundred and some in cash. Our ensemble, on SouthWest Flight #6969 from LAX to PHEE-NEX! as the wacky shorts-sporting steward sang when he saw the entourage board the plane, which consisted of:

Crew: Jorge, Janice, Me, and Geoff.

Cast: Jason Daw, Tommy Matthews, Vince Colby, Andrew Jacobs, Rex Andrews, Douglas Corwin, Logan Taylor, Taylor Dallas, etc.

Cameos: Drag Queen Chantee, in full gear.

And: Orland "Orrie" Bernfeld, our executive producer, and the owner of Starz Video Co. LLC, our film production company. Starz Video Co, LLC, it turned out, had among its quality titles *Gobs O Guys, Cocktails, Little Pee Master* and *Surf Punk Holiday*. I didn't even hear about him until the day we flew. Basically he was the money man, and he expected to enjoy the shoot like a little vacation with all the porno/rent boys he could get his hands on.

I spent the first drink of our flight muttering to Geoff that if one money shot was lost up or on the body of our benefactor, then he could direct the damn thing.

"Don't worry," Geoff assured. "I brought lots of Metrex."

"What?"

"Makes the boys come better. Tastes better, too."

Across the seat from me, Tommy Matthews tapped my foot and made a joke about engineered sperm. I liked him.

I'd gotten to know the guys a bit on each of their one-day shoots for the retro scenes. But adjusting the lines to accommodate their thespian limitations turned each shoot into more of a perfunctory chore, except Tommy Matthews.

With the full-tilt musical number scrapped due to budget limitations, I instead saved Tommy for a solo scene, since he'd said he could sing and dance "a little." With the money we saved from a full production number, I convinced Geoff to rent a run-down porn theatre for a day, the Tomkat on Santa Monica Boulevard.

With a top hat and cane, in a black toreador tux jacket and almost too-tight pants, Tommy pretended to rehearse a soft-shoe number in front of a rented vaudeville-style backdrop we hung in front of the screen. The footlights we brought added the right retro glow. His pants' bulge becoming more pronounced, he eventually pulled them down and, after some fully nude moves (albeit the top hat and shoes) with his bouncing boner adding panache, he engaged in some self-love that ended with his trademark far-flung finish, only to be applauded from the audience of one by an appreciative booking agent (a two-line role played by Douglas Corwin).

He wasn't at all like Lance with his muscles and dark hair, nor Tulsa, but it worked for me.

Now they each sat in nearby plane seats, talking to each other, comparing notes about their separate scenes while ignoring admiring glances from the male flight attendants.

I'd wanted to bring my tape player to enjoy the takeoff, but Tommy and Jason and I sang Annie Lennox's "Little Bird" and enjoyed it anyway. I love taking off on planes. Someday I want to have sex and come at just that moment. Talking to Tommy made me forget we were even airborne. Just talking to a guy you've already had mad imagined sessions with, and after making a few actually happen, is a grand form of afterplay.

Airport, rental car hell.

We all had to wait half an hour for the two vans to be found and approved. We would face a weekend of disappointment, missed cues, and odd ironies, but we somehow enjoyed it.

The hotel rooms were strangely situated. I'd reserved my own but Jason decided to share mine. The crew had been arranged on one side, the cast on the other. Geoff's doing? It worked in everyone's favor. Royalty on one side, the barn in the other.

The only problem was my room number.

The boys had 664. Janice had 668. I was in the middle.

Vince subtly asked if Janice could be his roomie so they could guard the equipment, and she said yes. How could I not give her the perks? All the boys seemed to behave with her around.

We were saying all this under the knifelike gaze of our reservations attendant, Charlene, who had a crucifix dangling from her large neck. She glared at me.

"Your room number is 666. How appropriate."

Surrounded by drag queens, and friends, hunky muscled men, her hatred still scared me.

I taped a NON MOLESTE on the front door, then left it open. I set up shop, shot lists, and garbage. Boys started walking in and out of my room, and once the conjoining rooms were opened and the hallways doors bolted, they started trimming, shaving, and showering in a cross-referenced Marx Brothers Muscle Beach scene. Geoff strolled from room to room, tossing douche kits to the cast. Scatological jokes ensued.

I felt like some young Fellini-esque auteur. I scribbled away, made drawings on the bed, planned shots, let the boys flirt with me one by one, some not at all. That intrigued me, too. I told them all to keep secret about their own solo and duo scenes, and I loved watching them gradually betray themselves. I opened myself completely to their wildness, and it washed away the feeling of evil the hotel clerk implied.

That's what I think the evil is, the 666 being badness in the shape of confusion and disarray, not sexuality, not dark urges. Our sexual urges will prove to be light, and sweet, and daring and comfortable.

I called a meeting in my room.

Jason and Geoff herded the cast, who seemed to hover over me from all directions.

"So, when are we going to shoot?" somebody asked.

They looked like a 3D Versace ad. Bruce Weber's Private Collection.

"Well, um," I turned to face them all. "We have the Pride event today, then the nightclub tonight, and after that, the morning off. Y'all better get some rest, cause I want some sunset action out in the desert tomorrow, which will go late, then you take the day off except for a duo scene with ..."

Then I paused, and I swear all those chests just puffed up slightly, like sayin' "Pick me," and I almost went for Tommy's bazookas first when I noticed Jason giving me this glare; Hello, who is Miss Top Billing?

"...Oh yeah, um, Jason and Tommy."

Some faces scowled then, so I continued. "Then tomorrow night, until late, like, midnight, after an early dinner, we go out in the desert and set up there, where we do a night group scene."

"At night?" Jake said.

"In the desert?" Andy added.

"That's why they call it work."

"That's why they call it a night scene," Tommy said before Jake chest-punched him.

I continued. "We want to get there well before sunset, for the lighting. Jorge has some lovely costumes, which you will all recall were your original costumes."

"Wow, they're all beat up."

"Dissssstresssssed," Jorge hissed as he waltzed in and out, showing off the worn fatigues, the tattered bellbottoms.

Tommy said, "So, it's like a time thing, like we're all coming out of the past for this ritual, right?"

It sounded right to me, even though I hadn't thought of it. I said, after everyone laughed, "That is exactly it. No, guys, I'm serious. Tommy, you are brilliant."

"I got a Master's Degree."

"In Masterology!" somebody quipped. The room became more locker roomy then, so I played coach. I felt like Officer Krupke, or that actor in *West Side Story* who looked like Uncle Sean imitating Officer Krupke. I imagined appropriating that shot for this film, jotted it down.

"So, yes. So, again, guys, I know you have this club thing tonight. Who's gogo dancing?"

Three hands were raised.

"Cool. I'll shoot some of that for B-roll, but you're really doing the club thing tonight. Don't worry about the tape until tomorrow. I will need all of you from four o'clock tomorrow afternoon until possibly midnight. You all have maps. Who's driving?" Two more hands. "Oh, and no guests. Actors and crew only."

"And make sure the police aren't following you," Jason said. The laughter from that broke up the meeting. I realized I was sweating. The guys dispersed, tossing out other questions.

Doug whistled. Our only African American actor, he'd volunteered to camera-assist in between nude scenes. "Midnight? My camera work's a little shaky by then."

"We brought a tripod, dearie." Jason said. "You can just stand about in ya jodhpurs. We're the ones'll be humping on rocks to capture your grand vision."

"You're wicked."

The boys were dispersed, and I discussed other particulars with Jason.

"I know how I've worked, and I know how I'd like to work, if you're game."

"Such as?" he asked.

"Let's do some opening shots at the Gay Pride."

"Can't have extras without model releases."

"We'll get Geoff to do that. Pass 'em around like candy. They'll be crawling over each other to get in. Besides, it'll give Geoff something to do."

"You've got it all planned out, doncha?"

"Naw, I'm just thinkin' on my feet."

"I like that." Jason patted my back. I'd seen him fuck on his feet, too, with the other guy's feet nowhere near the ground.

Janice had arrived late and begged off on the Pride visit so she could stay at the hotel and enjoy a spa treatment after crunching a shot list.

She didn't miss much. The Pride "event," spread out on some soccer fields way out of town, was a bust, the sun fading at strange glinting angles. I kept getting those sparkly prism effects. Guess who forgot to rent filters?

With Jason as my apparent escort, we assembled in the lobby and poured into the two vans for the Pride Day.

The porn boys crowded around a booth for a nightclub, The Works, which was sponsoring a Meet the Stars event that night, and paying for our airfare, thank you, which was a fabulous connection Geoff worked out. It pleased Orrie, too, since he didn't have to pay.

We were looking good in the sun. I was in the shadow of the nation's best cocksmen that season.

Off in another booth, Chance Caldwell was posing with folks as a fundraiser. He looked like a lone cow at a sad petting zoo. I felt sorry for not casting him, but hey, it's my movie. I wouldn't even use Lex Baldwin anymore. I want men that move. Statues are for museums.

Jason was sweet, and I felt worthy, being jostled and chatted with by the other boys, who were notably snotty, except Rex, who's just shy. In greeting, he kissed me! He doesn't talk much.

Pride keychains, T-shirts, swatches, red ribbon removable tattoos, all of it the scrappy, cluttered remnants of what was supposed to be a gay community. We watched bad drag queens lip-synch, watched boys watch us. I felt proud and arrogant in the company of Rex and Geoff and Jason and the others, the stares each nudging my back up a little higher, making me a little more happy just to be me, and ever so blasé about my illustrious company.

I shot a few B-roll crowd scenes, we ate greasy little chicken sandwiches made by lesbians, had lesbian lemonade. None of the crowd would chat with us, so we sat and watched folks dance. I saw a studly little pup with a crewcut and a mustache dance wildly, his firm back bending like Gumby, his grin tight and impervious to the silly tented dance floor situation.

I took an ice cube and trailed it up and down Jason's back and behind his ear, a translucent pink from the sun. It melted in seconds. I went to get my camera, got another ice cube, and shot the moment again, the ice melting on the valleys of his skin.

We got some shots that gave the impression of gay amusement, but the extras kept leering at the boys, even from twenty feet away. The drag queens demanded payment up front, which Geoff provided. The sun glinted at severe angles, and gave it an eerie, sad slant.

So they all left, and Geoff and I and Chantee, our drag queen, walked ahead to the van.

"I gotta get outta these heels. They just don't work on tundra."

I laughed as I put the equipment away in the little bags, locking things up securely. Orrie, our executive producer, approached. "Well, that was a sad little thing."

We achieved an odd sympatico when Chantee said, "Well, here we are, standing in a parking lot in Phoenix, waiting on a herd of rent boys. This is a new low."

But we got in the van, porno boys in tow, and argued about radio stations. It had a cassette player! Damn, wish I'd brought tapes, but I didn't want to chance losing one of my precious mixes while on some unknown road trip guerrilla dick flick.

Orrie proved to be a pest, a pleasant enough barrel of an older gent with a long history of interesting escapades. Unfortunately, he liked to tell about them while people were trying to engage in conversation. He proved to be more of a monologist without an editor. It got on my nerves, but I tolerated it for the evening. He would have to be "entertained elseways."

We caught up to the others at the hotel's big over-designed burger restaurant. The center plaza resembled something out of *Logan's Run*, which became a new joke, aimed at Rex Logan. It seems a recent porno closing credit shot included Rex running naked with a hard-on, thus *Logan's Run*. It was the best shot of the film, which is probably why the other porn boys kidded him about it.

Despite my directorial authority, and our smaller previous days' shooting, these boys didn't know me or Janice, while Jorge fit right in. I felt the usual awkwardness of joining a group and being the eleventh wheel, with no room to eat and nothing to say. I ducked out of the awkward seating situation by going to the john, my KOX T-shirt feeling horribly out of place, shocking in its redundancy. Passing through the crowds of straight vacationing couples, I couldn't help but wonder what they thought of these men whose company I was in. They all look famous, but why? I ended up having to sit next to Orrie, looking like his boy, I suppose. But Chantee was fun even out of drag, and Jason kept ducking down close to share private jokes with me and Janice. But Vince flirted hard with her, so her attention was tough to get.

Rex sat silent, snagging a choice seat by Doug, with whom he'd shared the previously-shot soldier-sailor duo scene. Unable to find a complete train car set, we settled for a leftover rented men's room set, and the pair's cramped stall action sufficed. Their uniforms gave it an extra appeal, particularly with Doug's brown skin contrasting with his sailor dress whites. We finally got a good groove going.

At a conversational lull, out of nowhere, I asked Jason, "Have you ever seen the movie *Jason and the Argonauts*?"

"That's the one with the fighting skeletons!" Tommy almost shouted from the far end of the table.

"Exactly," I smiled.

"Is that the plot of our movie?" Jason asked.

Before I could answer, Tommy added, "I read *The Odyssey* in college," to a snort from one of the others. "It's not in the movie, but there's a chapter with an island where the men get turned into pigs."

"Figures," Vince chimed in. "Except we already are pigs."

The bursts of laughter all around drew stares from other restaurant guests, but no one dared to complain.

The waiters loved us. They recognized a few faces. We got a lot of extra fries, and drinks, and desserts.

Satiated, the others left, but Jason, Tommy, Janice and Vince (who were getting along nicely), and Rex stayed. Tommy moved past empty chairs to sit next to me; fitting, as he'd shown himself to be the most engaged, sober, and intelligent cast member. After a bit of conversation about other books and movies, I took the opportunity to ask what I figured in such company to be an inappropriate question.

"So, what got you into adult films?"

Tommy sighed.

"Unless you don't—"

"No, it's fine. I was always sexual, and by college, which I paid for myself, after I realized I could attract any guy I wanted, I started hustling to pay for school. This was in Seattle, and my parents were poor, and well, I'm kind of into older guys, and they were generous, and then I posed for some guy for money, and I liked doing that. Then one of the photo shoots got in a porn magazine, *Mandate*, and the photographer hooked me up with a producer who saw them, and I moved to L.A. Sorry, too much coffee."

He pushed his cup away.

"No, that's great. So no unpleasant experiences?"

"A few; some creepy johns, a few poorly shot cheapo productions. But I kept a few day jobs and got more finicky about who I worked with."

"Huh."

"What about you? This is your first porno, right?"

"Pretty much." I explained my nom-de-softcore videos, my other films, omitting the Ricky backstory.

"So, it's just a job?"

"No, no, it's… It's something I wanted to get out of my system. I've always been a bit obsessed with porn." I told him of my and Jorge's video store days, and the abstract short film that got Jason's attention. "I thought that diving in and treating it like work would help me get over it."

"Sorta like not doing AA and binge-drinking instead?"

I stared at him, stunned, then forced a laugh.

"Sorry, it was just a joke."

"No, no, it's… you're a very perceptive guy."

Tommy patted me on the back, friendly, until he let his big palm linger, lightly rubbing, then grazing lower. More than his touch, his intuition turned a key inside me, making him more handsome than before.

He leaned in, whispered, "You know, it's too bad I have to save myself, what with you and all these other hot guys here."

I blushed.

"You're sort of with Jason for the shoot, right?"

"You really are perceptive."

"Oh, that much is obvious."

I smiled at him.

"Just do me a favor."

"Anything."

His hand moved to grip my leg under the table. "Just make sure to get my money shots up close. I want you right near me. I haven't even jacked off in a week, and, as you saw from my little tap dance number, I'm a big shooter."

I returned a grip to his thick thigh. "I'm quite familiar with your work."

We finished our coffee, and walked through the lobby to our rooms. Two old folks wandered into the elevator with us.

"Y'all together?" the elderly lady shouted.

"Sometimes," muttered Tommy, as he goosed me.

"Wha?" she said as I glanced up to the metal ceiling's reflection.

"Rugby team," Jason announced.

The man's ears perked up. "Where from?"

Tommy blurted, "Denver."

Rex, at the same time; "Ireland."

The elevator shook with our laughter the moment the doors closed.

After a short nap, as I showered in the bathroom, Jason entered. Guess who left the door open? He was very nonchalant as we talked over the noise of the water. But when I stepped out, he appraised me. I smiled. So did my dick.

He asked me to drop my towel so he could lick my bum. "Just once."

I loved watching him change clothes, and then us going into the other boys' rooms to watch them get dressed up. Even though they were still clipping their toenails and plucking stray hairs, they were all nearly naked. Jason jumped on my back in the hallway, and we entered the room like that, in just our shorts.

Vince pranced about naked and showed off his gorgeous bod and thick, uncut wiener. Catlike eyes and buff bod. Yummy, but a head case. He was intent on proving his bisexuality with Janice, who was doing some homework in her room. I'd forgotten to say I wanted him unshaven, and he was neurotic about being smooth as glass. I wanted more diversity of fuzz.

We finally got to The Works, a sprawling nightclub with a big disco and smaller alternative room and an outdoor pool lounge area. Jason was swamped by adoring fans, so I mostly hung with Rex, who drank nothing but water.

I was worried about drinking and smoking and doing drugs with Jason, since Geoff said something about him wanting to be around people who don't do drugs. Coulda fooled me! I got buzzed on two beers and watched the silly photo sessions, with Joe and the others posing as they raised money for a local AIDS charity, while an increasingly obnoxious half-straight crowd leered.

Jason, Rex, Doug, Tommy and I got taken into the office of the owner, a nice fellow, but too chatty and in our faces. I think he wanted a part, or was disappointed when I didn't want any shots of him on-camera. His office was nice, though, with antique sculptures of Ganesh and other neat things. He showed us a plastic clear dildo with electric strips on it for jolt dildo sessions. I got queasy.

We eventually ended up in the upstairs dressing room watching boys change and being silly with increasingly pushy Chantee, in full drag, posing and giving funny attitude.

In the tiny dressing room, while four other boys changed into gogo wear, Jason and I pissed in a tiny sink. Jason had honestly tried to piss in the public loo, but the mob scene was very unpleasant. "Some poor fellow popped his head on a wall," he smirked.

"Like they never saw that before," one of the boys hooted.

It took all my reserve not to guzzle Jason's pee like he'd jokingly asked, but he did piss on my fingers. I licked it in front of him.

"Couldn't resist," I said.

Back out under the beat, I tried to get more footage of Tommy and the other guys dancing, but the lighting was flashy and harsh. The guys kept moving about, but Rex stayed by me, so silent, so small and sweet, like a little doe you want to take care of. As I shot more footage of Vince and Tommy, then Jake and Doug taking turns dancing on platforms, Janice said she loved watching her 'date' strip for a crowd that, "reminds me of Chippendale's."

Geoff left for a bathhouse nearby, saying he'd catch a cab, only after asking if he would be needed before tomorrow. I said, no, and neither was Daddy Warbucks. Then there was a hell of a time trying to all get back together, the annoying techno started driving us mad, and we finally got pissed and almost left without Orrie, but he pulled up as we stood outside, waiting for someone to find the van. A bit of drama ensued, Rex holding the car keys like a little beautiful lawn jockey.

But no one except the departed Geoff knew where the van was parked.

Vince came by with Janice and bitched about losing some items in the makeshift dressing room. Sorry, no help from us. She calmed him down with some private conversation.

Jason, Tommy and Rex wandered the parking lot to find the van. Even though we were exhausted, we went back to the hotel. The rest of the cast called it a night.

"We've been invited to a late party," Jason casually noted in our hotel room as he removed his shirt and chose another. I again enjoyed watching Jason change, and after recruiting a few others, off we went.

Tommy decided to drive since he hadn't drunk any alcohol and didn't like ecstasy, which was a good idea. Vince and Janice had disappeared to her room, so I mentally crossed Vince off the cast list for the finale. But then, I thought, Oh, well, this is gonna be an Antonioni kind of weekend.

"Wait. Tommy. Pull over. Let's go back to the hotel, boys. We're bringing the equipment."

53. moan here like an alive rock spirit

The 'party' turned out to be in really-out-there bumfuck, and at a tiny faux-Santa Fe ranch house with religious relics cluttering up the place, and only four guys awake. Three others were crashed on a bed next to the bathroom, with no door. So I felt awkward.

The X had hit, too little for my taste, but Rex got the shivers and I cuddled him on a sofa. I stood next to guys who smoked cigarettes, happy to not need a smoke but okay with catching a contact high. Inside Jason played DJ, then he and I kick-lined to "Go West."

Then Jason said, "Let's go shoot out in the back yard. Let them help out and watch."

I first thought he meant sex, then I realized he meant sex and filming. Jason led me out to the back yard, which included—surrounded by rock-filled landscaping—a blue-lit swimming pool.

"This'll do," I said as Jason found Tommy, and they got naked. It added nothing to the "epic" story line, but with two naked guys and a well-lit swimming pool, I was more than accommodating.

"Should we swim first?" Tommy suggested.

"Yes, but my kingdom for an underwater camera."

The pair were actually very artistic, and even did some great rhythmic shimmer effects with the reflectors, then some water effects over the boy's bodies when Jason and Tommy emerged from the pool, dripping wet, then sucked each other between smooches.

The best shot, I think, is the one where Jason stands on a big rock above Tommy, who's reclining, his cock arcing up from his groin like a bowsprit, while Jason mouth-fucked him. Then Jason lowered and parked his cock atop Tommy's chest. But before that is a wide angle shot from below, Jason's cock lowering down from the top of the screen, in the shadow of a lamp we dragged from the living room, his ass like a pair of descending melons from heaven.

It took me lying on the concrete poolside, preoccupied by scenery, to get the shot. Jason simply appeared over my shoulder while I waited for he and Tommy to "get in the mood" for some fucking after Tommy made a brief visit to the bathroom. "Always come prepared!" he beamed as he extracted a spare enema kit from his duffel bag.

Meanwhile, Jason got in the mood by parking his cock on his director's face. The weight of it made me appreciate the benevolent nature of the gesture, as if Jason were placing his cock before me for safekeeping.

After some serviceable thrusting, with Tommy deftly switching positions between breaks, Tommy asked Jason to service him.

"Hold on. Gotta have a slash." He padded off to the bathroom.

"Would you like to do the honors?" Tommy teased.

"You want me to fluff you."

"I'll pay extra." He stroked himself, still not exactly hard.

I complied, gratis.

Upon his return, Jason chuckled, pried me from my kneeling position, handed me the camera, with which I shot them in close-up for a long while as the two more professional fellators lovingly performed on each other, until Tommy asked me where I wanted him to cum. Jason offered his chest, and, true to his word, Tommy delivered, in abundance.

After the boys took over the bathroom to clean up, where I heard Tommy jokingly chanting, "Stan sucked my di-ick. Stan sucked my di-ick!" we thanked our sleepy host, handed him some cash, drove on back, making jokes about anything, babbling as sober Tommy played chauffeur. Jason started making jokes about my inability to make a point, and he just started saying "dot, dot, dot" whenever I said something without a punch line, which was always. Then, to prove I could manage humor on call, I told the joke I heard from Chantee. "What did Jackie O say when she got to heaven?"

Nobody knew.

"Where's that blonde bitch?!"

Even Tommy didn't get it.

The buildings kept going by. I shot them sideways, so it would appear as a zooming ascension. This would be shown under the opening credits, I thought, or as a segue, or nothing. Circle K after lube shop after Wendy's after auto store, then the whole thing again and again, like the windows and doors in the house when Fred Flintstone is running, but they didn't get that since they never saw the show.

Up front, Jason and Tommy made jokes about British TV stars and raves and other stuff, "naff." I often couldn't understand Jason, his accent muffled by the music.

We made jokes about his two vampire pornos. He thought they were silly, but I thought they were frighteningly appropriate.

Somehow, we got along, even with Rex being sleepy, and Tommy saying little, but me treasuring each response. Then Jason started singing a Marc Almond song, leaning back between the front seats, and Rex and I beamed, still cushy from the buzz, Jason's sweet little boy voice coming out of that tall lanky sex god bod.

I turned the camera off. I was sleepy.

Back at the hotel rooms, we found a pile of guys on one bed, with Chantee looking like a mod version of *The Women* fur coat scene on the other, a stack of pizza boxes on a table. Everybody was too exhausted to fuck or leave. I lay down with Chantee and Jason on either side. We were quiet for a while, until Tommy resumed his little chant, whispering it like a lullaby. "Stan sucked my di-ick."

Thankfully, Jason asked if I wanted to be alone in our room, away from the giggling others.

We were gone in a second.

Oh, happy day.

We crashed, slept off the X, and then later I woke up with a hard-on and walked it to the john. After I peed, I noticed Jason was showing his backside off by pushing away the covers. I figured, what the hey.

We hugged. I nestled my nose near his armpit. It smelled of burnt coffee and salt. I rubbed him, then licked him and then, joy, his boner popped out from under the sheet. I slurped on his beautiful big uncut erection, and we got down, but then Rex knocked on the unlocked inside door while entering, asking how we were doing. "Oops." He retreated as Jason rolled me over, lapped at my ass with casual amusement.

I kept thinking, gee, how does he *really* like it, not just what he does in tapes and what I expect of him? Is he always this sexual; I mean, he's being so polite.

We never got too gymnastic, or even close to fucking, since I was probably the only person in our entourage who hadn't douched, so we stopped.

"No worries," he almost whispered. "I need to save it for the last scene, right?"

We cuddled some more, then I massaged him and caressed his smooth backside, and nestled my face in his lovely ass. I came just doing that. After all, I didn't need to save myself.

We slept like spoons.

Rex woke us up later, walking in with a raging hardon, stroking it, looking for condoms.

"Oh yum. Seconds," I said as his wanger pointed inches from my face. He had Tony, a little muscle cub from the club, back in his bed, promised to "save my juices" and then said Geoff had returned and to give him a call.

Wait. We had to shoot the fucking finale.

I didn't want anything. I didn't want to eat or see Geoff. I wanted to sleep in Jason's arms all weekend and let him do whatever he wanted, better still, with Tommy joining us.

We went back by the Chantee 'n' Boy pile room, and she said, "Well, the prodigal sons of bitches return." I felt a great sleepy glow. Trent came in, being loud and funny, sitting on Chantee, and then making a line about Jason packing a powerful tool, and me just smiling catlike.

"You all need to get your rest, get to the gym, whatever. We have the big finale to shoot tonight."

I could have gone another round, but Jason wanted to sleep some more, so Rex, Tommy, Geoff and I went to Jacqueline's, a schmaltzy faux-something diner. Rex and Geoff had healthy fruit while Tommy and I pigged out on Eggs Benedict, making funny silent glances with Rex across the table while Geoff rambled on, still speeding about his fucked-up family life and emotions and stuff way too heavy for brunch chat. Above us, the awnings occasionally hissed water.

We had four hours until we had to be set up out in the desert. I wondered how long we had before the cops would show up. The problem with getting film permits is you usually have some herd of the city's finest who want to see some movie stars.

I kept telling the boys money shots were not our goal, but most assured me they were still up for it, so to speak. They should just let go, but at the same time I tried to give them a sense of choreography, how I wanted them to disrobe, to fall into place, to go with the music, which I assured we would dub later to match the tunes to their gyrations.

At one point, I noticed they were all just standing around, impatient to get out of the setting sun, but I was really waiting for the right light, so we would only have to rely on a bit of the floodlights attached to one of the vans' batteries.

The portable lighting was harsh, but the sex action was fun because the boys were actually doing it in the shadow of sunset. I shot them either silhouetted or side-lit, but never front-lit. I would later touch it up in post, colorizing it. Real flat, hyper Balinese puppets.

What you do get on the Starz Video version of that night is called *Time Cocks*. In that is more plainly-shot fucking and sucking. Hey, they had the rights to redo whatever they wanted. What you get from my film, *Reel to Real*, is something altogether different.

I parked myself behind one of the camouflaged cameras, feeling like Marlin Perkins, testing the shot. The sun was just about to hit a far mountain. I moved the camera to off-center it. Then I went back to the center, where the fire would be lit. I stood on the periphery of the unlit pile of wood, looked at each of my indolent icons, my dream whores, and pointed.

Jorge emerged from the van with small carpets of fuzzy fabric.

"We're gonna shoot the intro now," I said. They looked collectively perplexed. "Take a piece of the fabric to go with your costumes, turn around, and walk until this spot is just a blip on the horizon, then turn around and walk back. When you get here, lay the fabric down, furry side up, on the chairs and rocks and stuff. Watch Jorge, then slowly strip and dance, then go for it. Do whatever you want to whomever. The rubbers and lube are here." I pointed to the little boxes and jars we'd placed on blankets around the fire. "Don't worry about camera angles or any of that shit. Do what you want. Okay? I'll see you in about twenty minutes."

"Ten minutes out, ten back," said Jason.

A few of them stared at me as if I'd lost my mind, except Tommy, who understood, but then Jason turned and walked, and the rest dispersed in outward directions. I wondered if they'd come back, but of course they would. Other than per diems, they hadn't been paid yet.

Jorge emerged from the van wearing a simple caftan, holding a turban and a pair of scissors. He set the scissors down and fiddled with the small turban.

"I'm almost ready for my close-up, Mister DeMille."

I smiled, seeing the sun spill through the sheer fabric. "Ready when you are, Bachir."

Jorge danced, slowly, teasingly, up to the sky. I followed him on the handheld, sometimes just shooting his hands, sometimes his face. I stopped and asked him to get hard. He asked me to help. I blushed and turned to see Geoff shrugging and turning away back at the far camera. I lifted his garment and tasted him until he sproinged up. I hated to pull away, but duty called. He danced with his cock tenting his gown, and the boys began to arrive, one by one, from the horizon. I pulled back, taking them in, getting them all as they arrived, flopping down the carpets.

"Finally, the golden fleece," Jorge announced. Then the guys laughed. Most got it, others were schooled as Jorge's fabric choice, a golden brassy shag rug faux-fur, shimmered by the firelight and small portable lamps.

They danced, and as I had hoped, the sun fell in great orange slats on the mountaintop, while the fat, full moon rose over the other side. I shot Jorge lighting the fire, the light dancing over the increasingly bare bodies of my icons; the sailor, the soldier, the farmboy, the dancer. They all became one, a part of a tribe of heat. The boys smiled, dropping the pretense of character, laughing, kissing, humping, standing, dancing freely, their boners wet as they withdrew from mouths, bouncing free in the dusk light.

By the time the sun had set, most of the men had taken up groupings around the fire, settling into duos, trios and occasional watching solos. I copped close-ups of butts being fucked, cocks and mouths and faces, always remembering to place whose organ was plowing in and out of whom. It was never just drilling, but drilling between people.

One of the guys grabbed my shorts. I succumbed for a few minutes, but then had to pry myself from them to resume shooting. I checked back with Geoff, who was doing fine at the far shots. I'd managed to stay out while he zoomed in, glancing up at his waves as he pulled out. It was frantic, and I feared we'd only get a good few minutes out of these hours of performed passion, but we were all so caught up in it, we didn't seem to care.

"Stan, come here," Jason called out. I pulled over to Jason, camera first, as he cranked his cock over Rex's sweat-glistened chest. With his usual professional acumen, he held back until I'd comfortably positioned myself, then he let go with a gush that drew audible moans of admiration from the others. Rex began to twitch underneath him, and I signaled Jason to lean down and kiss Rex, who spewed onto his own thigh.

The other guys took a little longer. I missed a few cumshots, but it happens. Tommy surprised me with yet another admirable finish. Nobody felt like they hadn't worked. They'd all worked, that was for goddamn sure.

As the guys foraged in their own duffel bags for their shorts, sweatpants and T-shirts, I handed out towels smartly pilfered from the hotel by Jorge, who also handed out bottles of water.

"Thank you all. Thank you so much. This is gonna be, well, either a great little video, or the biggest piece of shit you've ever been in."

Laughter all around. I started to pack up the camera. Jason stood behind me, still naked except for his boots.

"We all want to show our appreciation for your hard work, Mistah Grozniak," he said. All the others were behind him, waiting like my zombie bodybuilders in *The Manipulator* sequel, only this time they weren't green, plus they were a lot friendlier.

"Uh, gee that's okay, you don't have to..." And then I had an idea of what they might have in store. I was the only one who hadn't come.

Tommy said, "You have to be immortalized, too," or some such nonsense.

It wasn't that I didn't want to be smothered in affection by the bodies of these men. I just thought I'd make them work for it. That's why I took off running. By the time they dragged me back to the fire, stripped me down and, well, did sexy things to and on me, Geoff already had the camera set up, and well, that's one scene that didn't make the cut, one I won't be showing to any but a few select houseguests.

Panting, exhausted, regenerated with every breath, "Okay; one more shot, before you get dressed," I pleaded. "I want you all to dance some more."

"Dance?"

"It's very simple," I said. "Just do a little conga line, but in a circle."

It sounded so simple, as if I'd only thought of it that minute, like a lark. That's how they all like to tell it.

The fools. I'd been choreographing this shot for years.

I had them dance, half-clothed, then naked, a slow grooving compilation of every ethnic, funky, butt-bumpin' cock-flopping move I ever wanted to see a herd of men do around a campfire. Through the magic of later edited slow repetition and Geoff's steady camera work, we got it. The boys looked great, and they danced by the firelight, under the moonlight.

Jorge brought out a tray of sandwiches. We kept the fire going with the help of some siphoned gas. I imagined superimposing shots of Hel from *Metropolis* getting burned at the stake, but then I saw her burning, poor dear, and the film of her, and my poster of her, and everything burning away fresh, and it was oh so good, that or I was getting too dehydrated and almost started to hallucinate.

"Are porn shoots always like this?" I asked.

Three guys said at the same time, "Never!"

The guys shared stories, mostly about sex, but we veered off to other topics. We played some music on a portable radio someone had brought. After the last of them sat exhausted, cuddling together, most of the guys decided to head back to the hotel in the second van.

Jason and a few others wanted to stay, camp out until sun-up, make breakfast, tell stories. There was still some food. I asked Tommy to stay, since it was already about five o'clock in the morning. I wanted a sunrise scene, and no way was anybody coming back here again for just one shot. He was happy to comply.

It's the one I used with the end credits. We didn't dare use the whole score. Mister Sondheim would never go for such a rip-off, no matter his possible appreciation of my homage.

The shot is merely this: with no music, Tommy stands by the highway, maybe thumbing a ride, maybe not. He's wearing his tight black pants, his white shirt open, and his top hat lying in the dust, a chorus boy who fell from the tour bus. He keeps trying to get one step that eludes him. As his fumbling feet take him down the highway, he keeps repeating the phrase, "All I need now is the... All I need now is the..."

54. would you lie still beneath forest shadow ?

The shoot over, our merry crew disintegrated into a pack of whining children in the bodies of linebackers.

Some of the boys had a noon flight. Others stayed another night, just playing or having rounded up some escort business. We were all released from responsibility to each other.

I was hanging out, commencing the vacation portion of our trip. We said goodbye and see ya later. I tried to crash, while Orrie held court at the hotel bar and bragged about his wonderful night at the baths, which got onto discussing other bathhouses, then movie theatres, like The Adonis.

Somebody mentioned The David, and another guy just blurted out, "Oh, that's where I think I got the clap." Quick as a whip, Orrie snapped, "Well, nobody told you to eat the popcorn!" And everybody laughed so long and loud, we all had to go off to our rooms because the manager asked us to please keep it down.

One of the Andrews came back with a new weekend fuck buddy, a stringy boy who was nice enough to bring cookies. They talked about his overheated car and rich local fags, and I was exhausted, and they finally left and I got some sleep. I didn't get up until dusk. Even with Jason sleeping in my bed, I wanted to see Tommy, but they were sleeping, so I went to the pool and had almost an hour all alone.

Birds cawed and flew overhead, one sounding exactly like a small car horn. Another bobbed up and down over a small puddle of pool water, craning its straw of a beak in and out. Palm trees stood guard, still in the flat wall of air. Pool water rippled in moody glows from the lights under the surface, and I sank down many times, hearing my own heartbeat, as if in a womb, the only sound under the water.

As I swam down under it, my ears clogging, the creak of my limbs reverberated though my body. The twilight was a spooky, eerie time. A single star popped up, a planet perhaps, and I made the simplest of impossible wishes, to make love with Jason once again. I could have become horrified at what had become my complacency, my silence amid so much silence. The landscape, the hotel, was a great slumbering machine of pleasure, topiaries of cactus comfort, and I a lost blip of flesh floundering in a wet cement puddle.

A straight couple came by and lounged, then invaded the pool, so I retreated to the room.

Three messages. Orrie, Jason, Geoff and Tommy.

I ordered a pizza and went next door, where Jason and Orrie were chatting about Whitman. We were all wearing nothing but shorts, Orrie's roly-poly body reddened from the day's sun.

We showered and ate pizza and watched an *I Love Lucy* episode where she spends way too much money on new furniture for her country home. Hideous stuff, all of it. It reminded me of the younger times in Brookside, before we made a shift and got new furniture and stopped having dinner in the kitchen, before the dispersal of our center. I started to try to explain it to the guys. Orrie was getting it more than Jason, who started in on the "dot, dot, dot," line about me rambling. I don't know. Maybe he was pulling away, making it easier when you really have to pull away.

That night, The Works' manager let us have free reign of his place after I declared an informal wrap party, still letting Geoff play candid camera man. Maybe something would happen. Janice had already headed back north.

The party started out slow, but got fun when Vince got down to his red Speedos and swam in the tiny pool. We watched while Jason whispered exacting instructions, making Vince pose for him, shucking his Speedos, never taking them fully off.

Jason later read me a poem, in the midst of the party chitchat and music playing. He read it, about warmth and closeness, a heart beating. It was a bit sentimental, but he read it to me first. I was honored and charmed and embarrassed. I vowed not to fall in love with him.

Jason and I stripped down and swam, chatting with others as we sat in the pool and the Jacuzzi. Our serene joy was only interrupted by Geoff's new burst of slightly drunk silliness and the club owner's constant industry chatting. Difficult to make cracks about a place when the guy who runs it is in your face. I kept looking for Tommy, wondering where he was.

Jason introduced me to strangers as a "famous film director," and I shied away from it. I wasn't famous, even by gay or cult standards. These desert people were so sunstroked, nothing impressed them anyway. It was cruel to make them engage in the "making excuses why they live here" conversation. Not everyone needs to live in L.A. Fuck regional elitism.

But I knew it was time to go when a girl who'd been flirting with Vince came by, fangs in her mouth. She said something about how if we went in and out of the hot and cold water it would stimulate electrolytes and we could live forever.

"That or drinking fresh blood," I said. "Jason bares his fangs once in a while, but only under a full moon." He gave me a hurt look, and I said, "Sorry, Lestat, didn't mean to blow your cover," then sank under the water, away from the strange woman and off from the pool.

The rum and Coke felt good, and I felt an obligation to remain sociable, but I'd just filmed and participated in an ultimate desert orgy. Nightclub chat paled by comparison.

I dried off and dressed, then began the goodbyes. Orrie parted from his little beach chair chat with a Latino kid, and I almost bummed a few cigarettes from him, but remembered my vow to Lance.

About an hour after I'd settled in my bed, I heard a soft knock. At the door, Jason grinned. "Forgot my card."

"Where's Tommy?"

"You've got a little crush." He smirked. "He's off to the airport. He's got work in the morning, poor thing." He flopped on to the bed.

I watched a bit, admiring his prone body. I got up, eased the veranda door open, since the breeze outside was cooler than the clammy air conditioning. Lying close together, we had a nice chat about my work and the gay cause, and got to talking about the 1993 March on Washington.

"I saw many people again, a few for the last time in their lives, and I saw famous people and made out with a boy in the mall in front of the National Gallery," I half-whispered. "We kissed inside in front of a Jackson Pollock and someone took our picture."

My throat clogged with a sob, and I thought of him, and hoped he was doing okay. Jason and I chatted some more and then said goodnight. I listened to the hum of the distant traffic outside.

Jason had mentioned something about his T-cells in the car to Geoff, and I realized I had been riding with two men who might not live ten more years. I was so saddened, but then touched when he talked in bed about his little nephew and niece, how he's the gay uncle, how he's the nice sweet man in that little kid's life. Jason taught him songs and fairy stories and that telling Paki jokes was bad and if he ever did it again he would go away.

I was trying to listen and not get misty. It was okay. I could cry. It was dark. I just felt really glad to have met Jason, and how he got me to do this. He would definitely be the hero of this film. He was the bright spark amid the thick valley of heat in this place. I thought, despite the fact that he might not live another twenty years, how he will rise again in his little nephew and then his nephew's nephew or cousin, and that is how we regenerate, by sharing and seeing the queer spark in our others and letting them know any way we can, that they're incredible.

55. crush me man, from body to bed

With all the tripods, lighting equipment and videotapes (except my little cameo scene), taken back with Geoff, he and Orrie left with the raw video footage we'd edit sometime later next week back in the sprawl of L.A.

It was just down to me and my star.

I was lying in his arms mid-day after another massive breakfast, telling him secrets. We'd considered doing something, but after a long walk up and down the vacant sidewalks, all we could agree upon was returning to bed.

Jason listened, let me keep my hand on his penis, petting it, amazed by its sheer … everything.

"So you see," I told him of my official first time, "it was nothing foreign for me to consider 'being seduced in the basement.' Even though my little bones creaked as I took ten minutes to stand, slip out and up to my room, the lair had been christened."

"Okay," Jason said. "Me mother caught me out back with a boy. Coupla times. After the third time, she just gave up."

He stood up and over me on the bed, his cock dancing with him, his thighs straddling the wobbly mattress. "You wanna see me dance now?"

"Do you want some music?"

"Sing."

I did. He danced for me, my favorite most private show. So private, I won't describe another moment. It is lost to vision altogether.

I slept in his arms, covered in him, wearing him like a fleece.

We woke up later, since I'd left the drapes open.

"So, what are your plans after this?"

"Lunch, first. No, coffee first."

"No, silly. I mean after we leave."

Jason growled as he rubbed my buzzcut.

"Back to L.A., then New York, then Paris, the Ibeetha." He grinned at the pronunciation.

"Circuit parties?" I asked.

"Sort of. I have a … benefactor who likes to travel."

"Is he cute?"

"His wallet is quite handsome." He patted my butt. "And you? Another movie?"

"Nothing's planned yet. But it probably won't be anything like all this was."

"And what of love?"

"What of it?"

"The guy you mentioned."

"Lance."

"He sounds like a catch."

"Yup, I think I caught him. Took twenty years."

"Worth the wait, I hope."

He gave my cheek a kiss before jumping up for a shower. Before I joined him, I sat, feeling a bit sorry for him, then tossed that thought. He was living his life as fast as he could.

With a few hours before his flight, we drove around and up Camelback Mountain, where the wealthy folks live, the secret enclave. The birds were singing their songs, and the slow curving drive up was broken over and over by No Parking and PRIVATE DRIVE NO TRESPASSING signs. The rich had bought a million-year-old mountain and cut it up, slotting in their hideously beautiful homes, where they all slept.

I hadn't brought my own camera, but craved one to capture the view of the city as if it were already stolen. It sprawled low like a puddle, the mountains jutting up in an amusement park backdrop. The rocks were color-coordinated with the driveways. It was all scary proportions, unreality down to the last shrub. Two bunnies froze on a rock garden, and I stared them down, wondering if they were actually security cameras.

We drove back down away from them and sat in the van, overlooking the view. I wanted to remember the parade of men I'd seen naked and flirting, but the rocks and the sun and Jason were all I had left.

Jason sat on the steps of the nearly abandoned hotel while I checked out. I toyed with bringing him along on the next leg of my trip, then realized it was impossible. We needed time to think about each other, to miss each other again. He was going back. He needed the money.

"See you in L.A.?" I asked.

"After my travels, hopefully."

"Sure."

Even after our hug goodbye, I longed for him, but also felt content to end it, my hedonistic epic. I let my sex god, my Argonaut captain, move on his next journey. I wanted to be out in the heat, driving further into the desert, where I had a memory to fully burn off.

56. in space there are lakes of rust no zone past whisper

Interstate 10 opened up plain and flat. I considered a stop at Joshua Tree National monument since I'd never seen it, but I figured that could wait until afterward. Maybe.

After returning the van at the airport, I'd splurged on a sturdy SUV. Once past Blythe, that funny little border town on the Colorado River, I felt easier, secure in where I was going and what I was doing.

I drove through the desert town, looking for the address, but first checked my *Damron Guide* for the nearest gay anything. Force of habit, I guess. I love to see how the locals do it.

It wasn't a sin. It wasn't my fault. Don't any of you blame me. When I grew up, pre-teen singers were being marketed as sex symbols on the back of cereal boxes.

He came with a purpose, to hurt. He just happened to be lucky enough to find me ready and willing to enjoy being hurt. What wrecked the train was finding out he wasn't touching me to please me, but to hurt me. If a man wants a boy and wants to give him something, how can it hurt? How can popping a cork before it reaches full body hurt the wine?

It can. A boy may know what he wants and what it looks like, but he doesn't know control. He doesn't know how swiftly passion twists to love through obsession and into despair. Abuse is hurting someone who can't tell the difference.

I never have and never will do anything like that, but by God I will defend to my death my right to say I wanted it. At twelve, at thirteen, and all the way until "legal age" I wanted it. I wanted those goddamn closet college boys to teach me, to let me feel their hairy bodies. I wanted passage.

57. " you shot my Sasquatch !"

Uncle Sean's house was small and unimpressive, a little place your Aunt Edna might retire in until she's found dead of a stroke with her cats licking her face.

The lawn was bare, shrubless.

I walked to the door and knocked, then saw him in jeans and a T-shirt through the screen door.

"Remember me?"

"You're my sister's kid."

"Right."

"You come to kill me?"

"No."

"Then I guess I oughtta let you in." He stood a moment before opening the door.

Any house that's been lived in has a smell, a warm, fried dog breath kind of smell. It's vacant in some homes, but even that smell of cleanness or something living wasn't present here. It was as if he only stayed here sometimes. It was merely an address.

"So. What do you do with yourself these days?" I asked him.

"Go to meetings, AA. Work in a shop. Try to stay out of trouble."

"Do you?"

"Yes."

Once again, I trusted my Uncle Sean. "What's it like living here?"

"Quiet. Too quiet. Gets dark early. You can see the stars real good. They don't have many streetlights, so the observatory can see above the light pollution."

"Light pollution."

"Yeah. Get you something?"

"I thought you didn't drink."

"Diet Coke?"

"Ew. Juice or water's fine."

He fixed some drinks in the kitchen. The clinking glass and ice was so domestic. It made me shiver. I let him return, sit and drink. I didn't talk. Too long I'd always been the one conducting, keeping things pleasant, rolling along. I didn't have to do that anymore. I let him do it.

"It's so flat out here, it's scary. One time I meant to leave, just drive away. Got out to the desert, no one around anywhere. Just got out of the car and screamed. I felt better. Went back home."

"You came to our house to ruin it."

He sipped.

"Were you just testing a theory?" I asked.

"Listen, I was out of control then. Your mother? She got all I never had, made a life I couldn't. She got out young."

"That's your problem."

"You're right."

"You know, you were the first, really." Except for Ronnie in that sleeping bag, my saving grace.

"But not the last, I hope."

"No. In a way, it was great. It was everybody else's shame I took on. Would have enjoyed it if I hadn't found out you hit on my brother."

"You're like me?"

"I was never like you."

"I mean..."

"I know what you mean. I wanted it when I was ten and kissed you goodnight that other time you visited. When you brought the cheesecake all the way from Pittsburgh?"

"They don't make 'em the same anymore. Get 'em anywhere now. All those additives."

"You hadn't shaved for two days. I tasted you then."

He got up and fiddled with the stereo, but didn't turn it on.

"You wanna hit me?"

"Part of me wants to."

"Ya wanna kill me?"

"Maybe." I wanted. What I wanted. I wanted to still find a desire for him, to tie him down, fuck him without a rubber, wish I had a virus to give him, a huge dildo to batter his ass with, a big palm to slap him bloody.

I settled for a soft, wet, tender kiss on those old lips, then I turned away from that scrawny frame. Turning back, I hauled off with the best, most secure, good-feeling punch I'd ever landed on a man. It felt good because he looked like he enjoyed it. He sat up from the floor.

"That's from your son."

I went into the bathroom, acting like I had to piss, when I really needed some cold water on my hand, and there it was. Old Spice. I took it.

I returned to the living room. As I thought, he merely rose up to sitting. I walked over to his television and picked up a *TV Guide,* leafing though the pages. "You got cable?"

"Yeah."

I tossed the little magazine on the floor. "Thursday. Showtime. Ten o'clock." I walked out to the door, swung the screen door open, then turned back. "G'-bye, Unc. I love you."

"I know you do, kid." He spat out blood.

I called the rental place about just driving the car all the way home. Extra hundred dollars, or $98.79, according to Lee-Anne, my Service Representative.

"That'll be fine," I heard myself say.

Some hours and rest stops and Stuckey's and the airport rental car return booth later, rolling in the back of a taxi swerving off La Cienega and into Santa Monica, I was so tired I wasn't even there. I was no longer someone for a porn star to beg attention from. I was an obnoxious success. I was someone once again. I was me. I was home.

58. claim time to do an afterlife séance no zone past whisper

With two films in the can, I felt I'd overcome post-production depression. Punching out my uncle sure helped.

After I got home, slept for a day, and answered a slew of messages, I made an appointment with an old friend. Let's get 'em all taken care of before upgrading to Stan 4.0.

The address was the same as ever. Of course, when I first visited, all of Hollywood was a blinding glare of cheap sidewalk glamour. I've since learned how to work in the shade, the moist arms of ferns nearby, the clammy stucco of a wall behind me.

I found Guy LeDrac. We talked. His home had the same murky quality. Maybe it just didn't seem so bad because I'd since then often found ecstasy in better places. Either way, I was still thrilled as the kid I once was, just to see him again.

He walked me in through the immense doorway. The stairs loomed. He began a tour, almost like that when I was a boy, but then cut himself off. "But you've seen the place, of course."

"Through different eyes," I said. I let it fall. I wouldn't push.

We talked in his dining room. Dinner was exquisite. I chatted about my film work. Fortunately, Guy had seen my recent works, so we got to talk about my first love, *The Manipulator* series, and its merits and flaws.

"I think I still have a one-sheet from the first release."

"Ah, keep it. It may pay for dinner someday."

We laughed, and as he invited me into the library, by his major arcana, I couldn't help but search. Where was it? Where was she?

I got around to discussing *Say Uncle*, and then on to a new film I was toying around with. Of course, I made it sound ready to cast. There was a part for an elderly gentleman. Actually, it was Edmund's life story, which he'd already commissioned as a script, but I wasn't selling it as that. I was just trying to pay for next year's dinner.

We made jokes about Norma Desmond, and I assured him it wasn't anything like that, sort of Ed Wood meets Gregg Araki.

"Of course, it would be quite amusing to step in front of the camera again, after all this time."

"The fans still flock to you at the conventions, I hear."

"Yes, well, it's all Trekkies now, you know. This cyber stuff has just got the best of me. Not much call for old Karloff photos anymore."

"Maybe not." I decided to make my move. "But there's one artifact I remember, that I don't see."

"And which one is that?"

"The *Metropolis* poster."

"Ah, yes. Hel. For her, we must rise."

It was upstairs, over his enormous bed. I stood and gazed at her while he spoke.

I began pulling my T-shirt off and unbuckling my pants.

"What are you doing?" he asked.

"Payment," I said. "For this, and all those *Scream* years of happiness."

"That's hardly necessary," he sputtered.

"Unnecessary," I agreed, dropping my pants as Hel looked down on us. "But essential."

Driving home, ever so slow, afraid to break the framed glass that protected my Hel in the back seat, I felt complete, but a bit hollow, as if after a massive shopping binge. I finally knew what it was like to be satiated.

59. as woman need love a good gown's a **diamond**

Fortunately, despite the problems, Showtime managed to find a shred of acceptance among the mass mailing from Fundamentalist Theme Park numbers one through six hundred-sixty-six.

What saved it?

Focus groups. High advance screenings, pre-second and third re-edit. They wanted the guys to go off hand in hand. No kiss. We threatened to steal the print if they cut the kiss. And we didn't even test in West Hollywood, either, but Pittsburgh, of all places.

It was that kiss, I like to think, that got us the Cable Ace Award nominations.

Edmund decided to throw what he called a Get Nervous Party, hours before the awards, at his place. He said it would be a little bonding experience for us.

I said all of three words to him before being swept up by a slew of film students and wannabes among about fifty people there. So much for a bonding experience. Lance was on the other side of the room, beaming, surrounded by new fans.

Edmund had splurged again and put out a great spread, clearing the living room for everybody who wasn't going to the awards to stay and watch. "And make sure to tape the damn thing!" he yelled to his substitute host.

In our tuxedos, we looked like waiters about to bail on the job.

Each of the male nominees—Barry, Edmund, Lance and myself—stood around in tuxes while everyone else sported comfy clothes, with just one drag queen present. She got to fawn all over us like we'd had nametags saying, FAMOUS PERSON, GET IN LINE. As he would at the Ace Awards, Edmund kept introducing me to people. In my occasional trips to the bar or bathroom, I took notes.

Lance finally found a moment to sidle up to me. We'd been spending more nights and days together since I'd gotten the porn epic out of my system. I'd surprised him with a few techniques I'd learned from the professionals. And yet our public pairings remained a bit awkward. I was about to embrace him when we were interrupted.

"I know your films," a man who wore sunglasses inside said. I tried hard not to immediately dislike him. "It betrays a certain distrust to the viewer, even in your most commercial work."

Lance tried to hide his eye roll.

"Thank you, I think." I know they say most egomaniacs think the world revolves around them, but at that moment, I swear it did. I offered Lance a glance. "What have you seen of my stuff?"

"All of it."

"Really?" I try to dismiss people who want to put me in boxes according to my work based on what they've seen. It shows me what they think they know of me, and what they haven't met.

The guy in sunglasses rattled off all the names, except *Keemoe*. I had him.

"You forgot one."

"Which one?"

"You'll have to find out," I smiled and started off. Lance grabbed my shoulder like reins on a horse.

"Would you excuse us?" After he steered me away, he muttered, "I have a feeling that after tonight you're going to have be nicer to your fans."

"You're the only one that matters."

"I'm not just one of your fans."

I patted his butt. "I gave you that."

Showtime offered to rent us a limo, but Edmund's Rolls looked better. We arrived together in his car, but I managed to divert the limo to Janice's house. She picked up Katsuo, and they snagged invites and dates with what must have been two swift cell calls, because they got there before us, even though they left Barry's party after we did.

It wasn't the Oscars, but it was pretty fabulous.

"Okay, whoever gets low hand has to come out," I joked.

Lance turned away from the passing Hollywood street and said, "I'm out."

"What do you mean?"

"I did three interviews."

"Where?" Barry asked.

"Gay papers."

"Which ones?"

"*The Advocate, Windy City Times,* and *Out.* Katsuo got 'em."

"Edmund did *The Advocate*," I said.

Barry said, "I'd do *The Advocate* if I can have another date with that hunky editor, but not *People.*"

"There's a hunky editor at *People?*"

"I don't even have an Emmy or a husband and puppies for the photo op, what do I want with *People?*"

"So listen, are you guys gonna speak if we get one?"

"What's the order? Who got asked?"

"I'm sorry, I didn't know—"

The discussion had turned into that of a nervous unsure quartet of squeaky borderline shy boys. Now it was a contest to see who could out (or re-out) himself more fabulously.

"Well, whether you do or not," Edmund said, opening his tux pocket, "I want you all to have these." He withdrew three pairs of sunglasses, and put a fourth on himself as he dramatically opened the sunroof.

"I don't wanna wear these going in," Lance said.

I nudged him. They were Polizia, from Milan. Two hundred bucks, at least.

"No," Edmund said, as he stretched his legs. "But on the way out..."

The cab was silent then, except for the huff of air from the sunroof. Then we burst out laughing.

"Are you drinking tonight?" Lance asked me.

"Duh."

"Just hold back until after you've hit the cameras, okay?"

"*Ja vol, mein Kommendant.*"

Edmund's driver pulled the Rolls up to an awning, a white rent-a-tent that covered the red carpet walkway to the door. The morning's rain had passed. The security guard who opened our door wore a yellow jacket, as did all the other burly men guarding the entrance of celebrities.

As we got out, I felt a communal sigh of disappointment among the throng of fans in the far-off bleachers. Poised cameras were held aside, cheers held back as four nondescript yet handsome men surrounded The Captain. "Oh, it's The Captain!" someone shouted. Cameras flashed, then subsided.

My mom taped it on *MovieTime,* or *E!* or *EW,* or one of those channels. She plays it for the neighbors. I don't even remember slowing down that moment to let Lance catch up. I do remember him taking my hand, and us walking in together.

I kept bumping into Joanne Woodward. There were lots of famous people, and producers and assistants and handlers I'd seen at parties or clubs. The other gay men all seemed to give each other silent nods of recognition. Did the ones with beautiful women on their arms think they were pulling something off?

Barry and Lance and I kept turning away from each other, distracted by the famous. A small herd of them seemed to be waiting for a moment in front of the bright flare of cameras, Leeza Gibbons and some other lesser interviewers were getting their assistants to corral the film actors toward them one by one. Ted Danson looked larger than life.

Some of the older woman looked uncomfortable in gowns, parts of them spilling out in odd ways. Others were so thin, their bodies seemed merely draped by dresses that might fall off at any moment. They clutched wraps and gazed around with a wary huntress look, searching out a camera or another famous face to commune with. I continued to gaze at the parade of glamour until a familiar voice whispered into my ear.

"Stan, why do I have to die again?"

The Manipulator II shoot.

Barney Hassel was peeved, or at least pretended to be when he'd started that line back in the old days. In addition to playing small parts, he'd stunt-doubled for my bad guys. This time, his muscles nearly bursting out of his tux, he wrapped me in a bear hug. We had a good long chat. Barney was doing some adventure cable show; rock climbing, that sort of thing.

When Barney worked with me on *Manipulator II*, he'd been killed off, and again in a subsequent TV series, and been blown to outer space two years before in a sci-fi action pic starring the muscled Brian Thompson. In the latest project he'd signed on to, he said he'd been cast as yet another villain, this time beheaded by a train while Kevin Costner or Harrison Ford (lead still not cast) would fight him in the climactic action scene. He'd be making twice what I got for *Say Uncle*.

I loved watching Barry and Lance try to figure out my relationship with Barney. I loved him still working me. I loved people working me. I loved working them. I love watching people I know succeed, especially people who owe me.

The speeches?

Yes, well, Barry read his much better. That's all I say to that. I just blubbered. I thanked Mister Woo, the owner of that little video store. I forgot to thank my parents or announce my boyfriend-ness to Lance, but I thanked Mister Woo. This should explain my hesitance to get before a camera. Fortunately, directors don't get much airtime on *E!*

Post-awards, beaming, my tie choked me, business cards flying in my direction, The sharp award's points nearly stabbing me, I felt good. I wore no underwear and my tux pants told all. I was half-hard just from the excitement, but usually managed to be seated at the time.

In the tent next to the building, with a forty-foot buffet table and a few bars, I schmoozed and boozed with Lance at my side, holding hands, nibbling nibbly things, gloating.

"What a lovely coming out ball this has been, my dear," chirped somebody with a microphone.

"Yes, indeed," I replied with a smirk.

"You know, the gossip sheets are gonna have a field day."

"As Wilde said, 'It is better to be talked about...'"

I let her finish the line, and made her think she was funny.

"So, what's your next project?" she asked.

"Well, I'm in post-production on *Reel to Real.*"

"Sounds interesting. Is it a ...gay film, too?"

"Quite."

"Oh, what's it about?"

"It's about ten guys fucking and sucking each other through film history. They all end up in a big orgy in the desert." I grinned into the camera as Lance punched my shoulder.

"You mean..."

"Yes, it's sexual."

"Rated X?"

"Unrated. We're not—"

"Distributing?"

"Yes, but—"

Meryl Streep was two feet away, diverting the reporter.

"Oh...well, thank you." She sort of shriveled away.

I love the press.

"That reminds me," I said as Lance clung to my side, obviously using me as boyfriend material to wrench himself free of a "producer" who had attached himself to him. "Where is Katsuo when I need her? Interviews set up for tomorrow. We need some sit-down at my place to do a studio shot."

"What?"

"Some outdoor scene. Pretend we're already shooting for our next film. They'll eat it up."

"Who's the writer this time?" Lance asked, caught up in the ridiculousness of it.

"What?"

"Well, you see, Mister Grozniak, I have this treatment I'd love you to read."

I leaned in, as if in league with some terrific new project.

Lance assumed an announcer voice: "The Life Story of the Shampoo Guy!"

The producer laughed, as if getting it. He didn't. I had to wait for music to interrupt us. I pulled Lance away. "Excuse me, sir, but I've got to dance with my star."

We guzzled another fluted glass of champagne and twirled on the floor. They were playing a song by Melissa Etheridge, but I was singing to myself.

"Strings come in. Now we waltz."

"What are you singing?" Lance hummed in my ear.

"You don't remember?"

"It sounds so familiar." He grinned wide, nineteen-year-old dimples peeking out of his forty-something face.

"Show tunes, dear. They can save lives."

never **swallow** the **moon**
it's **enormous**

You'd think that after the success, the award, a rekindled romance that was once taboo, I'd become a happy man.

I was, for a while.

Lance's eccentricities sometimes annoyed me, as mine did him, so we too often tabled those discussions, because they were irrelevant. He cherry-picked from his faith, and after a few visits to his gay-friendly church gatherings, we both let it go.

He kept hinting about me moving in with him. It made sense. His house was nicer, but I couldn't see any space for all my stuff. Then I had to remind myself how lucky I was to have this boyhood crush become a full-fledged love.

After the award wins, the scripts I received from my agent Sal were either too much like *Say Uncle* or so trite I couldn't finish them. Want to write a cliché-ridden gay screenplay? Most gay screenwriters do.

Lance got work in some local theatre, a few showcases, but no lead roles. His agent then booked him another modeling job, as one of a few handsome men on boxes of No-Grey For Men.

"They hadda Photoshop the grey into my hair," he laughed the day he took me to Musso & Frank for a celebratory dinner after depositing his first check.

Barry continued to pitch the gay superhero movie, but *X-Men*, by then in pre-production, would upstage that, in a way. He got a few commercials, then wrote some perfunctory industrial scripts for trade shows, which I directed, all while he rewrote one of his novels, which didn't lend itself to a screen adaptation.

I wasn't set to re-establish myself as yet another "gay" director. Everyone else in my field, Todd Haynes, Gregg Araki, had moved on. Why couldn't I?

Meetings with executive producers who thought the world needed another car crash gunfight action movie nauseated me, even when they paid for lunch.

As DVDs became more popular, Sal called me with the news that whatever corporation owned the *Manipulator* films had found the original prints in a film storage warehouse and decided to reissue them with audio commentary by me and whomever in the cast I could round up. Sal negotiated for a small payment, but the project languished as my films kept getting bumped by other B-movies in the Corman genre. I felt almost relieved. The idea of talking about Ricky while watching him on-screen for six hours brought a lump to my throat.

It took a Vietnamese funeral to get me out of my rut. Mister Woo of Woo Video had died.

At the wake, I met Mister Woo's niece, an eloquent, fast-talking travel agent, who promised to hook me up with some underling at the Vietnamese Consulate, and free round-trip tickets and hotel stays in several cities in exchange for a cheery tourist-oriented travel documentary. So I went to Saigon with Lance.

We enjoyed the travel filming so much, with he as the innocuous host, I considered a career change when Lance shared some interesting news.

After several auditions, Lance's German had come in handy. An eager L.A.-based casting agent had helped him snag the role of a goofy American living in Berlin in a sitcom to be called *Die Glückliche Familie (The Happy Family)*. Although not a lead, his role was that of a hapless American neighbor who'd get the most laughs with bilingual malapropisms.

"Will you come with me?" he asked, his face beaming with hope and trepidation. "It doesn't start for a few months, and it prob'ly won't last a season, but we can travel on my off days. See Europe!"

It took me all of a few seconds to say yes. Inside, those few seconds became crammed with a dozen worries. Could I leave? Would they let us back in the U.S.? What about my home, all my stuff? Could I ever learn German? Would I need to? Could I get more work there?

But a second later, none of that mattered. I began to enjoy the idea of not being in America and not dealing with its realities. I would be with Lance.

"Yes."

The idea of traveling for months at a time gave me a sense of fresh desire towards Lance. He didn't have to beg me to shoot a short homemade documentary about his crew of long-distance cyclists. But he did have to coax me to get my chunky ass on a bike.

While Lance always said he admired my husky frame, he knew I only needed a little push toward getting more consistently athletic, which included joining his gym. Any excuse to be together was made, and anything nudging us closer to a fully orchestrated partnership-marriage-whatever you call it became possible.

By 2000, having acquired a new digital camera, I absorbed myself in a series of small projects. They also gave me an excuse not to move in with Lance too soon, although I spent a lot of time with him before he preceded me to Germany. It would be nice to have a clean uncluttered home to visit for editing sessions, then escape to the beach while I considered potential subletters.

One phone call to my teen star Brendan, by then nearly an adult and aching to leave his parents' home, solved that problem. Who better to trust with all my toys than a budding film director?

Well, not all of them. As I boxed up some of my belongings to clear some space for Brendan, Jorge sorted through my porn collection with a finicky precision before letting it all go; well, most of it. Jorge was possibly the only person with whom I could joke about it while being specific.

"I'll take *Hot Rods*, but you don't have *Hot Rods Two*?"

"It lacked Aristotelian structure."

A few days later, Lance came by to help me finish, and take most of my clothes later to his house. I guess I was sort of going to move in with him for the months when we'd be back in L.A.

"Storage, my house, or trash?" He asked as he stood over what was left from Jorge's forage through the porn videos and magazines pulled from under my bed.

"I don't suppose Goodwill would be interested," I shrugged.

Lance took me in his arms and whispered, before a light kiss, "I'll be your porn star."

We could have continued, but I still felt antsy with so many undecided options for my stuff. "I'll call The One Institute. They have a great porn collection."

Lance looked around. "So, what else?"

"Look in the kitchen and see if there's anything you like."

The books were the easiest to save, since Lance said he'd buy a few more shelves. Among them was a new addition. As a belated thank you gift, Tommy Matthews had somehow found my address (most likely from Jason) and just showed up one day with a vintage copy of *The Odyssey*. I pondered whether to tell Lance that I'd enjoyed a little post-film off-camera scene with Tommy, or propose, eventually, an affectionate yet no-strings threeway. Not just yet, I told myself, dropping the book into a box.

Amid our mutual sounds, the rips of packing tape, the clank of pots and pans in the kitchen, Lance called out to me.

"What about all this?" He gestured to the Magnetic Poetry phrases clustered all over the fridge door.

"Save that for later."

Soon, after the bigger objects are sorted, I would pluck the hundreds of tiny word magnets from the refrigerator door, and place them back in their little boxes for Brendan to start his own story.

"In fact, let's save this all for later, after our trip to Ohio." I wrapped him in my arms, we shared a kiss, and looked for a clear space to make out, which, fortunately, left only my bed.

This is the real ending: me and Lance getting along, becoming a couple across borders and on swift EuroStar trains. I email him from Prague or wherever else I get a job as Second Unit Director for the Travel Channel or other nondescript yet well-paying gigs while Lance fumbles his actually quite proficient German on-set in Berlin. Sometimes we meet up in Paris or London or just hole up in the ancient apartment the sitcom's producers lent him.

Even though the next chapters—back to Brookside one more time— are the last, I'm giving you the extended cut of *Whatever Happened to Stan Grozniak?*

This is the real ending: half of the year, a husky film director shares a vagabond life with his equally aging boyhood crush, wondering what he's supposed to dream about when his dreams have come true. Running away from Hollywood to live out your own multilingual musical comedy in real life?

It could happen.

61. say **gone** is a **moment**

"You have reached the message center for Daw Drop Productions. If this is a personal call, please press 1. If you're calling about Jason's health, please press 2 for the latest stats. If you are a healthcare professional, please press 3. If you are a video professional, please press 4. If this is a personal call to any of our hard-working staff, please press 5."

I call to see if Jason got any interest from one of his clients to find a distributor for *Reel to Real*, which has been sitting on a shelf.

Reel to Real was made in two forms. The commercial X-rated version, retitled *Time Cocks*, after my director's fee, got me a few hundred dollars in sales percentages. They'd included the special effects, but only for the first few minutes of each scene, dissolving into normal color devoid of saturated tones and retro film scratches; basically de-artified.

I'd presciently passed on outing myself as the director by not attending the 1996 Adult Video News Awards in Paradise, Nevada. *Time Cocks,* while nominated, lost the Best Specialty Gay Video to the appropriately titled *Pissed.*

My own version, still as sexual, but without plumbing shots, remained in limbo for three years. Nobody would touch it to distribute as an 'erotic art film,' so I'd lured Katsuo into handling it as an executive producer. In between her Showtime job, she had written up grant requests and Gay/Queer/Whatever applications for film festivals in Berlin, Paris and London. No one bit. Still, her Rolodex of Life turns and turns.

Leaving a message for Jason from my parents' house in Ohio seems so damned incongruous, as if he'd need a visa just to call back.

I give up on reconnecting to L.A., and settle into being here in Brookside a while longer, where my fame is more connected to my mother and father than my last film.

Gutting the basement serves as an additional distraction from telling Mom what happened when I met her brother. She keeps hinting, but like my porn video epic, some things remain unspoken.

I've held off long enough thinking that she or anything else could distract me from my task here. Besides the rotting paneling, other problems arise.

I've surfed every channel, all of it aflutter with Election Night jitters. Something odd is going on in Florida. TV screens show repeated images of Bush and Gore, ballot boxes, and 'dangling chads.'

Thinking I'd truly crossed over to simple narrative, heartwarming scripted stories may have worked for a while. I could even continue believing it with a guy like Lance. He had gotten a last-minute audition for a commercial, and assured me he'd fly out to Ohio as soon as it was finished, but possibly only for the day of Professor McCabe's tribute. I tried to get over my disappointment of not flying in with Lance, that sense of victory, returning home with my boyhood crush on my arm. Oh well. Reshoot.

But that old documentarian instinct distracts me. Something strange is going on in TV land, and I need to capture it now, before everybody forgets.

Mom's unopened stack of videotapes ripped of their plastic wrapping, I pop a tape in the VCR, set it to CNN, and hit record. Upstairs, in my parents' room, NBC. Record. I capture what feels like a new polluted wave of lies coming on. I'll need the footage for a new video I know will emerge next, a sort of *Keemoe* collage, but of a different cancer altogether. Another birth of future filmic agitprop will need fuel.

The rented equipment sits in the basement, a gas-powered water blaster. But first, I have to tear down those paneled walls, gut the remnants of that basement, and rip it down to its bare, dead cement walls.

The first thing I notice, other than the smell of mildew, are the veins. Ripping away the paneling, rotted from the bottom up after years of flooding and damp decay, each panel comes away like fungus candy bars.

But underneath it, a vast network of tree roots like capillaries trail along the cement wall. Blasting the coat of scaly paint flecks down to the grout between cement bricks, they leave the basement walls raw, skinned.

The gas fumes of the machine nearly choke me until I set up a fan by the doorway. After a third round of dumping the stacks of rotten paneling in the garage, I need a break, but return again to the basement after checking the TVs. Bush, then Gore, then news talking heads. Yes, something very strange is going on in Florida.

I can't process my gut horror at what I, and some on the news, are alleging is about to happen. I retreat downstairs.

I look for a new box of garbage bags. And then I find a wrinkled packet of Eves. On instinct, I sniff, savor the aroma, find a lighter from among Mom's candles near the washer, and light up.

Inhaling, I become sick to my stomach. I toss the pack in the fireplace, and after scooping out the soot, begin to gather kindling for a new fire.

62. worship a peach at purple blow pond

Ohio is at its best when it's ripe with crisp autumn. So my visit for Arthur McCabe's tribute fits in nicely.

Wrapping up a last few days at my parents' home, I'm struck with little urges to pack more things up and send them back before they show up missing. After packing up old cassettes, books and toys, I don a jacket and tie and drive five blocks with my parents to Brookside College.

The celebration honoring Arthur McCabe is held in the college's large event hall, a bland yet sufficient array of circular tables set for the dinner, with a single podium and a large projector screen behind it, where, during the program, a series of images of Arthur directing also include a few press photos from *Gypsy*. At the moment Lance's face shows on the screen, he as Tulsa, my heart thuds. Where is he? Are his parents here?

While it's nice to see so many old faces, some reminded who they are by my own parents, most of them having thickened a bit or lost hair among the men. I do my best to take in the good news that Dick Thorson is a tenured technical director at Oregon State University, balanced with the bad news, that he won't be attending the tribute. He has a wife, three kids, and a production of *Candide* opening that weekend. I just wanted to see if he still sports that fiery beard, those lionesque eyes, to hug him, breathe in his scent, and see, hope against hope, if he remembers. But more, I want to show him that I found the right guy from those misdirected teenage lustful days. I make a private note to myself to find any screenplay set in the Pacific Northwest.

My speech lauding Arthur McCabe is over, and he beams with pride from his table. I'm not sweating too much. I don't even have time to get a drink. Just before I get up, a few people come in late. That makes me nervous, thinking they might all be too sloshed to hear. I won't get a chance to even offer a greeting until after it's over, but I see Lance approach.

"I told the parents I'd be a little late," he says as he approaches me. Our relatives have merged into a handshaking cluster a few yards behind us. I give him a tight needy hug, which seems to surprise him.

"I didn't see you when I started talking."

"Oh, I heard it all. I was worried you might thank Arthur for giving you a chance to see me nekkid." He smiles.

"I should."

"Anyway, we got a big family dinner planned on Sunday." His Ohio accent has returned in full force.

"Well, my man, when are you free after that?"

"Oh, you're invited, kinda obligated," Lance explains. "Bring yer family. Might as well take advantage of meetin' the parents, now that we're uh…"

"Together?"

"Sumpin' like that. And I'll tell you, your mother may do Polish cookin' good, but my Aunt Wilhemina," (he said it 'Ont') "she makes a fried chicken and gravy with biscuits you will wanna take to go to heaven."

"You want me to go to Wooster to have my family meet your family."

"I told you. I am out to all, and those that don't like it can get stuffed."

I'd asked my parents to go on to the dinner and let me wait for Lance to come back into Brookside to pick me up and put my bags in his rental car. My dad fusses about the illogic of it, but I want to kiss Lance in my bedroom, of course, and I do, plus a bit more, and Lance understands. But even he doesn't understand when I ask him to go out to the car and wait a few minutes. I have to shake it all off.

From the cluster of cassette mixes in my luggage, I put Pearl Jam's "I'm Still Alive" on the stereo, blast it, and run around the downstairs of the house, through the living room, the dining room, the kitchen and again, running, dodging furniture and lamps, running, chasing it away, making the tiger melt, melt away, as the guitars thrash and burn it all away, me out-running him, my Boogie Man, getting away, finally, getting away.

We've both got stuff to process. Lance and I decide we will fly back to L.A. together the day after his little family picnic. Maybe a few days. Maybe a few weeks. Whatever it takes. All of Europe awaits.

We need the time not to talk more, which we might, but more to enjoy the silence, the luxury of not having to explain a thing to the person sitting next to us. We've also learned the benefit of a good exit.

My parents are a bit uncomfortable among these folk, and they are folk. I can tell Mom wants to take me aside and beg me to stay, but I remind her I've been three thousand miles away for years. They make the best of it, my mother befriending the matron of the Holtzer clan, coaxing stories out of her about Depression-era farm hardship, anything to avoid the inevitable arguments over the strange presidential non-election, and the technological fears of the coming New Year.

At some point during the picnic, which has rockers and a big red and white-checkered tablecloth straight out of a Pepperidge Farm commercial, Lance takes me for a walk in his woods. His parents still own the land, but it's grown a bit fallow since most of the other children have also gone off in other directions for their lives. He asks me what I'd like to do in Germany.

"Drink beer?"

"Seriously, you don't think leaving L.A. will limit your work?"

"I don't think Barry's project is gonna pan out, but maybe the travel shows will."

"You could always make more porn," he half-jokes.

"I think that phase of my illustrious career is over. *Reel to Real* was a bold step backward," I declare to the trees, suddenly realizing I am in a space where my opinions, voice and life are irrelevant. I shut up and enjoy the scenery.

I could have told Lance about a story I still long to film, about a ship-load of men who meet with some strange creatures along the way, and that I could film it all in magical castles, animated with action figures.

But I shutter away thoughts of movies. Be here, my little inside director commands. I want to thank his grandparents from Dutch Germania and my alleged Tsar-hating elders and hesitant parents who brought me to him.

"I was born for you," I want to shout to him, all the way to the pond's far side.

Lance smiles at me in the way you see a man go off the deep end but can't help but admire his conviction.

"Okay, no more shop talk," he says, as he leads me to the pond.

Trees surround the far edges, reflecting upside down in the water. It's better than any swimming pool, open, dark, yet bouncing the light with a brilliance I will never try to capture on film, as we peel off our clothes and my dick shrinks as soon as we step in.

"Wetsuits would come in handy about now," I mutter.

Yet we wade in toward the pond's center and swim. I let Lance frolic ahead, his butt mounting over the water as he dives. He is the star of a movie whose title escapes me.

Trout nibble my toes. The water's edge tickles my neck as we swim. I let the sun's watery reflection blind me, paddling away the question of what I want to be when I grow up.

His. I want to be his.

He is *Finding Tulsa*, an autobiography I have yet to write.

He is, like me, just a naked guy swimming in a pond.

Acknowledgements

In the two decades of developing this novel, many people assisted. First, thanks to Mark Hemry of Palm Drive Publishing for his steadfast help. Early critiques from Trebor Healey, K.M. Soehnlein, and Stephen Leblanc inspired many rewrites, as did my editor Jerry Wheeler. Special thanks to musicians Peter Fogel and Kippy Marks for their beautiful contributions to the book trailer. Thanks also to my colleagues for their praise: David Ehrenstein, Jack Fritscher, Marc Huestis, Sam Irvin, Tim Miller, Felice Picano and John Weir. My Los Angeles friends aided in ways they may not know: Eric Gutierrez, Marcus Kuiland-Nazario, David Touster and others. Max Leger made the book's cover design great. For their behind-the-scenes support, special thanks to Scott Wazlowski and Michael Yamashita, Ken Bunch, and my early IndieGogo campaign backers Bud Gundy, Alex Gildzen, Carrie Euype, Alex Gildzen, Jim Cartwright, and Peter Fogel. And thanks to my brother Paul Provenzano, who knows what is and isn't fiction. To the many others no longer with us—too many to name—this is for you. Thanks for watching.

Photo by Dot

About the Author

Jim Provenzano is the author of *Finding Tulsa, Now I'm Here*, the Lambda Literary Award-winning *Every Time I Think of You*, its sequel *Message of Love* (a Lambda Literary Award Finalist), the novels *PINS, Monkey Suits, Cyclizen*, the stage adaptation of *PINS*, and the short story collection *Forty Wild Crushes*.

Audiobook adaptations include *PINS* (narrated by Paul Fleschner) and *Every Time I Think of You* and *Message of Love* (narrated by Michael Wetherbee).

Born in New York City and raised in Ashland, Ohio, he studied theatre at Kent State University, has a BFA in Dance from Ohio State University and a Master of Arts in English/Creative Writing from San Francisco State University. A journalist, editor, and photographer in LGBT media for three decades, he lives in San Francisco. www.jimprovenzano.com

Critical acclaim for Jim Provenzano's other works

Now I'm Here

"In *Now I'm Here*, a Queen show serves as backdrop to a burgeoning romance. In addition to conveying the power of listening to music, Provenzano captures the intensity of making it: When Joshua, a piano prodigy and would-be rock star, sets fingers to keyboard, Provenzano beautifully renders his passionate character's combination of fugue state and frenzy." —*San Francisco Examiner*

"This storytelling method effectively and passionately conveys the lengthy, turbulent evolution of their compelling, inspiring and uplifting relationship... The love story of Joshua and David reminds the reader how to appreciate the extraordinary in the ordinary. Professionally speaking, neither of these men achieves fame or accomplishes anything especially newsworthy, but what they share emotionally is nothing short of remarkable. Some books you read for laughter, intrigue, debate or information. *Now I'm Here* makes you feel." —*Edge Media Network*

"California author Jim Provenzano joins the great novelists who have written important and lasting novels about men in love, and while he has won prizes for his work it is now, with his publication of *Now I'm Here* that he joins the ranks of the major authors who have had a lasting imprint on our society and the LGBTIQ community. André Aciman, Andrew Holleran, Colm Toibin, Edmund White, and now Jim Provenzano are important artists whose impact is significant." —*San Francisco Review of Books*

"Provenzano reminds us of a swath of gay men and boys who remain largely overlooked; the small town, Midwestern gays whose psyches, like their turf, have been regarded as flyover country. As Provenzano traces the friendship and falling outs between Eric and his two closest friends through the 1970s and 1980s, we hear untold tales of sexual awakening among the decidedly un-'woke,' we see the long- nailed finger of HIV/AIDS scratching far beyond big cities, and we are reminded how limited our sense of 'gay community' can sometimes be." —*Passport*

"Provenzano has honed his craft and takes you on this dizzying ride with the able assurance of a pro. His rendering of the mid-Seventies is deadly accurate ... and will bring a smile of remembrance to your face if you were coming of age then. He never missteps or falls short of the mark emotionally, either. The characters are all organic, built and embroidered on with well-chosen detail, and this never once feels false or contrived as many romances do. So, even if you're not exactly a Queen fan (and why not, I wonder?), you'll enjoy this supremely well-plotted and populated romance. Highly recommended." —*Out in Print*

"Joshua and David come to life through Provenzano's prose, as does the town of Serene. The story beautifully conveys the exhilaration of love, the power of music, and the profound sadness of loss. The late '70s and '80s were, in many ways the last remnants of a more innocent time. Provenzano's deft writing whisks readers back to those halcyon days."
—*Prizm News*

"Set in a fictional Ohio town like the one Provenzano grew up in himself, *Now I'm Here* is the story of Joshua and David, two teenagers who fall in love in 1978. Their passionate affair grows into a life together in the face of religious intolerance, 'rehabilitation therapy,' and—perhaps most significantly—the heartbreak of AIDS." —*Los Angeles Blade*

Lambda Literary Award winner *Every Time I Think Of You*

"Provenzano artfully works in the theme of nature to suggest hope for Everett's physical recovery as well as, in a difficult moment in Reid's and his relationship, the recovery of love … Their love is a force of nature." —*Lambda Literary Review*

"A remarkable, uplifting story." —*Windy City Times*

"Provenzano's characters are rich and complex. His sense of pace and plotting are dead on, and his prose is straightforward and never showy. It's a well-told tale whose aim to inform as well as entertain certainly hits the mark." —*Out in Print*

"A beautiful story of friendship, devotion and love." —*Echo Magazine*

"Their romance, simple and pure, yet heated and passionate, is strikingly genuine." —*Edge on the Net*

Reviews of the Lambda Literary Award finalist *Message of Love*

"An earnest, heartfelt and refreshing continuation of a young couple's adventures that leaves the reader excited, amused and inspired."
—*Edge Media*

"A brilliant retelling of young love and the transformations it undergoes as lovers grow from adolescence to adulthood." —*Philadelphia Gay News*

"Pure genius on Provenzano's part. I'll say it again: his writing is gorgeous and sweeping and strong." —*Boys in Our Books*

"A wonderfully satisfying and uplifting novel, certainly one of the best of 2014." —*Scattered Thoughts & Rogue Words*

Praise for Jim Provenzano's debut novel, *PINS*

"Provenzano has a swift and flexible style that cuts against sentiment and reveals, in moments of grace, something like true feeling. Most urgent, he shows how gay bashing is still an outlet for kids who grew up in the so-called gay '90s." —*The Advocate*

"Fully captures the reader...a descriptive writer of the Ernest Hemingway model; terse, stripped down, and to the point." —*Lambda Book Report*

"The author brings evident personal knowledge and a crisp, uncluttered prose style to this coming-out saga." —*East Bay Express*

"What starts off as yet another coming-of-age tale of gay youth in suburbia takes a dramatic turn and careens into a full-fledged miracle of writing."
—*NY Blade News*

www.ingramcontent.com/pod-product-compliance
Lightning Source LLC
Chambersburg PA
CBHW020426030726
47495CB00006B/1674